PRAISE FOR DAVID MORRELL

"The father of the modern action novel."

—Vince Flynn,
New York Times bestselling author of *Kill Shot*

"Fast-pace, intelligent, exciting and hard-hitting."

—Nelson DeMille,
New York Times bestselling author of *The Panther*

"A master storyteller."

—James Rollins,
New York Times bestselling author of *Bloodline*

"Grabs you by the short hairs of your soul and your brain and does not let go."

—James Ellroy,
New York Times bestselling author of *LA Confidential*

"A titan among thriller writers."

—Joseph Finder,
New York Times bestselling author of *Paranoia*

"David Morrell has written more good thrillers than just about anyone else alive."

—*Chicago Sun-Times*

"The best thriller writer of this or any generation."

—*Providence Journal*

PRAISE FOR THE NAKED EDGE'S PREDECESSOR
THE PROTECTOR

"A text on how adventure suspense should be done, with a sense of real knowledge about weapons and security technology that is rare in these days of make-it-up-as you-go-along writers."

—Dean Koontz,
New York Times bestselling author of *Odd Apocalypse*

"The action unfolds quickly, accelerates to warp speed, and hurtles on to a stunning climax . . . A wonderfully entertaining action adventure."

—*Booklist*

"Spectacular action backed by the author's hands-on research . . . It has more twists and turns than any other Morrell novel . . . One of the best of the genre."

—*Associated Press*

"Impressive action . . . plenty of twists . . . most notable, though, is the advertised 'tradecraft'—from clever ways to modify one's ammo and armor to the very best method of taking out a car you're chasing."

—*Publishers Weekly*

BY DAVID MORRELL

NOVELS

First Blood (1972)
Testament (1975)
Last Reveille (1977)
The Totem (1979)
Blood Oath (1982)
The Hundred-Year Christmas (1983)
The Brotherhood of the Rose (1984)
The Fraternity of the Stone (1985)
Rambo (First Blood Part II) (1985)
The League of Night and Fog (1987)
Rambo III (1988)
The Fifth Profession (1990)
The Covenant of the Flame (1991)
Assumed Identity (1993)
Desperate Measures (1994)
The Totem (Complete and Unaltered) (1994)
Extreme Denial (1996)
Double Image (1998)
Black Evening (1999)
Burnt Sienna (2000)
Long Lost (2002)
The Protector (2003)
Nightscape (2004)
Creepers (2005)
Scavenger (2007)
The Spy Who Came for Christmas (2008)

The Shimmer (2009)
The Naked Edge (2010)
Murder as a Fine Art (2013)

ILLUSTRATED FICTION
Captain America: The Chosen (2007)

NONFICTION
John Barth: An Introduction (1976)
Fireflies: A Father's Tale of Love and Loss (1988)
The Successful Novelist (A Lifetime of Lessons about Writing and Publishing) (2008)

EDITED BY
American Fiction, American Myth (Essays by Philip Young)
edited by David Morrell and Sandra Spanier (2000)
Tesseracts Thirteen (Chilling Tales of the Great White North)
edited by Nancy Kilpatrick and David Morrell (2009)
Thrillers: 100 Must Reads
edited by David Morrell and Hank Wagner (2010)

DAVID
MORRELL

THE
NAKED EDGE

To Dennis Martin, a true warrior who taught me about the fighting techniques of legendary W.E. Fairbairn—and to Marcus Wynne, who is not only an authentic runner-and-gunner but also a fine thriller novelist

There's a line between living and dying, between being a survivor and being a victim. Like a sharp blade separating predators and prey, that line is called the naked edge.

PART ONE: TELLTALES

1

The sniper had a partner. That was a given. To do the job properly, which meant not only making the hit but also escaping, the shooter needed eyes in the back of his head. All the time he sighted through the scope on his Remington .308 rifle, which he loved more than anything else in the world, he needed the freedom to concentrate only on the job at hand, an area of a few inches 700 yards away, and *that* meant he needed a spotter to concentrate on the objects around him: whether a threat was approaching from the side, whether a cloud was about to cast a shadow, whether something or someone was about to obscure the target. He needed a partner he could depend on, who shared his instincts, who knew what he was thinking. A lot of marriages weren't as close.

They hiked in from the neighboring valley, taking the most remote route through the roughest terrain so they wouldn't be noticed. Aerial photographs aligned with topographical maps showed the slopes that had the best cover while still providing a line of fire toward the target. Moving cautiously along the tree-capped ridges, they rejected two vantage points, chose the third, sank behind boulders, opened their backpacks, and assembled their equipment.

2

Telltales. In Cavanaugh's former line of work, noticing them had kept him alive. Runners-and-gunners tended to have identifying characteristics: baseball caps covering their military-style short hair, for example. The cropped hair wasn't a macho fetish. Rather, it was a hygienic necessity because they couldn't predict where they'd be assigned, possibly a desert, possibly a swamp. Contrary to the famous speech in *Lawrence of Arabia* about how clean the desert is, sand could be almost as insect-infested as a swamp, making long hair a likely nest.

Similarly, runners-and-gunners never wore loafers but instead had thick-soled, lace-up shoes that could serve as weapons and wouldn't fall off in a fight. They liked fanny packs and loose-fitting, casual clothes that gave them numerous places to hide weapons. They needed a thick belt to support the weight of a hidden pistol and ammunition magazines. They had an inconspicuous black metal clip over the outside of a pants pocket. The clip was attached to a folding knife that could be easily drawn and flicked open with the press of a thumb against a stud on the back of the blade. They were fond of "safari" vests, the kind with numerous pockets, ideal for hiding weapons. For the same reason, they liked pants that had extra pockets at the outside of the knees.

But attention to detail was itself a telltale. Most people stumbled through life in a state of profound inattention that noted handgun expert Jeff Cooper called Condition White. In contrast, Cavanaugh maintained a state of persistent alertness known as Condition Yellow. It was second nature to him. Whenever he left or entered a new space (a vehicle or a building, for instance), he always paused and scanned his new environment, assessing whether it presented threats. He was a connoisseur of mismatched details. If something didn't fit an expected pattern, internal alarms sounded. But it takes one to know one, and in a society of minimal consciousness, someone with Condition Yellow attention is so uncommon that he or she becomes a mismatched detail.

In the present case, the two men spotted Cavanaugh about the same time he spotted *them*. This was at an isolated gas station/convenience store twenty miles from Cavanaugh's ranch. The place had a log-cabin style that was popular in Wyoming's Jackson Hole valley. As he'd driven north from doing errands in Jackson (the names of the town and the valley were often confused), he'd noticed that the fuel gauge on his Taurus was below halfway. In the remote area where he lived, he never allowed it to get any lower, so he steered from Route 89 and headed along the sagebrush-flanked road toward the pumps. It took him only a moment to notice the two men watching him.

They stood across from him, in front of the convenience store. They were in their late twenties, not tall, not short, not thin, not heavy. Both wore baseball caps. They had hiking boots, camping pants, sturdy belts, safari vests, fanny packs, and knife clips overlapping their pants pockets. In glorious aspen-yellow October, in the camping paradise of Wyoming's Grand Teton National Park, none of those potentially suspicious details was unusual. No mismatch. Except for the alertness in their eyes.

Strong-looking without being conspicuously muscled, the two men gave Cavanaugh a thorough once-over: his cowboy boots, his jeans, thick belt, and unbuttoned shirt hanging loose over a blue T-shirt. They checked to see if he had the contour of a knife in a pants pocket (he didn't, but he did have a sheathed fixed-blade under his shirt on his left side, next to a spare ammunition magazine). On his right side, also concealed by his shirt, was his SIG Sauer 229 pistol, chosen because that nine-millimeter's compact design made it an effective concealed-carry weapon.

Cavanaugh avoided eye contact when he walked past the men and entered the convenience store. He paid for the gas and returned to the pump. Every motion became a study in casualness. He put the nozzle into his car's fuel tank. He squeezed the lever and pretended to enjoy the autumn sun's warmth. He glanced behind him toward the breathtakingly close Tetons, the towering peaks of which would soon be covered with snow. In the old days, the tallest of the cone-shaped mountains made winter-bound, female-starved trappers think of a woman's breasts, hence the range's name, which derived from the French word for teats. After an appropriate time admiring the mountains, Cavanaugh glanced over toward the convenience store.

Now the two men stood next to a dark van. The side door was open. One of them leaned in, rearranging camping equipment. The other man looked over at Cavanaugh and then away.

Could be off-duty cops on vacation, Cavanaugh thought.

Then he saw another set of Condition Yellow eyes, this time from a young man (late twenties, camping shoes, loose pants, thick belt, safari vest, knife clip, fanny pack, baseball cap) watching from next to a dark Ford Explorer. Not to be obvious, the man broke eye contact and walked over to a trash can, depositing the wrapper from a candy bar. To the left, a similar-looking man glanced away from Cavanaugh, opened a cooler in the back of his SUV, took out a soft drink, opened it, sipped, and glanced again toward Cavanaugh.

Without being obvious, Cavanaugh noticed six other attentive men walking from cabins opposite the convenience store.

Or maybe this is a rendezvous area for a team of protectors, he wondered. Jackson Hole attracted an unusual amount of celebrities, financiers, and politicians. A former vice president of the United States had a home in the valley. This could be a security team checking the route along which a powerful client would be traveling.

Or maybe these guys are what a security team would be watching for.

None of my business. It hasn't been for five months.

As a few cars came and went, Cavanaugh finished putting fuel in the tank. Driving back to Route 89, continuing north through the sagebrush-dotted valley, ignoring the Snake River on his left, he glanced toward his rearview mirror.

No one followed.

3

Even in Wyoming where SUVs and pickup trucks were king, Cavanaugh's Taurus was so commonplace that it didn't stand out. The ubiquitous model was a habit from his former life. On protective assignments, a Taurus tended to be invisible, especially if the client was extremely wealthy, with adversaries who couldn't imagine their target in anything except a luxury automobile. Plus, unlike an SUV, the Taurus wouldn't roll if Cavanaugh needed to perform a 180-degree turn or any other emergency tactic.

His version of the vehicle, which he had driven when he'd worked for Global Protective Services, was slightly longer than the standard design and had the powerful engine that the Ford Taurus racing team used. Its windows were bullet-resistant. Concealed along its interior were dense ceramic plates that protected against rounds from high-velocity rifles. In the unlikely event that a bullet passed through the fuel tank's armor, the container had a rubber liner that sealed bullet holes, preventing fuel from leaking. To accommodate the extra weight, the suspension was reinforced, which allowed the vehicle to use Wyoming's rough back roads. Its tires were reinforced also, and as a further precaution, Cavanaugh borrowed an idea from the Secret Service, arranging for the center of each rim to have a strong, plastic disc, a kind of tire within a tire, upon which the vehicle could ride if the outside tire became nonfunctional. There were additional modifications, such as high-intensity fog lamps in the rear that could be used to blind pursuing drivers.

He reached an intersection called Moran Junction. A turn to the west would have taken him north toward Yellowstone National Park. Instead, he headed east past grassy fields on which elk grazed, eventually coming to isolated Buffalo Valley Road. After several curves, he disappeared among lodgepole pines within which a security camera watched. A sturdy metal gate opened when he pressed a security code on a remote control.

"Pizza Hut," he said into a walkie-talkie.

After a moment, a female voice responded, "Plenty of pepperoni?"

"All they had was ham."

"It's not a pizza if it doesn't have pepperoni."

The all-clear exchange having been completed, Cavanaugh drove through, pressed the remote control, and closed the gate. Past another security camera in the trees, he emerged into a grassy canyon flanked by wooded bluffs, his rearview mirror showing the magnificent Teton Mountains in the distance behind him.

4

The spotter heard the Taurus before he saw it. A sentry had radioed him that it was coming. He thought he was prepared emotionally. Even so, his pulse increased until he felt pressure in his veins. Not because of what would soon happen. Instead, because of what *had* happened.

As he and the sniper sank lower on the ridge, he had a sudden painful memory of two boys wading in a stream filled with goldfish. Another memory, equally painful, followed: an old man pounding a hammer onto an anvil, sparks flying from a strip of glowing metal.

Peering between boulders, watching the car emerge from the pines, the sniper murmured, "I can do it as soon as he gets out of the car."

"Not until I tell you."

"But—"

"There's a schedule," the spotter insisted. "The backup team needs to be in place, ready to cut the phone line to the house. That way, nobody can call the police. Otherwise, with only a couple of roads out of the valley, the authorities could seal us off."

"The survivors could still use a cell phone."

"This area's too remote for one."

"You're sure?" the sniper asked.

"I drove by and experimented, trying to phone restaurants in town. The calls wouldn't go through. Later, I confirmed it by asking the phone company. The canyon walls prevent transmissions from reaching here or going out."

The shooter gazed longingly at the car as it crossed the canyon. "So when will the backup team be ready?"

The spotter touched his left ear, securing the bud of a radio receiver. "They're saying ten minutes."

Staring toward the canyon floor, he concentrated on the figure in the driver's seat. Even at a distance, the solid-looking shoulders and chest were all too familiar, impossible to be mistaken. The intelligent brow and handsome jaw had always been attractive to women, although amazingly the target had a talent for minimizing his appearance when he was on duty, dimming the glow in his hazel eyes, lowering his shoulders, making himself almost invisible. He still wore his sandy hair in a professional neutral cut.

It's been close to three years, the spotter thought. *How the hell are you doing, good buddy?*

A painful combination of anger and affection seized him.

"He'd dead, but he doesn't know it," the sniper said. "Ten minutes? Sure. I can wait that long. This is what it feels like."

"Feels like?"

"To be God."

5

Driving across the pasture, Cavanaugh smiled at the half-dozen horses grazing near a stream. A mare galloped toward him. She was a five-year-old quarter horse named after her color, Chestnut. As she ran parallel to the moving car, Cavanaugh lowered his window.

"Guess what *I* have?" He nodded toward a paper bag next to him.

The horse kept thundering next to him.

Cavanaugh pulled out a big red apple. "Want it now or later?"

Chestnut snapped at it.

"Hey, where are your manners?" Cavanaugh tossed the apple over Chestnut's head and watched her veer toward where it landed in the grass.

The five other horses, one of them a colt, realized what was happening and galloped in Cavanaugh's direction.

"I suppose I need to be fair." He dumped the bag of apples onto the grass and drove on.

Beyond the pasture was a three-story lodge. Made of logs, it had a wide, welcoming porch. Ten years earlier, while working in the area (his client: a political columnist threatened by a stalker), Cavanaugh had heard about a dude ranch for sale. Investigating while off-duty, he was so impressed by the peaceful feel of the canyon that he did one of the few impulsive things in his life and bought it.

It was expensive. For the down payment, he needed to hand over every dollar he'd saved as a protective agent and to accept two high-paying, extremely dangerous assignments. Thereafter, most of his income went toward the mortgage. But he never regretted his decision. Between jobs, sometimes convalescing from injuries, he came back to his magical hundred acres, which had the equally magical name of "home."

As Cavanaugh drove toward the lodge, he saw Jamie standing on the porch, attaching a walkie-talkie to her belt. Smiling, she stepped out into the sun, which glinted off her brunette ponytail. She was five feet ten, her jeans emphasizing her figure, her cowboy boots lifting her heels, making her legs seem to stretch up forever toward her hips. Her face had the narrow chin and high cheekbones of a classical beauty. But her green eyes, a mixture of amusement and intelligence, were what most captivated him.

He parked in front of the lodge and got out of the car.

"That Pizza Hut thing made me hungry. I don't suppose you actually did bring a pizza," Jamie said.

"Nope."

"Bummer."

"Something better."

"A Philadelphia steak sandwich?" she asked.

"How can you be so thin and think so much about food?"

"Because that's all I do is think about it. You feed the horses, but you never feed *me*. Come on, 'fess up, you brought Kentucky Fried Chicken, right?"

"Sorry."

"Double bummer."

"Even better than KFC." Cavanaugh leaned into the car and picked up a small case indented with the words HECKLER & KOCH.

"Awww," Jamie said, "you're right. It *is* better than KFC. You really know the way to a woman's heart. I just love it when you bring me a gun."

"But not just any gun."

"Don't keep me in suspense. What makes this one so special?"

"It's called the P-2000."

"My, yes, that certainly sounds special."

Their boot steps echoing, they crossed the porch and entered the lodge. A spacious "communal room," as the real-estate brochure described it, had a wide staircase, a huge stone fireplace, a battered upright piano, a long table where lodgers had eaten during the dude-ranch days, and several ceiling light fixtures in the shape of wagon wheels.

"Do you remember the first rule of choosing a handgun?" Cavanaugh asked.

"The gun has to fit the hand."

"Right. If the grip's too large, your finger can't reach the trigger without stretching. The gun twists to the side and ruins your aim."

Reaching the kitchen, Cavanaugh looked at a row of monitors under a cupboard. Linked to security cameras, the screens showed various areas of the property. Satisfied that everything appeared normal, he turned toward where Mrs. Patterson rolled a pie crust. A sixty-year-old widow whose children and grandchildren lived in Jackson, she had worked for the dude ranch and agreed to stay.

"What kind of pie are you making?" Jamie asked.

"Pumpkin."

"Maybe I'll skip dinner tonight and just eat the pie."

Cavanaugh shook his head in amazement at Jamie's appetite. He opened a cupboard, took out a box of nine-millimeter ammunition and an equipment bag, then headed toward the back door. "It's going to be loud for a while, Mrs. Patterson."

The gray-haired woman set down her rolling pin, pulled a Kleenex from her apron, tore it in two, and wadded the halves into her ears.

The screen door banged shut as Cavanaugh and Jamie walked toward a shooting area next to a barn. Feeling the intense sunlight, they stopped at a weathered wooden table and faced metal targets twenty-five yards away, a mound behind them. Each target had the outline of a human head and torso.

Cavanaugh opened the case, took out the pistol, and showed Jamie that there wasn't a magazine in it. Then he locked back the slide to reveal that there wasn't a round in the firing chamber.

"Cold gun?"

"Cold gun," she agreed.

He set the pistol and the gear bag on the table. Then he opened the box of ammunition. With practiced efficiency, he and Jamie loaded ten rounds into three magazines.

"It always amazes me that you don't break your fingernails," Cavanaugh said.

"That's how little attention you pay. Hanging around with you, I *don't have* any fingernails. So tell me about the P-2000."

"Even Goldilocks would like it." Cavanaugh showed Jamie three polymer strips labeled S, L, or XL. A strip on the back of the weapon's grip was labeled M.

"You're telling me you can size the grip…?"

"To fit the hand. Try it."

Although the pistol was still "cold," Cavanaugh approved of the way Jamie pointed it down range, as if it were loaded.

"Not quite comfortable," she said. "Slightly too big for my hand."

"Then we'll reduce the grip." Cavanaugh pulled a hammer and a punch from the equipment bag. With a few taps, he removed a pin from the strip. He took it off and attached the one marked S. "*Now* try it."

"Perfect," Jamie said.

Cavanaugh was fascinated by the problem of hands fitting grips because his own hand was small in comparison to his six-foot frame. Prior to his Delta Force training, he'd been obligated to use the Army's standard sidearm, Beretta's fifteen-round nine-millimeter. For a magazine to hold that many rounds, it needed to have two columns of ammunition. The result was a grip too large for him. He'd managed to compensate and control his aim, but like someone forced to wear tight shoes for a long time, he was now obsessed with proper size and comfort.

"Put some rounds through it," he suggested.

"Ladies first? Gosh." Jamie shoved a magazine into the grip and pressed a lever on the side. A similar lever was on the opposite side, making the weapon ambidextrous, another rarity. The slide, which had been locked back, rammed home, chambering a round.

"I need my fashion accessories," she told him.

They put on their protective glasses and ear guards, then approached the targets, stopping ten yards away, a standard shooting distance. Most gunfights occurred within half that space.

Jamie raised the pistol, both arms straight out, both hands solidly on the grip, both thumbs pointed along the side as a further way of aligning the barrel with the target.

Cavanaugh considered the freedom with which she lifted her arms. No evident discomfort, no stiffness to indicate her bullet wound five months earlier.

She pulled the trigger.

6

Hidden among the trees on the ridge, the spotter frowned toward the back of the lodge. The target and the woman were out of sight behind a barn.

Interesting that I want to objectify him by calling him "the target" instead of using his name. Doesn't seem a day older. Kept in shape. Picked a damned good-looking wife.

You son of a bitch.

The spotter unclipped a polished ebony knife from his pocket, thumbing the blade open and closing it. "Target practice," he said in response to the gunshots.

"A handgun," the sniper commented.

"Yes. Sounds like a nine-millimeter. Must be a metal target. Hear the bullets hitting it?"

"Accurate shooter."

"Oh, he's definitely an accurate shooter," the spotter said. "That's why we're up here and not down there."

The sniper counted. "Nine, ten, eleven, twelve."

"Thirteen, fourteen, fifteen."

"Large magazine. Sixteen, seventeen, eighteen. *Hell* of a large magazine. You know any handguns that hold that many rounds?"

"No," the spotter said. "After ten, a slight pause. Hard to notice. That's when the magazine got changed."

"Damned fast magazine change."

"Twenty-two. Twenty-three. After twenty, another slight pause."

"Yeah, a super-fast magazine change," the sniper agreed. "Well, I'm here to blast his eye out at seven hundred yards, not have a gunfight with him."

Amid the shots echoing across the canyon, they heard an approaching rumble.

7

Ear guards muffle sounds but don't eliminate them. Cavanaugh listened to the rhythmic thunder and peered toward the southern rim of the canyon, from behind which a helicopter appeared, its dragonfly shape getting larger, silhouetted against the cobalt sky.

Jamie lowered the pistol and glanced at her watch. "He's early."

"Yeah." Cavanaugh took off his ear guards. "A half hour. I was hoping he wouldn't come at all."

"You still don't know what he wants?"

"Only that he said it's important. But I can guess. He plans to offer me a job."

As the helicopter roared closer, Cavanaugh was able to read the name stenciled in red across the side: Global Protective Services. Memories rushed through him...of the clients he'd protected, some wealthy and powerful, others ordinary people whom he'd persuaded GPS to help, all sharing the common denominator that they were prey...of the protective agents he'd worked with, all of them linked by their hatred of predators and their devotion to being guardians, even at the cost of their lives.

Jamie said something, but the growing din of the chopper prevented him from hearing her. Or perhaps it was the memories.

"What?" he asked.

"Are you going to take the job?"

Preoccupied, Cavanaugh reached under his loose denim shirt and removed his knife from its sheath on the left side of his belt. A rugged utility knife, useful for work around the ranch, it was a gift from his friend, Gil Hibben, commemorating Gil's induction into the Knifemakers Hall of Fame. It had the balance for what Cavanaugh did next. Releasing the emotions that memories of his dead friends had caused, he drew back his arm and hurled the blade toward a post fifteen feet away, expertly judging the number of flips the knife had to make.

It struck solidly, the force of his throw and his emotions embedding it.

"No," he said. "I won't take the job."

"I think you should."

The chopper was nearer, louder.

Ignoring it, Cavanaugh turned toward Jamie. "Five months ago, you nearly died. I still have nightmares about it."

"You didn't force me to go along. I made a choice. It wasn't your fault I was shot."

"I'm never going to put you at risk again."

"But a lot of people need help."

"Somebody else will have to give it to them."

The helicopter hovered over a section of grass between the barn and the lodge.

"We'd better not be rude and keep him waiting," Cavanaugh said.

"In other words, you're changing the subject."

Cavanaugh shrugged. He retrieved his knife, then followed her to the weathered table, where they put their eye and ear protection into the equipment bag.

Jamie dropped the magazine from the pistol and caught it in the air.

Impressed, Cavanaugh reloaded it, not looking where the helicopter landed, the roar of its engine diminishing.

"Now we *are* being rude," Jamie said.

"Do you suppose it's a clue that I don't want to talk to him?"

8

"Early," the sniper said.

"Yeah." The spotter kept opening his knife and closing it.

"Complicates things. I told you I could have done it when he got out of the car. Now—"

"Now we'll just have to wait a little longer." The spotter readjusted the radio bud in his ear, listening harder. "The backup team isn't in position to cut the phone line yet."

Two men got out of the chopper.

"Getting crowded," the sniper said.

9

The first man who climbed down from the helicopter was forty-three, but his permanently pensive expression created wrinkles at the corners of his eyes and mouth, making him look older. His dark hair was as immaculately cared for as his handmade shoes and his custom-tailored suit. His broad shoulders and proud chest gave him a further imposing look. He carried a leather briefcase that shone with polish. His contact lenses had a similar sheen, the intelligence in his eyes magnified by them. What his smile lacked in warmth was offset by the brilliance of his perfectly capped teeth.

"William." Cavanaugh shook hands with him.

The man's last name was Faraday. A ruthless corporate attorney, he didn't just defeat his opponents' clients but also destroyed them, in the process acquiring numerous enemies. Cavanaugh had once saved his life when a disgraced executive hired someone to try to kill him. In gratitude, William did much of Global Protective Services' legal work in exchange for ready access to world-class protectors.

"You remember Jamie," Cavanaugh said.

"I do." William shook her hand. They'd met when he prepared their wills. "Have you recovered from your injury?"

"Yes. Thanks for asking."

William nodded, as if not accustomed to displaying soft human emotions or being complimented for it.

"Angelo," Cavanaugh said to the chopper's pilot. "It's been too long."

"Since Puerto Vallarta," the husky man replied, "and that stock market analyst we protected. Remember how he was afraid angry investors were waiting for him behind every corner."

"Hell, one of them *was*." Cavanaugh shook his hand warmly. "How are the llamas you were raising?"

"They were sissies. They never bred."

"You're sure you had male and female?"

"You think I can't tell the difference? They spent more time spitting than trying to fornicate. Right in my eye. One of them spat right here." Angelo used a middle finger to point at his eye.

Cavanaugh couldn't help laughing.

"Then they jumped the fence. By the time I found them, they'd been run over by a cement truck. If I'd been smart, I'd have eaten them instead of trying to breed them."

"They taste good?"

"I have no idea, but now I raise ostriches. *Those* you can eat. Plus, they lay eggs the size of basketballs."

"True?"

"I exaggerate only slightly."

Cavanaugh laughed again. "*Hombre*, I missed you."

He led them toward the lodge. In the kitchen, he scanned the monitors again, saw that everything was normal, and introduced Mrs. Patterson as she spooned pumpkin mix into the pie crust.

"Want something to eat or drink?" he asked his guests.

"Thank you, no," William answered. "We have business to discuss. Then I need to get to Denver."

"What's in Denver?"

"A Vietnamese businessman with a problem."

"Ah." Knowing William's reluctance to confide, Cavanaugh knew that the Vietnamese businessman might actually be a Japanese baseball player. "I hoped you'd stay for a while. Both of you are welcome. You'll never forget the color of the sunset behind the Tetons."

"Another time."

10

The office looked the same as when the property had been a dude ranch. Next to an old desk, a wall of photographs showed children fishing, swimming, riding horses, and pitching their tents in the meadow next to the lodge. Another wall had shelves with slots for mail and messages. Everything retained the vague smell of pipe smoke from long ago. On occasion, Cavanaugh was tempted to clear everything out, but then he remembered the two men in their thirties who'd arrived a couple of years earlier. They drove Winnebagos. They had beer paunches, their wives looked bored, and their kids kept shoving each other. The men asked Cavanaugh if it was all right for them to show their families what the children's camp had been like. They'd spent the happiest summers of their lives here, they said. They couldn't get over that everything was the same.

Their happiest summers. Cavanaugh had found it sad that they knew their lives hadn't gotten any better.

Now William sat in a dark leather chair and opened his briefcase while Cavanaugh and Jamie watched from wooden chairs across from him.

"I came all this way because—"

"You might as well know right away that I don't want a job."

"A job? You think I came here to offer you a *job*?"

"Didn't you?"

"The word 'job' doesn't quite describe it." William looked amused. "I'm offering you *everything*."

"What are you talking about?"

"'Lock, stock, and barrel,' as I believe they say out here."

"You're not making sense."

"You've got it all, my friend."

"All of *what*?"

"Global Protective Services."

Cavanaugh was certain he hadn't heard correctly. Then his heart lurched, and he took a long breath.

"Duncan gave it to you in his will," William said.

Again, Cavanaugh was overwhelmed by memories. Tall and wiry, with a mustache, Duncan had been Cavanaugh's Delta Force instructor. After leaving the military, Duncan had founded an international security agency that flourished, thanks to the quality of the personnel Duncan hired, all of them from special-operations units around the world, many of them having been Duncan's students. When Duncan had been killed on an assignment, there were Global Protective Services branches in New York, London, Rome, and Hong Kong, with another planned for Tokyo.

"His will?" Cavanaugh subdued the anger he suddenly felt. "You're telling me about this five months after he died?"

"There were reasons."

"What reasons? Jesus, we could have talked about this at Duncan's funeral. We could have—"

"No," William said, "we couldn't have."

Cavanaugh noticed Jamie looking at him with concern.

"I'm sorry," he told William. "I didn't mean to sound like I was criticizing you."

"Of course not. Anyway, you're in mourning. You're allowed. One of the reasons you didn't hear about this until now is that it was difficult to verify Duncan's death so that the probate process could begin."

"Verify his...?" Then Cavanaugh understood. The bullets had mutilated Duncan's face so completely that his teeth couldn't be used to establish his identity. What the bullets hadn't accomplished, a fire had. "God help him."

"There were indications of healed broken ribs and a similarly healed broken collarbone."

"Occupational injuries." Cavanaugh felt sympathetic twinges in his own healed bones.

"Unfortunately, there weren't any recent x-rays of those areas of his body, so I still couldn't prove the remains were his. Finally, I went to the Pentagon and asked to see Duncan's medical file. The Army was as protective of him in death as if he'd continued to be a Delta Force instructor. It took a phone call from a former client, a ranking member of the current administration, before the file was released to me. My concern was that the injuries occurred *after* Duncan left the military, in which case the x-ray films would have been valueless. But in fact, the broken ribs and collarbone were visible. I was able to make my case."

"You said '*one* of the reasons' I didn't hear about this until now."

"Another is that Duncan was a better protector than he was a corporate executive. Without consulting me, he made a number of business decisions that brought the continuing existence of Global Protective Services into doubt. There almost weren't any assets for anyone to inherit. Fortunately, I've been able to disentangle those problems. But still another reason that I didn't pay you this visit until now is..." William held up a sheet of paper. "Duncan willed Global Protective Services to a man named Aaron Stoddard."

As Jamie gave Cavanaugh another look of concern, he sat straighter, his back hardening.

"The problem is, nobody at GPS ever heard of a man with that name. Duncan didn't have any surviving family, so it wasn't possible to seek that avenue of help."

"You could have asked *me*," Cavanaugh said.

"You made clear you didn't want to be contacted. But what would you have answered if I *had* come to you and asked if you knew Aaron Stoddard? Would you have told me, or would you have remained determined to separate yourself from your former life?"

Cavanaugh didn't reply.

"In the end, the Pentagon complied with another of my requests. Aaron Stoddard, it turns out, once belonged to Delta Force also. In fact, he was one of Duncan's students. Then Duncan hired him for Global

Protective Services, but by then, for security reasons, Aaron Stoddard was using another name. *Your* name."

Conscious of his heartbeat, Cavanaugh leaned back. He needed a few moments before he could respond.

"Back then, my mother was still alive. My stepfather. My half-sister. My friends. When I joined GPS, I realized that one of the weaknesses in the system was that predators might target a protective agent as much as a client. They could grab a protector's family and friends and try to use them as leverage to get the protector to betray the client. I decided that I couldn't put my family and friends at risk. I needed to look out for their safety just as I did a client's, and the easiest way to do that was to assume a false name and identity that would keep predators from discovering my background."

"Well, you certainly succeeded. I believed Cavanaugh was your true name. I've never heard you supply a first one, so I was surprised that in GPS's personnel files, you list a first name of James."

"Which I never use when I'm working."

"Establishing a mystique as a protective agent with only one name. Do you agree?"

"That I'm Aaron Stoddard? Yes." He looked over at Jamie, to whom he'd long ago confided the truth about his identity. "Now that I'm no longer a protector, it doesn't matter if anybody knows who I really am. My mother's dead now. My stepfather has a heart condition. He'll probably be gone soon, also. My half-sister is the only relative I need to worry about. And *you*, of course," he told Jamie. "I'll never stop protecting *you*."

"What I meant was," William said, "do you agree to abide by Duncan's wishes and accept ownership of Global Protective Services?"

"William, did anybody ever tell you you've got a pushy manner?"

"My second and third wives. But I tried not to take it personally."

"Really, I'm sorry you came all this way."

"You won't accept?"

"I made a promise, and I'm keeping it. From now on, Jamie's all I care about."

"Duncan didn't indicate a second choice. GPS isn't a publicly traded company. There's no board of directors. No one except Duncan's heir can make decisions. If your refusal is absolute, ultimately the company will need to be dissolved."

"I'm afraid there's nothing I can do about that," Cavanaugh said.

"Perhaps you should take a couple of days to consider the implications."

"No," Cavanaugh insisted.

"Can we speak privately?" Jamie interrupted.

Cavanaugh looked at her.

"Outside," she told him.

11

Behind boulders on the ridge, the spotter studied the lodge through binoculars that were shielded to keep the sun from reflecting off their lenses.

"They could be inside for hours," the sniper said.

"The backup team's in position now. The moment you're sure you've got the target in your sights, I'll tell them to cut the telephone line. The timing has to be right. If we do it sooner than we need to, he might try to use the phone, wonder why it doesn't work, and realize he's being set up."

"In that case, tell them to get ready." The sniper peered through his scope. "The target's on the back porch."

12

Jamie closed the screen door after she and Cavanaugh stepped outside. "I want you to own Global Protective Services."

"But I promised you I was out of the business."

"I'm freeing you from that promise."

13

"Beta, get ready to cut the phone line," the spotter said into the radio.

"On your signal," a voice replied.

"Stand by." The spotter turned toward his partner. "Can you get the shot?"

The man lay on his stomach, his left hand gripping the rifle's stock, his left forearm resting on his knapsack. His right hand clutched the rifle's grip, his finger at the trigger. The bolt-action Remington 700 was one of the most accurate sniper rifles. A favorite of the U.S. military as well as law-enforcement SWAT teams, it accurately delivered a .308 bullet up to 900 yards. The sights had one-minute-of-angle accuracy. The trigger was adjusted to a gentle two-pound pull. The powerful scope had a holographic sight with a red dot that indicated exactly where the bullet would strike the target. The state-of-the-art sound suppressor prevented the sniper from disclosing his position and drawing return fire.

But precise equipment was only one element of accurate long-distance shooting. Training, experience, steadiness, the ability to craft handmade ammunition and adjust sights based on conclusions about distance, temperature, altitude, and wind, the Zen control of breathing, temperature, blood pressure, and heart rate, the focus of a lifetime into one steady confident pull on the trigger—the accumulation of all these and more were what made a great shooter.

"I said, Can you make the shot?" Receiving no answer, the spotter peered through his binoculars and inhaled with annoyance when he saw the problem. "Damn it, the woman's in the way."

14

"Sometimes, you don't listen to yourself," Jamie said.

"That's because I don't enjoy one-sided conversations."

"Angelo was talking about his llamas and his ostriches, and he made you laugh so hard, you said you missed him."

"Just a figure of speech. Hey, we aren't going to start shopping for furniture or anything."

"You *do* miss him. You miss *all* the agents you used to work with. You miss Global Protective Services and—"

"How can you be sure? I've never said *anything* about that."

"Sometimes, I see a far-away look in your eyes, as if your mind's somewhere else, doing things in places a lot more exciting than here."

"No."

"You *do* have that look." Jamie's hands were on her hips, her back to the sun-bright pasture and the aspen-covered eastern slope of the canyon. "It reminds me of tigers and lions in cages in zoos. The look in their eyes. The controlled frustration. It's like they know there has to be a better way, but they also know there's nothing they can do about it. Well, this is your chance to do something about it."

"There's no place else I'd rather be, and no other person I'd rather be with."

"You gave up a huge portion of your life for me," Jamie said.

"But look at what I got in return." Cavanaugh gestured toward the stream flowing through the pasture, sunlight glinting off it, the horses leaning down to drink.

"You still wear a gun and a knife."

"The world's a dangerous neighborhood."

"You still drive an armored Taurus."

"A sturdy, dependable car. The faraway look you see in my eyes isn't longing. It's nervous relief that I don't live that way anymore. It's amazement that I ever did."

"I don't understand."

"Risking my life for people I didn't know and often didn't like. I used to say I had my professional standards. I wouldn't protect child molesters or drug traffickers, anyone who's an obvious monster. But what about the monsters who aren't as obvious? That stock analyst Angelo and I protected. He was in bed with the companies he was supposed to be making judgments about. He let greed mean more to him than the trust investors put in him. A lot of people counted on him for the security of their pensions, and all he had was contempt for them. I *hated* that man. Part of me was delighted when a ruined investor tried to attack him. Oh, Angelo and I made sure the analyst wasn't injured, but he sure was scared, and I was glad to see him scared. But that was wrong. A protector needs to be absolutely committed to his client. He needs to be willing, if necessary, to die for that client."

Jamie's eyes reacted.

"Now that I'm away from it all," Cavanaugh told her, "I realize how many of my clients weren't worth risking my life for. They were special only because they were rich or powerful or uncommonly attractive. What made them unique poisoned them."

"Not all of them," Jamie said. "You told me *some* clients were remarkable. Saints, you called a few of them."

For a moment, Cavanaugh did long for his former life. "There was one politician I thought could have made a difference. Unfortunately, his party chose somebody who looked good on TV. There was a billionaire who told me, 'All my life I've been taking money out of the system. Now I'm putting it back.' He had exciting plans for ways to use his money to improve education. But then he got cancer and died, and his heirs fought over his estate. There was an entertainer who spent significant portions of his time performing benefit concerts for children's hospitals."

"What's the downside to *that* story?"

"Actually, there isn't one. The entertainer still performs benefit concerts, and the children's hospitals keep getting money."

"Who'd want to hurt a man like that?"

"He has several obsessed fans. Plus, he had a manager who was furious because the entertainer fired the guy after discovering how much money was being skimmed from the hospital fund. In Mexico City, where the entertainer was performing one of his concerts, kidnappers tried to grab him for a ten-million-dollar ransom."

"You're right. The world *is* a dangerous neighborhood." Jamie took a deep breath. "But maybe you're being given an uncommon opportunity to make things better. Maybe you could be the equivalent of that billionaire you mentioned."

"I don't understand."

"Maybe you could change the way Global Protective Services does business. Take from the rich. Give to the poor. By which I mean, hold your nose and protect people you dislike so the company can afford to protect people who deserve to be alive."

Cavanaugh studied her. "It would mean the end of all this." He gestured toward the canyon. He tried not to look at the helicopter and all it symbolized.

"We could come back whenever we wanted."

"We?"

"You don't think I'd let you go by yourself."

"Maybe *you're* the one who's feeling restless."

"Not for somebody else, believe me, lover. But maybe happiness isn't enough. Maybe human beings need to be useful."

15

"She isn't moving." The spotter stared through his binoculars at where the woman stood on the porch, her back to him.

"I can see his head."

"Behind her? Bullshit. All I see are his hands gesturing to one side of her or the other. His head? No way. From this angle, the porch roof interferes."

"I'm telling you, I see about an inch or so of his head."

"A guaranteed kill?"

"No."

"What about shooting *through* her?"

"Remember the JFK assassination?" the sniper asked.

"How the hell old do you think I am?"

"One bullet boomeranged all over the place, in several impossible directions, hitting Kennedy and Governor Connally."

"Yeah, the magic, slip-sliding bullet—if somebody's dumb enough to believe Oswald was the only shooter."

"What I'm saying is, I can hit her square in the neck on an angle that I think will go down and out the soft tissue and into his chest. But that bullet might just as easily hit the top of her spine and shatter or change angle, blast along a rib, and slam into the post beside her."

"So you can't guarantee a kill."

"Not even if the bullet does go through her neck and into his chest."

"But he'd be down, and you've got other ammunition in that rifle. How fast can you chamber a fresh round?"

"A lot faster than that dick Oswald. Wait. She's stepping out of the way. I've got a shot. This'll be just like that time in Rome."

"Beta," the spotter said into the radio. "Cut the phone line."

16

In the office, William pressed buttons on his cell phone, waited, but didn't get a response. Impatient, he stood, left the office, and crossed the communal room to enter the kitchen.

Mrs. Patterson was removing the pie from the oven. Angelo watched her.

"Smells like Thanksgiving," Angelo said.

The phone rang.

William, who disliked pumpkin pie, glanced around at the stainless steel appliances in the otherwise rustic kitchen.

"Get your business done?" Mrs. Patterson asked.

"They're discussing it." William turned his attention to the security monitors on the counter next to him.

The phone rang a second time.

Mrs. Patterson went to the wall next to the refrigerator and lifted the phone off its mount. "Hello? … Hi, Tina. How's little Brian's cold? I've been worried it'll turn into… Hello? … Tina?"

"Problem?" Angelo asked.

"The line went dead."

"Are these men supposed to be on the property?" William inquired.

"*What* men?" Angelo turned.

"The ones on this television monitor."

17

Three shots made Cavanaugh flinch. From behind him. From the opposite end of the porch. *From the kitchen* was all he had time to think as his startle reflex engaged. Even the most seasoned operators, accustomed to bullets being fired near them, couldn't control that reflex. He grabbed Jamie and lunged sideways, seeking the only available cover:

the lodge's wall. Simultaneously, he felt something snap past him and wallop onto the porch's floor, tearing up splinters.

Two shooters. One in the kitchen. One on the ridge.

He kept lunging, holding Jamie tightly, turning so his back led the way as they crashed through the screen that covered his office window. The window was raised. His head grazed past the wooden frame. He fell, holding Jamie, banging onto the floor.

"Cavanaugh!" Angelo yelled. Then William and Mrs. Patterson also shouted his name. He heard footsteps rushing toward the office.

But all he cared about was Jamie. *Are you all right?*

She didn't answer.

"Jamie!"

"I'm okay. Got the wind knocked out of me."

Cavanaugh rolled from under her, scanning her body, looking for blood.

"What happened?" she wanted to know.

Angelo and the others charged into the office. "Cavanaugh?"

He drew his pistol from under his shirt. "The kitchen? Who shot—"

"*I* did. Three bullets into the wall." Angelo's pistol was in his hand. "Men on the grounds. The phone line's been cut. I didn't know how else to warn you in time."

"The eastern slope. Sniper," Cavanaugh said.

"I didn't hear any shots from up there."

"He must be using a sound suppressor. William, I hope you know how to handle a gun."

"Not even in my worst nightmares."

"You're about to learn."

18

You dumb bastard. After all your bragging, you missed!" the spotter said.

"Hey, it wasn't my fault! How was I to know somebody'd start shooting down there? How was I to know the target would—"

"Quit making excuses! *How are you going to fix this?*"

"Wait for another shot."

"Now that he knows he's a target, you think he's just going to waltz outside and show himself?" the spotter demanded.

"To get to the car maybe. Or the helicopter. Hell, he's got to do something. He knows he's stuck. He can't phone for help. Sooner or later—"

"He's got food. Water. He can stay there for *days*. But *we* didn't come prepared for a damned siege."

"So you make mistakes, too, huh?"

"And you're one of them. Do this right!"

With a sigh of impatience, the shooter reached into his backpack and selected a box of ammunition. He worked the Remington's bolt and ejected the two remaining rounds from the rifle. Then he inserted four rounds from the fresh box of ammunition. Each cartridge had a red tip.

"Tracers?"

"Incendiaries. I brought them in case this turned out to be a night shoot. For the same reason, I also brought an infrared scope. If he tries to leave when it's dark, I'll get him."

"But it won't be dark for another four hours!"

"Doesn't matter." The shooter steadied his aim toward a large white tank beside a shed about fifty yards from the lodge. "I'll get the target out of the lodge if I shoot one of these babies into that propane tank. Hell, the explosion will probably level the place."

"No. *Don't.*" The spotter was appalled.

"What's the matter?"

"The neighbors in the other valleys are used to hearing shots on this property. But an explosion would attract every police officer and emergency crew from here to Jackson."

"Yeah, there's that, I suppose. Okay, I've got another way." The shooter switched his aim toward the lodge. "Tell Beta the target'll be outside in fifteen minutes."

19

Heart pounding, Cavanaugh raced across the communal room and tugged open a door next to the battered upright piano. He pulled out an AR-15, the semiautomatic civilian version of the M-16.

He gave it to Angelo, along with a loaded thirty-round magazine. "Watch the front."

"Got it."

"Wait. Take this." Cavanaugh grabbed a walkie-talkie off a shelf and tossed it to him.

As Angelo hurried toward the front windows, Cavanaugh took out another AR-15. "I'll watch the east and try to locate the sniper. Mrs. Patterson, get down in the basement."

"No. Tell me how to help."

"Stay out of sight."

"I'm not going to hide." Fear made her voice tremble. "There's a revolver in a kitchen drawer. You taught me how to use it."

"Stay behind cover!" Cavanaugh yelled as she ran toward the kitchen. "Keep your walkie-talkie close! *Jamie?*"

"I'll take the back," she said.

With no AR-15s remaining, Cavanaugh gave her a Ruger Mini-14, a streamlined semiautomatic rifle favored by ranchers. He stared into her eyes, praying she wouldn't be killed.

"You can count on me," she said.

He touched her hand. "I know." He felt his throat tighten as she grabbed a box of ammunition and hurried away.

"William, come with me."

Cavanaugh tugged the attorney back into the office.

"The good news is, the log walls of this building are so thick, we don't need to worry about bullets coming through."

"You're implying that in most houses bullets *can* come through walls? Dear God, what's the *bad* news?"

"The windows are the only target the sniper now has. He'll focus on them."

"Then how are we supposed to look out there and see if anybody's attacking?"

"Stay to the side. Keep your face from the opening. Peer out at an angle." Cavanaugh spoke those words into his walkie-talkie. "Mrs. Patterson, did you hear that?"

Her voice was staticky. "Yes."

"Angelo, see anything?"

"*Nada.*" His voice came from the walkie-talkie.

"Jamie?"

"Clear."

"Mrs. Patterson?"

"Nothing."

"What about the security monitors?"

"All I see are bushes and trees."

"Maybe it's finished." Breathing loudly, William crouched near Cavanaugh against a wall in the office. "The sniper that fired at you. Now that he missed, maybe he's gone."

Cavanaugh inched toward the undamaged eastern window, the one behind his desk, trying to get a glimpse of where the shooter might be hiding on the aspen-covered ridge. He eased closer to the window.

Its screen bulged inward. Something snapped through the room and struck the leather chair that William had earlier sat in. The glowing object plowed through the chair and hit the wall. Smoke rose.

Cavanaugh yelled into the walkie-talkie, "The shooter's using incendiaries!"

Crawling in a direction that didn't make him a target through the window, he reached a closet, tugged at its door, and took out a fire extinguisher. As flames writhed from the chair and the wall, he aimed the nozzle and pulled the trigger. A pungent cloud spewed toward the fire, smothering it.

"Still nothing." Angelo's voice crackled from the walkie-talkie.

"Same here," Mrs. Patterson's voice said.

"Nobody," Jamie's voice reported.

"He's definitely using a suppressor!" Cavanaugh told them. "I can't place where the shots are coming from!"

With a snap as from a whip, another tracer tore through the screen, this one shattering a lamp. More smoke rose. Flames wavered. Cavanaugh pressed the extinguisher's trigger, another cloud of retardant gushing over the fire.

William coughed from the assault to his throat and lungs.

"Mrs. Patterson," Cavanaugh said into the walkie-talkie. "There's a fire extinguisher in the kitchen. Get it ready."

20

On the ridge, the sniper worked the bolt on his rifle, chambering another round.

"Clever," the spotter said, peering through binoculars at the haze in a ground-level room down there.

"I'm just getting started. Check the attic window on this side." The sniper shifted his aim toward the top of the building. With practiced ease, he pulled the trigger and absorbed the recoil as the rifle's sound suppressor made a noise similar to a fist hitting a pillow. Keeping his eye on the powerful scope, he saw a hole appear in the attic window. "Keep handing me ammunition."

"Still incendiaries?" the spotter asked.

"What else? When you were a kid, didn't you like to play with fire?"

"No, I just tortured animals."

"Tortured…? That's a joke, right?"

"Of course."

"Man, sometimes you worry me." The shooter squeezed off another round, then quickly reloaded.

In an amazingly smooth, fast series, he pumped incendiary bullets through every window on the eastern side of the lodge's second level.

21

As the haze from the fire retardant settled, Cavanaugh said, "He's concentrating on this window. I can't take the chance of looking out. Let's go." He tugged William toward the door.

Entering the communal room, he saw Jamie crouched next to a screen door at the back, a log wall protecting her as she scanned the meadow and the ridge to the north. He noticed that she now wore her pistol in a holster on her right hip.

"Even if the horses can't hear the shots, they sense what's going on," Jamie said.

"He'd better not hurt them." Cavanaugh heard them whinnying in alarm. Then he realized that hurting the horses was exactly the right tactic for the shooter to use. Wound, but not kill. Make the horses scream in pain. Make Cavanaugh's rage get the better of him. Force him to do something foolish.

No. He strained to channel his adrenaline, to make his body do what was necessary, to shut out every thought and emotion that didn't contribute to survival.

"Come on, William." Cavanaugh passed the long table and reached the staircase.

"I'm going to try to get a shot from an upper window," he told Angelo, who was braced next to the front screen door, staring toward the pine trees to the south.

"We know the shooter's got friends. William saw them on the monitor," Angelo said. "Why don't they make a move? What are they waiting for?"

Cavanaugh paused on the stairway. From above, he heard faint thumps, a muffled crackle, as if somebody were crumpling newspapers.

"William, run back to the office and get the fire extinguisher."

"But what if he keeps shooting into that room?"

"He won't. Then get the extinguisher from the kitchen."

"But how do you know he won't shoot into the office?"

Cavanaugh heard several more thumps above him. The crackle became louder. Smoke appeared at the head of the stairs.

"Because he's shooting through the upstairs windows now!" Cavanaugh charged up. "Get the extinguishers! The bedrooms are on fire!"

Sweating, he heard the horses galloping out of control past the front of the house. They snorted in terror. He raced to the top of the stairs and saw smoke drifting from the four bedrooms along the eastern side of the house.

A frenzied sound on the staircase came from William charging onto the landing with two fire extinguishers. The attorney's perfect shoes, suit, teeth, and hair looked absurd amid the chaos.

"We'll each take a bedroom!" Cavanaugh set down his rifle and grabbed one of the extinguishers.

To the right, debris burst from a wall at the end of the corridor. A tracer bullet had come through a bedroom's window, hit the inside wall (which was of ordinary construction, unlike the log exterior), and rammed through into the corridor, bringing wood and plaster with it, striking a farther wall.

Another bullet burst through a closer wall.

"Jesus, we'll be hit!" William said.

"Get down!" Cavanaugh warned.

As they sprawled on the floor, a bullet slammed through the wall above them, plaster and splinters spraying them.

"Something's burning me!" William said.

Cavanaugh saw an ember on the back of William's neck, another in his hair, smoke starting to dance. He flicked them off as a bullet hit the bedroom to their left, sending debris through the wall into the corridor.

"He's moving his aim back and forth along the side of the building," Cavanaugh said.

Whack! Another bullet erupted through the wall above them. The smoke thickened.

The moment a bullet burst through a wall to the right, Cavanaugh scrambled to his feet. "Hurry before his shots come back in this direction!"

As William took the bedroom on the left, Cavanaugh ducked into the one in front of him. Choking from the smoke, he pushed the trigger on the extinguisher. With a *hiss*, the retardant's haze surrounded the fire. He saw the flames weaken and kept squeezing the extinguisher's trigger. He heard a bullet wallop into the farthest bedroom on the right. Continuing to spray the retardant, he heard the next bullet hit the bedroom immediately to the right. He released the trigger, shouted to the bedroom on the left, "William, get down!" and dove to the floor. A tracer cracked through the air above his head.

"William!"

"I'm down! I'm down!" came the reply as an incendiary hit the bedroom on the left.

Cavanaugh tensed, waiting for more bullets to march back and forth along the building. But what had been a steady sequence faltered. One second became two, then three, the pause lengthening. Four. Five.

"Maybe he's out of ammunition," William said.

"Or else he hopes we'll get careless."

Cavanaugh sprayed retardant against the wall, then coughed so hard that he needed to get away from the smoke. He staggered into the corridor, where he was stunned to see William, his hair mussed, his face smudged, his suit rumpled, spraying retardant into the bedroom on the left.

"What are you staring at?" William wanted to know. "Don't you realize attorneys feel at home in hell?"

Cavanaugh started to grin, but the impulse faded as he glanced up toward the ceiling and noticed smoke seeping from it.

"No."

"What's wrong?" William aimed his fire extinguisher.

"The attic's on fire!"

He raced to a trap door in the ceiling, reached for a short rope dangling from it, and pulled. As stairs unfolded, he lurched back from flames that blocked the entrance to the attic. Coughing, he and William sprayed retardant. For a moment, through a gap in the haze, he saw the flames retreating. Yelling, he started up the steps, aiming the extinguisher. The flames kept retreating.

He climbed higher, straining to ignore the heat as he spewed retardant.

Abruptly the extinguisher quit hissing. With a curse, he threw the empty tank at the flames and turned to William. "Give me yours!"

"It's empty!"

"No!" Cavanaugh's smoke-seared throat felt as if it would burst.

The flames regrouped. Roaring, they advanced.

Now the situation was reversed—William was tugging at *him*.

Pushed by the growing heat from the attic, Cavanaugh took an angry step downward.

"We can't stay!" William tugged him harder.

34

Cavanaugh reached the landing and stared desperately at the fires in the bedrooms.

Amid the din of the flames, William said something about "other fire extinguishers."

"We don't have enough."

"You're going to need this."

"Need…?"

"*This.* You set it down."

Through raw eyes, Cavanaugh blinked at the rifle William handed him.

"Yes," he vowed. "I'm going to need this."

22

In the pines to the south, a man wearing a baseball cap gazed through shielded binoculars toward the smoke and flames spreading from the lodge's upper windows. "Cooking nicely, Alpha," he said into a microphone on his shirt collar. "Won't be long now."

"Beta, is your team in place?" the spotter's voice asked.

"On every side."

"They know they're to stay within cover?"

"Affirmative. No need to advance when the target'll do us the favor of leaving *his* cover. In the confusion, it might be hard to distinguish him from the people with him, though."

"Don't even try. Do them all."

"Repeat, Alpha."

"All. Kill them all," the spotter's voice commanded.

Across the meadow, on the eastern part of the roof, the parched wooden shingles of the lodge exploded into flames.

23

Cavanaugh's face was streaked with soot and sweat as he and William hurried down the staircase.

Angelo remained by the front door, peering out. "No sign of them."

Cavanaugh pulled his walkie-talkie from his belt. "Jamie? Mrs. Patterson?"

The staticky voices quickly responded that they didn't see anyone.

"What about the security monitors?"

"They're not working now," Mrs. Patterson's voice reported.

"*What?*" Angelo flicked a light switch on the wall. Nothing happened. The electricity had been cut.

"The fire's spreading too quickly," Cavanaugh said. "We'll soon need to leave."

"But they'll pick us off," William objected. "The basement. Can we hide down there?"

"No. The fire would suck out the oxygen. We'd suffocate. Or the building would collapse and crush us."

"The helicopter."

"Too far," Cavanaugh said.

"Hey, I'm doing my best!" William complained. "If you don't like my ideas, come up with one of your *own*."

At the back of the hall, Jamie heard parts of what they said. Her voice came from the walkie-talkie. "The car's closer. It's armored."

"There," William said. "What do you think of *that* idea?"

Smoke came down the staircase, the fire crackling on the upper level.

"If we stay here much longer," Cavanaugh decided, "we'll need to soak our hair and clothes and breathe through wet towels."

Mrs. Patterson heard in the kitchen. From the walkie-talkie, she said, "Without electricity, the pump for the well won't work. We can't get water from the taps."

William moaned.

Mrs. Patterson's sixty-year-old voice continued unsteadily from the walkie-talkie. "The toilet tanks. The only place there'll be water is in the toilets."

"Where *are* they?" William asked.

"One off the kitchen," Cavanaugh explained. "Another next to my office. Angelo, I'll watch the front. Go with him. Bring me a vest from the munitions closet when you come back."

Braced behind the log wall next to the front door, Cavanaugh saw the Taurus parked in front of the lodge. The passenger side was toward him. It was only twenty feet away. If he kept low…

Angelo returned with a soaked towel wrapped around his neck. Water dripped onto his clothes. "Here's the vest. I assumed you wanted body armor, not Kevlar."

Cavanaugh understood. Kevlar fibers were designed to block pistol bullets but were useless against high-powered rifles. Only the metal plates of true body armor could stop the latter.

He took the vest from Angelo and hefted it in despair. So much weight.

"While you're standing here thinking, you're cooking," Angelo said.

"What?"

Turning, Cavanaugh discovered that he'd been too preoccupied to realize that the fire was starting down the stairs. Flames licked the ceiling. The heat became overwhelming.

"No time. Jamie," he said into the walkie-talkie. "Mrs. Patterson. Get to the front. We're leaving. William, take my rifle."

"I don't want it." He had a wet towel around his neck, his once-beautifully tailored suit a drenched mess.

"For God's sake, do what I tell you. I need my hands free." Cavanaugh strapped on the bulky vest. "There's a round in the chamber. All you need to do is point and pull the trigger. Just don't shoot any of *us*."

He yanked his car keys from his pocket and pressed a button on the remote control, unlocking the doors. When he pressed another button, the engine started. He took a deep breath so hot it warned him that he couldn't wait any longer. A flaming chunk of wood crashed onto the stairs.

Go! he told himself.

24

Burdened by the heavy vest, he banged the screen door open, leapt off the porch and kept running the moment he landed. He focused all his attention on the passenger door. Something snapped past him as he pulled the latch. The moment he yanked the door open, a bullet whacked it, the door's armor preventing the projectile from going through.

Another bullet struck his vest, pounding an area between his shoulder blades, knocking him forward. Gasping, he didn't allow himself to think of anything except lunging into the vehicle and sprawling across the seat as bullets struck the open door. Fragments spun toward his eyes. Averting his face, he rammed the gearshift into reverse and stomped the accelerator. The vest squeezed him. His back hurt.

Tires ripping up earth, he sped backward until he was away from the lodge. With sharp rapping sounds, bullets hit the front, rear, and driver's side of the car. They cracked against the reinforced windows on those three sides. Straining to ignore them, he shifted into forward, swung the steering wheel toward the lodge, and sped so close to the porch that he almost hit the front steps. He stopped on an angle so that the rear of the car was closer to the porch than the front was, providing cover just as the open front passenger door did.

Awkward in the vest, straining to catch his breath, he leaned into the back seat, fumbled for the latch, and thrust the porch-side rear passenger door open.

"Come on!" he yelled.

When he saw the flames looming inside, he realized that he didn't need to shout encouragement. The door burst open, Jamie and Mrs. Patterson rushing out while Angelo shoved William. The soaked towels draped over their heads were steaming. The group pounded across the porch, Jamie shoving Mrs. Patterson into the front passenger seat, Angelo thrusting William into the back, scrambling in after him, screaming, "My arm! *Mierda.*"

Next to Mrs. Patterson in the front, Jamie slammed the front door shut. Angelo did the same with the back.

"How bad are you hit?" Cavanaugh shouted to Angelo, speeding away from the lodge. He needed to raise his voice—the bullets striking the car sounded like hail.

"Grazed me! I can still use the arm! *Hijo de puta*, the bleeding!"

Jamie yanked open the glove compartment, grabbed a roll of duct tape, and threw it back to Angelo.

"The gunfighter's friend." Angelo gave William his rifle, then unclipped a folding knife from a pants pocket, thumbed it open, and cut off the sleeve on his left arm. Cavanaugh got a glimpse of him wrapping duct tape around the wound as the Taurus rushed across the meadow, bullets pelting the vehicle.

"Seat belts!" he warned, fumbling to secure his.

The bullet-resistant windows developed stars. While the reinforced glass could withstand widely spaced bullets, it could be shattered if several struck the same spot. Cavanaugh flinched as more stars developed in them.

Then he worried about something else. Tensing his hands on the steering wheel, he felt his right front tire shudder from a bullet's impact. A tire with a bullet hole could support a car for perhaps five miles before the tire completely deflated. But repeated bullet impacts were another matter.

These tires are reinforced, though, Cavanaugh fought to assure himself. *It's fine, it's okay, it'll still do its work.*

The gunmen in the trees didn't have sound-suppressed rifles. To Cavanaugh's left, the horses galloped insanely, the din of the shots overwhelming.

"Somebody'll hear and call the police," William said.

"The nearest neighbors are a couple of miles away. They hear us shooting all the time." Cavanaugh pressed the accelerator, throwing up dust. "It's a private canyon. The ridges muffle the shots. Nobody pays attention."

"But they'll see the smoke and call the authorities," William said.

"It'll take time before the smoke rises above the canyon. Then it'll take more time before emergency crews arrive."

"Couldn't you lie to me just once?"

The horses reached the trees to the left and veered in panic.

Don't you dare hurt them, Cavanaugh silently warned the gunmen in the trees.

Out of control, the horses galloped toward the Taurus now. More bullets starring the windshield, Cavanaugh aimed toward a gap in the trees: the lane that would take him to the road. The horses threatened to cut in front of him, making him afraid he'd hit them.

Blood spraying, a horse flipped, its momentum twisting it over and over.

In a fury, Cavanaugh veered around it, then urged the Taurus into the gap between the trees. Now the gunmen at the eastern and western sides of the canyon couldn't see the car. Only the shooters in the woods to the south could be a threat. The left front tire felt mushy, the same as the one on the right, but the lane was only a quarter mile long.

We'll soon reach the road, Cavanaugh hoped. Rounding a thickly treed curve, he pressed the button that would open the gate, only to realize that the button was useless—the electricity wires had been cut.

His thoughts were shattered by the sight of a van parked sideways, blocking the lane. The trees were dense on each side, giving him no room to veer around it. He'd be forced to ram it, striking the van where it had the least weight—at the fender behind the rear axle. The mass of the Taurus's armor would give it enough force to shift the van and allow the Taurus to squeeze past. But the moment Cavanaugh flicked a switch to deactivate the Taurus's air bags, he noticed how low the van was. Something in it was enormously heavy.

I'll never be able to force it aside.

As a man stepped from behind the van and fired toward the Taurus's windshield, beads of glass flew inside the car. Cavanaugh stomped the brake pedal and skidded to a stop, his passengers jerking forward despite their seat belts. He yanked the gearshift into reverse and sped swiftly backward along the lane.

A bullet whacked through the front windshield.

"Everybody down!"

Cavanaugh sped backward around the curve. He reached an area where the lane widened, took his foot off the accelerator, and simultaneously twisted the steering wheel a quarter turn. The Taurus spun a hundred and eighty degrees, grazed a tree trunk, and now faced ahead. Immediately, Cavanaugh shoved the gearshift into forward and pressed the accelerator. The rear wheels threw dirt toward the pursuing gunman, who fired at the Taurus's rear tires, the dust ruining his aim.

But Cavanaugh knew that it wouldn't be long before the rear tires had bullet punctures, also. Already, the deflating front tires made his steering hard to control. The stress from the 180-degree turn had worsened their damage. As he sped from the trees and into the meadow, he felt the front wheels settle onto the plastic ring that he'd attached to the center of each rim, a tire within a tire. Without the cushion of the normal front tires, the Taurus jounced and slammed over holes in the lane.

"We're all going to die!" William exclaimed.

"Wrong!" Cavanaugh stared ahead through the shattered windshield and saw that the entire lodge was aflame. The dense smoke didn't rise. Instead, a breeze kept it low, carrying it in Cavanaugh's direction, and as he approached it, he shouted to William, "Hand me the rifle I gave you!"

Reaching back, taking it, he told Jamie, "Switch places with Mrs. Patterson! Get ready to drive!"

He steered to the left of the burning lodge and sped into the smoke, which was so thick that he couldn't see ahead of him.

Jamie crawled over Mrs. Patterson, squeezing next to him.

"Angelo, check your watch!" Cavanaugh yelled. "Tell Jamie when it's ninety seconds from now!"

"What do you want me to do?" Jamie asked.

"Drive forward until Angelo tells you it's time. Then drive back this way until you reach the smoke."

"Why? What are you going to—"

"When you come back, stop just before you get to the smoke. I'll step out of it on your side. Be careful you don't shoot me."

Cavanaugh floored the brakes, the solid inner tires digging violently into the ground as the car stopped. He took a deep breath, shoved the door open, and lunged out into the smoke.

Hearing the door bang shut behind him and the car speed forward, he ran to the left in the direction that the breeze took the smoke. Despite holding his breath, he had a desperate urge to cough, the smoke stinging his eyes. His nostrils and throat felt irritated.

The air lightened, the smoke getting thinner. He saw an opening. Sunlight revealed the stream where it wound through the canyon. He rolled down its bank, feeling the impact of his armored vest against his ribs. At the smoke-free bottom of the streambed, he took a deep breath, feeling cool sweet air fill his lungs.

Rising to a crouch, he hurried along the stream until the smoke was behind him. Then he crept up to the rim. Peering carefully across the meadow, he scanned the pines and aspens. The smoke behind him prevented the silhouette of his head from showing as he aimed toward the trees.

He remembered the Condition Yellow operators he'd seen at the gas station where he'd stopped on the way home.

Why? I'm not in the game any longer. Why am I suddenly a target?

This much he did know. If this *was* the same group, there were ten of them. He'd taken a count while he stood at the pump. Plus, there was the sniper on the eastern ridge. And no doubt a spotter for the sniper. Twelve.

Behind him, the burning lodge roared and crackled. Inside it, something heavy collapsed, rumbling like an explosion.

Twelve, he repeated to himself.

Well, let's see if we can lower the odds.

Hearing the Taurus speed toward the northern part of the canyon, Cavanaugh estimated that the car would have emerged from the smoke by now. The men in the woods on this side of the valley would chase it.

With the Taurus gaining distance from them, they'll choose the easy route and run through the grass next to the trees.

And here they come, he thought as he squinted to the south, toward the gunman who'd been in the lane. The man raced into view, sprinting next to the trees, pursuing the Taurus.

Cavanaugh sighted along the AR-15, squeezed the trigger, and blew a hole in the man's throat. The man fell as if someone had yanked a rope attached to his ankles.

Switching aim, Cavanaugh scanned the trees, saw a gunman racing along it, and blew part of his head off. A third gunman, racing farther along, sensed that something wasn't right and paused to look back. Even at a distance, the fear on the man's face was evident as he saw his downed teammates and charged for the cover of the trees. But not in time. Cavanaugh's bullet shattered the back of his head. The man became a rag doll whose lifeless legs folded, his momentum pitching him forward.

Farther along, a fourth man definitely realized something was wrong. As Cavanaugh switched aim, the man darted into the trees. Cavanaugh fired toward his retreating figure, seeing him lurch into a pine bough, blood spraying the green needles, the man's arms flying up as if in surrender, his hair seeming to part as a second shot caused more blood to spray, and suddenly he was falling.

Cavanaugh switched his aim yet again, but no targets presented themselves.

They realize what's happening, he thought. *They've taken cover. Now they'll...*

He rolled to the bottom of the stream a moment before bullets tore up dirt above him. *Four. I got four of them. Out of twelve.*

He heard the sound of the Taurus's engine change as Jamie turned the car and started back. Retreating farther along the stream, he took a deep breath before he reached the smoke. Then he climbed up, letting the smoke envelop him.

Keeping his eyes closed, he approached the sound of the returning Taurus. His nostrils and throat felt burned.

The drone of the Taurus became louder.

He stumbled faster. *Come on, Jamie!*

Then he heard the car stop ahead of him. Opening his eyes, which immediately began to weep, he stooped and emerged from the smoke. Coughing, he saw the car. Only partially visible through the bullet-starred side window, Jamie's strained face reacted with relief when he opened the rear door and climbed in, only to realize that the window across from him had a hole in it. The smell of blood permeated the car's interior. Angelo was slumped forward, unmoving.

William was covered with gore. He stared straight ahead, catatonic.

"Two windows are shattered!" Jamie said, pressed low in the front seat. "The others can't take much more!"

Desperate, Cavanaugh strained to decide what to do. To the south, the lane through the trees was blocked. To the west, most of the shooters were dead. But that still left shooters to the east and north, plus the sniper on the eastern ridge.

"Back up. Get a little farther from the smoke," he told Jamie.

Immediately, the car was in motion.

Cavanaugh pulled William down as bullets hit the no-longer protective window, chunks of glass flying.

With a clear view of the burning lodge, Cavanaugh told Jamie, "Stop."

She did.

"We're getting out."

She didn't hesitate.

Cavanaugh dragged William from the back seat. Jamie and Mrs. Patterson joined him, scurrying down into the streambed.

"I shot four of them on this side," Cavanaugh told Jamie, pointing to the west. "I think there's only one more shooter over there. If we can get into the woods, we can take him. Then we're home free."

The expression "home" struck him with bitter force as he thought about the burning lodge.

"But we'll be shot if we show ourselves and try to run to the woods," Jamie said.

"Unless we have a distraction."

Behind him, another car window burst apart, glass flying, too many bullets having struck it.

"What kind of distraction?"

"Give me a gun," William said, his catatonia broken.

"What?"

"Give me a gun. Bastards. Sons of bitches. Give me a gun. I'll shoot them until their whore mothers won't recognize them."

"Hold that thought, William. Glad to have you back with us."

Cavanaugh squirmed to the top of the bank and risked showing himself to what he assumed was now only one gunman on the western side of the canyon. But he didn't face the west. Instead, he peered toward the burning lodge. He studied a shed behind the building. A large white propane tank was next to it. But a non-incendiary bullet wouldn't detonate it.

"Jamie."

"What?"

"Cover your ears. Make sure William and Mrs. Patterson cover theirs."

He sighted his rifle toward the burning lodge, toward the fiery back porch, toward a barbecue grill on the porch. The grill had a small white propane tank. When he shot a hole in it, the flames caused the gas in the tank to explode, the porch heaving, its roof flying. Burning chunks arced toward the shed.

Immediately, Cavanaugh swung his aim toward the huge white tank behind the lodge, shot a hole into it, and tumbled down the slope, pressing his hands to his ears.

But nothing happened.

I didn't time it right. All I did was blow a hole in the tank. Now the gas is escaping, but if the fire doesn't reach it—

The ground shook. Even with his hands over his ears, the roar of the explosion stunned him. A shockwave jolted him, knocking him even closer to the ground. As the canyon walls captured the roar and thrust it back in a massive echo, Cavanaugh yelled, "Now! Run to the trees!"

He grabbed William, and thrust him up the side of the streambed. Jamie and Mrs. Patterson ran next to him, chunks of smoking metal and burning wood thudding around them.

"Faster!" Cavanaugh yelled, ignoring something hot that fell on his left arm.

Any moment, he expected a bullet to knock him flat. But more chunks of metal and burning wood kept falling, and he kept charging, and at once, yet another explosion shook the canyon, its shockwave so powerful that it threw Cavanaugh and William onto their chests.

"*Jamie?*" Cavanaugh's ears rang. "*Mrs. Patterson?*"

"We're okay! What was *that?*"

"I think it was the helicopter!"

Cavanaugh tugged William to his feet and pushed him, urging him to run. Cavanaugh's body armor made him feel suffocated. Another hot object struck him, this time on his neck, but all he cared about was the forest looming before him as he and William burst through undergrowth into the trees. He yanked William down with him and waited tensely for Jamie and Mrs. Patterson to crash through bushes and dive behind trees, landing next to him.

Only then did bullets from the opposite side of the canyon wallop into the woods. *Too late*, Cavanaugh thought in triumph.

The shots faltered, ending.

"They know the explosions can probably be heard all the way to Jackson," Cavanaugh said. "The smoke's above the canyon now. Police and emergency crews will be coming. The shooters need to get out of here."

He let thirty seconds elapse and decided it was safe to peer between trees. What he saw made him inhale sharply. The exploding propane tank had indeed caused the helicopter to explode. The combined force had flattened the lodge. Burning timbers were everywhere, igniting the grass.

25

"You prick!" the spotter yelled. "You swore you could do this!"

"How was I to know the target would—"

With a look of contempt, the spotter drew a handgun and shot his companion four times in the face. Then he took out his knife and cut off the sniper's fingertips.

"That's what *I* know," he said.

The act wasn't impulsive. It wasn't motivated by anger. The truth was, he'd been ready to kill the man, whether the attack was successful or not. The sniper had exemplary professional habits before an assignment, first-rate preparation, but afterward, he drank and talked too much. His usefulness had come to an end. In fact, the execution was the only thing about this assignment that felt good.

"*Abort*," he shouted into his walkie-talkie. "*Abort. Abort. Abort.*"

PART TWO:
THE GOSPEL ACCORDING TO FAIRBAIRN

1

"Those last four shots are too low-pitched to be from a rifle," Jamie said, puzzled.

Cavanaugh nodded. "Sounds like they came from the ridge where the sniper was. But we're too far away for anybody to expect to hit us with a pistol from there. It doesn't make sense."

Jamie studied their surroundings. "We need better cover."

"Right. For all we know, there's still at least one shooter on this side of the canyon. Keep down," he told William and Mrs. Patterson. "Move back."

Deeper into the woods, they found a depression circled by trees and squirmed into it.

"Mrs. Patterson, face this way," Jamie said, watching the elderly woman take her small Ladysmith revolver from her apron. "Aim toward the trees."

"William, you face *this* way." Cavanaugh unholstered his pistol and gave it to the attorney. "Keep it pointed away from us. Don't pull the trigger unless I tell you."

Cavanaugh and Jamie sank low, every quadrant occupied.

"When I get out of this—" Emotion made William's voice thick. "—I'm going to take shooting lessons. Karate lessons. Every damned lesson I can find. I won't feel helpless like this again."

"I'll be glad to teach you," Cavanaugh said, trying to distract William from his fear. "Especially about Fairbairn."

"Fairbairn? Who's *he?*"

"But here's your first lesson. Stop talking. We need to be quiet so we can listen if someone's sneaking up on us."

"Oh." William's face turned red with embarrassment. "Yes."

They waited and watched the forest. Cavanaugh's need to protect helped distract him from his rage. He wanted to get his hands on whoever had ordered the attack, to slam that person's head against a rock until bone cracked and—

No. Fantasies about revenge were a liability. Anger got in the way of clear thinking.

Concentrate on keeping everybody alive.

A minute passed. Cavanaugh's ears continued to ring because of the explosions and the shots he'd fired. He worked to filter out that sound, to listen beyond it, trying to detect any noise in the forest.

Ten minutes. Fifteen.

Sweat oozed from under his body armor. His back hurt from the force of the bullet that the armor had stopped. As he aimed toward the trees, his heart thumped against the ground.

There! A branch snapped deep in the trees. Cavanaugh steadied his rifle in that direction. Another branch snapped, and now Cavanaugh's finger slid onto the trigger.

He relaxed as an elk poked its head from the underbrush, its antlers blending with the dead branches of a tree behind it.

Maybe this is going to be all right, he thought. *The elk wouldn't be wandering in this direction if somebody with a rifle is out there, creeping toward us.*

Then another elk appeared, and Cavanaugh became more hopeful.

At once, the animals bolted, their hind legs kicking as they crashed through the forest. *Somebody* is *out there.* Cavanaugh again touched the trigger. But then he realized what had spooked the elk. Not somebody creeping among the trees.

A noise. Far away but getting louder. A high-pitched cluster of sirens. The police and the emergency crews were finally coming.

Cavanaugh studied the forest one more time and murmured to the group, "I think we're going to make it."

"Whatever pressure you put on me, I can take," William said.

"What?"

"I went to Harvard Law School. Nothing's more brutal than that. I'm holding you to your promise to teach me. And while you're at it, who the hell is Fairbairn?"

"When this is over, I'll tell you." Taking refuge in his protector's role, Cavanaugh distracted William from present fears by projecting him into the future.

2

They stayed within the forest, moving southward along the edge of the smoldering meadow.

"You think the sniper might still be on that ridge?" William kept glancing in that direction.

"He might have risked staying, in case we get careless when help arrives. It's better if we don't step into the open."

When the sirens stopped, Cavanaugh turned toward the silence. Through a gap in the trees, he saw scattered, burning timbers: all that remained of the lodge. To subdue another burst of fury, he focused on movement within the smoke, relieved to see that five of his horses had survived. They gathered nervously near the one that had been killed. Sickened, he shifted his gaze toward the countless bullet holes in his car, its windows starred, some of them shattered. Thinking of Angelo's body inside it, he felt his fury intensify.

Immediately, the horses bolted as a highway patrol car, dark chassis, white roof, flashers on, emerged from the lane. Even at a distance, Cavanaugh detected the shock on the face of the uniformed driver when he saw the damage.

Then a forest-service fire truck emerged, and *its* occupants looked stunned, also.

They managed to move the van that was blocking the lane, Cavanaugh thought. A further idea struck him: *Or maybe some of the gunmen drove it away.*

With Jamie watching the trees behind them, he led William and Mrs. Patterson around the southern curve of the forest and only then stepped into the lane, the trees still shielding them from a sniper.

At almost the same time, a highway patrol car came around a curve, the driver slamming on his brakes at the sight of them.

"Set down your weapons," Jamie warned William and Mrs. Patterson as she and Cavanaugh put down their own.

"Let him see your hands are empty," Cavanaugh emphasized.

The state trooper, a captain, had his fingers on his holstered pistol as he got out of the car, but then he gave Cavanaugh a closer look. "Aaron?"

Cavanaugh had used his legal name when he'd bought his property. If an enemy who knew him only as Cavanaugh had hoped to track him down by searching through land records, the effort would have been useless.

"Nice to see you, Garth."

The trooper looked surprised. "My God, with all that soot and dirt on you, I didn't recognize you."

"We had a little trouble."

"So I hear. On the radio, the first officer to get here told me your place looks like a war zone."

Garth had a solid build from weightlifting. He was tall, with strong cheekbones and a dark mustache. He spent so much time outdoors that his face had the grain of weathered wood, his tan emphasized by the green of his uniform and trooper's hat. Like any expert police officer, his eyes were constantly alert, even off duty when he, Cavanaugh, and Jamie sometimes ate dinner together in Jackson.

Those eyes were very alert now. "Jamie, is that blood on your shoulder?"

"Yes, but it isn't mine."

Cavanaugh thought angrily of the blood spatters inside the Taurus after Angelo was shot.

"Lillian…" Garth frowned at Mrs. Patterson. "You're wavering. Come over to the car and sit down."

With an unsteady hand, she pushed gray hair from her face. Dirt streaked her apron. "Thanks, Garth. It's been a long afternoon."

"You'll find four dead men in the western edge of the meadow," Cavanaugh said.

"Dead? How?"

"Shot."

"Who pulled the trigger?"

At this point, Cavanaugh would normally have requested a lawyer to make sure that he didn't say something that became misinterpreted. But he had one of the best attorneys in the country standing next to him.

"*I* did," Cavanaugh said. "You'll find a fifth body in my car, or what's left of my car. One of the other guys pulled *that* trigger."

3

Mrs. Patterson's late husband, Ben, had been a Wyoming state trooper who died in a shootout with a gang trying to hijack a truck filled with pharmaceuticals. Known as Lillian to every officer assigned to Teton County, she was interviewed first, then escorted back to the waiting room at the highway-patrol barracks ten miles south of Jackson.

"I phoned your son-in-law to let him know you can leave now," Garth said. "He'll soon be here to drive you to your daughter's place. Your family's eager to see you."

"I'll wait with you in the front hallway," Jamie told her.

William was the next person taken to the interview room. Twenty minutes later, he came back, the satisfied look on his face indicating that, while he might not know anything about guns, he knew how to conduct himself with law officers. Now that he was in lawyer mode again, his torn, filthy suit somehow looked dignified.

Jamie went next. Cavanaugh had taught her to answer police questions directly but never to provide more than what was asked and never to attempt to deceive.

Then it was Cavanaugh's turn. The room had harsh lights, plain walls, two chairs, and a small desk. Focusing on minutiae helped keep his emotions in check.

"Want some coffee?" Garth pointed toward a carafe and some Styrofoam cups on the desk. A tape recorder was there, also.

"I could use the caffeine," Cavanaugh said, pouring a cup. His watch showed that it was half past ten. But now that his adrenaline had dissipated, he felt as if it were four in the morning.

"Ready?" Garth asked.

"When you are." The stench of smoke radiated from Cavanaugh's jeans and shirt. His neck and arm hurt. His back felt bruised where the bullet had struck his armor. But at least his legs and chest felt lighter, relieved of the heavy vest.

Garth pressed buttons on the recorder. "This is Captain Garth Braddock. The interview is with Aaron Stoddard." He gave the place, time, and date. "Tell me what happened."

While waiting, Cavanaugh had taken the opportunity to get his narrative in order. Only after concluding his description, did he allow his emotions to show. "I haven't the faintest fucking idea what's going on."

"We found your sniper."

Cavanaugh leaned forward. "Is he answering questions?"

"It's a hard to get answers from a corpse. Somebody shot him four times in the face."

Cavanaugh took a moment to adjust to that, finally saying, "That explains the four pistol shots we heard."

"Fragmentation-type ammunition. Mutilated his features enough that even people who knew him would have trouble identifying him. His teeth were so damaged that comparing them to dental records will be useless. The question is, who did that to him?"

Cavanaugh thought about it. "The only available candidate is someone on the assault team. But that doesn't make sense. Did he have ID?"

"No."

"Did you send his fingerprints to the FBI?"

"Couldn't. The tips of his fingers were cut off."

Cavanaugh took a longer time to adjust to that.

"The four men you killed," Garth said.

"Was *forced* to kill."

"*Their* fingerprints got a really quick response. Those men were fresh out of prison. Within the past six weeks."

"Six weeks?"

"I can't imagine how they came to be together. They served time in four different penitentiaries. Pennsylvania. Alabama. Colorado. Oregon." Garth slid a sheet of paper across the table. "Recognize any of these names?"

Cavanaugh studied them, hoping, but finally had to say, "No." He grasped at a thought. "Four different prisons? They must have known each other *before* they went to those prisons."

"Not according to their criminal records. There's no indication they ever crossed paths before. But they did have *one* thing in common. Armed robbery. Gang shootings. Rape. These were really violent guys."

"Before everything started, I think I saw them and the rest of their friends at the Moose Junction gas station." Cavanaugh said. "They didn't handle themselves like street criminals. They weren't wired and jittery and unfocused. These guys had stillness and control. They looked like operators."

"But their records indicate they *were* street criminals. So how, all of a sudden, did they get to be…'operators,' you called them? Unusual word. I don't often hear it. That car of yours. When I got a close look at what was left of it, I found bullet-resistant windows, armor plating, tires within tires…Tell me again what you used to do for a living."

"I was in the security business."

"The bodyguards I see around here—"

Cavanaugh hated the word.

"—are usually hired by entertainers and sports stars on vacation. Mostly for show in a quiet community like this. To remind us how important they are. But you never fit the profile of the thugs some of those celebrities use for bodyguards."

"I'm an unassuming guy."

"Obviously, you don't like being called a bodyguard."

No answer.

"Are you holding back anything I need to know?"

Cavanaugh hesitated. "Yes. I was what's called a protector. I worked for an international security firm called Global Protective Services. I used the professional alias of 'Cavanaugh.'"

"Professional alias?"

"I saved the lives of people who show up on CNN and the front pages of *The Washington Post* and *Wall Street Journal*. These are the kind of people who need the reassurance of knowing they can absolutely trust me with sensitive information, that nobody'll come around later and persuade me to answer questions about them."

"You mean like the *police* asking questions?"

"My former clients will stonewall you."

"It's been tried."

"And they'll never trust me again."

"Again? I got the impression you'd retired."

"My retirement just ended."

"Is that another way of saying you intend to run your own investigation?"

"If a former client decided that he or she can't let me live with certain information, I have ways to find out."

"You're not a law enforcement officer. Keep that in mind."

"I will."

"I'm serious. I wouldn't want to see you in front of *two* grand juries. 'Cavanaugh.'" Garth tested the sound of the name.

"The idea was to keep my private life and my professional life separate."

"Looks like it didn't work."

4

A state trooper came over when Garth escorted Cavanaugh from the interview room.

"Did you find any of them?" Garth asked.

The trooper looked at Garth, as if to suggest that they speak in private.

"It's okay. You can talk in front of him."

In the background, Jamie and William listened to the trooper's reply.

"No sign of the shooters."

"They were dressed as campers," Cavanaugh said.

"Which makes them fairly invisible around here," Garth pointed out. "Even so, how do you suppose they got out of the area near your property so fast?"

"When you drove me from the ranch, I noticed that the van that had blocked the lane was gone. Did any of your team move it?"

The trooper shook his head *no*.

"Some of the shooters probably drove it away. The tires were low from weight in the back, but even so, they could have driven it. As for the rest, I'm guessing a couple of cars picked them up as they emerged from the trees. Using two-way radios, they could have easily coordinated it so they didn't show themselves if there were police cars or emergency vehicles in sight. Plus, you didn't know what you were dealing with and didn't start searching until thirty minutes after the explosion. Plenty of time to get away. They could have been in Jackson by then."

Another trooper entered the room. "A lot of reporters and a TV crew in the parking lot."

"Swell," Garth said.

"We can't assume they're all legitimate," Cavanaugh warned. "That hit team isn't going to fade away. They'll watch the building. They'll try to follow us when we leave."

"Spend the night here."

"There's nothing I'd rather do. But in the morning, we'll still have the same problem. Not to mention, they'll be organized by then. No, the best time to leave is when they least expect it. As soon as possible."

"How? And where will you go? What will you use for transportation?"

"I already made the arrangements," Jamie said.

5

In the harshly illuminated parking lot, dozens of reporters straightened as the barracks door opened. The lights from within silhouetted Garth, who stepped from the building and walked toward them. The weather had shifted, cold enough to bring frost from his mouth. Garth had no idea how the media had gotten word of the attack so quickly. If one of his officers was responsible, he swore to find out who it was and give him the worst duties imaginable. Since Jackson didn't have a TV station or a large newspaper, most of the men and women converging on him must have come from Idaho Falls (a driveable 180 miles away) or from Casper, Laramie, and Cheyenne (much farther away—to get here this soon, the reporters would have needed to charter planes). Then it occurred to Garth that the person who alerted the media might have been somebody on the hit team. Get as many reporters and TV cameras here as possible. In the ensuing chaos, the gunmen could blend. Any of the supposed news people shouting questions at him could be a killer.

"Is it true that six men were shot—"

"Ranch thirty miles north of—"

"Explosion destroyed—"

"Sniper—"

"Helicopter—"

"Okay, all right." Garth gestured for quiet. "If all of you talk at once, I can't hear your questions." The television lights glared at him, hurting his eyes. "I have a brief statement. At four-thirty this afternoon—"

Suddenly, the front door to the barracks banged open. As Garth turned, he saw a trooper hurrying toward him, a concerned look on his face.

"What's the matter?" Garth asked.

Cameras flashed as the trooper motioned Garth away from the reporters and spoke in urgent hushed tones.

Garth spun toward the reporters. "This'll have to wait. There's been a—"

"Captain!" a trooper yelled from the front door.

A siren wailed in the fenced-off parking area behind the barracks. Roof lights flashing, a highway patrol car rounded the building and skirted the reporters. An officer was silhouetted in the front seat as the car reached the main road and sped north toward Jackson, disappearing around a curve in this sparsely populated section of the valley. Moments later, a second patrol car followed, lights flashing, siren wailing.

Some of the reporters raced for their cars.

Or possibly they aren't reporters, Garth thought.

Others stayed, demanding to know what was going on.

"Tell us what happened this afternoon!"

"Are these incidents connected?"

Headlights blazing, a state police van hurried past, reached the road, and followed the three civilian cars that chased the cruisers.

6

Opening and closing his knife, the man who'd shot the sniper watched from a road on a bluff across from the police barracks. He was forty years old, tall and lean, with an etched face. His powerful forearms resulted from years of pounding a hammer onto an anvil, forging blades. He used various names. Currently, his devotion to knives had prompted him to choose the alias of Bowie. Sitting in his car, he used a night-vision magnifier that wasn't affected by the stark contrasts of light and darkness in the parking lot a quarter mile from him. While he listened to the sirens, he studied the sequence of vehicles speeding away: the first cruiser, the second cruiser, the three civilian cars, then the police van.

Damned smart, Bowie thought.

He spoke into a two-way radio. "It's a shell game. The target's in one of the police vehicles. The question is which."

A voice from one of the pursuing civilian cars said, "I vote for the van."

"Or maybe the target's still in the barracks," Bowie replied. "Maybe those police vehicles are decoys. We don't have enough personnel to follow everybody."

"Wait!" the voice blurted. "Ahead of us. One of the police cars is pulling to the side of the road."

"For God's sake, don't stop," Bowie ordered.

"But we need to act like real reporters. Real reporters would stop."

"That's what they *want* you to do. You'd be caught between the cruiser that stopped and the van behind you. Meanwhile, the *first* cruiser would get away. That must be where the target's hiding."

"Okay," the voice said five seconds later, "I didn't stop. In my rear-view mirror, I see the other cars—the reporters who left with us—*they're* stopping. Shit. The cruiser ahead of us. *It's* stopping!"

"Drive past it!"

"It's turning sideways! It's blocking the road!"

7

Cavanaugh crouched out of sight in the police car's back seat. Feeling the state trooper expertly skid the cruiser sideways to block the road, Cavanaugh braced himself and reminded the driver, "Leave room for them to drive around!"

There was always the chance that actual reporters were in the pursuing car. On a hunch, the reporters might have decided to ignore the patrol car that stopped and to follow the one in the lead. If so, with the road blocked, the driver of the pursuing car would now stop and demand to know what was going on. But members of the assault team would want to get away.

Hurrying from the cruiser, Cavanaugh and the policeman took cover behind the engine, the only place in an unarmored vehicle that would stop a bullet. The pursuing car took advantage of the space the patrolman had left and veered toward the shoulder, passing the cruiser's back fender, throwing up dust. As it sped farther down the road, Cavanaugh aimed a powerful flashlight, centering the beam on the license plate.

"Got it!" He shouted the numbers and letters to the trooper who repeated them into a radio microphone attached to his collar.

The second cruiser arrived, and Jamie hurried from her hiding place in the back seat. Meanwhile, Cavanaugh's driver chased the escaping car, his siren wailing.

A moment later, the van arrived. William got out.

"It worked," Jamie told Cavanaugh.

"Not just yet." As the other cruiser joined the chase, Cavanaugh walked along the road, in the direction from which he'd come. The trooper who'd driven the van followed him, accompanied by Jamie and William. Cavanaugh turned left toward a dark lane that led into a gravel pit. He aimed the flashlight and saw a shadowy pickup truck parked between mounds of earth. In case there'd been a gunfight, the occupants would have been out of the line of fire. Even so, they'd obeyed instructions and taken cover behind the truck's engine.

"Mrs. Patterson? Kyle?" As Cavanaugh shone the light, keeping it away from eye level, he saw two people rise from behind the truck.

"More excitement," Mrs. Patterson said. "I don't know how my husband ever put up with it." But something in her voice suggested that some aspects of the excitement were enjoyable, that she now understood why her husband had liked being a police officer.

The man next to her—stout, bearded, with wooly hair—was Mrs. Patterson's son-in-law, one of the best horse trainers in the valley. "Good directions, Jamie."

"Thanks." When Kyle had picked up Mrs. Patterson at the barracks, Jamie had explained what needed to be done. "You won't be safe with your family," she'd told Mrs. Patterson. "The people who attacked us know you matter to us. They might try to grab you and use you against us. Plus, your family won't be safe if somebody on the assault team follows you to them."

"Jamie told you I need a favor?" Cavanaugh asked Kyle.

"The loan of my truck. Sure. Anything to keep Lillian safe."

"Count on it," Cavanaugh said. "This officer will make sure no one's following his police van when he drives you home."

Kyle gave Cavanaugh the keys to the truck. "Where are you taking Lillian?"

"Can't tell you in case a couple of guys with guns come around and ask you."

"Anybody who tries'll be dodging slugs from a deer rifle. No matter what, I wouldn't tell," Kyle emphasized.

Cavanaugh thought, *But what if they put a gun to your daughter's face?*

In the distance, the pursuing sirens echoed.

8

"The cops must have radioed ahead!" the voice blurted from the two-way radio. Sirens shrieked in the background. "We're in Jackson! They've got two police cars parked sideways, blocking the street! The other police cars are still chasing us!"

Saddened, the man who called himself Bowie shook his head. He had spent the past month with the team he spoke to. He had shared meals with them, slept in the same room, and gotten to know all the pathetic, painful outrages that had been done to them throughout their lives. Social conservatives would argue that those outrages were nothing more than excuses these men used to justify their outrageous acts. There was truth to that viewpoint, Bowie thought. No matter how damaged people were, they needed to accept responsibility for their actions. They needed to exert control over themselves. Without discipline, chaos reigned. He had learned that lesson with great difficulty.

"I'm going to do a one-eighty!" the voice yelled.

Leaning closer to the radio receiver, Bowie heard tires squealing.

"They're blocking us that way, too!" the voice yelled.

Yes, chaos needs to be eliminated, Bowie thought.

Melancholy, he reached for a transmitter next to him. He pressed its "on" button and saw a red light appear. When he pressed another button, a green light appeared.

In the distance, a sound like thunder rumbled through the night.

9

Speeding toward the car, the state trooper stared beyond it toward the flashing lights of the Jackson police cars that blocked a main street through the small town. *Almost got them*, he thought. *One thing they're not is reporters.*

Suddenly, the quarry ahead executed a 180-degree turn. With equal abruptness, the trooper pressed his brake pedal enough to give him traction but not lock the brakes. He swerved so that his patrol car blocked the left side of the almost deserted street. The cruiser following him performed an equivalent maneuver, blocking the *right* side of the street.

He scrambled outside, drew his Glock .40, and took a position behind the engine area, aiming toward the vehicle that sped toward him. His fellow officer did the same. If the car tried to ram them, they would flee toward the protection of the storefronts on each side. If the car stopped and its occupants decided to try shooting their way to freedom, the troopers would teach them the error of their ways.

The car sped closer, veering to the right, hoping to slip between the cruiser and the sidewalk.

It exploded, the shockwave hurling the trooper backward, slamming him onto the street. The flash seared his vision. The ringing in his head was agony. As his mind spun, he felt pressure in his chest, air being sucked from his lungs.

Wet. Why does my face feel wet? He pawed his cheeks. *Blood. My God, I'm bleeding.*

Chunks of metal crashed around him. Something soft and wet fell on him. Beyond the ringing in his ears, he heard the other trooper screaming. Then he realized *he* was the one who was screaming.

10

As the pickup truck worked its way up a slope, Cavanaugh heard the blast from the direction of town. Using only parking lights so that the truck would be difficult to follow, Jamie drove, Mrs. Patterson and William sitting next to her. With no more space in the cabin, Cavanaugh sat in the truck's uncovered back.

He felt the explosion as much as he heard it. In the murky distance, a fireball illuminated the night, showing him that the explosion came from the direction of town.

The truck's back window slid open. "My God, what caused *that*?" Jamie asked through the opening.

Cavanaugh was reminded of what Garth had said when he'd arrived at the ruin of Cavanaugh's home—*looks like a war zone.* "This is beginning to feel like Bosnia did."

He sensed Jamie thinking as the truck jounced along a deep rut. "You never told me you were there."

"It's not something anybody who was there wants to remember. One thing you could count on—just when things got quiet, somebody'd start shooting again or blow something up."

The lane got bumpier, sending vibrations that jostled Cavanaugh in the back of the truck. From the direction of town, he heard sirens. A lot of them. Through another break in the trees, he saw that the flames silhouetted the hills close to town.

"How much farther?" William asked, uneasy.

"Five minutes."

The faraway sirens persisted.

"Who's Fairbairn?" William prompted nervously.

Cavanaugh studied the slope they'd been climbing. He didn't see any headlights following them. "Fairbairn invented the basis for some of those lessons you swore you were going to take."

In the back of the truck, he turned to look inside. The faint dashboard lights revealed that the attorney's face was stark with fear.

Maybe it's time for a bedtime story, Cavanaugh thought.

"Fairbairn was a police officer in Shanghai," he said through the open rear window. "In the early nineteen hundreds. When Shanghai was the most dangerous city in the world."

William raised his head and looked at him with interest.

"You're sure you want to hear about this?" Cavanaugh asked.

"For God's sake, would I ask if I didn't?"

"If *he* doesn't, *I* do," Mrs. Patterson said.

"One night, while Fairbairn was patrolling a particularly rough district, someone attacked him. He woke up in a hospital and vowed he'd never be caught off-guard again, so when he saw an advertisement for somebody named Professor Okada, 'master of ju-jutsu and bonesetting'—I love the bonesetting part—he decided to take lessons. Eventually, he became an expert in several Oriental martial arts and adapted those systems into a few simple, deadly movements that anyone could learn in a couple of hours."

"Hours?" William asked.

"Shanghai's violence gave Fairbairn plenty of chances to test his methods. He created the first SWAT team. He also invented the shooting house: a series of rooms with various obstacles and pop-up targets of bad guys aiming weapons. Sometimes, the pop-ups show a woman carrying an infant or a bad guy holding a hostage. The point is, as you proceed through a maze, anticipating a threat around every corner, you can't start shooting every time there's movement. Instant decisions need to be made. Control has to be maintained. Anybody who's ever gone through a shooting house—Fairbairn called it a mystery house; the British SAS calls it a *killing* house—knows how tense and draining the experience can be."

In the darkness, the truck leveled off in what seemed to be a meadow.

"And?" William asked.

"In 1939, at the start of the Second World War, Fairbairn went back to England and joined the War Office. There, he taught what he called 'gutterfighting' to the British commandos. After that, he went to America and taught the OSS, which eventually became the CIA. He and his colleague Eric Sykes invented the Fairbairn-Sykes dagger that the British commandos used. His students went on to teach other students. *Those* students spread the gospel according to Fairbairn until his close-quarter combat tactics became pretty much universal in any unit that truly knows what it's doing. Not only are Fairbairn's tactics easy to learn, but they stick with you. In the 1990s, the CIA tested his theories on some behind-the-lines World War II agents. Those eighty-year-olds hadn't forgotten any of what Fairbairn taught them. The system was so simple and logical, it came back to them automatically and proved that you didn't need to be young and strong to protect yourself."

The truck stopped.

"We made it," Jamie said.

"See?" Cavanaugh told William. "That five minutes didn't take long." Wary, he climbed down from the truck, assessing the murky outline of a cabin. "Jamie, here's the key Garth gave me. While the rest of you get settled inside, I'll check the perimeter."

"Wait," William insisted. "You're just going to stop? What about the specifics of Fairbairn's system?"

"There's work to be done, William."

11

Garth stepped from his cruiser into a nightmare. Ahead, on East Broadway, one of Jackson's few main streets, lingering flames as well as the headlights and flashing lights of emergency vehicles showed the wreckage of five cars. The vehicle in the middle had been ripped apart by an explosion. Fiery debris had struck and ignited the four police cars, eventually setting off the fuel in their gas tanks. Now the cars were just smoking metal frames. Paramedics put unconscious state troopers onto gurneys, wheeling them toward two ambulances. The air smelled of cooked flesh. *Dear God*, Garth thought, watching the ambulances speed away.

Movement caught his attention. Jackson's chief of police finished an urgent conversation with a fireman and walked toward him. Jackson had about 8,200 all-year residents, with an additional 10,000 ski-season residents and three million tourists who passed through during the summer. The huge influx of visitors meant that the area's law enforcement, emergency, and medical systems needed to be first-rate, but even so, they weren't accustomed to gunfights and explosions, let alone two in less than twelve hours.

"You radioed ahead to warn us about the pursuit," the police chief said. "I sure hope you know what's going on."

Sickened, Garth scanned the shattered store windows on each side of the street: Pendleton's, Jackson Mercantile, Chico's, Häagen-Dazs ice cream. The wooden sidewalks were smoldering. So were some of the cottonwoods in the town square. One of the four elk-antler arches that served as entrances to the square's small park had been blown into pieces. Thousands of chunks of gray-white antlers covered the street like dirty snow.

"This is connected to the attack on Aaron Stoddard's place."

"And what was *that* about?"

"No one's sure." Garth outlined the facts that were available, then asked, "What did they have in that car? A bomb? What set it off? Bullets?"

The police chief pointed toward a crowd at the far end of the square, shocked residents and tourists wearing hastily put-on clothes, some only in housecoats. "A guy walking his dog saw the whole thing. He said there were a lot of sirens and squealing tires. But no shots. Definitely no shots. Several people who live nearby and were wakened by the sirens say they didn't hear shots, either."

"So what set off the explosive? Whoever was in that car, were they so determined not to be questioned that they blew themselves up?"

"I don't see how they could have," the police chief said.

"What do you mean?"

"They couldn't have reached the explosive to detonate it. The blast split the chassis upward. From the middle. From underneath."

"*Underneath?*" Garth asked in confusion.

"We'll need crime-scene investigators to confirm it, but at the moment, it looks as if the bomb was mounted under the car."

"They didn't know it was there?"

"Seems that way. If it was their explosive, they'd have kept the bomb in the trunk or in the back seat, where they could get to it in a hurry. But this way…"

Garth understood. "Yes. The only reason to put the bomb *under* the car was to hide it from the people inside."

12

The man who called himself Bowie drove west over the rugged Teton Pass, leaving Wyoming. Dark mountains hulked on each side. His destination was a motel in Idaho Falls, two hours away. He'd rented a room there two days previously. He'd made his preparations and left yesterday before dawn, arriving in Jackson Hole with plenty of time to accompany the sniper on his hike to the ranch. At midday, the motel's maid would have cleaned his room and made the bed. There was no way for her to be aware that for much of tonight, the bed would not have been slept in. Tomorrow, after he got a few hours sleep, she would again make the bed, nothing unusual about his patterns. By then, he'd have checked out, gone to the Idaho Falls airport, and flown his plane to his next destination.

As he drove through the darkness, his tortured thoughts tugged him back to a long-ago summer when he and Aaron had played in the shadows of the trees in the park at the bottom of their street. Someone had built a new subdivision a few blocks away. To make the location more attractive, the owner had put in a lake, stocking it with goldfish. What the owner didn't count on was the effect of heavy rains. The lake overflowed, fish and water spilling into the stream that wound through the park. Aaron and Bowie had sat by that stream, spellbound by the magic of the six-inch-long fish, their speckled gold shimmering beneath the water.

"We could go home and get buckets," Aaron had suggested. "Trap a couple of fish in each bucket."

"And then what?"

"Try to convince our parents to buy us each a fish tank."

"I don't think my father would go for that. He'd probably knock me on the floor for suggesting it."

"I don't think my stepfather would go for it, either," Aaron said. "But, hey, we could still get the buckets. What we'll do is catch the fish and carry them back to the lake."

"It'll take all day," Bowie said, although his name had been different back then. "Besides it wouldn't make a difference. The next rain, all these fish will flood back into the stream." He removed his knife from his pocket and opened it. "I know what to do."

Aaron stared uneasily at the sunlight glinting off the blade.

Bowie saw a dead branch on the ground and cut off its twigs. He was about to sharpen its tip and suggest that they use the fish for target practice, but the look on Aaron's face told him to make a different suggestion. "Let's get some string and safety pins. We'll fish. We'll pretend our helicopter crashed in the jungle."

"Cool." A doubt clouded Aaron's eyes. "But if we catch any, I don't want to eat them. They're not very big, and I'm not sure goldfish taste good."

"Who said anything about eating them? We'll put them back in the lake after we catch them."

But they never did catch any fish, no matter how hard they tried throughout that muggy summer, most of which they spent in the shade of those dense trees, pretending they were the last two members of a Special Forces team trapped behind enemy lines. They became so skilled at hiding from the enemy that kids bicycling past or men and women strolling hand-in-hand along the path didn't see them crouching among the bushes.

As things turned out, it didn't rain again for a long time. The stream evaporated until there were only four inches of water. Most of the fish suffocated. By then, he and Aaron had gotten tired of fishing and instead lay among the bushes, reading Bowie's knife magazines. Sometimes when Bowie's father got even drunker than usual, bragging about what a hot-shit football player he'd been and how Bowie had damned sure better be as good, Bowie went down to the park on his own. He speared a couple of the surviving fish. His knife was so sharp that it made him feel as if he cut through butter when he sliced their bellies open. After all, what did it matter? The fish would have died anyhow.

13

"By the time I concluded that you and Aaron Stoddard were the same person, I'd learned a lot about your alter ego," William said in the cabin. "Aaron Stoddard is part of Jackson Hole's search-and-rescue team. He volunteers to coach basketball at a local school. He teaches children's groups about wilderness camping."

"A hell of a swell guy," Cavanaugh said. Knowing that he'd been investigated made him feel vulnerable. If William could find him, others could. In fact, they *had*.

The cabin—a hunting retreat that Garth leased from the government—had a living/cooking area, a bedroom, a hand-pumped well, and an outdoor toilet. After scouting the perimeter, Cavanaugh had waited in the woods, listening, satisfying himself that the night was quiet.

Meanwhile, Jamie had closed and locked the interior shutters. When he entered, he saw her put a lamp in a corner, where it wouldn't help a gunman who peered through cracks in the shutters and tried to use its feeble light to guide his aim. Mrs. Patterson (tireless, wonderful Mrs. Patterson) used the cabin's Coleman stove to heat cans of soup that she found in a cupboard.

"You're going to get your wish," Cavanaugh told Jamie after a long silence.

She looked confused by the apparently out-of-nowhere reference.

"I'm accepting what Duncan gave me in his will. I'm assuming control of Global Protective Services."

The stove hissed. William and Mrs. Patterson watched him.

"I think the only way to catch whoever's responsible is to offer myself as bait," he continued, "and that's an awfully good reason to own Global Protective Services. It'll give me access to the best operators in the business."

The stove kept hissing.

"All my life, I tried to protect people," Cavanaugh said. "Even when I was in Delta Force, I thought of it as protecting. Against terrorists. Against all the cowards and sadists who think they can kill anybody in the name of God or because they believe *they're* God. But this is something new for me. This is the first time *I've* needed protecting."

14

Venice.

The suite in the hotel—a converted twelfth-century Doge palace—had a dramatic view of St. Mark's piazza. Crowds persisted, despite a chill spray from rising waves.

"Glassmaking," the Internet tycoon said.

"Glassmaking?" The head of his protective detail frowned.

"Nobody comes to Venice without taking the boat across the lagoon to Murano," the tycoon's wife said. "For certain, *I* don't. Murano's the most famous glassmaking town in the world. Its pieces are museum quality."

The protective agent nodded. "Give me twenty-four hours to set up the security."

"In twenty-four hours, we'll be in Madrid," the tycoon's wife told him.

"Madrid? That isn't on the schedule."

"We decided during breakfast. This city's too damp."

The agent, a former member of Britain's Strategic Air Service, nodded again. "Yes, all those canals." One hundred and fifty of them, to be exact. Four hundred bridges. One hundred and seventeen islands, every nook and cranny of them a security nightmare.

"So that's the plan." The tycoon's wife dropped her napkin onto a half-eaten bowl of fruit. "In ten minutes, we leave for Murano."

There wasn't much to be said after that. The agent, whose name was Miller, had five men at his disposal, three of whom were resting after the night shift. Because the change in schedule was last-minute, a predator couldn't know about it, so there wasn't any point in sending a man to scout the location. Miller took some consolation that he didn't need to be overly concerned about a long-distance threat from a sniper. With a business executive, the likely threat was kidnappers wanting a ransom.

The bumpy twenty-minute lagoon crossing made the tycoon and his wife slightly nauseous. As Miller's eyes roamed the choppy water, on guard against any boats that might speed toward them, he studied the island of San Michele, Venice's main cemetery. Several boats were docked there, draped with funeral cloths and wreaths. He'd read somewhere that, with land so scarce in the Venice area, soil had to be brought to the cemetery so that it could continue accepting coffins.

He switched his gaze toward Murano, the heart of which had two rows of Renaissance buildings separated by a canal. Yellow and brown, the long, stone structures adjoined one another, almost all of them glassmaking factories.

My God, if we need to go into every one of these buildings, Miller thought, *we'll be here all day.*

But the tycoon and his wife had made phone calls and knew precisely where they were heading. Miller instructed one of his men to stay behind and guard the launch, to make sure it wasn't tampered with. Then Miller and his remaining agent flanked their clients, never looking at them, always peering outward at potential threats. The tycoon and his wife ignored the tourists, crossed the street next to the canal, and entered a building, where two well-dressed owners waited for them.

Miller didn't like the shadowy corridor he faced—or the roar at the end of it. He entered a large area that consisted of several blazing furnaces, their hatches open. Men wearing fire-retardant aprons and gloves held metal poles into the flames, turning them, softening the large pieces of glass suspended from their tips. At a precisely judged moment, one of the workers removed the pole and applied various tools to the molten glass, cutting, twisting, and shaping it, sometimes blowing through a tube to expand it into a globe.

Keeping his attention on the corridor through which they'd entered, Miller heard a conversation behind him, the two owners using English to explain to the client and his wife how time-intensive a hand-crafted piece of glass was, how it could take all day to make one perfect vase and certainly much longer to fashion a glass peacock, its fanned-out tail as multicolored as that of an actual bird. The most ambitious pieces, the most complexly contoured and layered, required centuries of glassmaking experience. The techniques were handed down from generation to generation.

Miller straightened as a man and woman came along the corridor. In their mid-thirties, pleasant looking, they wore shorts and sandals. The man's shirt was tucked in. So was the woman's blouse. No outline of a gun or a knife. No fanny packs. Nothing to cause concern. The man had a camera around his neck. He nodded to Miller, a little puzzled that Miller wasn't watching the activity around the ovens. Miller nodded in return.

Behind him, the two owners were telling the tycoon and his wife that the almost finished vases they saw on a table required one more procedure and then would be ready for exhibition.

"Twenty of them. How much will their total value be?" the tycoon asked.

The answer was a very long number in euros.

More tourists entered.

Miller scanned them. Nothing threatening.

"How much in dollars?" the tycoon asked.

Miller heard fingers tapping a calculator. "Four hundred thousand."

The tycoon said, "I assume they can be safely packaged and sent by air."

"Of course."

"Signore," one of the executives said, presumably to a tourist who'd entered, "photographs are not permitted."

The man answered in French that he didn't understand.

The executive switched to French and repeated that photographs were not allowed.

The room became more crowded.

"No, don't touch that," the other executive said in Italian.

Glass shattered.

The startle reflex cannot be eliminated. It's hardwired into the human nervous system. Knees bend. Shoulders hunch forward. Hands rise to the chest, palms outward. These movements provide an instinctive defense against an attack. His reaction unwilled and automatic, Miller swung his gaze from the corridor toward the scene behind him, where the two executives and Miller's clients gaped at an almost finished vase that the man with the camera had knocked over. Chunks of colored glass lay at their feet.

"I'm so sorry, so sorry," the man kept saying in French.

Miller suddenly felt light-headed. His leg was wet. He peered down, gasping when he discovered that his right pant leg was cascading crimson, that he was standing in a pool of swiftly spreading blood.

Femoral artery was all he could think. *Somebody cut my—*

A knife slash with a sharp blade almost never caused pain unless delivered with force. As the skin parted, there was only a stinging sensation. Spinning, Miller saw the woman who'd followed the group into the factory. Shorts. Sandals. She walked along the murky corridor toward the bright sunlight that formed the exit, looking once over her shoulder.

Abruptly, Miller's vision turned gray. Groping to find something to keep him from falling, he stumbled toward his client's wife, who jerked away in horror. Somebody screamed, but Miller barely heard. The roar of the furnaces became muted. Their blazes dimmed. Despite the heat radiating from them, he felt cold. Reaching, falling, he struck the table, upended it, and sent the remainder of the vases crashing onto the floor.

With his head sideways on the concrete floor, he stared at colored chunks of now-worthless glass shimmering around him. Their luster faded, as did his vision. The last he saw were the chunks being covered by his blood.

15

Sunlight glinting off its bullet-resistant windows, the helicopter landed in the meadow in front of the cabin, the wind from its rotor blades bending the grass.

"But when will I be able to come back and see my family?" The noise from the chopper's engines forced Mrs. Patterson to strain her voice.

"When we're sure you're out of danger," Jamie explained.

"Which is the same as saying when *Aaron's* out of danger." Mrs. Patterson nodded toward Cavanaugh.

Jamie had gotten so used to his assumed name that she felt a sense of unreality when people referred to him as Aaron.

"It's for your family's protection as much as yours," Jamie told her. "Believe me, you'll be well cared for."

"New York?"

"Yes. Manhattan."

Mrs. Patterson thought a moment. "Is Radio City Music Hall there?"

Jamie almost smiled. "Ten blocks from where you'll be staying. We've got some nice-looking young men who'll be pleased to escort you."

Behind her, Cavanaugh told Garth, "William phoned Judge Canfield and got permission for us to leave the state until the grand jury convenes."

"He certainly has the power to get things done in a hurry." Garth didn't sound happy that influence achieved results. "We're checking every hotel and motel in the area. We're especially interested in the cabins at Moose Junction, where you saw the assault team. We're also checking the airlines and the local rental car agencies."

"The car that blew up. You're sure the bomb was *under* it?"

"The crime scene investigators confirmed that."

"What the hell is going on?" But even as Cavanaugh asked the question, the answer was obvious. "Whoever hired those men was afraid of what they might say if they were captured and interrogated. Ditto the sniper."

In the helicopter, the pilot motioned for everybody to get aboard.

"Thanks for your help, Garth."

"I'm just glad you got out of this alive."

Except for Angelo, Cavanaugh thought, anger burning inside him. *I'll find who did this.*

The chopper lifted off, gaining altitude to clear the bluffs. Its destination was eastward. But as it flew from the Teton valley, Cavanaugh did something he'd promised himself that he wouldn't—he asked the pilot to fly north first. He wanted to see his ranch. Above his canyon, he surveyed the scattered wreckage of his home, the charred timbers, the craters where the propane tank and the helicopter had exploded, the flattened lodge, the burned meadow.

He and Jamie looked at one another.

Yes, I'll find who did this, he thought.

16

Albuquerque, New Mexico.

The newly constructed jail was on the outskirts of the city. The state's hottest time was from the middle of June to the middle of September. But this had been a drought year, the heat lingering into the fall. Even now, in the middle of October, at mid-morning, the temperature was eighty-five. Although Bowie's car windows were open, the absence of a breeze made the interior feel hotter than the air outside, his brow beading with sweat, his wet shirt sticking to the back of the seat. But he had trained himself to ignore inconvenient sensations and focused all his attention on the glass doors at the front of the jail.

Fifteen minutes later, a lanky Hispanic stepped out. His hair was cut so short that his scalp showed. He wore sneakers, jeans, and a white T-shirt with short sleeves that revealed tattooed gang symbols on his arms. Bowie knew that the man, whose name was Raoul Ramirez, was twenty-three. Raoul had been a member of an east-side gang called the Blades, a name Bowie appreciated, although he wondered if Raoul had the awareness to know that "blade" didn't mean only "knife." Raoul's blade had certainly gotten him into trouble. He spent five years in prison for forcibly restraining a woman in a motel room and raping her. In addition, his police record listed arrests for assault, theft, shooting at an occupied building, and torching a car that belonged to a member of another gang. Except for the rape, every arrest had resulted in probation.

Because of overcrowding in the state's prison system, Raoul had been allowed to serve his final months in the relative ease of the spacious new jail. Now the sneer on his face and the sociopathic dullness in his eyes became more pronounced as a low-riding car stopped at the curb.

Raoul got in. Gang handshakes were exchanged. The car pulled away. Maintaining a careful distance, Bowie followed to the modest, single-story home of Raoul's parents, where relatives and friends parked and hurried in. Music and the smell of barbecued chicken drifted along the street. Bowie took for granted that one of the ways Raoul would celebrate was with alcohol. Around two in the afternoon, when the booze had its effect and the urge to have fun took control, Raoul left his parents' home, got in the lowrider with his friends, and drove down the street.

The car stopped next to Bowie, who assumed that neighbors had phoned Raoul's parents about the man watching the house. A window slid down. Pounding music boomed out. Raoul glowered.

"I'd like to talk to you," Bowie said.

"I did my time. Why don't you *chingado* cops leave me alone?"

"I'm not a police officer."

"I was innocent. The bitch lied."

"I've got a business proposition for you."

Raoul lapsed into a string of hate-filled Spanish.

Bowie surprised Raoul by answering in Spanish. "I'm serious. I've got a business proposition for you."

Raoul spat on Bowie's car. The window went up. The car moved on.

Bowie followed. Raoul and his friends reached an Allsup's gas station, where they bought two twelve-packs of Tecate beer. They drove over to Interstate 40 and headed west.

Bowie continued to follow as they left the crowded highway and turned north onto a deserted, narrow road. Bowie noted the mountains in the distance and the cacti around him.

The paved road became gravel and, except for the two vehicles, was now totally deserted as it rose toward a low hill. From a quarter mile back, staying clear of the dust their car raised, Bowie had an occasional glimpse of them drinking beer and knew that in their quest for fun they'd decided that he would provide it.

Their car went over the hill. Following, cresting the hill, descending, Bowie saw what he expected: the car blocking the road, an embankment shielding it from anybody watching from a distance.

Raoul and his three friends were propped against the lowrider, drinking beer, watching him stop. As he got out, the sun weighed on him, but he ignored it, focusing his reflexes, leaning sideways when Raoul threw his empty can at him.

"That's what I think of your shitface business proposition," Raoul said.

The can clattered over stones, but Bowie wasn't distracted. The jeans that Raoul wore from the jail had been replaced by baggy, big-pocketed pants that hung low on his hips like the pants his friends wore.

The pants aren't hanging down to their butt cracks just for style, Bowie thought. *It's because of weight. They have weapons.*

76

"You cops shouldn't be harassing me." Raoul seemed proud that he knew the word. "It's against the law."

His friends thought that was hilarious.

"I told you, I'm not a police officer," Bowie assured him.

"So this isn't entrapment." Another big word Raoul was proud of. "I won't be charged for stomping a cop."

"Or cutting you," a kid next to Raoul said, drawing a knife.

"Or maybe I should just give you a red hole in your head." Raoul pulled a semiautomatic pistol from his pants. It was small, a .32.

"You wouldn't enjoy doing that," Bowie said.

"No?"

"You ever hear of Carrie Fisher?"

"*Who?*"

"The actress. Debbie Reynolds is her mother."

"What the—"

"She played Princess Leia in the first three *Star Wars* movies."

"Man, I might as well shoot you to keep you from talking me to death."

"She also writes novels and screenplays. Her best line is, 'The trouble with instant gratification is, it takes too long.'"

Raoul looked as if Bowie was speaking Martian.

"You won't shoot me," Bowie said, "because it's too quick. It wouldn't be as much fun as prolonging the foreplay by cutting or stomping me."

"Foreplay?" For a moment, Raoul looked confused, as if the concept wasn't familiar to him. "Yeah, you got that right."

"Can I have him, Raoul?" one of the kids asked. "Let me take a piece of him."

Raoul thought about it.

Perhaps he's beginning to suspect, Bowie thought. *If so, that's encouraging. I'm not wasting my time.*

"All of us'll take him," Raoul decided.

They pushed away from the car and spread out. One of the kids finished his beer and threw the can. So did the others.

Bowie had no trouble avoiding the cans.

"What'll it be, Raoul?" a kid asked. "Stomp?"

"Or cut?" The kid with the knife grinned.

"Want to make a bet?" Bowie asked.

"That your arms and legs are gonna be busted? That's a sure thing."

As they came closer, Bowie folded his left arm across his chest and raised his right palm to the side of his face in an absolutely nonthreatening pose.

"Well, well, look at how chilled this guy is," a kid said.

"He won't be after we stomp him."

"I'm serious. You want to make a bet?" Bowie asked.

They came even closer. Bowie kept his left arm across his chest, his right palm on his face.

"For what?"

"The money in my wallet."

"We're gonna have it anyhow," Raoul said, holding the gun.

"But don't you want to know what the bet is?"

They were almost to him.

"So what's the stupid damned bet?" Raoul wanted to know.

"That you can stand twenty feet away from me, holding your gun at your side."

"Yeah? And?"

"I can get to you before you shoot me."

Raoul snickered. "Yeah. Right."

"Believe me."

Raoul snickered again and turned to his friends.

At that point, Bowie could have taken them.

"And what'll I tell the cops when I put a bullet in your guts?" Raoul asked.

"Self-defense."

"You've been smokin' too much crack," one of the kids said. "A gun against fists ain't self-defense."

"Well, maybe if I had something that the police would agree was a threat."

"Like what?" Raoul asked.

"Oh, I don't know. A knife maybe."

"This is *loco*." The kid with the knife sneered. "He wants me to give him my—"

"Wait. Shut up while I understand this," Raoul told him. "I stand thirty feet away."

"I said twenty."

78

"Thirty."

"That's the length of a good-sized room," Bowie pretended to object.

"And you stand over here with a knife."

"Yes."

"And you bet I can't shoot you before you get to me?"

Bowie nodded. "And if you do shoot me, it's self-defense because I've got a knife. You can tell the cops how I followed you. Stalked you."

"I'm telling you this guy is *loco*," the kid with the knife said.

"How about it, Raoul? You've been away five years. Didn't you lie awake, dreaming of action? And now here you've got it. And it's perfectly legal. Your first day out."

Raoul studied him.

As the sun became more intense, Bowie waited.

"Forty feet," Raoul said.

"You're taking advantage. The bet I offered—"

"Was forty feet," Raoul said. He turned to his friends. "Right? Forty feet."

"Sure, Raoul. That's what he said."

"Okay, if you want to be tough about this," Bowie said.

Looking amused, Raoul took forty steps backward. Generous steps.

The kid with the knife said, "I ain't givin' him this."

"Then I'll need to use mine." Bowie still had his left arm folded across his chest, his right palm to his chin. With his left hand at his right armpit, he reached into the short sleeve of his loose shirt and brought out a five-inch folding knife that he had secured under his arm with Velcro on a hypoallergenic strap wound around his chest.

His handcrafted knife was different from the one with the polished ebony handle that he liked to play with. *This* knife was for business. Its action was butter-slick as he thumbed the button at the back of the blade, flipping it open. Anodized black, forged from 440 C steel, it was sharp enough to slip between the fibers of a Kevlar vest. Its handle was made from a grooved, laminated, almost indestructible plastic called Micarta. The grooves were important because they allowed Bowie to keep a tight grip, even if his fingers were slippery with blood.

"Where the hell did *that* come from?" a kid exclaimed.

Raoul raised his pistol.

"Take it easy," Bowie said. "I just need this for the bet. If you kill me, it needs to look as if you're defending yourself."

"If? There's no if about it." Raoul's eyelids lowered. "The bet was fifty feet. Right?" He took another ten steps back.

"Aw, come on," Bowie complained. "You want this to be fair, don't you?"

"Fifty feet is fair."

"But you need to keep the gun at your side. You can't raise it until the bet starts," Bowie said.

"Sure." Across the vast distance, Raoul smirked. "At my side." He lowered the gun.

Bowie lowered his knife and braced himself without seeming to. "Who's going to do the counting?"

"Counting? Nobody said anything about—"

Screaming at the top of his voice, Bowie charged. "*I'm going to rip your guts out, cocksucker!*" he shouted. "*Cocksucker! Cocksucker!*" Reaching full speed almost immediately, he hurtled across the distance, his motion so violent, his face so contorted with fury, that Raoul flinched. Instead of raising the gun, aiming, and pulling the trigger, he lurched backward. Off-balance to begin with, he became more off-balance when his knees bent with a will of their own. His arms jerked protectively up toward his chest. The instinctive motion caused the gun to point upward instead of toward the target who rushed at him, screaming, "*Killyoukillyoukillyou!*"

The scenario was a worst-case nightmare for anyone who earned a living with a gun. Law-enforcement officers, special-operations personnel, protective agents—any professional knew that someone with a knife could scream and race across those fifty feet and kill you before you overcame your surprise and defended yourself. The only defense was to avoid the scenario and shoot that s.o.b. dead the moment you saw the knife. Then, if you were in law enforcement, you had to justify your actions to a review board and maybe a grand jury. Almost certainly the relatives of the dead piece of shit would complain tearfully, "It wasn't fair. A gun against a knife. The cop had the advantage. He didn't need to shoot." And you'd think, "I damned well did need to shoot. And if I needed to do it again, I'd nail that sucker just as dead as he is now." Because, in the popular imagination, the person with the knife stops running, gets set, and then jabs with the knife, wasting a valuable second or two in which time the person with the gun overcomes the startle reflex and starts blasting. But in reality, the person with the knife doesn't stop but keeps rushing, using all that raging momentum to slam into the person with the gun and send him or her flying backward, crashing against a wall or onto the ground, and then the assailant drops onto the victim and goes to work with the knife.

That was close to what happened now. Raoul gaped, knees bent, arms thrust uselessly upward, as Bowie seemed to cross the no-longer-vast distance in hardly any time at all. Using his shoulder, he rammed into Raoul with such power that Raoul's lungs emptied. His feet left the ground. His body arched backward. His head made a sickening crunching sound when he landed.

At that moment, Bowie could have used a curving downward motion to slice Raoul's throat. Instead, he yanked the gun from Raoul's hand and spun toward his gaping pals, ready with the knife and the pistol.

"Want to make a bet?" Bowie asked.

"Jesus, man, don't shoot me," the kid with the knife begged.

"Farthest thing from my mind." Bowie put the gun under his belt. "Raoul, are you watching this? I want to make sure you see it."

"Uh," Raoul murmured. "What?"

"Damn it, are you *watching* this?"

"Uh, yeah, uh."

Bowie folded his knife and clipped it onto a pants pocket.

"You," Bowie told the kid with the knife. "I asked you if you want to make a bet."

"Bet?"

"That the three of you can't take me."

The three kids kept gaping.

Bowie again assumed his absolutely nonthreatening position, folding his left arm across his chest, raising his right palm and pressing it against the side of his face. "Come on, for God's sake, do something!"

The kid with the knife took his chance. As he lunged with the knife, Bowie whipped his right hand down and deflected the knife. At the same time, he turned his left hand so that his palm was outward and slapped the kid as hard as he could, the blow so powerful and covering so large a portion of the kid's face that his eyes rolled up.

In the same motion, Bowie spun so that the edge of one of his thick-soled shoes caught the side of the second kid's leg, hitting a nerve that temporarily disabled the leg and sent the kid screaming onto the dirt. Meanwhile, the kid with the knife sagged to his knees. Bowie thrust his right palm upward under the kid's chin, holding back just enough force that he didn't break the kid's neck when he struck. He kicked the third kid in the testicles, and when *that* kid pitched his head reflexively forward, Bowie jabbed a palm to *his* exposed chin also. Both dropped, unconscious.

That left the one whose leg was paralyzed, the pain so intense that he could barely make himself fumble for something in a pants pocket. As the kid pulled out a shitty, short-barreled .22 revolver, Bowie kicked him in the chin, taking care that he only broke the jaw and didn't kill him.

Raoul lay on the ground, struggling to catch his breath, blinking in disbelief.

"And what did you think of *that?*" Bowie asked.

"Uh."

"How'd you like a job?"

"Uh."

"How'd you like to learn to do that? Be an operator. Win friends and cause a world of pain."

"Job? What kind of—"

"Working for me." Bowie pulled a money clip from his pocket. The steel clip, handcrafted by him, had a knife so skillfully concealed along the side that he never had trouble taking it through security check-points. "Two thousand dollars as a sign-up fee."

"Two *thousand?*"

"You get room and board, free clothing and equipment."

"Two *thousand?*"

"The sign-up fee. Then you get three thousand a month. You never got that much robbing liquor stores."

"What do I need to do?"

"Prove you can learn. And then..."

"Yes?"

"Do what you're told."

17

"A slap?" William asked, as if Cavanaugh were joking.

Cavanaugh felt subtle pressure in his stomach as the Gulfstream G-200 soared away from the airport in Casper, Wyoming. Jackson Hole's airport could have handled the jet, but there was too great a chance that the attack team would watch that airport. Better to use the helicopter to fly 240 miles east to Casper, where the Gulfstream had been instructed to land and wait for them. GLOBAL PROTECTIVE SERVICES was stenciled across the side. Club chairs, a conference table, living-room-style seating for up to ten passengers, a spacious galley, a sophisticated entertainment system, a transcontinental fuel range, quiet engines, one-hundred-percent filtered air, plenty of natural light.

"You think a slap sounds like a sissy kind of thing?" Cavanaugh asked.

"Well, certainly," William said.

Jamie came from the bathroom, where she'd put on a white blouse, blue blazer, and gray slacks, clothes that William had instructed the pilots to bring. Turquoise earrings brought out the deep green in her eyes. She'd undone her ponytail, her brunette hair hanging to her shoulders.

"It's actually very serious," she told William.

"Fairbairn wanted his close-quarters combat techniques to be simple," Cavanaugh said. "Easily taught. Easily remembered. When condensed to essentials, there are only a few moves. But just as important, Fairbairn's system ensures that the person making those moves doesn't get injured in the process."

Mrs. Patterson stopped admiring the Gulfstream's appointments and listened.

"A punch, for example." Jamie made a fist and pretended to hit the wall. "I'm going to hurt that person, no question about it. But I'm probably also going to hurt my hand. At the least, my fist will swell and throb and become useless if I try to keep punching. At the worst, I'll break bones, incapacitating me with pain and shock. I don't care how tough you are—you can't will yourself *not* to experience shock."

Cavanaugh added, "So Fairbairn asked himself, 'What are the parts of the body that can administer force with little risk of injury?'"

"Since we're talking about slaps, I assume one of them is the palm of a hand," William said.

"Yes, but when we say a slap, we're not talking about anything dainty," Cavanaugh told him. "We're talking about a slap that's as hard and fast as you can make it. The full force of your body. Your palm covers a lot of area, almost the entire side of someone's face. If you don't knock the opponent out, you'll daze him enough so that when you slap the *opposite* side of his face, he'll go down."

"What are the other parts of the body that Fairbairn decided were the best to use?" William asked.

"The feet, if you wear thick-soled shoes. You can stomp down hard and break somebody's toes. Fairbairn recommended a variation in which you stomp the side of your shoe all the way down your opponent's shin before you hit the toes."

"Ouch," William said.

"The knee," Jamie said.

"To the groin?" William asked.

"Definitely."

Mrs. Patterson kept listening.

"The elbows," Cavanaugh said. "You can break ribs with them but not hurt yourself."

"You can chop the edge of your hand against someone's throat and not hurt yourself," Jamie said.

William winced, imagining the damage to the other person.

Mrs. Patterson leaned forward.

"And you can shove the palm of your hand up under someone's chin, gouging their eyes with your fingers while you thrust back your opponent's head and…"

William looked more uncomfortable.

"Why didn't my husband teach me any of this?" Mrs. Patterson demanded. "He never taught me about the guns he kept around the house, either. He was a good husband, but he always treated me as if I was weak."

"Now's your chance to make up for lost time." Jamie motioned for Cavanaugh to stand. "Fairbairn recommended combinations."

She crossed her left arm over her chest and raised her right palm to the side of her face.

"I'm defenseless?" she asked William and Mrs. Patterson.

"Pretty much," William said while Mrs. Patterson nodded.

"That's what you want the opponent to think. The idea is to make him feel overly confident and then to engage his startle reflex when you do something he isn't expecting."

Cavanaugh pretended to strike at her stomach.

Her right hand swept down to knock the blow away. Her left hand whipped, palm outward, in a pretended slap across Cavanaugh's face. She mimicked a kick to his groin, and when he bent forward in pretended pain, she delivered a slow-motion palm thrust to his chin, fingers near his eyes, pushing his chin back.

"The slap would have so stunned him that he couldn't defend himself," Jamie concluded. "Fairbairn wrote a book: *Get Tough*. We'll find a copy for you."

"Which reminds me, I have something for both of *you*," William said.

They watched with interest as William opened a drawer in a storage compartment that resembled a side table.

He took out a briefcase. "You told me to arrange to have a bug-out bag delivered from GPS headquarters and put on the plane, but I confess I haven't the faintest idea what a bug-out bag is."

"It's something you need when you bug out," Cavanaugh said.

"What?"

"An emergency kit for when you expect you'll be on the run. Most operators have a bug-out bag stashed somewhere."

Cavanaugh opened the case and revealed knives, nine-millimeter ammunition, an extra magazine, an easy-to-conceal SIG Sauer P229 pistol, lock picks, a miniature flashlight, an ample supply of twenty-dollar bills, fake ID, small rolls of duct tape, and assorted seemingly non-tactical items such as safety pins and zip ties, the thin, supple plastic strips that were used to bundle wires or close garbage bags.

"What are *they* for?" William asked.

"Pinning things and tying things."

William gave him an unamused look. "Right. And I suppose the duct tape is for sealing leaky pipes."

"Or veins."

"Some day, you'll need to teach me about *that*." William turned to Jamie. "This is for *you*." He handed her a black plastic case the size of a laptop computer. SIGARMS was stenciled on it.

"How thoughtful," Jamie said. "Everybody wants to give me firearms."

"You'll also need *this*." William handed her a holster.

"No," Cavanaugh said.

Jamie looked at him.

"You're not in danger if you're not with me," he said.

"You're suggesting…"

"Stay with Mrs. Patterson. Keep away from me."

"The attack team might still try to find where I am and use me to get at you," Jamie said.

"You'll be well guarded."

"See this ring on my finger," Jamie said. "I'm in this as much as you are, babe. There's no way I'm going to hide while you're out making yourself a target."

"It's the safest thing for you."

"I don't give a damn about what's safe for me. If this were reversed, if I were the target, would *you* hide?"

"Of course not. But that would be—"

"Different? How? Because I'm a woman and you're a man?"

"You know I don't think that way. It's just…if we do this together, if things go wrong and something happens to you…I couldn't bear losing you."

"You think I could bear losing *you*? You won't get a better, more motivated protector than me."

"I know."

"And I'm good at it, as you often told me. Together?"

Cavanaugh's emotions made it difficult for him to speak. "Yes. Together."

PART THREE:
"DO YOU LIKE TO PLAY VIDEO GAMES, RAOUL?"

1

Oaxaca, Mexico.

The movie star surprised Dominic by being polite and compliant, not at all what he was used to when protecting celebrities. Her name was Shana Lane. Twenty-one, with a knock-'em-dead figure, she'd had five hit movies, one of them good enough to earn her an Oscar nomination. But then she disappeared for a long, hot summer. After police, private investigators, and the media looked everywhere, she finally turned up drugged out of her mind, staggering down the main drag of a small town in Nova Scotia, Canada, where she was on her way, she thought, to buy a racehorse. Nobody, including herself, was ever able to figure *that* out. The authorities did some investigative backtracking and found the cottage where she was staying with her boyfriend.

A *possessive* boyfriend, who was also a crack addict. They returned to Los Angeles after paying fines and listening to a judge's lecture about the pointlessness of wasting a talented life. But despite Shana's determination to clean up her life and sever their relationship, the boyfriend persisted in wanting to see her. He showed his love and determination by burning her BMW and strangling her cat, then vanished and waited until the police became weary of guarding her.

That was where Dominic came in. For an enormous fee paid by a movie studio desperate to protect its investment, Dominic and five other protectors went to Shana's film location in Mexico. Working in shifts of two, they made sure the boyfriend didn't show up. They made sure of something else—that, in keeping with the plot line of a movie about drug smugglers, Shana didn't get tempted to go back to sampling the real stuff.

To Dominic's amazement, Shana behaved in an exemplary fashion, following instructions, arriving at the set on time, with her lines prepared, never once complaining about the twelve-hour shooting schedule and the rigid control of her time off the set. Sundays were her only free days, and she used them (accompanied by Dominic and another protector) to buy rugs, pottery, and carved animals from nearby towns or to visit Oaxaca's baroque cathedral, the vaulted interior of which had dazzling gold ornaments.

On this, his second-to-last evening of the assignment, Dominic and another protector stood separately at the shadowy sides of the Hotel Victoria's patio restaurant, watching the various approaches to it as Shana and the film's director ate dinner together. On a lower level, cast members splashed in a swimming pool.

Then dusk thickened. Dominic and his fellow protector escorted Shana to her room, one of a series in a long low building next to the restaurant. Pleasant-smelling flowers lined the softly lit walkway. While his partner watched the approaches to the building, Dominic unlocked and entered Shana's room, making certain that it was safe for her.

Only when they heard Shana secure the numerous locks on her door did the two protectors relax.

"After we escort her back to the States, do you have another assignment?" Dominic asked his partner.

"No. I'm thinking about coming back here with my wife. What are *your* plans?"

"New Orleans. I'm scheduled to be part of the security at the World Trade Organization conference. After the devastation from Hurricane Katrina, the WTO wants to show support for the New Orleans recovery effort by meeting there."

"The last time I worked at a World Trade conference, the protestors rioted and shut down the city. Talk about an elevated threat level. I was on Condition Orange for a week. Then I *slept* for a week."

They pulled out their room keys and unlocked the units that flanked Shana's. From there, they could easily get to her if she pressed a button linked to alarms in their rooms. When they opened their separate doors, they encountered the embodiment of a local proverb, *You won't find a doctor to cure a bite from this snake*, as a machete hissed toward each of them, slicing off their heads.

2

The fourth major airport in the New York City area (after Kennedy, LaGuardia, and Newark International) was Teterboro, a so-called "reliever" airstrip that catered to charter, corporate, and private jets, relieving congestion from the larger airports. From there, a twelve-mile drive via the George Washington Bridge could have taken Cavanaugh to Global Protective Services' corporate offices in midtown Manhattan. But because the attack team might have anticipated that he was headed in that direction and might have put Teterboro under surveillance, he decided against the risk of using an automobile and instead took a helicopter.

Manhattan had three heliports. Cavanaugh chose the one farthest from GPS headquarters, reasoning that it was the least likely to be under surveillance. An armored van drove him and the others through sparse midnight traffic to the secure garage under the Madison Avenue building in which GPS had its fortieth-floor offices. A team was expecting the van's arrival. They escorted Cavanaugh and his group into the elevator and through the upper security checkpoints.

The view from the conference room was spectacular, lights gleaming throughout the city. But even though the windows had bullet-resistant glass, Cavanaugh pressed a button that closed the draperies the moment he and the group entered the room, the draperies so thick that silhouettes couldn't be seen through them. He glanced at the plush carpeting and oak-paneled walls. Every chair at the long conference table had its own computer terminal and phone console, one of which he used to summon three GPS officers who'd been alerted to remain after business hours.

"Looks like you're settling into authority nicely," William said.

"How do we make it official? Don't you have documents for me to sign?"

"I instructed my assistant to go to my office and bring them," William answered. "He ought to arrive shortly."

"It can't happen soon enough."

"Mrs. Patterson, if you want to get some sleep, we can find an empty office that has a couch," Jamie offered.

"Thanks, but I napped on the plane." Mrs. Patterson clearly didn't want to miss anything.

But Cavanaugh couldn't allow it. "This is where you need to step out of the loop. The less you know, the better it is for you."

She looked crestfallen.

"Think of it this way," Jamie said. "You had an interesting ride while it lasted."

"Interesting? I'm having trouble understanding why, as frightened as I was, it was just about the most exciting time of my life."

"Winston Churchill once said, 'There's nothing more exciting than to be shot at and to survive.' The thing is," Cavanaugh added, "we don't want to get excited like that too often. William, when did Duncan put me in his will?"

"A month before he died. Why do you ask?"

Three people entered the office.

The first was from East Indian parentage, born in Akron, Ohio. Late-thirties. Short, thick, black hair. Compact build. Strong, square face. Steady, dark eyes. Muscular shoulders. His name was Ali Karim, and when he'd served on a Special Forces team, his specialties were languages, medicine, and explosives, as well as the ability to blend into an Asian environment. He was currently in charge of recruiting, training, and monitoring GPS's protective agents.

The second person was Chinese, female, early thirties. Kim Lee. Raised in Seattle. Her lustrous black hair hung to her waist. Five feet four, slender, with thin, delicate but attractive features, she looked too vulnerable to work for a security corporation. But anyone who acted on the foolish assumption that she was defenseless quickly discovered that she was a black-belt instructor of aikido and jeet kune do. She was one of the few employees of GPS who had not been in special operations, but her expertise didn't require military training. Duncan had hired her because she was once a notorious computer hacker and virus designer, skills highly desirable in a company that defended against electronic assaults as well as physical ones. Cavanaugh wondered how Kim and Jamie would get along inasmuch as Jamie, too, was a computer specialist.

The third person was white. Gerald Brockman. Early forties. A handsome, solidly built Afrikaner who once belonged to South Africa's Reconnaissance Commandos: experts in working behind enemy lines in the most hostile outdoor environments. One of the unit's endurance tests involved surviving for five days among the lions, elephants, and fires of Africa's bush country with no food except a tin of condensed milk, half a day's ration pack, and twelve biscuits, the bulk of which students discovered to their dismay had been soaked in petrol by their instructors. In addition to his elite military background, Brockman had superior administration skills that qualified him to be the interim CEO of the company.

All three paused. Special operators were trained to control their emotions. Even so, it was clear that they were surprised.

"Cavanaugh?" Brockman stared.

When William had contacted Global Protective Services, he'd followed Cavanaugh's instructions and told Brockman only that William would be arriving with the new owner.

Brockman looked at Jamie and Mrs. Patterson, eliminated them from the possibilities, and said, "*You're* the new CEO?"

"But…" Kim turned her attention to the attorney. "William, for the past five months, you've been asking me to search our computer records for someone named Aaron Stoddard. I got the impression *he* was the person Duncan willed the company to."

"That's true," William replied. "Now that I have my client's permission, I can finally tell you—Aaron Stoddard inherited GPS."

"*I'm* Aaron Stoddard," Cavanaugh said.

The room became silent.

"I had a theory that a protector would be vulnerable if the bad guys learned about his private life," he explained. "Pressure could be put on his family and friends in order to put pressure on *him*. So I decided to use a pseudonym."

"But how could the bad guys get that information?" Ali asked. "Between Kim and me, those records are absolutely secure."

"Wrong," Cavanaugh told him. "Yesterday, a hit team attacked my home."

"*What?*"

"My *home*, for God's sake. The deed's in Aaron Stoddard's name. The people where I live know me only as Aaron Stoddard." Anger forced Cavanaugh to work to control his breathing. "But somehow the hit team found me. The only way that could have happened is through GPS's search for somebody with that name."

"What about *William's* office?" Ali suggested. "William's the one who started the search."

"I assure you I informed no one, other than the three of you, that it was essential to find a man named Aaron Stoddard." William turned toward Cavanaugh. "For reasons of confidentiality, I couldn't mention the terms of Duncan's will. But they quickly made the connection."

"What the hell are you implying?" Brockman demanded. "That *we* sent the hit team to keep you from inheriting the company? To give *us* a chance to gain control of it?"

"Until now, the thought hadn't even occurred to me," Cavanaugh lied.

"This is bullshit." Ali's perfect American idiom contrasted with his East Indian features. "As if we don't have enough problems, now we've got a guy who told us he doesn't want to be in the business any longer who decides he *does* want to be in the business and comes back to tell us we're all working for the other side."

"Time out," Cavanaugh said.

"It really is bullshit," Ali insisted.

"Honestly, time out. Did Duncan keep any whiskey around here?"

"You've become a *drinker?*" Kim asked in astonishment.

"No," Cavanaugh said, "but maybe if we hit each other over the head with the bottle long enough, we'll start talking sense. Duncan trusted the three of you absolutely. *I* trust you absolutely. But that doesn't change the security breach we need to find, and it doesn't change the problem I've got. Somebody's hunting me, somebody with a lot of money and resources. Just because the first attempt failed doesn't mean the threat's over. I've got to believe there'll be another attack, bigger and better organized."

Brockman ran a hand across his shaved head. Ali exhaled slowly.

"Sorry," Kim said. "I guess we're all reacting to stress."

After a knock on the door, a security guard brought in a package. "Mr. Faraday's assistant delivered this."

Cavanaugh gave the bulging, legal-sized envelope to William, who spread the contents onto the conference table.

"Where do I put my autograph?" Cavanaugh asked.

"Aren't you going to read it first? As your lawyer, I strongly advise you to study what you're signing."

"Is there anything in it you don't approve of?"

"It's elegantly simple. You accept the bequest. You assume control of the company, with all its assets and, I emphasize, its liabilities."

"Yesterday, you told me Duncan made some questionable business decisions."

"He expanded the company too quickly. London, Paris, Rome, Hong Kong. The new office planned for Tokyo. Granted, after Nine-Eleven, first-rate security has never been in greater demand. But right now, GPS has more money going out than coming in. There's a risk of bankruptcy."

"Bankruptcy?" Ali frowned at Brockman. "Nobody told me anything about—"

Cavanaugh signed the document.

"We need a witness." William looked at Jamie. "But it can't be your wife."

"Wife?" Kim looked stunned.

"Hell, I'll do it," Mrs. Patterson said, happy to have continued to be part of the group. She signed where William indicated.

"So the company's mine now?" Cavanaugh asked William.

"Down to the paper clips and the water coolers."

"Then let's get started. Gerald, cancel the Tokyo office. Merge the Paris office with the one in Rome. Ali, Mrs. Patterson needs to be protected around the clock. Put her in a safe site."

"And assign some handsome young men to watch her," Jamie said.

"William needs a safe site, too," Cavanaugh added. "The hit team can use both of them to get at me. Kim, do a computer search on every assignment I ever had. There's a chance the attack on me was meant to keep me quiet about something I learned. I want the best protectors to escort Jamie and me. Send for Rob Miller, Dominic Benuto, Hans Dietrich, and…"

The somber looks he received made him stop.

He suddenly processed two incongruous statements that Ali and Kim had made. Ali had said, "As if we don't have enough problems." Kim had said, "I guess we're all reacting to stress."

"What's wrong?" he asked.

Kim drew a breath. "They're all dead. Within the past twenty-four hours."

At first, Cavanaugh was certain he hadn't heard correctly.

"Miller was in Venice, protecting a corporate executive and his wife," Ali explained. "Dominic was in Oaxaca, escorting a movie star. The others were on equally unrelated assignments. All of them were killed with sharp-edged weapons."

Cavanaugh leaned forward, pressing his hands on the table.

"All the blades were covered with a rapid-acting poison," Kim added.

Cavanaugh couldn't speak.

"The clients survived." Brockman sounded troubled. "They weren't harmed in the least. Nobody attacked them."

"Nobody? But that doesn't make sense," William objected.

"Sure, it does," Cavanaugh said. "If the clients weren't attacked, it means the protectors were the targets."

"But why not just use guns?"

"Because there's something creepily intimate about being stabbed," Cavanaugh replied. "A victim often doesn't feel the cuts or have any idea how serious the wound might be. There's a video that knife trainers use. The tape came from a security camera mounted to the ceiling of a bar in California. You see a bunch of Anglo tough guys beating up a short Latino man. They really put the boots to him. Finally, the worst of the attackers has the Latino on the bar's pool table, whaling the hell out of him. On the video, you see a little movement to the left, the Latino's hand trying to get out from under the bad guy, struggling to reach into his jeans pocket. Then you see a lot of quick little movements. The hand's a blur. Then the bad guy straightens, as if he pounded the Latino as much as he wanted to. He turns, and his stomach's wide open, but he's in shock and doesn't know he's been cut. Everybody runs. The bad guy looks puzzled by their reaction and walks over to the bar. He sits down. The Latino, who's covered with blood, gets off the pool table, puts his knife in his pocket, straightens his clothes, and walks out. The bad guy sitting at the bar orders a drink. He's still in so much shock that he doesn't know how many times he's been cut. He sits there a moment longer, shakes his head as if he's a little confused about something, and falls over dead."

William looked appalled.

"Most security personnel are so worried about a knife threat, they make sure they carry at least one knife so they can scare somebody with it if the situation gets that bad. *Several* knives are preferable so you've got a better chance of drawing one of them. Attached to a break-away chain around the neck." Cavanaugh opened his shirt, displaying a short, black knife in a nylon scabbard: part of the contents of the Gulfstream's bug-out bag. It was called La Griffe, a French word for "talon," which described its shape.

"And here." Jamie pulled back her blazer, showing William a utility knife holstered above her left hip, something else from the bug-out bag.

"And here." Cavanaugh unclipped a five-inch tactical folding knife from the inside of his pants pocket. The clip attachment made it easy to find and retrieve the knife. On the back of the blade, a hook snagged on the pocket. The resistance caused the blade to open as the knife was being drawn. "I had years of training with blades. A master knife maker taught me to forge them. But I hate the thought of being attacked by one. Believe me, a lot of protectors will feel cold and naked when word gets out they're being stalked with blades."

"But *you* weren't attacked with a blade," Jamie told him. "What's the connection?"

3

Raoul had no idea where he was being taken. After he used a pay phone to tell his parents that he was heading north to find a job in Denver, the stranger drove him to a small airport, Double Eagle, west of Albuquerque. There, the stranger returned his rental car. No security check was required as they walked toward a small jet. A few minutes later, they soared into the cobalt sky.

"I use small airports," the stranger explained, as if Raoul understood what the hell he was talking about. "I stay below eighteen thousand feet. That way, I don't need to file an instrument flight plan, and I don't turn on my transponder, which is how radar would otherwise track me."

Raoul had trouble concentrating. Until now, he'd never been in a plane. Vertigo threatened to make him vomit. But there was no way he'd let the stranger realize he was afraid. Although his palms were slick with sweat, he kept them firmly on his knees. He forced himself not to tremble.

The secret was not to look down, he decided. He began to wonder if this was some kind of sex thing, that the stranger would be like the predators Raoul had fought off in prison. But the stranger made no moves of that sort. In fact, after paying Raoul the promised two thousand dollars, all he wanted to talk about was fighting.

"Ever want to join the military?" the stranger asked.

"Hell, no." The jet engines were muffled through the earphones the stranger had given him.

"Don't you think it would be cool to carry a handgun and an assault rifle as part of your job?"

"*That* part. But who wants to go through all the bullshit of taking orders?"

"One goes with the other." The stranger had powerful-looking forearms. His sun-darkened face was gaunt, with a crease down each cheek, and an unusual intensity in his hazel eyes. "Nobody's going to give you a gun without telling you how and when to use it."

"I already *got* a gun."

"That piece of junk thirty-two? Even if you'd shot me with it, I could have reached you, grabbed it out of your hand, and shoved it down your throat. We'll get you some *real* guns. Ever fired an MP-5?"

"A what?"

"A submachine gun. Do you know the difference between a subma-chine gun and an actual machine gun?"

Raoul didn't even know there was a difference.

"A submachine gun fires pistol ammunition. Nine-millimeter. A *machine* gun fires rifle ammunition. A point two-two-three cartridge, for example. The kind that goes in an M-16. Wicked. The bullet flips end over end when it hits something. Rips the target to shreds. Ever fired a submachine gun?"

Raoul hesitated, afraid he'd lose face if he admitted the truth. "No."

"We'll make up for that deficiency. There's nothing as sweet as firing an MP-5 on full auto, thirty rounds zipping through that gun in two seconds. Raoul, you might not have made love to the most beautiful woman. You might not have tasted the greatest whiskey. You might not have driven the fastest car. But I'm telling you, when you put thirty full-auto rounds through an MP-5, you can definitely say you've shot the world's best submachine gun. But to be given the chance to do that, and to get the further money I promised, you need to follow some or-ders. I mean, that's in *any* job, right?"

"I realize nobody's gonna give me money and not expect me to do something," Raoul said. "But you asked if I ever wanted to join the army. There's no way I'm gonna make bunk beds and bounce quarters off them and shit like they show in the movies."

"Movies, Raoul? You like movies?"

"Sure."

"Did you see any movies when you were in prison?"

"On TV."

"Sounds like a cushy prison."

"Try it sometime. See how cushy *you* think it is."

"Oh, I've been in prison, Raoul. Believe me. But the kind I was in didn't have TVs. What they had was red-hot needles under my finger-nails and electrodes on my testicles."

Raoul noticed the scars on the stranger's fingers.

"When you're not learning about MP-5s and fun stuff like that, you're going to have a different kind of fun, watching a lot of movies," the stranger said. "Quite a job, huh? To get paid three thousand dollars a month to watch movies?"

"*What* movies?"

"Action movies. I think we'll start with *Thief.* Michael Mann directed it. James Caan's the star. Ever seen it."

Raoul had no idea who the hell Michael Mann and James Caan were. "Sounds like an old movie. I don't watch old movies."

"I guarantee you'll love this one. At the end, Caan goes into a house and blows away a bunch of gangsters, using a handgun. It's one of the first times a gunfight had an accurate look in a movie. Mann uses terrific technical advisors. The way Caan holds the pistol. His balance. His footwork. Amazing. I've got a bunch of other movies like it. *Ronin. Proof of Life. Spy Game. The Recruit.* The thing is, Raoul, you need to ignore the plots and concentrate on the individual scenes, on what the characters do and the way the actors handle themselves, because those movies had terrific technical advisors too, and except for a few spots, they're accurate in their tradecraft."

"Tradecraft?"

"The way operators—*professionals*—do things. You'll catch on to the vocabulary as we go along. You'll watch *Black Hawk Down,* of course. And the TV series *The Unit,* which is about Delta Force. And *Dark Blue.* Kurt Russell plays a corrupt cop. The director, Ron Shelton, got a really good technical advisor. The gun stuff is accurate. And there's a moment when Kurt gives a speech and says, 'I'm a gunfighter. I come from a family of gunfighters.' That's a first. I never saw a movie before in which somebody like a police detective who earns his living with a gun calls himself a gunfighter. In life, of course, privately they do call themselves that. Gunfighter. You like the sound of that word, Raoul?"

"Sounds like an old western."

"A western. Good idea, Raoul. I'll make sure you look at *The Wild Bunch.*"

The sun was behind them. The expanse of the landscape changed from mountains to flats, from brown to green. Sunset occurred swiftly. Soon they flew in darkness. Raoul controlled his dizziness by staring at the faint glow of the lights on the cockpit's dials.

"You impress me," the stranger said.

"What are you talking about?"

"You're afraid to fly."

"Who says I'm afraid?"

"But you don't show it."

"*Who says I'm afraid?*"

"Not me."

Raoul continued to stare ahead, surprised by how much light was on the ground. Towns glowed. Cities glared. Headlights blazed on freeways. There were seldom stretches of pure black. He hadn't realized how many people there were and how bright the night could be. When they reached one of the few sections of black, the stranger aimed the jet toward the heart of it.

Immediately, two rows of lights appeared in the gloom. As the stranger guided the plane down toward them, Raoul's stomach rose toward his throat. He repressed the urge to be sick. But by God, he wasn't going to show the stranger any of what he felt.

Descending, he suddenly had the sense of high trees on each side of the lights. Then the lights got big, and he felt a nudge through the plane as the wheels touched down. The stranger steered to the right, toward other lights, which were in a corrugated-metal building that had its large doors open. At once, the lights on the runway went out, but not before Raoul looked back and saw men scurrying across the runway, pulling something over it. A net. They were covering the runway with a camouflage net. The stranger shut off the plane's engines. In the blessed silence, their sound still echoed in Raoul's ears.

When the stranger opened the exit hatch, humidity enveloped Raoul. Sweat moistened his face and threatened to make his clothes stick to his skin as they stepped from the plane. The air weighed on him.

Where the hell *was* he?

There was too much else to think about. Three men waited for the stranger and him to climb down. They wore thick-soled camping shoes, pants with numerous pockets, loose shirts hanging out, and baseball caps over what their short sideburns suggested was closely cropped hair. One was Anglo. One was black. One was Hispanic. The latter made Raoul feel less isolated. It took him a moment before he noticed that, although he thought of them as men, two seemed younger than his twenty-three years, but something about the way they carried themselves made clear they were definitely men.

"Everything's on schedule?" the stranger asked.

"Yes, Mr. Bowie," the black man said.

At last, a name for the stranger.

"This is Mr. Ramirez," Bowie said, indicating Raoul.

Despite his uneasiness, Raoul felt proud to have been introduced in that formal manner. Mister. No one had ever called him that before.

"He's smart," Bowie said.

No one had ever spoken about Raoul in *that* way, either.

"He'll be an excellent contribution to our group." Bowie turned to him. "Won't you, Mr. Ramirez?"

"Yes." Then an amazing thing happened. Raoul didn't think about the next thing he said. He just did it. "Yes, sir."

"See?" Bowie told the three men. "An excellent contributor. Get him squared away. Clothes, equipment, something to eat. Show him where he'll be bunking. Mr. Ramirez, as you can tell from these representatives of our group, this is not a white-bread operation. If you have any problem relating to various races, you'll need to get over it in a hurry. We follow the one true god here, and that is Discipline."

Sudden gunshots made Raoul flinch. In an instant, he tucked down his head, bent his knees, and raised his hands to defend himself.

"Quick reactions," the Anglo said.

The shots came from behind the building.

"He shows promise," the Hispanic agreed.

The shots persisted: a steady rattle. His stomach on fire, Raoul stared past the plane toward the rear of the building. He had no idea how thick its corrugated metal was, and the only thing that kept him from diving to the concrete floor was that no one else in the group seemed alarmed.

"It's a night-training exercise," Bowie told him. "You'll be involved in them soon enough."

Out there, something exploded. Again, no one else reacted.

"And when you're not training," Bowie said, "you'll learn to sleep despite the noise. Sleep is the operator's friends. Fatigue is among the legion of his enemies. Always sleep and eat whenever you get the chance, although you won't have much time for rest here. Do you like video games, Raoul?"

"Uh, video games?" The seemingly weird question made Raoul frown as he glanced nervously again in the direction of the shots.

"Video games, *sir*."

"Sir. I used to. In the joint, there weren't any."

"Well, that's different now. Here, when you're not in classes or watching movies, you can play video games as much as you want. The latest versions. *Soldier of Fortune. Mortal Kombat. Doom.* The U.S. military licenses that one and encourages its soldiers to play it. *Medal of Honor. Brothers in Arms. Men of Valor. Full Spectrum Warrior. America's Army.* We've got every action video game on the market. Hone your reflexes. Have a ball."

4

"Don't you think you should try to sleep?" Jamie asked Cavanaugh from the shadowy doorway to the bedroom.

Duncan, who'd sometimes worked twenty-hour days, had put his living quarters next to his office. That Duncan's personal and professional lives had been so severely joined made Cavanaugh wonder how his own life and Jamie's would change now that he'd assumed control of the corporation.

He sat at Duncan's desk, a thick computer printout spread before him.

"I doubt I could sleep." Eyes sore with fatigue, he ran his finger down the list that Kim had prepared: his former assignments.

It depressed him to realize the number and extent of the protective details he'd worked on. Politicians, corporate executives, movie celebrities, sports stars, real-estate barons, on and on. There'd been hundreds, but only a few had seemed special apart from the money, power, or fame they had. The work had been what he'd cared about. As Duncan had insisted, "Unless they're obvious moral monsters, it isn't our place to make judgments about our clients. The only thing that's important is, they're somebody's prey, and predators are always the enemy."

"That list will look fresher in the morning," Jamie said.

"But in the meantime, what if somebody dies because I didn't do my job? I have to believe, somewhere in these past assignments there's a clue about why the hit team tried to kill us and why those other agents were killed. Or maybe the attack was revenge because of an assassination or kidnapping I prevented. I don't know where else to look."

"You can't do your job if you can't think straight."

"I've gone without sleep a lot longer than this."

"I hear it makes a person psychotic."

Cavanaugh had to grin. "You say the sweetest things."

"I'm serious." Jamie massaged his shoulders. "The list will look fresher in the morning."

Cavanaugh thought about it and sighed. "All these assignments. When this is over—"

"Making me think about the future so I don't worry about the present?"

"I'm projecting *myself* into the future so *I* don't worry about the present. When this is over." Cavanaugh set down the pages. "You're right. Let's get some sleep."

He put his arm around her and guided her toward the bedroom.

The phone rang.

He paused.

It rang again.

He turned.

"Don't answer it," Jamie said.

He stared at the desk. *Not Duncan's desk. Not any longer. Now it's my desk.*

"Whatever it's about can wait until morning," Jamie told him.

"No," Cavanaugh decided.

But when he reached for it, the phone stopped ringing.

"Couldn't have been that important if the caller hung up," Jamie said.

Cavanaugh pointed toward a light on the elaborate phone console. "Somebody else answered. Maybe after a specific number of rings, the call gets transferred to another phone."

He stared at the constant light on the console. Next to each light was a name. In this case, the name was Brockman. "If it was a wrong number, he'd have hung up by now. I'd better go find out what's wrong."

"What makes you think something's wrong."

"Was there ever a call at three in the morning that *wasn't* about something wrong?"

They entered the corridor.

Cavanaugh had the feeling of being lifted, of him and Jamie being thrown through the air and striking the corridor's wall, of dropping to the floor. Immediately, his senses caught up to him. The roar behind him. From the office. No, from *beyond* the office. From the *bedroom*. The searing flash. The shockwave punching air from his lungs. Groaning, he rolled toward Jamie as chunks of plaster and wood fell over him. Despite the ringing in his ears, he thought he heard Jamie moan. Then he heard her curse, anger giving her the energy to paw rubble off her.

He smelled smoke. Struggling to his hands and knees, he peered through the doorway into what had been the office. The wall between the office and the bedroom had been ruptured. The lights had been destroyed, but flickering flames allowed him to see into the gutted bedroom. The window's bullet-resistant glass was spread across the bedroom floor. An October wind howled through the jagged opening, fueling the flames.

An alarm went off. Overhead sprinklers gushed water into the bedroom and the office.

Somebody pulled Cavanaugh away—Ali. Somebody else pulled Jamie. Belatedly, Cavanaugh realized it was Kim. Brockman had a fire extinguisher and charged into the wreckage, spraying foam where the flames resisted the water from the sprinklers.

Then Cavanaugh was clear of the smoke and the dust. Ali set him down in the conference room and turned on the lights. Jamie squirmed next to him, blood running from her nose.

Cavanaugh realized that blood ran from *his* nose, also.

Through blurred vision, he stared at the draperies that covered the conference room windows. "Get us out of here." His voice seemed to come from far away.

"What?" Ali asked, as if Cavanaugh spoke gibberish.

And maybe Cavanaugh did speak gibberish. He pointed toward the windows. "Get us out of this room." He tried to say it as distinctly and forcefully as possible, his throat raw, his lips numb.

"The glass from the other window," he managed to say.

"What about it?"

"...sprayed *inside* the bedroom. The explosion came from outside. It must have been..."

"A rocket," Kim realized.

Handheld types were only thirty inches long. At this late hour, with midtown Manhattan mostly deserted, one could have been easily launched from the opposite sidewalk.

"Hurry." Ali helped to pull Cavanaugh and Jamie from the conference room into the lobby.

But they didn't stop there. Brockman was suddenly with them again. Dropping the fire extinguisher, he helped Ali yank open doors that led to a bank of elevators.

A bell rang. An elevator opened.

Brockman, Kim, and Ali drew their guns.

5

The man who emerged from the elevator wore black pants and a black leather jacket. He stared at the weapons, stopped chewing gum, and raised his hands. "Whoa," he said.

Slowly, the pistols were lowered.

The man was Eddie Macintosh, one of the protectors Cavanaugh had sent for. He studied the blood trickling from Cavanaugh's nose. "Tell me what to do."

"Have you got a car?"

"In the parking garage downstairs."

From the gaping window down the hall, they heard the wail of approaching sirens.

Jamie sat up. "Get us out of here."

"To the hospital?"

"No. We'd be targets there."

"And we'd be defenseless at a police precinct." Cavanaugh forced himself to stand. "We can't assume every police officer and fireman who arrives is genuine."

Through the shattered window, the sirens sounded closer.

Cavanaugh wavered, then helped Jamie up. "How did they know to hit our bedroom?"

"Maybe they saw its light go on," Brockman said.

"No. That light was off," Jamie insisted. "What was that phone call about?"

Brockman's tone was stark. "Another agent's been killed."

"What?"

"Jack Gantry. He was in Vancouver, protecting a TV anchorwoman from a stalker. He escorted her home. When he walked back to his car, he got hit. A crossbow. Those things are almost as powerful as some pistols. No sound."

"A crossbow?" Cavanaugh's confusion made him feel as if the floor shifted. "Kim, do you have a backup for the printout you gave me?"

She fumbled in her suit coat and gave him a memory stick.

"Tell the police we'll contact them when we're safe." Unwilling to trust the elevator, Cavanaugh motioned for Jamie and Eddie to follow him toward the fire door.

6

The stairs felt cold. Cavanaugh tried to assure himself that was why he shivered. Footsteps scraping, the group descended from the fortieth to the thirtieth floor, where he surprised Jamie and Eddie by opening the door.

Eddie looked puzzled. "You said we were leaving the building."

"The others don't need to know."

Cavanaugh glanced inside and made sure that the softly lit corridor was empty. After they went in, he held three fingers in front of Jamie. "How many?"

She told him.

"Blurred?"

"No."

"Headache?"

"Yes." Jamie wiped blood from her nose.

"We need to wait and see if it's a concussion."

"How will we know?"

"If you throw up or feel sleepy."

"Sleepy? At this hour? Imagine that." Jamie turned toward Eddie. "We haven't been introduced. Jamie Travers."

"Eddie Macintosh. Are you an operator? You must be new. I haven't seen you around."

"She's my wife," Cavanaugh said.

"Wonders never cease."

"And yes," Cavanaugh said, "she's an operator."

"Haven't seen *you* around, either. I heard you left the business."

"I tried. But now I'm back."

7

Cavanaugh led them to a door marked WILLIAM FARADAY LAW OFFICES. He raised his jacket collar, reached into a slit in the material, and pulled out the lock-pick tools that he'd taken from the Gulfstream's bug-out bag. He inserted one of the picks into the lock, probing to free the pins while he used another pick to apply torque and turn the key slot.

It took him thirty seconds. *Too long*, he thought. *I should have been able to do it in fifteen.* Perhaps he was still dazed from the explosions. But perhaps his lock-picking skills had atrophied during the months he'd stopped being a protector.

That made him worry about what other skills might have atrophied.

He opened the door and heard the intrusion alarm's beep. If he didn't enter the access code within thirty seconds, the alarm would blare. Leaving the lights off, he crossed the waiting room to the control panel and pressed buttons for the code that he and William had agreed on when the system was installed.

The beeping stopped.

Jamie locked the door behind them.

"*Faraday*," a voice croaked. "*Jerk*."

Jamie and Eddie drew their guns.

A dim nightlight revealed a parrot in a cage.

"*Faraday. Jerk*," the bird repeated.

"What the hell?" Eddie muttered.

"One of William's competitors sent the parrot after losing a case to him," Cavanaugh explained. "William thanked the rival attorney and promised to keep the bird in his reception room."

"*William* did that?" Jamie asked in surprise.

"He also swore to keep the bottom of the cage lined with photographs of the man who sent the parrot. William's clients find it amusing to look down and see bird droppings over the guy's face."

"Now *that* sounds more like William."

"*Faraday. Jerk*," the parrot squawked.

Cavanaugh hurried to the receptionist's desk and turned on its computer. Helped by its glow, he inserted Kim's memory stick and activated the printer.

As the machine went to work, he asked Eddie, "Are you armed?"

"Of course."

"Mind watching the front door while we clean the blood off us?"

Eddie pushed back one side of his leather jacket and drew a Beretta nine-millimeter. He had big hands and could handle the double-stacked fifteen-round magazine. He put another piece of gum into his mouth.

"Anybody who breaks through that door won't live to break through another one."

8

"Still got a headache?"

Cavanaugh used a moist paper towel to wipe blood from Jamie's face. The restroom didn't have windows, so it was safe to turn on the lights, which pained Cavanaugh's eyes.

"Not as bad. You?" Jamie wiped blood from *his* face.

"Shook up."

"You don't show it." Her voice echoed off the room's tiles.

"You're doing a good job of hiding it, also. Are you sure you don't feel dizzy?" The bright lights continued to hurt his eyes.

"You mean, do I think I'm going to pass out from a concussion? No. How do I know? Because I'm starved for a medium pizza with pepperoni and mushrooms."

"I guess you're going to live."

"For now."

"Yes," Cavanaugh said, the words sticking in his throat. "For now."

As he guided her toward the door to the hallway, she hesitated, no longer able to ignore her troubled thoughts. "How did they know to make the bedroom the target? I didn't turn the light on. They couldn't have known we were going in there."

"Maybe the phone call," Cavanaugh replied.

"You didn't answer it. They couldn't have known we were in that office."

"But then the call was automatically transferred to Brockman," Cavanaugh reminded her.

"You think *he* told them where we were?"

"I have no idea. He claims the phone call was about another agent who was killed."

"We'd need phone records to find out where the call came from."

"Yes, and while we figure out how to get them, here's something else that's been troubling me."

In the harsh light, Jamie's eyes narrowed.

"Duncan chose Brockman to be his chief-of-staff. It's a logical choice. Brockman's a first-rate administrator as well as a proven operator."

"So?"

"Why didn't Duncan give the company to him?"

"Because Duncan felt a bond with *you.*"

"But he also knew I hated working at a desk. We were close, yes, but Duncan saw Brockman all the time and must have gotten along with him if Duncan kept him as chief-of-staff."

"I don't see where you're going with this."

"According to William, Duncan decided to make me his heir a month before he was killed. What if he gave GPS to me because he'd begun to suspect something was wrong with the company?"

"Is that what *you* think? You told Brockman, Kim, and Ali you trusted them absolutely."

"I lied."

"In other words, we're not sure of anything."

"I'm sure of *one* thing. You."

9

Cavanaugh sat in a corner of William's office. Away from the draped windows. On the floor. A desk lamp was next to him, the light so dim and sheltered that it couldn't be seen from a building across the street. Eyes scratchy, he read the printout: the details of his Global Protective Service assignments.

Despite the windows, he heard faint commotion outside. Below on the street. Sirens. The rumble of what might have been fire trucks. Vehicle doors being slammed. Voices. He imagined what was happening in the opposite direction, ten floors above him in what was left of the GPS offices. Police officers and fire department personnel would be questioning Brockman, Kim, and Ali about the explosion. The authorities' frowns would deepen when they learned about the number of GPS operators who'd recently been killed. Teams would be rushing into buildings across the street, searching for an indication of where the attackers had placed themselves, hoping to find whoever was responsible for the explosion.

He concentrated on the printout. So many assignments. Hundreds and hundreds. They'd accumulated, blending in his memory until many of the names of clients were meaningless to him. How was it possible to devote oneself to protecting somebody to the point of being ready to risk dying for that person and not have the faintest mental image of what that person looked like?

He read about the powerful, the wealthy, and the famous, or else about average people under terrible threats, the helpless, the preyed-upon. As far as Cavanaugh was concerned, GPS didn't accept enough of those latter cases. The victims couldn't afford the company's services unless they attracted a protector's attention and the work was done *pro bono*, but if Cavanaugh survived this, he was determined to change things. Take from the rich and give to the poor.

He suddenly realized that he was projecting himself into the future to distract himself from the present. *No*, he warned himself. The only way to survive was to concentrate on now, but that meant concentrating on the past, and regardless of how much he tried, no summary of his former assignments jogged his memory about anything he might have seen or heard that would have made him a liability to a former client. His employers had always been careful to guard their secrets. As for the revenge theory, Cavanaugh had prevented so many assassinations and kidnappings that he found it impossible to single out any one incident for which an opponent might be determined to get even.

Even so, there was something about one of his assignments that nudged at the back of his mind, something that connected with the way the GPS operators had been killed, something about knives.

At once, Eddie came into the office. "Somebody's trying to get in the front door."

10

When Cavanaugh hurried into the dark reception room, he saw Jamie's silhouette crouched behind the desk, aiming her pistol toward the door. Next to him, Eddie drew his own gun, aiming. Cavanaugh noticed a slight shadow in the sliver of light that came through the bottom of the door. He heard the scrape of metal as someone worked to pick the lock.

Hearing it slide free, he tensed as he remembered that he hadn't reset the alarm. When the intruder opened the door and didn't hear the warning beep, it would be obvious that someone had entered and turned it off.

Imagining the intruder removing the lock picks and putting them away before turning the knob, Cavanaugh hurried across the reception room's carpet and pushed the alarm's "set" button. He got back to the desk as a different scrape of metal indicated that the knob was being turned. In the darkness, Jamie and Eddie kept aiming.

The door opened a few inches. From the hallway, a beam of light angled in. The warning beep began. Cavanaugh drew his pistol. A shadow obscured the beam of light.

How many are out there? he wondered. *The door's too solid for them to shoot through it or for us to shoot at them. They'll need to show themselves.*

"*Faraday. Jerk,*" the parrot croaked.

The alarm kept beeping. In fifteen more seconds, it would wail, summoning security personnel. The intruders (it was foolish to believe there was only one) needed to make a decision—assume that the warning beep meant that no one had entered the office, or else take the chance of bursting in and shooting as the alarm went off, knowing that they had to finish the gunfight before the police who were already in the building hurried to this floor.

No, there was a third option, Cavanaugh realized. Maybe the plan was for the intruders to throw in flash-bang grenades, temporarily blinding and deafening anybody in the office. Then they could easily charge in and finish anyone inside, avoiding a prolonged gunfight, gaining time to get away before the police arrived.

With no time to try to protect his eyes or his ears, Cavanaugh tightened his grip on his pistol.

And frowned as an object hurtled through the gap in the door, thumping onto the carpeting.

Only one object. If the intruders were using flash-bang grenades, they'd have thrown several.

The door was slammed shut. In the corridor, footsteps raced along marble.

"Get back!" Cavanaugh shouted as the alarm blared.

He tugged Jamie from behind the desk. Eddie retreated with them.

The object detonated. But not with a roar and a flash. Instead it made a *whump*ing sound that could barely be heard amid the alarm's wail. Even in the shadows, Cavanaugh saw a cloud burst from the object.

"Back! Back! Back!" he kept saying, tugging Jamie, almost tripping over Eddie. "Into William's office!"

They reached the corridor near the reception room. Looking over his shoulder, Cavanaugh saw the cloud obscure the murky furniture. Hissing pressure expanded it rapidly.

"Faraday," the parrot squawked. It didn't get a chance to add "Jerk" before it toppled to the floor of its cage, wings thrashing.

Jamie and Eddie ran into William's office. Cavanaugh followed and slammed the door.

"Poison gas!" His voice was barely audible amid the alarm as he recalled how much force the vapor had been under. "We can't stay here! It'll seep under the door!"

He pivoted toward a wall of shelves that had an array of imposing law books on them. After yanking down a book on the right of the middle shelf, he flipped a lever, then tugged at the entire section of shelves. The section was on rollers. It swung smoothly out, revealing a circular metal staircase that led down.

Jamie and Eddie looked surprised.

"William got so paranoid about his security, he insisted on another way to leave his office!" Cavanaugh flicked a switch that illuminated the stairs and motioned for Jamie and Eddie to hurry down.

About to follow, he balked and stared back at the closed office door. The gray haze was seeping under it.

Unable to subdue his protector's instincts, he lunged for the desk, grabbing the phone.

"What are you doing?" Eddie shouted from the staircase.

The building's security guards, Cavanaugh thought. *The police. The explosions put them on heightened alert. The alarm will bring them to this office. They'll burst in.*

They'll breathe the gas and die.

William's phone system had an emergency button that directed a call to the lobby's security desk.

"What?" a voice asked quickly, sounding harried.

Pressing the phone hard against his ear, holding a hand over his other ear, Cavanaugh thought he heard sirens and urgent voices in the background. "There's an alarm on the thirtieth floor!"

"We know! A team's going up there!"

Cavanaugh stared again at the crack beneath the closed door. More of the gray haze seeped under it. "Don't go into the office! It's filled with poison gas!"

He slammed down the phone and charged through the opening in the wall. The metal staircase echoed as he pulled at the section of shelves. Closing the barrier, he heard a latch click shut. Then he ran down the circular stairs, turning repeatedly, the echo rumbling.

Jamie and Eddie waited at the bottom.

A dead end.

"How do we—"

"That latch on the right!"

Eddie yanked it and pulled.

A section of the wall moved toward him. The light in the stairwell revealed a janitor's closet.

They closed the wall, unlocked the closet door, and peered out, checking the corridor.

After the dim light in the stairwell, the overhead fluorescents seemed bright when they emerged from the closet.

"The police will search the building," Jamie said.

"And emergency-response teams," Cavanaugh agreed. "Assuming they're all genuine."

He eased a stairwell door open. From below, footsteps and voices rumbled upward.

"We can't go that way."

11

I always get the shit duty, the fireman thought. His name was Ben Gutowski. Laboring up the stairs in complete firefighting gear, he felt sweat soaking his clothes. His legs ached.

Would you rather be in an elevator? he asked himself. *Suppose this is another World Trade Center attack. Suppose more bombs go off or rockets or whatever caused the explosion. Suppose the building collapses. How'd you like to be in a friggin' elevator then? And what's this alert about poison gas? You want to be trapped in an elevator with* that? *Maybe the captain did you a favor.*

Breathing hard, Ben reached another stairwell door. Twenty-ninth floor. Below him, other firemen in full gear struggled upward, checking other floors. He pressed his hand against the door, feeling for heat. He did the same to the doorknob. Normal. He put his oxygen mask over his face, breathed, and opened the door. Assuming he didn't encounter a fire and his air-testing meter didn't detect any gas, he would then take off his oxygen mask and lumber along the corridor, making sure nobody was in danger.

Bang! Crash! Clatter!

Elvis Presley sang "Blue Hawaii."

Surprise made Ben almost drop his ax. Ahead, a janitor took a wet mop from a pail and swabbed the corridor while a radio played music through the partially open door of a maintenance closet.

"What are *you* doing here?" Ben demanded.

12

While Elvis crooned, Cavanaugh peered up from mopping the floor. His gray janitor's coveralls covered the blood on his clothes and gave him the rumpled look of somebody who'd worked too many years on the night shift. The small radio was a bonus.

"What does it look like I'm doing?" Cavanaugh answered, annoyed. The fireman appeared genuine, but after the night's threats, it was foolish to make assumptions. "And what are *you* doing here?" He almost let go of his mop in apparent sudden realization. "Wait a minute, is there a fire?"

"Didn't you hear the explosion?"

"Explosion?"

"On the fortieth floor."

"*What?*"

"And poison gas," the exhausted fireman said.

"Poison…Jesus, don't tell me it's terrorists!"

"We don't know *what* it is. You need to get out of here."

"Buddy, I don't need convincing."

"Anybody else on this floor?"

"Nobody."

"You're positive."

"I've been up and down this corridor for the past hour. The place is deserted."

A bell sounded. Down the corridor, an elevator opened. A policeman charged out.

"This floor's clear!" the fireman shouted to be heard above the music. "I'm getting this janitor out of here."

"On the double! We don't know what else might happen!" The policeman ducked back into the elevator. Its doors closed.

"You heard him," the fireman said. "Go!"

"I'm outta here," Cavanaugh said.

He and the fireman hurried toward the stairwell door.

"Hold it, I forgot my coat," Cavanaugh said.

"Hurry!" The fireman turned and yelled down the stairs toward where footsteps and voices struggled upward, "Evacuee coming down!"

"I'm right behind you!" Cavanaugh yelled. "Check the other floors. Poison gas? God help anybody who's in the building."

Breathing hard, the fireman climbed to the next level. Simultaneously, Cavanaugh opened the maintenance room's door all the way. There, amid boxes of cleaning supplies, Jamie and Eddie waited. Only one other set of coveralls had been in the room. They'd been too big for Jamie, so Eddie wore them.

Jamie grabbed a box, holding it as if it contained something important.

Clutching his mop as if he was too startled to realize it was in his hand, Cavanaugh led the way through the stairwell door. Lights glared. Above, the door to the thirtieth floor banged shut as the fireman went in. Below, other firemen climbed and opened doors.

Cavanaugh, Jamie, and Eddie hurried down.

"One of your men ordered us out of here," he told the next fireman, four floors down. "I don't understand what's happening."

"Just do what he told you." The fireman breathed hard from the climb and the weight of his equipment. "Get out of the building. Evacuees coming down!" he yelled to his team farther below.

As Cavanaugh, Jamie, and Eddie hurriedly descended, the clatter of their footsteps added to those of the emergency team.

"Evacuees!" a fireman yelled to other men below him. "Are you hurt?" he asked Cavanaugh.

"No. Just scared."

"I hear you," the fireman said. Putting his oxygen mask on, he braced himself and opened a door.

They hurried lower. Passing emergency workers, breathing hoarsely, they reached the fifth floor, the fourth…

A few seconds after they passed the lobby door, it banged open. A fireman charged up the stairs, shouting into his two-way radio, "Affirmative! Poison gas! The thirtieth floor! Make sure the building's empty!"

With his attention focused on the upper floors, the fireman failed to see them below.

13

GARAGE LEVEL TWO, the sign said. Cavanaugh cracked the door open and listened. Hearing only stillness, he opened the door farther and studied the few cars. In an emergency that required a building to be evacuated, it was standard procedure for the teams to start at the bottom, moving upward. Subsequently, they assumed areas they'd checked didn't need to be revisited.

As he stepped into the parking garage, the overhead lights made everything a sickly yellow.

"Over there." Eddie pointed past three drab-colored Tauruses that Global Protective Services used.

Eddie's car was equally anonymous.

"Let's see if it explodes."

They crouched behind the farthest car and put their hands over their ears—except for Eddie, who could protect only one ear while he pressed an ignition button on his car's remote control. When the car started, Eddie relaxed. "Well, at least we don't need to worry about *that*."

"But there might still be a bomb," Jamie said.

Eddie agreed. "The attack team would have seen me drive in here. They'd have had plenty of time to hide one somewhere other than attaching it to the engine."

Cautious, they approached the car. Its nostril-stinging exhaust made Eddie press another button on the remote, shutting off the engine.

In the smothering silence, Cavanaugh reached under his sport coat, felt behind the pouch that contained his spare ammunition magazine, and unsheathed a small flashlight, another item from his bug-out bag. For its size—as long and wide as his index finger—it produced surprisingly intense light.

Jamie took out hers, also.

They knelt and aimed the beams behind the wheels and at every area of the car's undercarriage. Then Cavanaugh went to one side of the car while Jamie went to the other. He aimed his light through a window toward the rear of the interior while Jamie did the same from the opposite side. The idea was to concentrate on small areas, progressing from one tiny space to another in an ordered way. Cavanaugh had difficulty keeping his flashlight steady when he knew that at any moment the door to the parking area might bang open and what came through might not be an emergency team.

Through the windows, they looked for anything that seemed out of place. But the chances were a bomb wouldn't be that easy to notice. Sometimes, the only indication was a slight shadow.

The dashboard. The steering column. The brake. The accelerator.

What they mostly searched for was a wire. When a door was opened, the wire would tug a concealed igniter, and the car would explode. The extremely thin wire might have a non-reflective coating that made it difficult to detect.

Cavanaugh's mouth felt dry. "See anything?"

"No," Jamie answered.

"Time for the game." Cavanaugh referred to Rock, Paper, Scissors. He and Eddie made a fist and shook them three times. When they stopped, they had three options: to leave the fist closed (rock), to open the hand flat (paper), or to hold out the first two fingers (scissors).

Cavanaugh's scissors cut Eddie's paper. "Okay," he told Jamie and Eddie, "Get back behind the far vehicle while I open the doors."

"You didn't play the game with *me*," Jamie noted.

Cavanaugh studied her.

"Fine," he said.

They held up their fists and shook them three times.

Jamie's paper covered Cavanaugh's rock.

"I don't want you to do this," Cavanaugh said.

"I don't want to, either. But I'm part of the team, and I'm going to risk my life the same as everybody else."

"Yeah, you're tough," Eddie said.

Cavanaugh had never understood the expression "heart in my throat" until now.

"Do it slowly," he said. "Keep looking for wires."

The speed of his pulse made him sick as he and Eddie crouched behind the farthest car. He opened his mouth and pressed his hands over his ears to minimize the impact of an explosion. But even with his ears muffled, he was sure he heard Jamie open the doors.

A few instants lasted forever.

Then Jamie was standing in front of him, looking terrified but proud.

"Okay," he said, exhaling. "My turn. I'll check inside."

As Jamie and Eddie crouched behind the far vehicle, Cavanaugh aimed his small flashlight and cautiously leaned into the car, peering up under the dashboard. He checked under the seats.

Nothing looked suspicious.

As Jamie and Eddie rejoined him, he reached into his jacket pocket and came out with something else from the bug-out bag: a zip tie.

Without needing to be told what came next, Eddie unlocked the Taurus's trunk but kept his hands on the lid so that it opened only a crack. While Jamie aimed her flashlight, Cavanaugh inserted the zip tie into the crack between the lid and the car's chassis and drew it from one side to the other.

What he felt for was a taut wire. All an enemy needed to do was pick the trunk's lock, put a bomb inside, attach a wire to the bomb's detonator, close the lid until only the enemy's hand fitted inside, hook the wire to the inside of the lid, and then close the lid.

The twist tie was pliant enough that if it encountered a wire, it would bend without putting pressure on the wire. Sweat trickled down Cavanaugh's face. His hand wanted to shake, but he kept it steady. Five minutes later, he nodded to Eddie, who raised the lid slightly higher, while Cavanaugh and Jamie aimed their flashlights inside.

Finally, the trunk was all the way open. They searched among weapons and an armored vest, and to their relief found nothing that looked like a bomb.

Security specialists were paranoid about being held prisoner in the trunks of their cars. One of the first things an operator did when acquiring a vehicle was to inspect the trunk's interior and rig its latch so that it could easily be tripped from the inside. As a further precaution, a weapon and escape tools were hidden behind the trunk's lining and air holes were drilled, tubes leading from them to the vehicle's interior. Finally, the best agents had a secret stash of something else. Smiling, Eddie now displayed it, peeling off the lining on the right side of the trunk.

Cavanaugh grinned at a plastic bottle of water and a bag filled with energy bars.

"God, I love working with a pro."

They took turns drinking. Water had never tasted so wonderful. Cavanaugh wiped drops from his lips and bit heartily into a caramel-flavored energy bar, all the while staring toward the door that led into the parking garage.

He looked at his watch. Almost five a.m.

"We still need to check the engine and under the car."

Twenty minutes later, every part of the vehicle had been studied.

"Clean," Eddie said.

"But we can't leave the building yet," Jamie said. "The police and the emergency crews would see us and stop us. They'd probably take us somewhere and question us."

Cavanaugh nodded. "We need to assume the assault team's watching the building. They'd follow."

"I'm tough to follow," Eddie said. "Even so, yeah, we'd better stay put and get some rest."

After another round of Rock, Paper, Scissors, Eddie got the spacious back seat, Jamie the front, and Cavanaugh, who hated enclosed spaces, got the trunk.

It faced a wall. He set the weapons to one side. Then he crawled in, put his handgun beside him, saw a section of rope, threaded it through a rib in the underside of the lid, and lowered the lid until the trunk was open about five inches. He tucked the rope under him so that his weight would keep the lid at the level he wanted. If he needed to, he'd be able to release the rope and raise the lid in a hurry.

Jamie stepped back, pretending she was someone who'd just entered the garage. "It looks natural. With the trunk facing the wall, I can't tell it's partly open."

Eddie was already stretched out in the back seat. With both doors closed, Jamie couldn't see him unless she stood at the side of the car and looked directly in. She turned toward the trunk's lid and peered through the gap. "Sweet dreams, babe."

PART FOUR:
THE RULE OF FIVE MISSIONS

1

Dreaming that he was buried alive, Cavanaugh woke with a start. Having imagined the sound of dirt being shoveled onto his coffin, he knew that further sleep was out of the question.

Instead, he imagined Jackson Hole near dawn, the crisp autumn air, elk in the pasture.

Sounds interrupted. Opening his eyes, Cavanaugh clutched his pistol and listened to a door banging. He heard car engines, footsteps, voices. But there wasn't any sense of urgency. The police and the emergency crews must have finished their investigation, decided that the risk was over, and finally allowed the building to be reopened. As more cars arrived, he pulled the rope down, lowering the trunk's lid almost all the way. In the murky enclosure, he stared at his watch, waiting for his eyes to detect the faintly luminous dial. The hands showed that the time was eight minutes after one.

"Time for lunch, babe." Jamie's voice was close outside the trunk.

"Don't you think about anything except food?"

"And a bathroom," Jamie said. "But restaurants have bathrooms, so we're got everything covered. Incidentally, I'm pretending to unlock the trunk."

Cavanaugh released the rope and let Jamie raise the lid.

Her green eyes studied the enclosure. "Reminds me of the first dormitory room I had at Wellesley. Minus the weapons, of course. Nobody's watching. I'm partially shielding you. Come on out."

Cavanaugh's legs felt stiff as he stepped down to the concrete.

Eddie looked rested, putting a stick of gum in his mouth.

More cars entered the parking garage. Sounds and movement filled it. Men and women wearing business clothes walked toward the elevators. Cavanaugh heard bits of troubled conversation about rumors of what had happened during the night.

"Ready to go?" Eddie no longer wore the janitor's coveralls. Despite his beard stubble, his clean leather jacket and turtleneck made him look the most presentable of the three.

Jamie closed her blazer over the blood spots on her white blouse.

Cavanaugh decided that the coveralls he wore would attract less attention than the damaged clothes underneath. "Let's do it."

They got in the Taurus, Eddie behind the steering wheel, Cavanaugh next to him, Jamie in the back. Despite the care they'd taken to make sure the car didn't have a bomb, Cavanaugh tensed when Eddie turned the ignition key. But the only sound was the car's smooth drone.

Eddie drove up the ramp toward the building's exit, where he showed a GPS badge to a security officer. The crossbar went up. They emerged onto the noise and commotion of 53rd Street.

"It'll be hard to follow us in all this traffic." Eddie drove through noisy Madison Avenue and continued along 53rd.

"Unless they planted a location transmitter so small we didn't spot it when we searched the car."

"Unpleasant thought." Eddie checked his rearview mirror. "Where to?"

"Get us off the island," Cavanaugh said. He turned on the radio. Billy Joel sang about "A New York State of Mind." Cavanaugh pushed a button that switched the sophisticated radio to an extremely wide FM spectrum, a Global Protective Services modification. "Jamie, why don't you tell us the fascinating story of your life?"

Jamie hesitated only long enough to gather her thoughts before starting her monologue. "It *is* fascinating. First I was born, and then I learned to crawl, and then I was toilet trained..."

Cavanaugh proceeded up the FM spectrum on the radio. Most location transmitters used an FM setting, as did many eavesdropping devices—tuned to bandwidths that weren't employed by local radio stations and police or fire department radios. To discover if that type of beeper or bug had been concealed in the car, Cavanaugh needed only to continue up the FM spectrum and listen for Jamie's voice or the beep of a location transmitter to come through the radio.

"And then I went to junior high, and then I started dating boys, and then I went to high school, and I *really* started dating boys."

"You can skip that part," Cavanaugh said.

"And then I went to Wellesley, and I dated men."

"You can skip that part, also."

"And then I met *you*, and my life got weird, and…"

Cavanaugh reached the top end of the FM spectrum without hearing Jamie's voice come from the radio. "Seems like it's safe to talk." He didn't add his next thought, which was that if the attack team had used a radio transmitter that gathered conversations on exotic frequencies and sent them in microbursts, there was no easy way to detect it.

Eddie had his hands at ten o'clock and two o'clock on the steering wheel, his fingers slightly spread as a professional driver was trained to do. "How about the Lincoln Tunnel?"

"Good," Cavanaugh said. "Then head south on Ninety-Five."

"To?"

"Washington."

Eddie passed Fifth and Sixth avenues, then turned south onto Seventh, switching his grip on the steering wheel. The next light remained green. The many lanes of one-way traffic increased speed.

"Why are we going to…shit."

"What's the matter?" Jamie asked.

"Something…" Eddie took his right hand off the steering wheel and stared at it. "Stung."

"What?"

"Something stung me."

They kept with the rapid traffic.

"A bee?" Cavanaugh glanced around. "A mosquito or something? It's a little late in the year for—"

"No." Eddie's voice was thick. "Steering wheel. Something on the..." Eddie pointed toward the two o'clock position on the steering wheel. "Jesus." His breathing sounded labored.

"Hey." Jamie touched his shoulder. "Are you all right?"

"Don't feel...Cavanaugh, have you got a..." Eddie shivered. "Handkerchief?"

Cavanaugh frowned. "In my jacket." He pulled it out.

"Wrap it." Eddie gasped. "Your hand."

"What?"

"Grab the..." Eddie shivered more violently. "Bottom...steering..."

Suddenly, Eddie's head jerked back. He slumped.

2

When Cavanaugh had learned defensive and offensive driving techniques, one of the drills involved what to do if you're in the front passenger seat of a car, your partner driving, and the windshield blows apart from super-velocity bullets and the driver takes one in the head. You can't let the car veer off the road into a wall or a tree. You can't let it stop. The prime imperative is to get away from the shooting zone as quickly as possible. And that meant you had to do what Cavanaugh did now.

Conscious of the rapid traffic on either side, he undid his seatbelt and shifted close to Eddie. With his handkerchief wrapped around his fingers, he grabbed the lower portion of the steering wheel, far from where Eddie had gripped it, far from whatever had stung him. Simultaneously, Cavanaugh shifted his left foot over to the floor pedals, pressing the brake as traffic slowed and then stopped for a red light.

Seeing a police car ahead on the left, he blurted, "Jamie, lean forward! Prop Eddie up! Tilt his head so he seems to be looking forward! Make it seem like he's driving!"

Sweating, Cavanaugh propped Eddie's right hand on the steering wheel. As he neared the police car, he told Jamie, "Now lean back!"

Cavanaugh tried to put distance between him and Eddie, making the space between them look normal while still managing to stretch his leg toward the brake. Amid waiting traffic, he eased to a stop next to the police car, put the transmission in neutral, and moved back to the passenger seat, the idling engine allowing him to take his foot off the brake. Looking ahead, he pretended this was the most boring day of his life. From the left side of his vision, he had a blurred image of one of the policemen peering at the Taurus. The officer watched Eddie and Cavanaugh for what seemed an eternity.

The light turned green. Traffic shifted forward. The cruiser seemed frozen in place, the policeman studying Eddie. Then the van ahead of the police car went through the intersection, and the police car caught up to it, filling the gap.

Working to control his breathing, Cavanaugh slid close to Eddie, gripped the bottom of the steering wheel, put the transmission into drive, and eased his left foot onto the accelerator, matching the pace of traffic.

"Jamie, lean forward again. Put your head next to Eddie as if you're saying something to him. Put a hand on his shoulder. Keep him from slumping over."

In the middle of several lanes of traffic, Cavanaugh saw a space open on his right and steered into that lane so he wouldn't be next to the police car. A taxi blared.

3

Jamie had the sensation of spiraling downward. Since she'd met and married Cavanaugh (which wasn't even his real name), the abnormal had become the rule. Chases. Gunfights. Even getting shot five months earlier. She didn't understand how she'd managed to adjust to Cavanaugh's dangerous, upside-down world, where things were seldom as they appeared. He once joked that she must have been a protective agent in another life. Leaning toward Eddie, holding his shoulder to keep him from slumping, putting her head next to his to keep it from tilting while she pretended to talk to him—all this seemed insanely natural. From the listless feel of his body and the increasing coolness in the skin, she was certain he was dead. *Another first*, she thought. Touching a corpse. Talking to it.

I've gone crazy.

"What killed him?" She tried to keep her fierce emotions from affecting her voice.

Cavanaugh's face showed the strain of concentrating to keep the Taurus moving with the chaos of traffic. Ahead, a van's brake lights came on as an intersection's signal turned red. He stretched his leg over and pressed the brake pedal, stopping just before his car would have hit the van. "Eddie said something stung him."

"A needle on the steering wheel? Another pointed weapon? With some kind of toxin on it?"

"We need to find a place to park."

"In midtown Manhattan? Lots of luck."

"Which we seem to have run out of."

The light turned green. The van moved ahead. Cavanaugh shifted his outstretched leg from the brake to the accelerator. "I don't trust myself to try to turn a corner without hitting another car. We need to stay on Seventh Avenue."

Flanked by a limousine and a delivery truck, they headed farther south. A taxi veered from the left to get into Cavanaugh's lane. He barely stretched his foot to the brake in time to avoid smashing into it.

As Eddie's head threatened to list to the right, Jamie gripped the back of his neck tighter to keep it straight. His skin felt cooler. "Driving from the passenger seat. I guess that's something else you need to teach me."

"When we get out of this."

"Yeah. When we get out of this." The lovely concept of the future.

They kept heading south on Seventh Avenue, staying in the middle of the numerous lanes of traffic. Jamie had the sense of being on a runaway wagon, Cavanaugh struggling to keep it under control. A red light stopped them at 34th Street. Then they sped forward again, car horns blaring around them. Five more red lights later, they crossed below West 14th, leaving the rectangular grids of midtown for the randomly arranged streets of Greenwich Village.

Traffic became less crowded. Easing to the left toward Sheridan Square, Cavanaugh reached a No Parking zone in front of the spear-tipped metal bars of tiny Christopher Park. With no policemen in sight, he jumped from the car and ran around the front to get behind the steering wheel and push Eddie into the passenger seat. Meanwhile,

Jamie hurried from the back and fastened Eddie's seat belt. She closed the passenger door against him, then rushed to the back again and leaned Eddie's head against the passenger window as if he were sleeping. Cavanaugh pulled from the No PARKING zone.

Driving was still awkward because Cavanaugh had to grip the bottom of the steering wheel, keeping a handkerchief around his right hand, wary of whatever sharp object was embedded in the wheel. He steered around a block and got back onto Seventh Avenue, continuing south.

"The Holland Tunnel?" Jamie asked.

"Yes. Hoboken. A shopping mall."

4

In addition to fresh clothes, what they needed were a magnifying glass and a strong pair of tweezers, all of which were in bags Jamie carried to where Cavanaugh had parked in a remote area of the shopping mall's parking lot. Jamie had worn Eddie's leather jacket to conceal the blood on her top. To be thorough, she'd bought *two* magnifying glasses, and after she and Cavanaugh put on jeans and pullovers in the back seat, they leaned toward the steering wheel, careful not to touch it as they gazed through the magnifying glasses, examining it in painstaking detail.

"I see something glinting," Jamie said on her third pass over the wheel. She pointed. "There."

"Careful." Cavanaugh stared through the magnifying glass. "Yes. I see it." He raised the tweezers and probed at the back of the wheel, gripping something, pulling it free.

The needle glinted in the late-afternoon sunlight coming through the windshield.

Jamie shivered.

"Looks like the back end's been snipped off," Cavanaugh said. "After it was pushed through the padding on the steering wheel, it must have been trimmed so it wouldn't stick out on either side."

"But hidden the way it was, the driver wouldn't get pricked unless he gripped the steering wheel with a little extra force," Jamie said.

"Which Eddie would have needed to do when he turned the corner onto Seventh Avenue."

"Let's keep checking in case there are more."

But twenty minutes of further searching revealed nothing else. They dropped the needle into a plastic bag.

5

"Global Protective Services," the receptionist's voice said.

Using his cell phone, Cavanaugh stood next to the Taurus at the deserted edge of the shopping mall's parking lot. In the background, he heard objects clattering, as if workmen were removing debris from the explosion at the GPS office. "Mr. Brockman, please."

"I'm sorry. He's not available."

"Then give me Mr. Karim."

"May I tell him who's calling?"

"Mr. Stoddard. He's expecting my call."

"One moment."

Cavanaugh heard a click, then nothing. He held the phone closer to his ear as an eighteen-wheel truck roared past on a neighboring highway.

"Cavanaugh?" Karim's voice suddenly asked. "Where *are* you? We've been worried about—"

"What's your cell-phone number?" Cavanaugh worried that the office phones were tapped.

Karim told him the number.

"Go to encryption. I'll call you right back."

Duncan's justified mania about security had prompted him to arrange for all GPS cell phones to have a scrambler capability so that protectors could speak to one another while eavesdroppers with radio scanners would hear only garbled words. It was the only time Cavanaugh felt comfortable using a cell phone.

Immediately, he activated the encryption on his phone, then pressed numbers.

On the other end, the phone barely rang before Karim answered. "*Are you okay?*"

"We had another casualty. Eddie's dead."

"What?"

"A needle hidden in his car's steering wheel. It had some kind of poison on it."

The phone became silent for a moment as Karim reacted to this information. "A sharp object. Like the others. After Eddie parked and came up to the office, somebody must have gotten into the building's garage and rigged his car."

"Maybe," Cavanaugh said.

"How else would—"

"After Jamie, Eddie, and I went down in the elevator, did you, Kim, Brockman stay together?"

"Together?"

"Waiting for the police and the fire department. *Did you stay together?*"

"No, not all the time. We went back to your office, trying to save files and contain the damage. Each of us had different things to do. When the police and the fire department showed up, things got more confusing. Why? What are you getting at?"

"Would there have been time for one of you to go down to William's office?"

"I don't understand." Karim sounded more confused. "Why would any of us have wanted to go *there*?"

"Because one of you got information that *we* went there."

But *how?* Cavanaugh thought. Did someone have William's office bugged to find out if he learned who Aaron Stoddard was?

"Wait a minute," Karim said. "Are you suggesting one of us tried to kill you?"

"Where's Brockman?"

"I haven't the faintest idea. Home probably. Even if he's not the boss any longer, he's entitled. We spent all night at the office, remember." Karim's voice had an edge to it. "Or maybe he's as dumb as *I* am, and he's putting in another shift, meeting a client or whatever. Don't tell me you think Brockman—"

"I'm just trying to cover the possibilities. "

"Next, you'll be asking about Kim. I'll save you the trouble. She's not here. Did you think *she* had something to do with this? What about *me?*"

"I told you I'm just trying to cover the possibilities. There isn't time for this. We need to do something about Eddie. I'm in a parking lot at a shopping mall in Hoboken."

"Then I guess *I'm* not the only one having a fabulous time."

"Tell the police I'll leave Eddie with his car."

Cavanaugh told Karim the license number and directions to the shopping mall.

"Everything's the way it was when he got killed, except the needle's in a plastic bag on the seat next to him."

"The police won't be happy you moved the murder weapon."

"Would they rather somebody else died from being stung by it? Tell them to expect to find our fingerprints all over the car. But maybe they'll also find some evidence left by the killer. We'll call them later and answer their questions. But there's no way we'll take the risk of exposing ourselves by coming in."

6

On the mall, Cavanaugh and Jamie stood in a corner near glass doors, concealed by customers who came and went.

"Won't be long now," Jamie said. "The sign says it's supposed to come at four o'clock."

Air brakes hissing, a bus stopped outside the glass doors. The sign said, WEATHERVIEW RETIREMENT CENTER. As elderly people queued up to get on the bus, Cavanaugh and Jamie merged with them, the only young people in the group. Cavanaugh noticed that the driver wasn't collecting money. The bus was apparently some kind of community service.

"How'd the shopping go?" Cavanaugh asked a white-haired man ahead of him.

"Shopping? Don't come here to shop. I *walk*. Exercise. Know what I mean?"

"Sure do," Jamie said. "But why don't you walk in a park or some place nice?"

"And get killed?"

"Yeah, the streets aren't as safe as they used to be."

"The ozone layer's shot. Skin cancer. I'm talking about skin cancer. Know what I mean?"

"Sure do. Not to mention all the junk in the air. Smog. Car exhaust."

"That's what I mean."

As Cavanaugh and Jamie got on the bus, Jamie's rapport with the man made it seem they were together. When the man missed his step, Cavanaugh caught his arm, helping him inside. He gave the bus driver an "I need to keep an eye on the old fellow" look, then proceeded with Jamie and the elderly man toward seats in the back.

When the bus eased away from the mall, heading toward a busy street, Jamie touched Cavanaugh's arm and nodded toward the deserted part of the lot where they'd left Eddie in the Taurus.

Sirens wailing, three police cars sped toward the vehicle.

7

"Where to?" the taxi driver asked.

"Across the river," Jamie said.

"Manhattan? Gonna cost you." The driver ignored Cavanaugh, enjoying Jamie's figure and her captivating eyes. "Once I get over there, I'm not allowed to take a fare back to Hoboken."

"I don't have a choice. I've got a meeting I absolutely need to attend. I'll pay double, plus a twenty percent tip."

8

They got out at Times Square and went into a store that had CAMERA in its title but sold almost everything. They came out with two over-the-shoulder travel bags, went into a nearby drugstore, bought the toiletries they needed, and put them in the bags. They went into a clothing store and used some of the cash from the Gulfstream's bug-out bag to buy a few more clothes, including underwear and socks.

They walked east on 42ⁿᵈ Street.

"Having fun yet?" Cavanaugh asked.

"Loving every minute. God help me, I've been with you so long I can't tell the difference between being scared and feeling an adrenaline surge."

"Did I ever tell you about the rule of five?"

"No." Jamie made her way along the congested sidewalk. The time was almost six o'clock. Car horns blared amid stalled traffic. "But I've got nothing better to do, so why don't you tell me?"

"You're sure?"

"Can't wait."

"In the Second World War, instructors training American fighter pilots couldn't help noticing how many students died on their early missions. No matter how hard the instructors tried to teach the pilots the way to spot traps and get out of tough places, a large percentage of each class got shot down. So the instructors researched files that dated all the way back to the First World War, and what they discovered was a mathematical pattern. The majority of novice pilots were shot down within their first five missions."

Jamie looked at him.

"The same pattern showed up in the Korean War and in Vietnam. Five was the magic number. After that, their chances of surviving combat flights increased dramatically. During the first five missions, the tension of combat was so unfamiliar that the students had trouble using what they'd learned. They were too busy adjusting. It was only after *five* missions that they started to know the difference between fear and adrenaline. Once the pilots understood that adrenaline primed their reflexes and made them better able to track a target and pull the trigger in the split second when it mattered, they were on their way to being professionals. The pilots who survived five missions tended to survive thirty and forty missions. If you consider everything that happened to us…I'm not talking about the training I gave you since we got married. Training's only half of what it takes. The real thing, adjusting to fear— that's the other half. You graduated. You passed your five missions."

"Is that supposed to give me confidence that I…that *we* have a better chance of surviving?"

"We got *this* far, didn't we?"

As the evening became dimmer and cooler, they stared up at the imposing entrance to Grand Central Station.

9

The stocky black man jogged around a curve and increased speed down a straightaway through a wooded park in a suburb of Washington, D.C. He wasn't alone. At 6:30 in the morning, an army of his fellow exercisers primed themselves for another day's combat in offices throughout the nation's capitol. The chill of October had its effect, prompting the black man to wear a long-legged, navy exercise suit. Breath vapor blew from his mouth.

Hearing rhythmic rapid footfalls behind him, he waited for the faster runners to pass him. A white man and woman, each wearing gray exercise suits, came abreast of him. He maintained his moderate pace, waiting for them to surge ahead, but instead they kept even with him, one on each side, their footfalls matching his.

When he looked at one and then the other, he almost faltered.

"I do believe," the Southern Baptist said.

"I'll tell you what *I* believe," Cavanaugh said.

"I'm not sure I want to know," the black man, John Rutherford, said.

"I believe in gun oil and plenty of ammunition."

"I'm relieved. For a second, I expected you to say something you hoped would shock me."

"*Bull Durham*," Jamie said.

Rutherford nodded, jogging past a duck pond. "Baseball's an enjoyable pastime."

"So are the slow kisses Kevin Costner's character believes in," Jamie said.

"If you expect me to be shocked by *that*—" Rutherford breathed hard as he ran. "—I remind you I was married. My wife…God rest her soul…believed in slow kisses, also. How *are* you, Jamie?" His smile was genuine. "The last time I saw you, you were in a hospital bed. I'm glad you recovered from your wound."

"How's the guy who shot me doing?"

"Not well, I'm afraid. Prison doesn't agree with him. Seems he prefers solitary confinement to all the inmates who want to be his friend."

"What a shame. And how about *you*, John?" Cavanaugh asked. "How are *you* getting along? I understand congratulations are in order."

"You mean my promotion?"

"Director of the FBI's counterterrorist unit. I'm proud of you."

"Sure, you are."

They ran past a homeless man asleep on a bench.

"I hate to ask this. We're having such a great time so far," Rutherford said. "How are *you?*"

"Need a little help, John."

"Gosh, and here I thought you'd just happened to be in the neighborhood. You decided to drop by at the crack of dawn, say hello, and catch up on old times while you joined me for a little exercise."

"Exactly what we had in mind," Cavanaugh said. "But as long as we're here…"

"Let me guess. You want to talk about the Global Protective Service agents who've been killed."

"You know about that?" Cavanaugh looked at him in surprise.

"They're not the only ones. Protectors in various government agencies are being killed also."

"What?" Cavanaugh slackened his pace and veered from the path, stopping next to bushes.

Rutherford and Jamie followed him.

"The Secret Service. The U.S. Marshals. The Diplomatic Security Service. Three days ago, agents from all of them suddenly became targets." Rutherford took a towel from around his neck and wiped sweat from his forehead. "At first, it looked like they'd taken hits meant for the people they were protecting. But the casualties kept mounting, and most of the attacks happened when the agents were off-duty. We soon had to conclude—"

"The *protectors* were the targets."

"On a hunch, we checked the civilian protection agencies. The small ones didn't know what we were talking about. But a major one like Global Protective Services..."

"We took our share of hits," Cavanaugh said.

"'We'?" Rutherford frowned. "I thought you'd left the business."

"What's that line from one of the *Godfather* movies? 'Just when I thought I was out, they dragged me back in'? Now I'm not only *back* in the business. I *own* the damned thing."

Cavanaugh explained what had happened at the GPS office in Manhattan and later in Eddie's car.

"Eddie *Macintosh*?" Rutherford looked appalled. "He's one of the best drivers I ever worked with."

"That's how he died. Behind a steering wheel."

A group of joggers sped by. Rutherford stepped farther toward the bushes, trying to get out of hearing range of anyone on the path.

"Sharp weapons? Bladed ones?" Rutherford asked.

"That's the pattern. Up close and intimate. Except for the attacks against Jamie and me."

"But at the time of the first one, you were retired. Out of the game. Why would anyone attack you?"

"Maybe somebody found out who was set to inherit Global Protective Services," Jamie said. "Maybe that couldn't be allowed to happen."

Cavanaugh looked around the park. "Aren't you nervous being out here in the open every morning?"

"Protectors are the ones getting killed, not FBI agents. But now that *you've* paid a visit..."

"We weren't followed."

"After last May, it's no secret we're friends."

"Hey, so far so good. Nobody's made a move against us while we've been talking," Jamie said.

"I'm not consoled."

"At first, I thought this was a client from my past, trying to keep me from revealing something incriminating that I happened to learn," Cavanaugh said. "Then, when I realized how many top-rate GPS operators had been killed, I figured this was an attack directed at the company—to put it out of business, or to get even for an assassination or a kidnapping that we prevented. But now…Attacks this widespread. You're assuming this is…"

"Who's got the money, the organization, and the determination?" Rutherford asked. "The Bureau believes it's a terrorist network taking out key security personnel and trying to intimidate the others so we're not prepared for another major assault. Protectors are trained to be shields, not targets. Presumably, the bad guys figure our protective divisions will be so busy looking over their shoulders that they won't be able to do their jobs."

"It's a hell of a distraction," Cavanaugh agreed.

"'Hell' might be appropriate in this case," the Southern Baptist said. "Got any leads?"

"Every extreme faction in every country who hates us. Take your pick. These days, there are plenty to choose from. And as for possible ultimate targets, plenty to choose from there, also. For starters, the president."

"We'd better keep moving." Worried about directional microphones, Cavanaugh pointed toward a street next to the park, where traffic accumulated. "Over there. Next to the refreshing smell of automobile exhaust."

"And the noise of car engines?" Jamie asked.

"Hey, what's the harm in a few precautions?"

"You're going to ruin this place for me," Rutherford complained.

They increased speed toward the street.

"How did the government protectors die?" Cavanaugh asked.

"Sniper rifles, remote-controlled bombs, car ambushes."

"No bladed weapons?"

"A few, but no pattern. Nothing like what happened to your GPS operators."

"Then why was GPS singled out for that kind of weapon?" Jamie wondered.

"Last night, when I was studying the printouts of my former missions—" Cavanaugh breathed quickly as he ran. "—I couldn't find any client who might want to kill me because of things I knew about him. But the idea of knives reminded me of somebody."

"Who?" Rutherford asked.

"A former GPS agent. Can you use your Bureau resources to get a profile of a man named Carl Duran? And while you're at it, do a deep background check on Gerald Brockman, Kim Lee, and Ali Karim."

"But aren't they—"

"The top officers in GPS. Something's wrong there. Maybe it's got nothing to do with what's going on, or maybe it's got *everything* to do with it. Either way, I need to find out."

10

"Who's Carl Duran?" Jamie asked, lying next to Cavanaugh on a motel bed.

"Bad news." Preoccupied, Cavanaugh removed the magazine from his pistol and pulled back the slide, letting Jamie see that the firing chamber was empty. "Clear?"

"Clear."

He pressed the release lever, causing the slide to snap forward. Then, as was the habit of many operators, he practiced raising the pistol and lining up its sights. It was the equivalent of fingering worry beads. "Carl Duran and I went through Delta Force training together."

Jamie was propped against pillows the same as Cavanaugh was. She removed the magazine from her handgun, then pulled back the slide. "Clear?"

"Clear."

She too practiced aiming. The pistol came with a wide-notched rear sight that had a white dot on either side to encourage focusing. The front post had a similar, easy-to-distinguish white dot that made sighting easy.

"Some people have a misguided notion about special-operations personnel," Cavanaugh said. "They think we're beer-swilling bar brawlers. They don't understand that what our trainers are looking for is discipline and control, and anybody who acts like a thug when he's off-duty doesn't meet those requirements. In fact, the best operators are amazingly well mannered. They've been conditioned to unleash massive amounts of violence. They've also been conditioned to have a mental on-off switch and to turn on that switch only when it's appropriate. When they're not working, it's essential to remain calm."

"And Carl Duran didn't?"

"He almost got kicked off Delta Force."

"What was his problem?"

"Special operators are attracted to the profession because they enjoy the rush of taking risks. You might even say they're addicted to it. They crave the satisfaction of knowing they were in danger and had the strength and determination to survive."

Cavanaugh thought a moment, remembering Carl. "Special operators are also attracted to the profession because they like the reinforcement of belonging to an elite group. There's no place for a grandstander in a special-ops unit. As the old joke goes, there's no 'I' in 'team.' For most special operators, the bond they feel for their group is greater than what they feel for their family. They get a powerful satisfaction from knowing that they and their teammates survived unimaginable dangers, that they're among the most special human beings in the world, and that they can count on each other for support, even if it comes to dying for each other."

"Carl Duran was a grandstander?"

"He wanted to prove he was better than anybody else. For him, everything was a contest—not with himself, which is the way Delta wants it, but with everybody in his unit. He had to be superior. The best operator. The best gunfighter. And he had to make sure everybody knew it. Even when he was a kid, he acted that way."

Jamie quit aiming her pistol and looked at him. "You make it sound like…"

"I went to high school with him in Iowa."

"But you told me you were raised in Oklahoma."

"Until my dad beat my mom and me once too often, and she took me and left him. Eventually, we landed in Iowa City, where she got paralegal training, went to work for an attorney, and married him."

"How is it we need to be running for our lives before you tell me about your past?"

"Why should I talk about what I want to forget?"

"Your stepfather wasn't kind to you, either?"

"He didn't know how to react to a child. He was a better husband than he was a father. Let's put it this way, he disapproved of mistakes, and in *his* eyes, I made a lot of mistakes. But he didn't raise his voice. He didn't beat me. He didn't beat my mother or the daughter my mom and he had. By comparison with what we'd been through, he was a saint. I was grateful that he gave us a home. Still am. Even so, I did my best to stay out of his way. When it came to sternness, though, nothing could equal *Carl's* father. *That* guy was a pusher. In his youth, Carl's father played football for the University of Iowa. In Iowa, few things are as important as college sports. Carl's father had ambitions to be a pro quarterback. Might have done it, too. To hear him tell it, he was a fantastic athlete. But he broke his leg in a game in his junior year. It crippled him, and he never got over the bitterness. So the old man decided that *Carl*, by God, was going to be the pro quarterback in the family. He pushed Carl, and pushed him, until Carl was so determined to please his father that he needed to prove he was better than anybody else on the West High team. Needed to prove he knew more than the coach. Needed to prove he was smarter and tougher than anybody, and proved it so well that the coach kicked him off the team. So Carl's father beat the hell out of him and sued the school and—"

"What a mess," Jamie said.

"It got worse. Carl's father was a stockbroker. He was also a secret drinker. Finally, he got better at one than the other, and his company fired him. The drinking problem got so bad that the family was forced to sell their house. They moved to an apartment. Then they moved out of state, trying for a new start."

"And was it successful?"

"Eventually, word came back that Carl's father died from liver disease. Carl never went to college. He certainly never had a chance for that pro football career. But while we went to high school together, he and I were friends."

"I don't understand why you thought about him in connection with what's happening," Jamie said.

"Carl had a thing about knives."

11

Jamie looked at him. "Knives?"

"This was before those two kids shot up that high school in Colorado and suddenly every school had a zero-tolerance policy about bringing anything that might be a weapon onto campus. Carl was *obsessed* about knives. He carried one in his pocket every day he went to school. Or under his sweater. Or in his knapsack. He showed them to me when nobody was looking. Once, he even hid one under his uniform when he was playing football."

"And this was your *friend?*"

"It's hard to explain. We lived on the same street." Cavanaugh's memory was painful. "Hafor Drive. He was the first kid I met when my mother and I moved to my stepfather's house. There was a soccer field at the end of the street. Woods. A creek. Carl and I used to play in those woods a lot. He didn't like to go home. Neither did I. The thing about a friendship is, once it's formed, you get used to how your friend behaves. No matter how strange he acts, you think it's normal."

"You mean the knives."

"Folders. Fixed blades. Utility knives. Tactical knives. Fishing knives. Skinning knives. Carl and I had jobs delivering for one of the local morning newspapers, the *Gazette*. This was before newspapers decided it was safer and cheaper to have adults deliver them by throwing them from cars. My stepfather insisted I put the money I earned in a bank account. But Carl's father—at the time, I thought this was cool—let Carl spend his money however he wanted. I didn't think the knives themselves were cool. The truth is, they made me nervous. But Carl's father was really pleased with the knives, as if they proved Carl was macho enough to have a chance at being a pro football player. So Carl played with knives, and because he was my friend, I joined him. We had contests to see how fast we could pull them from our pockets and open them. We practiced throwing them. We imagined scenarios in which we saved somebody's life with one. Then Carl discovered in a knife magazine that a top knife maker lived right outside town, on a farm near a place called West Liberty."

"You're talking about a hammer and anvil and forge?" Jamie asked.

"The old-time real deal. One day, Carl showed up at my house to say that he'd phoned this knife maker and convinced the old guy to teach us how to forge blades. He was more excited than I'd ever seen him, so I thought, 'What the hell, I'll go along and see what it's like.' My mom wound up driving us every Sunday afternoon. It turned out that the old knife maker belonged to something called the American Bladesmith Society. He had the rank of master, a big deal when you realize there are only about ninety masters in the world. Making knives was the old man's life. His name was Lance Sawyer. The first time I heard it, I thought that name was hilarious. A knife expert whose name was Lance. He was seventy-five years old. He wore bib overalls. He was stooped and scrawny and bald and had brown tobacco juice on his white beard, but his arms were as muscular and strong as anybody's I've ever seen. For a year and a half, until Carl's father moved the family out of state, Carl and I learned how to stoke a forge, how to use a hammer and an anvil to shape a blade, how to cool the metal and then do the reverse, heat-tempering it. The old man made us use leaf springs from old pickup trucks as our rough material. It was hard, heavy work. My arms used to ache all week. But I must say we turned out some awfully fine-looking knives."

"Did you continue the lessons after Carl moved away?"

"For a while. But it wasn't the same without Carl's enthusiasm, and then the old man died. I wasn't there, but I heard he keeled over in the middle of hammering a blade. Went out happy, doing what he liked." Cavanaugh smiled wistfully to himself. "After that, I went to the University of Iowa. I'm pretty sure my stepfather wanted me to be what *he* was: an attorney. But I surprised him and my mom by leaving school before my first year ended and joining the military. That hatred-of-bullies thing I told you about. Eventually, I got into Delta Force." Cavanaugh paused. "And not long after, Carl showed up."

Jamie, who'd resumed aiming her pistol, now stopped and looked at him again. "Seems a hell of a coincidence, don't you think?"

"Except it *wasn't* a coincidence. From bits and pieces of what Carl told me, I eventually realized what happened. As his father's alcoholism got worse and the family's fortunes disintegrated, Carl kept looking back on Iowa City and his friendship with me and the lessons with the old knife maker as the best time of his life. He never went to college as his father planned. He never played football. He never had a chance for the big career his father wanted for him. He used to phone me a lot. The calls always felt as if they came from a ghost. I didn't talk long. Then one day he phoned, and my mother told him I was in the Army. As near as I can figure, he joined the Army shortly afterward. I realize now that he was hoping to get stationed with me and continue the ideal friendship he imagined we had. He kept following my career, taking special-ops training, eventually trying to get into Delta Force as he knew *I* had. Suddenly one day, there he was at the Fort Bragg Delta compound. I turned from completing a training exercise and saw him grinning at me. That was one of the few times in my life when somebody took me totally by surprise."

"Creepy," Jamie said. "It's like he was stalking you."

"Yeah. And it didn't help that the other Delta operators associated him with me. When he got too competitive, I could sense they wanted me to tell him to cool it. But Carl was in competition with me more than anyone. He wasn't about to let *me* give him advice. He knew enough to be a team player when it came to our missions. One time, in Iraq, in the first Gulf War, he saved my life. I made up for that by saving *his* life in Bosnia. The knives, though. He couldn't stop his fixation on the knives. In an effort to buy the team's friendship, he even went to the trouble of making tactical folders for everybody. But then he sabotaged any good will he created. Our team went on a mission to the Philippines to retrieve an American diplomat who'd been kidnapped by terrorists. Carl was supposed to take out an enemy sentry, using a sound-suppressed pistol. Instead, he crawled up to the guy and killed him with a knife. Almost jeopardized the assignment. Later, after we extracted the diplomat, our CO was furious. Carl claimed his pistol malfunctioned. He said his only option was to take out the sentry hand-to-hand. The CO seemed to accept his explanation. But Carl never got sent on another mission, and three months later, he was dismissed from the unit."

"So how did he get hired by Global Protective Services?"

Cavanaugh hesitated. "After Duncan retired from Delta Force and set up his business, Carl came to me, asking if I'd put in a good word. Even if it was sometimes strained, the friendship was there. He'd never done anything against me. To the contrary, he'd kept me from coming home in a body bag. Maybe his pistol *had* malfunctioned on that extraction assignment. For sure, his courage was never in doubt. Duncan and I talked about it. Duncan tried him on some low-level assignments. No problem. Some mid-level assignments. Again, no problem. Then Carl and I got assigned to protect a teenage female rock star who was getting death threats from a fan. The rock star was dating a sports celebrity, and the fan got jealous."

"I notice you haven't told me her name."

When Cavanaugh mentioned who she was, Jamie nodded. "Yeah, a knockout. The kind that flashes a lot of skin but claims to be a virgin."

"You can see how this nutcase fan felt conflicted. The singer had the money for a full-scale nine-operator team, including two female agents made up to look like her."

"Which is really *twenty-seven* operators, divided in shifts of three." Jamie did some rapid arithmetic. "That's a budget for some Third World countries."

"Then the police caught a man they were sure was the stalker. He even confessed."

"To get attention," Jamie said, anticipating where Cavanaugh was going. "But the *real* stalker—"

"Came at her after she'd reduced the protection detail to five operators. It happened outside her hotel. I was the agent in charge. I tried to convince her to use a hotel that had an underground parking garage so she could get into her limousine where there weren't any crowds."

"No anonymous car for *her*," Jamie said.

"Exactly. She needed to see her fans, she told me, and *they* needed to see *her*. It was great publicity, she said. *Entertainment Tonight* wanted to show her interacting bravely with her admirers. So we came out of the hotel, trying to part the crowd. I never would have agreed to the setup if I hadn't believed what the police told me—that they had the stalker. We moved in a standard square formation: two agents in back, two in front. The singer was in the middle with me next to her. The deal was, if somebody came at her, I was to shield her with my body and get her into the hotel or into the limo, whichever was closer. Meanwhile, the rest of the team was to surround us, to provide a barrier between her and the stalker and make sure he wasn't acting alone. The idea was to protect the client first and disable the attacker second. So when this man charged out of the crowd, thrusting a knife at her, I went into my covering mode. The rest of the team formed a ring as we backed toward the hotel. And that son of a bitch Carl broke ranks to have a knife fight with the guy."

"What?"

"Yeah, there they were in front of the Plaza Hotel, a couple of thousand fans, a ton of TV cameras, everybody screaming as the team and I hurried the singer back into the hotel, and Carl's out there, showing the guy how the business end of a knife works. Flash, flash, slash. Before the stalker died, I bet he was astonished by the enormous quantity of blood he lost. Carl was standing over the trembling corpse. Meanwhile, the crowd's in a panic, and the TV cameras are taking it all in, getting Carl's face in close-up. A little too much recognition factor for someone in the protection business. The grand jury called it a justified killing. Carl claimed that the guy was coming at *him*, to drop him and get through to the client. 'No choice,' Carl said. Privately, the members of the team knew that was bullshit. We knew Carl was so highly trained he could have disarmed and disabled the guy before the situation got lethal. He killed the guy because—"

"He wanted to have a knife fight," Jamie said.

Cavanaugh nodded. "Not that it was much of a knife fight, but yeah, I'm sure that was half his motive. And the other half? We're trained not to look at our clients when we're protecting them. The idea is to watch away from them, to see if there's a threat coming. But I noticed Carl giving the singer glances, checking her out, enjoying the view. I think the knife fight was Carl's way of trying to impress her, to earn a permanent gig protecting her."

"Did he get what he wanted?"

"What he got was fired, and this time, when he begged me to put in a good word, to persuade Duncan to rehire him, I told him to go to hell. The friendship had been strained for a long time. That broke it. I wanted nothing to do with him, even on a professional basis, because as far as I was concerned, he'd stopped being dependable. I wasn't the only operator who felt that way. No reputable protection agency would hire him. The last I heard, he was working for a Colombian drug lord."

"But now you think he's back?"

"Whoever arranged for all those protective agents to be killed with sharp weapons couldn't have done it without a thorough knowledge of how the protection business works. Combine that with a knife obsession—"

"And you get Carl Duran," Jamie said. "Maybe it wasn't the female rock singer he was trying to impress with the knife fight."

"Not her? Who else would he—"

"You. He has to assume you've made the connection between him and the blade attacks. He'll hunt you as hard as he can."

PART FIVE:
THE IRON MISTRESS

1

Rutherford almost drove past the place before he noticed it. It was in a seedy section of Alexandria, Virginia, a locale so unexpected that he was sure he'd misunderstood the address he'd been given. But then he looked harder and spotted the Hideaway Motel between a massage parlor and a porn-video shop. Shaking his head at what he hoped wasn't a practical joke, he turned left at the next intersection. He went up and down several streets at random and watched his rearview mirror to check if he was being followed. Finally, he headed back to the motel and steered into its lot, where he parked next to a Dumpster and knocked on a door.

Winos, drug dealers, and gang members watched as it opened and Jamie smiled.

Stepping in, Rutherford surveyed the grimy floor, cracked mirror, and sunken mattress. Years of cigarette smoke permeated the walls. He nodded to Cavanaugh, who stood behind the door, ready with his pistol in case Rutherford had unfriendly escorts.

"Homey," Rutherford said.

"Nobody here thinks it's strange if we pay with cash instead of a credit card," Jamie said, locking the door.

"They probably think you're a hooker."

"As long as we don't leave a paper trail, I don't even care if they think I'm a lobbyist." Jamie pointed toward a thick manila envelope Rutherford held. "What did you learn?"

"Gerald Brockman made several disastrous investments. He borrowed money to buy on margin. When the market collapsed, he needed to pay off the loans. Basically, he's broke."

"So, when Duncan was killed, Brockman might have hoped he'd inherit Global Protective Services," Cavanaugh said. "Except he had reason to suspect someone named Aaron Stoddard was set to inherit. Maybe he decided that getting rid of Stoddard would move him to the front of the line."

"Who's Aaron Stoddard?"

"Me," Cavanaugh said. "That's my real name. Word's getting around fast enough, you might as well be in on the secret."

"*Your real name?*"

"From time to time, it does a person good to be somebody else."

"Not me. I'm still trying to figure out how to be John Rutherford."

"What did you learn about Kim Lee?" Jamie asked.

"She has a drug problem."

"What?"

"Two years ago, she fractured a spinal disc during a martial-arts competition. Now she's addicted to big-time painkillers like OxyContin, so many pills a day that she needs a black-market supply."

"But she never gave the slightest indication."

"Some don't. If her stash runs out, though, she'll give you *plenty* of indication when she climbs the walls during withdrawal. It's as bad as trying to withdraw from heroin. Someone wanting information about Global Protective Services could blackmail her to supply it."

"What about Ali Karim?"

"So far, he appears to be squeaky clean."

"For a change, good news," Cavanaugh said. "And what about Carl Duran?"

"As you mentioned, after he got fired from GPS, he worked as the director of security for a Colombian drug lord." Rutherford paused for emphasis. "Until two years ago."

"What happened then?"

"He disappeared."

Cavanaugh frowned. "You mean his boss suddenly mistrusted him and had him killed?"

"No. There's not even a hint of that. We've got an informant who says Carl was considered irreplaceable. He was so furious about the way legitimate protectors turned against him that he went in the opposite direction and made the drug lord's security the best in the business. He even got his pilot's license so he could handle the drug lord's private jet in an emergency. Then one day, he was gone."

"Did your informant say if anything unusual happened before Carl disappeared?"

"As a matter of fact, he said the compound had a visitor. The newcomer was so important that the cartel's leader went out to meet the helicopter."

"Any idea who he was?"

"Not by name. But even after two years, the informant remembers what he looked like."

"Hard to believe," Jamie said.

"Not when you hear the description. The guy was in his forties. With a mustache. Solidly built. Intense eyes. Dark complexion. Serious expression."

"Doesn't help us."

"He came from Iraq," Rutherford said.

"Iraq," Cavanaugh repeated in surprise.

"Yeah, they don't see a lot of guys from that part of the world paying visits to drug-cartel compounds in South America," Rutherford said.

"At least, they didn't before Nine-Eleven."

Jamie looked mystified.

Rutherford explained. "After the attacks on the World Trade Center and the Pentagon, we started the in-depth investigation we should have been doing all along. Extreme religious terrorist groups figure that because we're corrupt, depraved infidels, they'll attack us through our corruption. A lot of terrorist funding comes through proceeds from prostitution and drugs."

"Drugs. A reason to pay attention to Kim," Jamie said.

"The stranger spent a lot of time talking to Carl," Rutherford continued. "The next morning, Carl and the newcomer were gone."

"So Carl was recruited because of his deep understanding of how the legitimate security community works," Cavanaugh said. "But he can't be doing this on his own. Too many agents have died. He can't be everywhere. He needs help. *Trained* help. Like the team who attacked us in Jackson Hole."

"Jackson Hole? You'd better bring me up to speed on that."

Cavanaugh told Rutherford about the incident.

"The men I shot turned out to have been released from prison, all within the past six weeks. They were each in a different prison, and it doesn't seem they'd ever met before they were convicted."

"So what brought them together after they were released?" Rutherford wanted to know.

"Maybe the right word is *who* brought them together," Cavanaugh answered. "And how did Carl change them so rapidly that in six weeks they became operators instead of thugs?"

2

Shots echoed through the swamp. Explosions rumbled. Even wearing ear protectors, Raoul heard the concussions as Bowie shook him, yelled obscenities, and spun him three times one way, then the other. Raoul wanted to push back, to shout at Bowie and knock him to the ground. But he didn't act on the impulse because he knew the purpose was to disorient him and get his adrenaline flowing.

Bowie shoved his face close to Raoul's, screaming, "Four bad guys ran into this building! They have automatic weapons! They have hostages! No time to negotiate! There's a bomb set to explode in thirty seconds! It'll level the block! Get in there, kill the bad guys, save the hostages, and shut off the bomb! Move!"

With a force that snapped Raoul's teeth together, Bowie pushed him into the building. It was actually a maze of walls without a roof, but Raoul's emotions were so engaged, he imagined it *was* a building. He was vaguely aware of Bowie rushing behind him, but all Raoul paid attention to was the pistol he drew from his holster, a target popping up, a man with a gun, shooting him, crouching, peering around a corner, another target, a man with a gun, an elderly woman next to him, shooting the man, pivoting, another target popping up, a woman hold-ing a baby, Bowie yelling, "She's got a gun in the blanket! Shoot her!" ignoring the voice, rushing forward, a guy with an assault rifle popping up, shooting him, the fourth guy, where was the fourth guy, where was the bomb, peering around another corner, a kid popping up, a priest popping up, pivoting in search of the fourth guy, realizing the priest had a gun, ducking, turning, shooting him, seeing a metal box on the ground, rushing over, flipping the "off" switch, and suddenly noticing how fast his heart was pounding, how sweat-soaked his clothes were.

Trembling, he looked up from the box, seeing Bowie and a couple of students grin at him.

"Three seconds before the bomb would have blown," Bowie said. "Every bad guy down. No hostages lost. You spotted the trick with the priest. Very good, Mr. Ramirez."

"Thanks." Raoul's voice was unsteady, remembering to add "sir." The emotional involvement in navigating a shooting house amazed him.

Outside, as more shots and explosions rumbled from the swamp, he watched Bowie approach more students. "Mr. Ferguson, you're next."

The tall, red-haired twenty-year-old didn't look enthusiastic.

"Let's go, Mr. Ferguson." Bowie pushed him, beginning the disori-entation process. He shook him, cursed, spun him, yelled orders, and shoved him into the shooting house so hard that Ferguson nearly fell.

Raoul and the students who'd passed the exercise followed Bowie.

Ferguson shot the first bad guy and the second, ignored the old woman, shot the third gunman, saw the woman holding the infant, pivoted in search of another target, and heard Bowie yell, "She's got a gun in the blanket!" He fired three times into the target. "You missed!" Bowie yelled. "Shoot her! *Shoot her!*" Ferguson emptied the rest of his magazine into the target. He did a rapid reload, hurried on, ignored the priest, and ran to the metal box, flicking the "off" switch.

Looking up in triumph, he frowned when he didn't receive the ap-proving looks he expected.

"Mr. Ferguson, it appears you're a menace to society," Bowie said.

"What are you talking about? I shut off the bomb, didn't I?"

"You'd have been dead before you reached it. That guy in the white collar would have dropped you."

"The priest? Give me a break."

"He's not a priest."

"How the hell do you know that?"

"The gun in his hand."

"*What* gun?" Ferguson groaned when he took a closer look.

"Even if you *had* shot him and disabled the bomb, it wouldn't have been any consolation to the woman and baby you killed."

"That wasn't a baby! The woman had a gun in the blanket!"

"No."

"But you told me—"

"I made a mistake."

"You lied to me."

"I tested you."

"This is bullshit."

"No, Mr. Ferguson. It's an exercise in discipline and control, qualities you apparently lack."

Ferguson seemed about to raise his gun. Bowie drew his knife from his pocket.

Ferguson stared at the knife and took his hand off his pistol. "I didn't come here to get bossed like I was still in the joint."

"No, you came here for a two-thousand-dollar signing fee and three thousand a month, plus room, board, and training."

"What good is the cash if I can't spend it anywhere?"

"Would you prefer to leave, Mr. Ferguson?"

"Does it show? All these damned mosquitoes. If I stay any longer, I'll get malaria or some fucking thing."

Bowie turned from Ferguson and faced Raoul, his tone hard. "Mr. Ramirez."

Raoul was taken by surprise. "Yes, sir?"

"After your next class, report to my office."

3

As Raoul crossed the packed earth of the compound's parade ground, he tried not to gaze around in continuing wonder at the sun-drenched encampment. Dense bushes and trees formed the perimeter. To his left were two wooden barracks mounted on stilts. Beyond, students shot at moving vehicles or learned to storm a building. Others practiced hand-to-hand combat, while still others learned how to handle knives. Raoul had no idea where all this was headed, but he knew that he couldn't be happier. Guns, movies, video games. The only thing missing was booze and women. Almost heaven. And he was getting *paid* for it. The weight of the pistol on his waist, the sense that he was doing something important and doing it well—these brought a straightness to his posture, a fullness to his chest.

He heard an instructor shout, "When you catch your enemy from behind and pull back his head, don't try to slit his throat. You might cut your hand. Grab his chin and mouth so he can't scream. Yank his head back. Stab a kidney. *That's* the killing stroke. A kidney. Almost instant renal failure."

Pausing outside a corrugated-metal shed, Raoul heard the clang of a hammer against metal. He had no idea why Bowie wanted to see him. His elation at having done well in the shooting house was replaced by confusion about the argument between Bowie and Ferguson and what it had to do with *him*.

The hammer's angry clang became rapid and insistent. When Raoul mustered the resolve to knock, the noise abruptly stopped.

"Come in."

4

According to the Bible, Cain had many descendants, one of whom was the first to forge iron. Carl enjoyed that idea, just as he enjoyed the notion that Hephaestus, the son of Zeus, was also supposed to have been the first to forge metal: the armorer of the gods. It was an interesting parallel, for Hephaestus's skill with a hammer and an anvil had an effect as terrible and long-lasting as Cain's murder of Abel. The Greek god's most ingenious creation was an elaborately engraved metal box that contained every evil and disease. The box was given to the seductress Pandora, and when she opened it, she released war, pestilence, famine, and a host of other darknesses. Only one evil did not escape before Pandora closed the box: cruel, seductive hope.

Carl wore gloves, a canvas apron, and safety glasses. Through their dense lenses, he watched the burning coke in his forge, the thick strip of steel beginning to glow the requisite orange color while he worked the bellows. Heating the metal for exactly the right amount of time and at the necessary temperature, he used tongs to remove it from the forge and set it on his anvil. With his powerful right arm, he wielded a hammer, pounding the steel into submission, flattening, shaping. The forge's heat softened the metal, making it malleable, allowing him to impose his will upon it.

Clang!

Aaron.

Clang!

Aaron.

Bittersweet memories seized him. The rhythmic high-pitched din of the hammer on the anvil sounded to him like ricochets, like screams of pain. He pounded harder, then sensed another sound and turned toward the door, where someone had knocked.

"Come in."

The door slowly opened. Raoul stepped apprehensively into shadows that were dissipated by the glow of the forge.

"Come closer. I want to show you something," Carl said.

Raoul did what he was told.

"The knife I'm working on is named after the one the first Jim Bowie carried. You've made the connection? Bowie? The Bowie knife?"

Raoul showed that he'd absorbed one of the lessons Carl had taught him—to admit what he didn't know. "I've never heard of it."

"It's the most famous knife of all time. Bowie was a land speculator along the Mississippi. A knife fighter. An adventurer. He died with Crockett and Travis at the Alamo. In 1827, he used a knife to kill one man and wound another in what's known as the Sandbar Duel. Nobody's certain what Bowie's knife actually looked like. The one I'm making is based on a design from a movie called *The Iron Mistress*. Alan Ladd played Bowie. But the knife was the true star. It was later used in other movies, Walt Disney's *Davy Crockett* and John Wayne's *The Alamo*. When you see the beauty of the finished product, you won't be able to take your eyes off it. A whole generation of knife makers was inspired to take up the craft because of this knife."

160

Carl remembered the first time he'd seen *The Iron Mistress*. The old knife maker had taped it off television and lent the video to Aaron and him. The start of the movie was boring: Alan Ladd in frilly clothes trying to make Virginia Mayo fall in love with him. He and Aaron had hooted at the television. But then Ladd went to a blacksmith and showed him a wooden model of a knife he wanted made. The blacksmith got all excited and said he had a piece of a meteorite that he would melt and add to the metal. The knife would have a bit of heaven, he said, and a bit of hell. In the next scene, the knife was finished. It flew through the air and stuck into a post. It had a long, wide blade, the elegant curving lines of which made Aaron and him shout, "Cool!" The handle was black wood with a brass cap. It had Bowie's name engraved in ivory and set into the handle. It had a silver guard and a brass strip on the back of the blade. The purpose of the brass strip baffled Aaron and him until they asked the old knife maker about it, and he explained that it protected the knife's owner during a fight. Since brass was softer that steel, it snagged an attacker's blade and kept the edge from slipping down the back of the knife and cutting whoever held it.

Aaron and he watched the best parts of the movie again and again. There were all kinds of knife fights, especially one in a dark room during a lightning storm, blades flashing. A bit of heaven and a bit of hell. But then the movie itself went to hell when Alan Ladd felt guilty about all the men he'd killed and threw the Iron Mistress into the Mississippi.

Carl came back from his memory. "Pay attention," he told Raoul. "The blade has to be carefully cooled."

Raoul concentrated as Carl used tongs to set the long, wide strip into a metal container of olive oil. That had been one of the old knife maker's jokes—to use olive oil to cool metal and then pour the oil over a salad.

But contrary to the way it was depicted in movies, Carl didn't put the glowing knife in tip first. Rather, he set the knife in lengthwise so that the oil didn't touch the back of the blade. The oil hissed.

After a few moments, Carl lifted the knife slightly so that the oil cooled only the blade's edge. Vapor rose, the smell like a hot, oiled frying pan before a steak was added. After another few moments, Carl removed the knife and set it on the anvil.

"People who don't know anything about forging think the entire knife has to be plunged into the liquid," Carl explained. "That could destroy the blade, because sudden cooling has only one purpose—to produce hardness in the metal. A blade that's been hardened one hundred percent shatters if you strike it against something. Instead, the cooling needs to be done in stages. Here, at the edge of the blade, I cooled it the longest because I want the edge to be hard enough to retain its sharpness. I cooled the middle of the blade for less time because I want it somewhat pliant as well as hard. And as for the back of the blade, I didn't subject it to *any* sudden cooling because I want it even *more* pliant."

"Pliant?"

"Capable of bending under stress."

Carl paused, hoping Raoul would demonstrate his intelligence by asking the appropriate question.

At last, he did. "I can understand why the blade needs to be hard to be sharp, but why does the back need to bend?"

"In order to be certified a master, a knife maker must produce a blade that passes four tests. First, the blade must be sharp enough to cut through a one-inch free-hanging rope with a single stroke. Second, the blade must be hard and sharp enough to chop through a pair of two-by-fours. Third, it must still retain sufficient sharpness to shave hair off the knife maker's arm. Finally, it must be pliant enough to be placed in a vise and bent ninety degrees without snapping. The only way to meet all of these requirements is to cool different parts of the blade for different amounts of time. The hard edge supplies the sharpness. The pliant back supplies the give. Otherwise, the knife snaps."

Raoul thought about it and nodded.

"Can *you* be like this knife?" Carl asked.

"I'll be anything you want me to be."

5

The door to the shed banged open. Raoul flew backward through the opening and landed hard on the packed earth. Carl stormed after him and kicked his side, sending him rolling.

At the nearest firing range, students sensed the commotion and turned, seeing Carl kick Raoul again and roll him farther across the parade ground.

"Nobody talks to me like that! Pack your stuff!" Carl shouted.

Raoul came to a crouch, barely avoided another kick, and lurched toward one of the barracks.

Carl stalked toward the students at the firing range.

"Ferguson! You, too! I'm sick of your sloppiness! Get your stuff! I'm driving you and that other asshole out of here!"

"But—"

"Now!" Carl twisted Ferguson's pistol from his hand and shoved him away. "You said you wanted out? You're *out*!"

"Do I keep the clothes you gave me?"

"And the money! That was the deal, wasn't it? I honor *my* word, even if you don't honor *yours*! Move! You and that other prick have five minutes!"

As Ferguson ran toward the barracks, Carl turned in a fury toward a pickup truck in front of the administration building. He pulled keys from his pocket, started the truck, and made so fast a turn that dirt flew. He sped toward the barracks, made another sharp turn, and skidded to a stop, waiting for Ferguson and Raoul.

Raoul got there first, holding his knapsack.

"Get in the back, damn it!" Carl yelled.

As Raoul climbed into the uncovered cargo space, Ferguson arrived with a duffel bag, breathing heavily.

"Inside!" Carl commanded.

Before Ferguson could shut the door behind him, Carl sped away, tearing up more dirt.

"*You're sure you got all your stuff?*" Carl demanded. "I want to keep my part of the bargain!"

"Quit trying to make me feel like a piece-of-shit quitter," Ferguson said.

"Isn't that what you *are*?"

"Who wants to put up with the bugs and the heat and the fucking humidity?"

"Obviously not *you*."

"And the snakes and the spiders and the damned rain most afternoons, and trying to sleep while those jerk-offs play those stupid video games. Bang, bang, bang. My ears haven't stopped ringing since I came here."

"You knew from the get-go you were being paid to learn about guns."

"I *know* about guns."

"Yeah, right. I've seen the way you shoot."

"And you didn't tell me I'd have to *clean* the damned guns after I shot them. And you didn't tell me I'd be humping heavy packs and crawling through swamps and…I might as well have joined the stupid army. Everybody telling me what to do. This is worse than when I was in the joint."

"Not hardly." Carl stared at the scars on his hands.

"And where the hell are we anyhow? How close to the nearest city? I want to get back to Chicago. Hang around with the guys. Find some action. Get laid. Man, that would be different."

"Wanting sex too much is what got you in prison," Carl said. "Maybe you should stick with guns."

"Just answer the question. How close is the nearest city?" Ferguson demanded.

"An hour. And it's not a city. It's a town."

"*What*? Why didn't we *fly* out of here? That's how you brought me into this mess."

"You're not worth the price of aviation fuel, buddy. You want to know a secret? You were part of a great experiment."

"Living in a swamp? Some experiment."

"About visualization."

"Whatever *that* means."

"First, I show you how to do something—shoot, use a knife, whatever. Then I make you close your eyes and repeatedly imagine doing what I showed you. I reinforce it by making you watch accurate movies of what I demonstrated, Hollywood stars doing things so smoothly you want to *be* those stars. Finally, I tell you to do what you imagined in the movie in your mind."

The truck hit a bump. Carl heard it jostle Raoul in back.

"The military discovered that, by using visualization, a four-week course could be reduced to three days," Carl said. "It's a form of self-hypnosis, reinforced by the video games."

"Yeah? Well, I've been here three *weeks*. How come it didn't work on *me*?"

"Nobody's perfect. You want to know *another* secret? A long time ago, this used to be a plantation."

"What's *that* got to do with anything? Drive faster."

"Then the plantation went bust, and the owners tried to keep the land in the family, and finally a private foundation bought it as a nature preserve."

"Tears, man. You're boring me to—"

"Then the CIA took over the foundation and all this land."

"CIA?"

"Finally got your attention? Strictly speaking, not the CIA. It was a company that worked for a company that worked for *the* Company. They call it 'compartmentalizing the risk. Plausible deniability.'"

"I call it yawning, man."

"The whole point was to build a private airstrip that hardly anybody knew about. See, to fly what you'd call 'spies' into hot spots…in those days, Central America had a *lot* of those…"

"Yawn, man."

The truck hit another bump.

"The CIA couldn't just pop their people onto a United jet and fly them to El Salvador or Nicaragua. They'd leave what's called a 'paper trail.'"

"You know what *I* call it?" Ferguson made an obscene gesture.

"So this company that worked for *the* Company made up its own airline and flew its people out of here straight across the Gulf to where the action was."

"Gulf?"

"Of Mexico."

Ferguson looked interested. "We're near Mexico?"

"But then times changed, and the hot spots moved to other countries, and the company that worked for the Company didn't have any more use for this place. Besides, it had started to attract attention, so they sold it to some drug smugglers they'd been working with."

"Drug smugglers?" Now Ferguson was really interested.

"Sure. The spy business is based on 'you scratch my back, I'll scratch yours,' the same as any other business. The spies had been working with the drug smugglers, getting tactical information from them, using them for cover, giving the spies an excuse to go in and out of various countries via secret airstrips. If you're a drug smuggler, nobody questions why you're so secretive. But if people think you're a *spy*, you're in trouble. So when it came time to get rid of the airstrip, it made sense to sell it to the smugglers, who were already using it. But eventually, the smugglers decided to switch locations, too, and the place was rotting until *we* bought it."

"Yeah," Ferguson said. "Rotting. Step on it, would you?"

"Can't."

Carl drove slower.

"*What are you doing?*"

"Stopping to take a leak."

"Man, can't you hold it till we get to town?"

"You want me to hold it for an hour?" Carl gave him a "get real" look and steered to the side of the road. He stepped out and went down a slope to the edge of the swamp. Under deceptively attractive Spanish moss—it was always bug infested—he undid his fly and urinated into the algae-covered water.

Ferguson banged the truck door open, stepped sullenly to the spongy earth, and walked to the water, fumbling at his fly.

Carl finished relieving himself, shook lingering drops from his penis, pulled up his zipper, and asked Ferguson, "You want to make a bet?"

Three shots roared. Crimson blossomed on Ferguson's shirt. Blood erupted from his face. He dropped on his back, thrashing.

The shots echoed across the water.

Carl turned toward where Raoul, on cue, had shot from the back of the truck. Under Carl's loose shirt, he had a Colt Commander .45. If Raoul had delayed, Carl would have drawn his pistol in a continuation of zipping up his fly, shooting both of them.

Raoul looked pale. The darks of his eyes were huge. Obviously, despite all his bravado, he had never killed anyone before.

Better distract him, Carl thought. "Very good, Mr. Ramirez. Two shots to the body and one to the head. Why were you taught that pattern?"

Raoul had to switch to a different section of his thoughts. "Uh…" He looked confused. His need to seek approval became greater than the shock of his emotions. "Uh…the target might be wearing a Kevlar vest, so I also shot him in the head."

"Your instructor explained that?"

"No." Raoul continued to look confused. "I just figured that was the reason."

"It *is* the reason. Your intuition is excellent. Did you do what I told you and sit with your head against the back window?"

"Yes."

"You heard what I said about the CIA?"

"Yes."

"Then you understand the necessity for what I ordered you to do. There are serious issues at stake that I'm not allowed to reveal to you. Not yet. But the target's lack of discipline would have made him talk about our camp. He would have destroyed us."

Using his shoe, Carl shoved the body into the scummy water. Immediately, an alligator erupted, snapping at the head, jerking the body under the surface. A second alligator fought for the corpse's right leg. Blood swirled amid the green scum.

"When I set up the camp," Carl explained, "I drove here once a day, urinated into the water, then threw raw steaks in. After a while, the alligators learned to identify food with the sound of the truck, my footsteps, and urine streaming into the water. Now those signals bring them here for dinner."

The turmoil in the water subsided. After the frantic splashing of jaws and tails, birds again sang.

Pleasing Carl, Raoul picked up his empty cartridges.

"Get rid of his duffel bag," Carl said.

Raoul took a chain from the back of the truck, shoved it into the bag, and hurled it into the water.

"Quick. Sharp. Obedient," Carl said.

Raoul's eyes brightened.

"I'm going to pull you from the group," Carl decided.

"*No.* What did I do wrong?"

"The reverse. You and a select few are coming with me."

"To do what?"

"Hunt an old friend."

6

Waking slowly, Cavanaugh felt as exhausted as when he'd gone to sleep with Jamie next to him. He reached to put his arm around her, discovered that she wasn't there, and opened his eyes, focusing on where she sat at the cigarette-burned table in their seedy motel room's corner. She wore a T-shirt and boxer shorts, her brunette hair hanging over her shoulders. She didn't notice that he'd wakened, too preoccupied re-reading the documents Rutherford had given them.

"You talked in your sleep," she said.

So I'm wrong, he thought. *She* did *notice I was awake.*

"Oh? What did I say?"

"'How much wood could a woodchuck chuck?'"

"Well, that's a relief. For a second, I was afraid I said another woman's name."

"You did mumble something about 'Ramona'."

"My third-grade math teacher." Cavanaugh pointed toward the documents. "Have you learned anything?"

"Didn't you tell me Carl's father died from alcoholism? Liver disease?"

"That's what Carl said in a phone call to me when I was still living at home."

"According to this police report, his father stumbled while he was drunk, fell on a knife in the kitchen, and bled to death in the middle of the night."

Numbed, Cavanaugh didn't react for a moment. He got out of bed, ignored the cold air on his bare legs, and went over to her. She indicated the bottom of a page.

Cavanaugh read the passage and felt colder. "The police report says Carl found the body in the morning. Since he knew for certain how his father died, why did he tell me it was liver failure?"

Jamie looked up. "You think Carl finally got tired of his father picking on him? He might have told you the cause of death was liver disease because that was an easy explanation. But bleeding to death from a knife wound…knowing Carl's obsession with knives, you might have started wondering. How old were you when he made that phone call?"

"I was still in high school. My senior year."

"Young to start to be a killer."

"If his father was his first," Cavanaugh said.

The room became silent.

"What do you mean?"

"Thinking about those days, I suddenly remember things. But I'm seeing them in an entirely different way."

"*What* things?"

"Our neighbor had an Irish setter named Toby. My stepfather was too buttoned down to allow a pet in the house, but the neighbor didn't mind if I played with Toby, so I sort of had a dog. The summer before my senior year, the dog ran away. The neighbor phoned the pet shelter. No sign of the dog. Nobody ever found him. A couple of neighborhood cats ran away that summer, also."

"Didn't anybody think there might be a pattern?"

"If anybody did, *I* never heard about it. Anyway, there was a lot going on that summer. Carl's dad was fired. In August, the family needed to move. Meanwhile, I was excited about beginning my senior year at West High, and to tell the truth, Carl demanded I spend so much time with him that I was relieved to see him go."

"So he practiced killing animals before he graduated to killing his father?"

"Or maybe…"

"What are you thinking?" Jamie asked.

"Do you suppose Carl killed *other* people before he mustered enough rage to go after his father?"

7

"Nashville, Tennessee?" Rutherford asked.

"That's where Carl's father took the family after losing his stockbroker's job in Iowa City," Cavanaugh explained. "Can you arrange for someone to investigate a rash of missing animals or stabbings while Carl was there?"

They sat at a corner table at a truck stop near Alexandria, Virginia. Cavanaugh and Rutherford drank coffee while Jamie dug into a cheese-and-ham omelet with hash browns.

"Stabbings?" Rutherford frowned.

"Homeless people. Drifters. Back-alley drunks. The sort of victims who wouldn't be missed and didn't look like they could defend themselves."

"This guy sounds scarier and scarier," Rutherford said.

"Maybe you should check Iowa City, too." Jamie looked up from her omelet. "And any other place Carl lived."

"And where he was stationed in the military," Rutherford decided.

"What about Ali Karim?" Cavanaugh asked. "Did you find anything?"

"Still seems squeaky clean. But Global Protective Services lost another operator last night."

Jamie set down her fork.

"Frank Tamblyn," Rutherford said.

"I know him." Cavanaugh's voice was stark. "A former Army Ranger. Eight years with GPS. Wife. Two children. Dependable, always ready to be the first operator out the door to check if it's okay for a client to leave a building."

"Apparently, he loved to bowl."

"Why is that important?"

"Last night, he got in his car to drive to a bowling tournament. Afterward, around midnight, he returned to his car. He probably checked it for explosives. Not that it matters. When he got behind the steering wheel, a spring-loaded knife burst from under the dash and hit him in the groin. There weren't any trip wires, so he wouldn't have spotted the device. It was rigged to a vibration switch. Death was so rapid, the blade must have been coated with poison."

8

Greenwich Village, New York.

Kim Lee stepped out of a martial-arts studio and turned left on Bleecker Street. Her cheeks were flushed, her eyes intense after two hours of practicing aikido. She wore jeans and a blue sweater, and carried a gym bag. Around the corner, she came to a café that, on this not-yet-chilly October evening, still had tables on the sidewalk, although most of the customers were inside. She sat, ordered tea, removed a magazine from her bag, and settled back to read.

But she seemed more interested in her surroundings than in her magazine. The tea came. She tasted a few sips, looked around again, reached under the table, detached something, concealed it within her magazine, and put the magazine in her bag. She paid for the tea and continued down the street, glancing behind her as she turned a corner. No one followed, and she soon fell into a comfortable pace, her cheeks no longer flushed.

At her brownstone, she took the elevator to the third floor, unlocked her apartment, stepped in, closed the door, locked it, flicked the light switch, and turned toward the living room, only to freeze at the sight of Cavanaugh and Jamie.

"*How did you get in here?*"

"Picked the lock," Cavanaugh said. "Maybe you're like a physician who forgets to have a yearly medical exam or an accountant who's too busy to balance her own checkbook."

"What are you talking about?"

"For someone who works at a security company, you don't pay much attention to your personal security," Cavanaugh said. "You should phone GPS and order a technician to install an intruder-detection system."

"Right. I'll do that just as soon as I call the police." Kim picked up the phone.

"Good idea," Jamie said. "I'm sure they'll want to know what's in your gym bag."

"Gym bag?"

"Black-market prescription drugs. Probably OxyContin."

Kim stared.

"At the café, they were taped under the table you used," Jamie said.

"This isn't funny." Kim scratched her arms.

"With so many operators getting killed, aren't you worried about walking around in the open?"

"Maybe if I *were* an operator. But there doesn't seem to be a bounty on computer specialists." Kim set down the phone. She picked up the gym bag and headed toward the bathroom.

"Time for another pill?" Jamie asked.

Kim didn't answer.

"I'm told getting off Oxy is a nightmare," Cavanaugh said. "Or maintaining your addiction when you can't find any more doctors to write prescriptions for you and you need to turn to dealers."

Cavanaugh gestured toward the living room, which was sparsely furnished, only a lamp, a canvas chair, and a small television, not even a rug.

"Been selling things to feed your habit?"

"Since we're being so candid, why don't I stop the charade of going into the bathroom?" The pupils of Kim's eyes were pinpoints.

She opened the gym bag and took out a plastic bag that contained a fist-sized quantity of white pills. With a look of defiance, she put two in her mouth and chewed.

Jamie frowned. "Why do you—"

"The pills have a time-release coating so the body absorbs the pain-killer over twelve hours," Cavanaugh explained. "If you just swallow them, you can't get a rush. You have to pulverize them and snort them."

"Or chew them," Kim said. "What the hell do you want?"

"GPS's assignment records," Cavanaugh said.

Kim looked baffled.

"You still haven't sold the computer in your bedroom," Cavanaugh told her, "so why don't you crank it up and get me some information I need?"

"*That's* what this is all about? For God's sake, why didn't you just come to the office to do this?"

"The last time I went to the office, I almost didn't leave it alive."

"I could have given you the information over the phone."

"Sure. But this way, I know the information hasn't been edited."

"You still believe someone at GPS can't be trusted? *Me?*"

"Distrust a drug addict? Perish the thought," Jamie said.

"You know, lady," Kim said, "I don't need to take crap from the boss's wife." She turned toward Cavanaugh. "You want to fire me? Do it."

"Just get into the GPS assignment records," Cavanaugh told her.

Kim's cheeks looked flushed again. She went to the bedroom and turned on its light, revealing that there was only a mattress on the floor but that a lavish computer setup occupied a desk in a corner. Cavanaugh went over to the window and closed the draperies against the thickening darkness.

When Kim touched a button on the keyboard, the monitor came out of sleep mode. Jamie stood behind her while Kim sank into a chair, wincing slightly.

"If you're in that much pain, maybe you need to ease off on your martial arts," Jamie suggested.

"Can't give them up."

"Just like Oxy," Jamie said.

"You don't know. I tried detoxing. Last spring." Kim glanced toward Cavanaugh. "Supposedly, I was in the Caribbean on vacation. But I was right here. I vomited for a week. My bones ached. My heart raced. Hot and cold sweats. Wobbly legs. Twitching. And that was the fun part."

"You tried it on your own?"

"Had to. Would anybody at GPS have relied on me if word got out I'd checked myself into a detox clinic?"

"Go ahead and check yourself into one now," Cavanaugh said. "Take advantage of our great medical plan."

Kim avoided the subject, turning toward Jamie. "You know anything about computers?"

"A little," Jamie lied. "I know the difference between a Big Mac and a Mac Apple."

"Always thinking about food," Cavanaugh said.

"You need to step away while I type in the security codes," Kim told her.

"Don't think so. I co-own the company. I get to see everything."

Kim looked questioningly at Cavanaugh.

"I just made her vice-CEO," Cavanaugh explained.

"Let's see those security codes," Jamie told her.

Kim's fingers flew across the keyboard, an elegant blur that made Jamie nod in wonder as she watched information flash across the monitor.

"This is brilliant." Jamie leaned forward, seeing security code after security code. "I never could have hacked this."

"I hope to God not." Kim's fingers kept working the keyboard.

"As you looked for more OxyContin," Cavanaugh said, "I don't suppose people ever offered you unlimited quantities in exchange for showing *them* the codes."

"No."

"Cross your heart?"

"I guarantee it."

"Hard to guarantee."

"Not really."

"How do you figure?"

"If I had unlimited quantities of Oxy in exchange for giving the bad guys information…" Kim's fingers kept flying.

"Yes?"

"Would I be forced to humiliate myself by paying a cheesy drug dealer to stick that plastic bag to the bottom of that table? A lousy hundred pills? I can go through those in a week."

"She has a point," Jamie said.

"Or maybe that's part of her cover story."

"I'm into the files. Tell me what you need," Kim said.

"All the GPS assignments Carl Duran was on." He watched Kim intently, checking for a hesitation, a slight narrowing of her eyes, anything that might indicate that the name meant something to her. "He was fired three years ago."

"Does the first name have a C or a K?"

"C."

Cavanaugh still detected nothing to suggest that the name was important to her. No pursing of the lips. No tightening of the cheek muscles. In his experience, most dopers couldn't repress telltales when they were under stress.

"Sorry," Kim said. "Carl Duran doesn't have a file."

"Doesn't…? You must have made a mistake."

"When it involves computers, I don't make mistakes."

"But GPS *always* keeps records about former employees."

Kim tapped more keys. "Nope. No assignment list. No photograph. Nothing."

"Duran must have deleted it," Jamie said.

"Couldn't have. At least, not on his own. Only three people know the codes to get that far into the system. Gerald, Ali, and—"

"You," Cavanaugh said.

"Another nasty mark against me, right? But before you get judgmental again, watch *this*." Kim tapped more keys. "The purging was so thorough, I can't retrieve Duran's file. But I *can* search every assignment we've ever had and tell the computer to isolate any that Duran worked on." Kim touched a final key. "And here you are."

The printer came to life, flipping out pages.

"Plenty of trouble at GPS," Kim remarked.

"Yes," Cavanaugh agreed. "Frank Tamblyn's the latest casualty."

"I mean *new* trouble."

The phone rang.

"And I'm afraid," Kim said, "that this'll be more."

9

The agent made sure his weapons were in place before leaving his house: his .45 semiautomatic on his hip under his suit coat, his nine-millimeter subcompact in his ankle holster, his tactical folding knife clipped to a pocket concealed by his suit coat, and another knife on a breakaway chain around his neck under his shirt.

Uneasy, he glanced back toward his wife, whose eyes were filled with equal unease as she held their baby boy.

"Meg, believe me, I'll be careful."

"But what about *us*? I don't mean to make it seem like the risk you're taking doesn't matter. But…" The baby squirmed under Meg's left arm. He had a slight fever. "What if whoever's doing this starts attacking…"

"Not just operators but their families?"

"I couldn't bear it if something happened to the baby."

"Stay inside. Keep the doors locked."

"I need to take Bobby to the doctor."

"There's a gun on the top shelf in the closet."

"Right. I'm going to hold the baby and blast away like in that John Woo movie you watched last night where the hero's in a nursery in a hospital with kids in his arms and guns in his hands. I kind of doubt it."

"Why don't you go to your mother's? I'm off this assignment in a week. When I get back from New Orleans, we'll take a vacation, someplace we feel safe."

"Wherever *that* is."

"Maybe I should take a pay cut and get a less dangerous job."

"If it was just the two of us…"

"What a joke. I'm a security specialist, but I can't make my wife feel secure."

Outside, a car beeped.

"The taxi. Listen, the client's got his jet waiting. He's obsessive about maintaining a schedule. I'll call you en route to the airport. We'll try to figure a way to handle this."

Meg nodded, unconvinced.

"Love you," he said.

"Love you."

As the taxi drove away, the agent glanced back at his house. He felt encumbered by his numerous weapons, but he knew agents who'd responded to the recent attacks by carrying *three* guns instead of his two.

He pulled out his cell phone and called headquarters for updates. While the phone on the other end buzzed, he continued gazing through the taxi's rear window toward the third house from the corner, the one with the bright flower boxes.

A huge fireball roared, chunks of walls, floors, windows, furniture, and bodies spewing from the churning core. The neighboring houses burst apart from the force of the blast, flaming debris hurtling across the street.

The taxi wavered to a stop. A brick struck the window, bursting through, but all the agent cared about was shoving the door open, lurching onto the street.

"Meg!" he shouted, running. "Bobby!" He felt the heat of the blaze but ignored it, charging closer. "No!" His shriek threatened to tear his vocal cords. "*Nooo!*"

10

Kim's knuckles whitened as she clutched the phone. All the while she listened, the shocked look on her face made Cavanaugh and Jamie remain absolutely still.

"Yes, Ali," she said. "Yes, I understand." She took a breath. "Nothing will help him, of course, but you're right—we need to do what we can."

She set down the phone.

"Another agent's been killed?" Cavanaugh asked.

"His family," Kim answered.

"His *family*?" Jamie looked stunned.

"Jim Driscoll. Word about what happened to his wife and child got around fast. Now our agents are calling their duty officers to say they're sick. We hear the same thing's happening with the U.S. Marshals, the Secret Service, and the Diplomatic Security Service. Only a few so far, but the trend's not hard to predict. Why should agents protect strangers when they themselves are the targets? And their loved ones. Those reporting for duty are either unmarried or else insisting on protection for their families while they're not home. They also want twice the operators they normally have on an assignment. The system's falling apart."

Kim nervously scratched her arms. Her brow glistened with sweat. Through the open bedroom door, she saw her gym bag on the living room floor. The bag of white pills was on it.

For a moment, Cavanaugh thought Kim would move toward it. His own move was toward the Global Protective Services information that she'd printed.

Continuing to stare toward the bag of pills, Kim asked, "You think this Carl Duran has something to do with what's happening?"

Cavanaugh took the pages from the printer's tray. He tried not to allow his emotions to tighten his voice. "At the moment, he's the only lead we have."

"Well, if you're willing to allow a doper to help—" Kim turned from staring at the pills. "—we'll *all* see if we notice anything."

They slid to the floor in the nearly bare room, their backs to a wall, reading the material: all of Carl Duran's assignments.

"Nothing about the clients he protected draws my attention," Cavanaugh noted.

"What about *where* the assignments took place?" Jamie asked.

They scanned the pages.

"Washington. New York. Paris. The same places *I* was usually assigned," Cavanaugh said. "Nothing suspicious."

"What about incidents on his assignments?" Kim asked. "I see there was something about a female rock star and an obsessive fan he stabbed."

"That's what got him fired."

"And here." Jamie pointed. "A client died on one of his assignments. A Russian oil tycoon."

"I heard about that, but I had no idea Carl worked on it." Frowning, Cavanaugh explained to Jamie, "It happened four years ago. The tycoon was in Rome, negotiating to lease oil tankers. He believed some of his Russian competitors were conspiring to have him killed. It turned out he was right. A sniper got him." Cavanaugh scanned another page. "Who was Carl's team leader?"

"And who were some of the other operators he worked with?" Kim drew a finger down a list. "Shit," she suddenly said.

"What?"

"Ali," Kim said. "*Ali* was the team leader when the tycoon was assassinated. That was before Ali got promoted to running our personnel department."

"That's not the only time Ali worked with Duran," Jamie said. "Here." She pointed toward the middle of a page. "And here." She pointed toward the top of another.

"And here," Kim said. "Duran and Ali worked together on several long assignments."

"The tycoon was hit by a rifle bullet that went through a window in his hotel suite," Jamie said, reading. "Ali was in the room with him, and then Duran hurried in from standing watch outside the suite."

"When an assignment ends that badly, we send an investigator to learn from our mistakes," Kim said. "The report concluded that nobody was at fault."

"Who ran the investigation?"

All three read the summary of the incident.

"Gerald Brockman," they said at once.

"Okay, okay, let's not jump to conclusions." Cavanaugh stared at the page. "These could all be coincidences. It doesn't mean something's wrong."

"Who else was on the team?" Kim asked. "Is there anyone we can ask who'll either confirm Brockman's report or insist it was a cover-up?"

"Four of them." Cavanaugh scanned the names, his stomach sinking as he read each of them. "Most are dead."

"What?" Jamie asked.

"Over the years, they—"

"Not most of them," Kim said. "I recognize these names. Leaving out Gerald, Ali, and Carl Duran, *all* the operators on that team are dead."

Kim hurried to the computer, set down the page she held, and typed names that were on it. She stared at the monitor. "One was shot on an assignment. The others…car crash, scuba accident, altitude sickness while climbing…"

"Mt. Everest," Cavanaugh said. "I was invited on that expedition. A job kept me from going. Carl went, though."

"Guy gets around," Jamie said.

"But if Carl was involved in a cover-up that Gerald and Ali were part of, Carl would never have allowed GPS to fire him," Cavanaugh said. "He'd have put so much pressure on Gerald and Ali, blackmailing them, that they'd have persuaded Duncan to let him stay."

"Good point." Kim scratched her arms.

"Are you okay?" Jamie asked.

"Couldn't be better." Kim's brow was beaded with sweat.

"Right. If you need it, chew more Oxy. This isn't the time to make another attempt at withdrawing."

"Just a little longer," Kim said. "When Duran was fired, Gerald was Duncan's second-in-command. He had the authority to stop Duran from being dismissed."

"But since Gerald didn't intervene, that suggests Carl didn't have any way to blackmail him," Jamie pointed out. "That leaves Ali. When was he promoted to running the personnel division?"

Kim's fingers tapped the keyboard. "A year after Duran was fired."

"He couldn't have suddenly demanded that Carl be rehired," Cavanaugh said. "It would have looked suspicious."

"But if Ali couldn't get Duran rehired, how else could Ali have been useful to him?"

"By giving Carl information about GPS assignments. We—"

A noise made Cavanaugh pause.

"What's the matter?" Jamie asked.

Cavanaugh glanced from the bedroom toward the front door.

The noise was repeated.

"Get down!"

11

The lock and the hinges disintegrated, presumably from thermite cord. As the front door crashed inward, three men charged in, firing muffled automatic rifles.

In the bedroom, Cavanaugh grabbed Jamie and dove to the floor. Chunks of the wall erupted. He and Jamie drew their pistols, but before they could shoot, the gunmen veered out of sight. Kim astonished him by squirming across and slamming the bedroom door, locking it.

"Stay down, Kim! They'll shoot through the door!"

"It's metal!"

With a ringing echo, the bullets struck the door but didn't come through.

The shooters returned their aim to the wall, firing holes in it, their sound-suppressed weapons no louder than sewing machines. Given enough time, they could level a portion of the wall and step through to finish their job. But they *didn't* have time. They counted on surprise and massive firepower to give them the advantage. Now they had another obstacle to overcome, and despite their muffled weapons, the din of bullets bursting through walls would alarm the neighbors. Cavanaugh prayed that someone would phone the police, that sirens would converge on the building. The shooters would worry about that. They would soon need to run.

The sudden silence in the living room supported his logic. They were leaving.

No. He was wrong. He heard a noise against the hinges and locks on the metal door.

"They're using thermite cord on this door also!"

Cavanaugh fired three times at the wall, not expecting to hit the attackers but wanting to make noise, hoping to panic neighbors into calling 911.

"Let's go!" He hurried toward the bedroom window, shoved it upward, and stared at a fire escape he'd noticed earlier when he'd closed the draperies.

Waving Jamie and Kim through, he squirmed to follow.

A dark, narrow alley was three stories down. A brick wall across from Kim's apartment had prevented the shooters from establishing a sniper's post.

"Faster!" Cavanaugh yelled, hearing Jamie and Kim scramble down ahead of him. The clang of their impact on the next landing was followed by the crash of Kim's bedroom door falling inward.

They realize we've gone, Cavanaugh thought. *They used all their time. They need to run before the police arrive.*

To assure himself, Cavanaugh spun and peered up, dismayed to see a face and a rifle barrel at the open window. The slots of the fire escape deflected the gunman's bullets, the ricochets loud in the confines of the alley.

"Go, go, go!" he yelled to Jamie and Kim.

He heard Jamie's desperate breathing as she surged down ahead of him. Kim's martial arts training allowed her to vault the railing, dangle from the bottom of the platform, and drop to the next landing. Cavanaugh rushed down next to her, seeing her straighten, an expression of pain tightening her face.

He stared up. The face was gone from the window.

We're two floors below them, he thought. *But there might be other gunmen on the street. We don't know what we'll be running into.*

He noticed that the windows next to him were dark.

"Look away! Protect your eyes!" he warned Jamie and Kim.

He kicked the window, glass flying.

Jamie reached through, freeing the lock, raising the window.

"Go!" he urged.

He crawled in after her. As glass crunched under his shoes, Kim gripped the inside of the window frame and swung in behind them.

181

Eyes adjusting to the dark, Cavanaugh hurried from a kitchen into a living room, put his ear against the door, heard footsteps thundering down stairs, unlocked the door, yanked it open, and slammed against a man with a rifle who tried to charge past. The impact knocked the man's breath out. A railing snapped when he struck it. As the man dropped his rifle and almost plummeted into the stairwell, Cavanaugh grabbed him, dragged him back, and gripped him in a restraining hold. Leverage pried Cavanaugh's gun from his hand.

Abruptly, more thundering footsteps made Cavanaugh spin toward where the stairs led upward. A second gunman charged into view. As the man raised his rifle, he lurched back, his eyes going blank, Jamie's bullets—two to the chest, one to the head—dropping him.

At the end of the landing, a door opened, an elderly woman peering out.

"Stay inside!" Cavanaugh shouted, struggling to keep the man in a restraining hold. "Call the police! *Where's the third man?*" Cavanaugh yelled to Jamie and Kim.

"There!" Kim shouted, pointing downward.

The last of the gunmen aimed from the bottom of the stairs. Cavanaugh lurched back as bullets disintegrated what remained of the railing. At once, a metallic scrape indicated he was reloading. Jamie leaned into the stairwell and fired repeatedly. The man groaned, slumping.

"There might be others! Get into the apartment!" Cavanaugh yelled, continuing to restrain the first gunman. As Jamie and Kim hurried toward the dark kitchen, Cavanaugh forced the man across the shadowy living room.

He winced when the man slammed a thick-soled shoe onto his right foot. Holding him from behind, Cavanaugh applied a strangle grip, feeling him squirm, hearing his labored breathing.

The man tried to reach behind him and grab Cavanaugh's testicles. Cavanaugh strengthened his grip and stomped the man's left foot.

The man grunted, lurched backward, walloped Cavanaugh against a wall, and rammed an elbow into his ribs. As Cavanaugh's grip loosened, the man charged free and suddenly had a knife in his hand. Cavanaugh blocked the exit from the apartment. The man pivoted toward the kitchen, where Jamie aimed her pistol toward him.

"No!" Cavanaugh said. "We need him alive!"

"I don't care!" Jamie told the man, "Take one step toward me, and I'll—"

The man swung toward Cavanaugh, jabbing with his knife. Cavanaugh leapt back and threw a lamp. While the man avoided it, Cavanaugh unclipped his knife from his pocket. By design, the hook on the back of the blade snagged against the edge of the pocket, the motion causing the blade to open as Cavanaugh yanked the knife out.

Kim jabbed the light switch. Cavanaugh saw her doing it, but the man did not. Surprised by the light and by how quickly Cavanaugh had produced his knife, the man thrust again. Cavanaugh parried, slicing the back of the man's hand, and now the crucial element was who acted faster. No staring at one another. No assessing. No calculating a clever move. Most knife fights took less than five seconds. Flick, flick, flick. Now you're bleeding. Now you're dying. Overwhelming primordial power would win. Cavanaugh believed that the term "martial arts" was a self-contradiction. When it came to combat, there was nothing artistic, nothing smooth and graceful about it.

As adrenaline dumped into Cavanaugh's system, his blood vessels expanded. His heart sped. Martial arts students claimed to be able to use Zen techniques to control their pulse during combat. But in Cavanaugh's experience, his adrenaline took charge, and as sure as death followed life, his heartbeat went ballistic. Fine motor skills, which use dexterity and hand/eye coordination to perform precise movements (accurate shooting, for example) disintegrate at 115 heartbeats per minute. Complex motor skills, which help muscle groups perform a series of blunt movements (kicks and punches, for example) disintegrate at 145 heartbeats per minute. But most hand-to-hand combat causes the heart to surge to 200 beats per minute. In that frenzy of adrenaline, the combatant becomes one of two large furious deadly animals charging one another.

Along with burnt gunpowder, the smell of testosterone filled the living room. Musk. A man smell of fierce power. Everything seemed fast and yet terribly slow. Sounds faded. Vision narrowed. All of this happened in an instant as Cavanaugh screamed, flicked his knife back and forth and up and down with a violent speed that the eye couldn't follow, and charged his opponent, using a buzz-saw technique against which his enemy couldn't defend unless he too used his knife as a buzz saw. But it was all happening so fast, so overwhelmingly that the opponent jerked back, screaming—not as Cavanaugh screamed, in massive aggression, but instead in abject terrified surrender. As blood flew from the man's arms and his chest, as the man tripped and fell backward, Cavanaugh was on him, kicking.

"No!" Jamie yelled.

But Cavanaugh couldn't stop kicking.

"You'll kill him!" Jamie shouted. "You said we need him alive!"

Cavanaugh's frenzy snapped, Jamie's urgency reaching him. He stopped. He stood over the unconscious man, breathing frantically. His clothes were soaked with sweat.

He was suddenly aware of sirens.

A voice yelled, "I told you to drop the knife and put your hands up! Lady, drop the gun! Don't make me shoot! Everybody, *hands up*!"

12

Chest heaving, Cavanaugh turned slowly and saw two policemen in the living room, their pistols aimed at him, Jamie, and Kim. In the open doorway, an intense man in a suit aimed a pistol also. Outside, more sirens joined the commotion as the man in the suit yelled, "For the last time, drop your weapons!"

Cavanaugh let go of his knife. It clattered onto the floor.

"My gun might go off if I drop it," Jamie told the man.

"Gently," the man said, aiming, "set it down."

Jamie obeyed, then carefully straightened, both hands in the air. Kim raised her hands also.

"Get the paramedics up here," the man told someone behind him. "*You three*," he said to Cavanaugh, Jamie, and Kim. "Over against this wall! Lean forward! Spread your legs! Get a police woman up here!" he shouted down the stairs.

"We were defending ourselves," Cavanaugh maintained as he leaned forward with his hands against the wall.

"Sure you were."

"They attacked us in my apartment," Kim said. "The third floor."

"Check that," the man told a policeman. He studied Kim. "So if you live *up there*, how did you get *down here*?"

"Lieutenant," an officer said, peering into the kitchen. "We've got a broken window."

"I think we're going to be a long time sorting this out," the lieutenant said. "Just so we don't have any misunderstandings with a judge and a jury, you have the right to remain silent. You know the drill?"

"Yes."

"Do you want an attorney?"

"Seems like I don't have a choice."

"You got *that* right." The lieutenant searched him from behind, lifted Cavanaugh's jacket, and found his empty holster. "Where's the gun that goes with this?"

Cavanaugh nodded toward where it had fallen. "Near the door."

"You better have a permit for this."

"I do."

"Why do you need it?"

"I'm in the security business. Global Protective Services."

"Yeah, I saw how you were protecting this guy on the floor, leaving impressions of your shoes on his kidneys. Global Protective Services, huh? I'm impressed all to hell."

Cavanaugh decided the conversation had just about come to an end. "How do I contact my attorney?"

"Unless you've got a supply of carrier pigeons, I suggest using *this*." The man pulled Cavanaugh's phone from his jacket.

"Now?"

"When I'm finished." The man patted Cavanaugh's chest and found his claw-shaped knife in a plastic sheath suspended by a breakaway chain around Cavanaugh's neck.

Meanwhile, a policewoman arrived and searched Jamie, removing her knife from her hip.

The man glanced from it toward the pistol and the knives on the floor. "Between these and the automatic rifles on the stairs, we've got enough weapons to outfit the military of a Caribbean country."

"Lieutenant," a policeman said at the door. "The apartment upstairs is shot to pieces."

"Just your normal Saturday night in Greenwich Village," the lieutenant said. "Sit on the floor," he told Cavanaugh.

Cavanaugh obeyed.

"Cross your legs."

Cavanaugh did.

"Here's your cell phone. Tell your attorney to be quick. Tell him Lt. Russell can't wait to talk to him."

Ambulance attendants crouched next to the man Cavanaugh had subdued.

"Is he going to live?" Russell asked.

"He'll be able to answer your questions. My, my, he's got a pistol under his jacket."

"And there'll be another knife somewhere," Cavanaugh said.

"Yeah," the ambulance attendant said, "on a chain around his neck." The attendant pulled it from under his shirt. "Looks like a claw."

"Like the one that was around *your* neck," Russell told Cavanaugh. "Are you guys making some kind of fashion statement?"

"And what's *this*? Another fashion statement?" Using forceps, the attendant probed the man's left ear and removed a flesh-colored object.

"An earbud radio receiver," Cavanaugh said. "If he's got one of those, he's also got a miniature microphone." Cavanaugh studied the man's blood-spotted turtleneck. "Probably pinned to the front of his collar. A mike the size of a dime."

"Damned if there isn't," the attendant said.

Lt. Russell yelled down the stairs, "Does the wounded guy down there have a microphone on his collar? And something in his ear?"

"Just a second, Lieutenant, while I…yeah!"

"Same with *this* guy!" someone shouted from the upper stairs, where the third gunman lay dead.

Russell inspected the microphone and pried off its back. Just before he pulled out a tiny battery, he asked Cavanaugh, "Who the hell did you take on? The CIA?"

13

"*The CIA?*"

Sprawled on a dark rooftop across the street, Carl listened to the radio transmission crackle and die. Like the men in the apartment building, he had an earbud and a miniature microphone. *Un*like them, he had a small black box the size of a pack of cigarettes. This box, a radio receiver and transmitter, had a switch that allowed him to communicate with each man separately. For the past fifteen minutes, until the microphone had failed, he'd been able to eavesdrop on the conversation.

He hadn't heard Aaron's voice in several years. It filled him with a welter of emotions: anger, regret, bitterness, a fond need to return to that long-ago summer when they pretended to be soldiers caught behind enemy lines and hid among bushes, watching men and women holding hands as they strolled through the woods.

Concealing himself behind a chimney, Carl raised an AR-15, sighted through its holographic scope, and waited.

14

The cell-phone numbers Cavanaugh pressed were for the landline at William's safe site. As the phone buzzed on the other end, he heard more sirens outside. Red and blue lights flashed beyond the window.

"Hello."

"This is Cavanaugh. Put William on."

"Maybe he'll talk nicer to you than he does to us."

The phone made a bumping sound. Then William's voice said, "I hope this means everything's back to normal and I can get out of here."

"Afraid not," Cavanaugh said. "There's been some shooting and—"

"*Some* shooting?" the lieutenant said in the background. "I was with the Marines in the first Iraq war. I think we used less ammunition."

"Why don't I let Lt. Russell explain it to you so I don't say anything I shouldn't."

"Name, rank, and serial number," William's voice cautioned. "Nothing else. Put him on the phone."

Cavanaugh handed the phone to the lieutenant, then looked at Jamie and Kim against the wall. Jamie impressed him with her composure, as if she'd been an operator all her life.

But Kim was another matter. The pupils of her eyes resembled pencil points. Her brow was beaded with sweat, her withdrawal symptoms accelerating.

Cavanaugh gave her a firm nod of assurance.

"At the precinct in half an hour," Russell said to the phone, then gave it back to Cavanaugh.

"Yes, William?" Cavanaugh asked into it.

"Name, rank, and serial number. No exceptions."

"I want you to call somebody." Cavanaugh gave William a name and a phone number. "Tell him I need help."

When William heard the name, his response was, "*He'll* get their attention."

"Okay, we're ready to move this guy," the ambulance attendant said.

The attendant and his partner lifted the semiconscious man onto a gurney and wheeled him from the apartment. Below, a clatter of equipment indicated that the gunman Jamie had wounded was being lifted onto a similar gurney.

"Hands behind your back," Russell told Cavanaugh.

The lieutenant clicked handcuffs onto him.

The policewoman did the same to Jamie and Kim.

"Is the van here?" Russell asked a policeman.

Cavanaugh managed to stand.

Preceded and followed by police officers, he, Jamie, and Kim left the apartment. On the stairs, a camera flashed, a medical examiner and his team inspecting the other gunman Jamie had shot.

Cavanaugh descended. The smell of burnt gunpowder widened his nostrils. He stepped over empty ammunition casings and left the building, confronted by the chaos of flashing lights, police cars, ambulances, and several hundred onlookers.

15

As Aaron emerged from the building into the kaleidoscope of lights, Carl almost pulled the trigger. Aaron had his hands cuffed behind him. He had policemen ahead of him, policemen behind him, and two women next to him. One of the women, Chinese, was the GPS computer expert whose apartment Carl had ordered watched. The other woman was the one he'd seen in Jackson Hole. Aaron's wife.

Carl studied her. Tall, wearing slacks, with legs that drew his gaze from her ankles to her inviting hips. Athletically trim, with upward-tilted breasts that made him imagine standing behind her, cupping his hands over them. Glossy brunette hair that he wanted to stroke. Eyes so intense Carl felt their power even on the roof across the street. *Aaron, you and I always had the same great taste.*

Do it, Carl told himself. *Shoot.* But no matter how much he wanted to, he mustered the discipline that he had not possessed while he and Aaron had been in Delta Force and later when they'd worked for Global Protective Services. *No "I" in "team"? I understand that now*, he thought.

No self-control? Not then. Not when I took out that sentry with a knife instead of obeying the order to kill him with a sound-suppressed pistol. Not when I stabbed that crazy fan when he pulled out a knife and attacked that rock-star babe. No, I learned my lesson, Aaron. You and Duncan taught me that lesson. I spent a lot of time on shit jobs learning that lesson. Stay cool. Keep the mission in mind. Don't get distracted. Don't screw things up for a moment's satisfaction. I learned that lesson so well, I could teach you. But if I shoot, I'll never get off this rooftop and make it to where Raoul's waiting with the car. Right now, there's only one thing more important than killing you, and I'm so cool, so disciplined, so in control, that's what I'm going to do.

Carl pulled a transmitter from his pocket. When he pressed a button, a green light flashed. Then he pressed a second button.

16

Uneasy, Cavanaugh stood at the entrance to the building. Partially blinded by the flashing lights, he watched attendants wheel the injured gunmen toward two ambulances. *We got what we need*, he thought. *When they're conscious, we can question them. We can find out where Carl trains his men.*

"I want an officer in each ambulance," Lt. Russell said.

Two policemen stepped toward the vehicles as the attendants shut the doors, and suddenly the ambulances heaved, explosions shattering their windows, blasting their rear doors open. The shockwaves knocked the ambulance attendants and the policemen to the pavement. Others stumbled back. Bystanders ran. Many screamed.

"*Bombs?*" Russell spun toward Cavanaugh. "What the hell's going on? How did—"

"Wyoming," Cavanaugh said, trying to recover from his shock. His skin itching from wariness, he nudged Jamie back with him into the cover of the building's vestibule. Kim noticed and retreated with them as Cavanaugh scanned the roof on the opposite side of the street. He lowered his gaze toward the windows and the entrances to the brownstones, but the emergency vehicles and the flashing lights made it difficult to see much of anything at street level.

"Wyoming? What are you talking about?" Russell demanded.

Emergency personnel ran toward the ambulances. Smoke drifted from the open doors.

"That's where this started." Cavanaugh stepped deeper into the building, Jamie and Kim following. "A hit team tried to kill me there, also."

Russell stared.

"When two members of the team were about to be captured, their car blew apart," Cavanaugh told him.

Russell stared harder.

"We think the team's leader planted a bomb under the car and used a remote control to detonate it—to keep them from being questioned. Earlier, somebody on the team shot a sniper working for them, presumably because he couldn't be counted on to keep his mouth shut."

"You're telling me, the guy who organized this attack watched from down the street and blew up his men when he saw them being carried out alive?" Russell asked in dismay.

"He might be out there even now," Cavanaugh said, prompting Russell to turn and scan the street with the intensity that Cavanaugh did.

"How the hell could he put a bomb on his men without them knowing about it or us finding it?"

A frenzied voice shouted from one of the ambulances, "They're blown in half at the waist."

"The plastic sheaths," Cavanaugh said.

"Sheaths?" Russell's voice was raw.

"For the knife each man had. Your people took the knives but left the sheaths. The plastic must have had explosive in it, along with a miniature detonator."

For the first time, Russell was speechless.

"Carl was here, watching us go into the building." Cavanaugh felt a chill. From the building's vestibule, he stared toward the crowd across the street. "Maybe he's *still* watching. Maybe he's up on a roof with a rifle. Lieutenant, have you still got that earbud and microphone?"

Russell pulled them from a suit pocket.

"Put the radio receiver in my ear," Cavanaugh said, feeling helpless with his hands cuffed behind him.

Russell hesitated, then did what Cavanaugh wanted.

"Please put the battery back in the microphone and raise it to my mouth," Cavanaugh said.

After less hesitation, Russell did.

"Carl?" Cavanaugh asked.

All he heard was static.

"Carl, I know you're out there. You're probably watching the entrance to this building."

More static.

"Carl, I think I know how you've been training your recruits. Remember those visualization courses our special-ops instructors arranged for us to take. We couldn't get over how fast visualization accelerates the learning curve. You used that technique reinforced by movies and video games, right? It's an efficient way to program someone."

Only static.

"I don't know what your objective is," Cavanaugh said into the microphone Russell held in front of him. "But I know you're behind all this, so there's no point in continuing to try to kill me. It won't make a difference. Nothing's going to divert suspicion from you. So quit taking the risk. I'm a worthless target."

Cavanaugh strained to listen to the plug in his ear, to ignore all the distracting shouts, doors slamming, the drone of automobile engines before him, the rumble of footsteps on stairs behind him.

The static changed subtly. Carl's voice, unheard for so many years, said, "You should have been a better friend."

Then the static changed again, as if the transmission ended.

191

Cavanaugh told Russell, "You can put the microphone away. He's gone."

"Carl?"

"Carl Duran," Cavanaugh said. "You and I have a lot to talk about."

Russell pulled a two-way radio from his belt. "Randall, get a SWAT team down here. Tell your men to check the roofs."

"What are we looking for?" a voice asked.

"If I'm to believe what I'm hearing: the prince of darkness."

"*Who?*"

"A guy who doesn't leave loose ends. I'll get you a description as soon as—"

"Six feet tall," Cavanaugh said. "Lean. Women find him attractive until they discover he almost never smiles. Strong arms, particularly his forearms, from working with a hammer and anvil."

"A blacksmith?" Russell asked.

"A master knife maker," Cavanaugh said. "He spends a lot of time thinking about blades and sheaths. I guess it finally occurred to him how sheaths could be weapons also."

Russell stared toward the ambulances and the blood on their shattered windows. "Yeah," he said, "you and I definitely have a lot to talk about."

PART SIX:
THE KNIVES OF OLD SAN FRANCISCO

1

Kim threw up again.

A policeman hurried toward a door in the harsh corridor, only to be blocked by Lt. Russell, who suddenly opened the door. Russell was accompanied by two other grim-faced men, one white, the other black: William Faraday and John Rutherford.

"…sick," the policeman explained to Russell, pointing toward the holding cell. "The Chinese woman's throwing up."

"My client demands medical help," William said.

"And believe me, counselor, she'll get it. I'll send for the police chief's personal physician if that'll make you happy."

"*Nothing* makes me happy."

"I already got that impression." Russell turned to the policeman. "Send for a doctor."

The group marched along the corridor, stopping in front of the cell, where Russell motioned for an officer to unlock the door.

"Hi, William. Hello, John," Cavanaugh said as they stepped in.

Kim threw up again.

"What's wrong with her?" Russell asked.

"Back injury," Jamie explained. "She needs a painkiller."

"Like more of those OxyContin pills we found in her apartment?" Russell asked.

"Those pills belonged to the attackers," William said.

"Yeah, right," Russell said.

"In the frenzy of the moment, the pills fell out of a gunman's pocket," the attorney said. "That's the sort of man who'd be capable of that kind of violence. A pill popper. A drug addict."

"Whatever you say," Russell told him.

"And *you* had plenty to say." William turned to Cavanaugh. "I told you to volunteer nothing but your name and your vital statistics."

"It's nice to see *you*, too, William."

"But the lieutenant tells me you pretty much gave him your life history. If you want to be your own attorney, why drag me down here?"

"Hey, I thought I was doing you a favor, freeing you from your safe site," Cavanaugh told him.

"Well, you didn't do *me* any favor—" Lt. Russell pointed toward the black man next to him. "—bringing in the FBI. At the start, I figured you were bullshitting me to try to talk your way out of that shooting. Now the director of the FBI's counterterrorist unit invokes national security."

"Bottom line," Rutherford told Cavanaugh, "You're coming with me."

"But that doesn't stop me from trying to untangle this mess," Russell said. "We managed to get fingerprints from the men who were killed in those blasts. It won't be long before we find out who they were. Maybe *that* information will lead us to your ex-buddy Carl Duran."

"Won't help," Cavanaugh said. "You'll discover they got out of prison recently. Probably within the past six weeks. They were doing time for violent offenses, but they each went to a different prison, and they didn't know each other before they went in."

Russell asked Rutherford, "Is this more bullshit?"

"Afraid not."

"Then enlighten me," Russell told Cavanaugh. "Show me how smart you are. How did these guys wind up together?"

"Carl approached them when they got out of prison, and in a brief time, he turned them from being rough criminals into operators."

"How?"

"I think Carl selects his recruits on the basis of their capacity for violence, their ability to learn, and their need to be somebody important. They're wannabes, guys who'd love to be in Marine Recon, the Rangers, Special Forces, or the SEALs, just to show how tough they are and force people to look up to them. But they don't have the character and the discipline to make the grade. Approach them when they're fresh out of prison with no prospects and no money but a powerful urge to let off the anger they've been building up. Pay them. Flatter them. Use visualization and other accelerated instructional techniques. Give them a chance to play with guns. Six weeks later, their egos are so pumped, they'll do anything to prove to Carl they deserve his respect. Just as important, they're the kind of guys nobody cares about and nobody'll miss. If Carl thinks they're in a position to be captured and questioned, he blows them up. It's like they never existed."

"That's quite a theory," the lieutenant said.

"Help me prove it," Cavanaugh said.

"You suggested I look at places where Carl Duran lived," Rutherford interrupted, "including where he was stationed in the military. We searched for a pattern of cats and dogs that disappeared. Or maybe they didn't disappear. Maybe they showed up in alleys or ditches, with their guts sliced open and their heads cut off. The police and the humane societies had records of clusters like that. In Iowa City, just before Duran moved away. In Nashville, Tennessee, just before he moved from there. In Columbus, Georgia, next to Fort Benning, where he started his Ranger training. In Tacoma, Washington, next to Fort Lewis, where he got more Ranger training. In Fayetteville, North Carolina, next to Fort Bragg, where Delta Force is trained. Especially just before Duran moved to another base or when he left Delta, there was a high incidence of mutilated animals." Rutherford paused. "Then the bodies started turning up."

"Bodies?" Russell asked.

"Winos and homeless people. All of them stabbed to death. Other winos and homeless people spread a rumor about a man who stalked them at night. Under bridges. In storm culverts. In parks and alleys, in abandoned buildings and junk-filled lots. The rumors were about this man kicking drunks awake or knocking cardboard boxes over and making homeless people crawl out. He gave them a knife and told them to fight. Then he went to work. But the patterns of the cuts showed that he took a long time to finish them off."

"Yeah," Russell said. "The prince of darkness."

Kim threw up again.

2

After the doctor left, Cavanaugh and Jamie studied Kim where she lay on the bunk.

"An ambulance is coming," Jamie assured her.

Pale, Kim managed to nod.

"The doctor says you're in stress from withdrawal."

"What time is it?"

"Two in the morning."

"Longest time I've gone without Oxy since last spring. At least I'm not shitting my pants yet."

"The doctor says he's taking you to a detox clinic," Cavanaugh said.

Kim nodded weakly again.

"He says you *asked* to be taken there," Cavanaugh added.

"Hey." Kim ran her tongue along her dry lips. "I'm into withdrawal *this* far. I might as well go all the way."

Cavanaugh noted that Kim didn't qualify her statement by saying she would *try* to go all the way. "Don't worry about your job. It'll be there when you come back."

Kim crossed her arms over her chest and shivered. "I'm not worried about *me*. It's the two of *you*…" She shivered harder, asking Jamie, "Do you remember the computer codes?"

"You bet," Jamie said. "Your security's so brilliant, I can't get in otherwise."

"Nail the bastard who's doing this."

3

Lt. Russell arranged for numerous cruisers to leave the precinct at the same time, so many that Carl's operators couldn't follow them all. But if any tried, the sparse traffic of two a.m. would make the surveillance obvious and easily intercepted.

Cavanaugh and Jamie hid in the back seat of one of those cruisers. They got out at Central Park's West Drive, slipped into the trees, and headed north. From time to time, they paused among murky boulders and bushes to check if they were being followed. Only the park's usual predators stalked them, but Cavanaugh and Jamie gave off such strong don't-screw-with-us vibrations that just four kids made a move, and what happened to them was so swift and decisive that word spread quickly—*stay away.*

Confident that they'd eluded Carl and his men, Cavanaugh and Jamie crossed Central Park West and proceeded along West 73rd Street. They reached a modest apartment building, outside which a man with a beer can in his hand seemed asleep behind the steering wheel of a car. Farther along, a man walked a dog. Still farther along, a van had a small air vent in its roof, the vent actually an aperture for a surveillance camera.

Outside the front door, Cavanaugh studied a list of tenants. He pressed the intercom button next to the name Zimbalist.

After a moment, a man's voice said, "This better be good. It's the middle of the night."

"Jimmy Lile sent us," Jamie said, mentioning a famous knife maker whose name they'd selected as a code.

A buzzer sounded. Cavanaugh opened the door and stepped into a warm, pleasantly lit vestibule. Halfway along a hallway, a door was ajar. A security camera looked down from a corner. They went up one flight of carpeted stairs and prepared to knock on door 2-C when it opened and Rutherford smiled.

"You two don't look so good."

"You don't need to seem so cheery about it," Jamie said.

"I'm just glad you're all right." He locked the door after they entered.

"What about William?" Cavanaugh asked. "Did he get back to his safe site okay?"

"Nobody followed the car."

In the living room, two men in white shirts had their suit coats draped over chairs, their holstered handguns visible on their belts. They watched a row of closed-circuit TV monitors that provided views of the street, the door to the building, the vestibule, and the stairs leading up.

"You ought to feel flattered," Rutherford said. "The Bureau maintains this place only for prized informants."

"The park." Cavanaugh rubbed his arms. "Cold."

"You've got your pick of two bathrooms to take a hot shower."

"Hungry," Jamie said.

"The pizza's already here," Rutherford said. "With pepperonis, right?"

"And anchovies and black olives."

"And salad and garlic bread. Everything you ordered."

4

"Are you okay?" Cavanaugh asked in the darkness of a bedroom.

"A few bumps and bruises. Nothing serious." Jamie lay next to him.

"I mean, are you *okay*?"

"Why wouldn't I be? It's just the usual, isn't it? Fear and trembling."

"You were talking awfully fast in the kitchen. You sound as if you're on speed."

"Adrenaline will do that."

"It should have worn off by now." The darkness seemed to compress around him.

"I guess I'm resistant," she said.

"I just want to make sure nothing's wrong." The darkness got even thicker.

Jamie lay unmoving next to him. Finally, she said, "You mean because I killed somebody?"

Cavanaugh exhaled. "Now that you mention it."

"He was trying to kill *us*."

"Best reason in the world to pull the trigger," Cavanaugh agreed. "You didn't panic. You didn't let the heat of the moment make your hands waver. You acted precisely. You saved our lives."

"Is this what the military calls an 'after-action report'?"

"It's useful to talk. To sort out your emotions."

"In other words, a cheap form of psychotherapy." Jamie remained motionless beside him.

"Imagine that you didn't raise your pistol fast enough. Imagine him firing the rifle, full auto, bullets tearing into us, blood and flesh and bone flying, you and Kim and me dropping."

"Trying some neuro-linguistic programming on me?"

"It's nothing I haven't used on myself."

"When was the first time..."

"First time?" Outside the curtained, bullet-resistant window, a car drove by, its lonely drone echoing in the night. "You mean, the first time I killed someone?"

Jamie didn't answer.

"Twenty years ago," Cavanaugh said. "In Peru."

Jamie turned toward him. "Isn't that where you told me Duran was held prisoner by revolutionaries?"

"They called themselves the PCP. The *Partido Comunista del Peru*. American soldiers were down there, helping prop up the government. Carl and I and some other Delta Force members were sent to teach the Peruvian soldiers how to put together their own version of Delta. Lord knows, enough officials had been kidnapped that the local government needed experts in hostage retrieval. We accompanied Peruvian soldiers on a mission to rescue a high-ranking politician. The PCP was threatening to kill him if the government didn't release some PCP members the army was interrogating. But somebody leaked the details of the mission to the revolutionaries, and we walked into an ambush. Carl was knocked unconscious by an explosion. The government soldiers he was with ran away. Later, we received photographs showing that Carl was alive, with a message that gave the government three days to release the PCP agitators."

Cavanaugh forced himself to continue. "Delta looks after its own. Within twenty-four hours, a full extraction team arrived from Fort Bragg. Twelve hours before the deadline expired, we got a lucky break, some excellent intelligence reports along with aerial surveillance photos that showed the mountain camp where Carl was being held. At night, we parachuted into a clearing about three miles away and converged on the target. The infrared satellite images we'd studied gave us a pretty good idea of where the prisoners, eight of them including Carl, were being held. About twenty revolutionaries were guarding the camp. We used night-vision binoculars to confirm what was on the satellite images. I was with the men assigned to get to the prisoners and protect them once the attack started. Basically, the tactic was coordinated sniper shots followed by overwhelming automatic fire and a hail of fragmentation grenades. It was a textbook assault, and it went perfectly. No casualties among the prisoners or the attack force. The revolutionaries were utterly outclassed."

"You killed some of them? That was your first time?" Jamie asked.

"I laid down covering fire, three thirty-round magazines, but I have no idea if any of my bullets connected. I need to assume I did damage, but it was as if I was destroying objects. I had no sense that I was actually killing people. My primary emotion was relief that Carl was safe and that I'd survived the mission."

"Then I don't understand. It doesn't sound like your first time."

"We radioed for evac choppers and set up a perimeter in case other revolutionaries heard the shots and came to investigate. When I found cover and waited, I had a sense that something was terribly wrong, a feeling that I was being watched, that something awful was about to happen. By then, it was dawn. I glanced to my left and saw a face in the bushes. A kid. He was maybe sixteen, raising a pistol. Before I realized what I was doing, I swung my rifle and emptied the magazine into him. Total reflex. Thirty rounds. Just about blew him apart. Even if I'd probably killed before, *that* was my first time. Up close and personal. The moment was so intense, I could see into the kid's eyes, past his fear-dilated pupils into his brain. Into his soul. I remember thinking, *You stupid kid, why didn't you hide? Why did you need to try to be a hero?* It was so pointless, so damned unnecessary."

"What happened then?"

"I threw up," Cavanaugh said.

"That's what *I* felt like doing."

"I had a lot of nightmares about that kid," Cavanaugh continued. "His chin had a wart. He had scruffy hair and a scar on his forehead. His clothes were filthy and ragged. He was so thin, he probably hadn't eaten a decent meal in weeks. The revolution was one of those 'share the wealth' deals: millions of poor people against a handful of rich landlords and financiers trying to control them. I'm sure the kid had been exploited all his life. He was probably consumed with hate. I bet he went to sleep every night longing for a decent future. A lot to sympathize with. But if I had the chance to do it again, I'd shoot him just as dead as I shot him the first time. Otherwise, you and I wouldn't be having this conversation."

Jamie's hand touched his. "And if *I* had to do it again, I'd shoot *that* man as dead as he now is, just to make sure you and I could be lying here like this."

"It's one way to decide if something was justified—whether you'd do it again," Cavanaugh agreed.

"But I hate that it needed to happen."

"Yes. I measured my life from that moment…before I killed and after."

"Rescuing Carl Duran," Jamie said.

5

His eyes feeling raw, Cavanaugh peered toward painful sunlight seeping past the draperies. With effort, he got out of bed. He opened the door a crack and saw a different pair of armed agents in the living room. With the attentiveness of their predecessors, they watched the numerous surveillance monitors.

Cavanaugh shifted his gaze toward a different area in the living room and saw Jamie seated at a table, tapping on a computer. Rutherford stood behind her, watching her fingers work magic. Jamie's fresh jeans and turtleneck were part of the safe-site resources.

He took the longest, hottest shower of his life, but tension insisted. He couldn't keep his mind off everything that had happened. Damn it, what was Carl's objective?

Khaki slacks and a brown shirt were on a bureau, along with fresh underwear and socks. Motivated by a sudden idea, he dressed so hurriedly that he continued to button his shirt as he walked into the living room.

"Morning, sleepy head." Jamie kept her gaze on the computer screen.

"Did I miss anything?"

"Breakfast."

"We left you a doughnut," Rutherford said.

"Haven't you heard of Dr. Atkins?" Cavanaugh picked up the phone and pressed the numbers for information. "Cincinnati, Ohio," he told a computerized voice. "F and W Publications."

Jamie and Rutherford looked at him.

"F and W Publications," a cheery voice said.

"*Blade* magazine. Steve Shackleford," Cavanaugh said.

"One moment please."

Cavanaugh said a silent prayer that Steve wouldn't be out of his office on an assignment. *Blade* was a favorite magazine of knife enthusiasts, but it was a mistake to imagine a redneck, good-old-boy reader with biker's boots, a beer gut, and a chain leading from his thick wallet to his belt. Instead, most of *Blade*'s 40,000 subscribers were attorneys, physicians, computer experts, and other white-collar professionals, their average income in six figures: a subscription base that many magazines envied. The magazine's avid readers had knife collections they'd assembled with the care of sophisticated art collectors.

Some of the knives were treasured antique Bucks, evoking pleasant memories of trusty jackknives from a happy childhood. Others were pocket knives crafted so painstakingly and with such elegance, those by Michael Vagnino, for example, that collectors who'd paid $2,000 for one of his folders felt lucky to have gotten a bargain now that he'd risen to the top of his field.

Some knives were valued because of the life-experience they symbolized, Vietnam veterans treasuring the rugged Ka-Bar combat knife that, in many instances, had meant the difference between death and survival. Other knives were valued because of their current reputation as a dependable tactical knife, those by Ernest Emerson, for instance, who in 1991 handcrafted tactical knives for soldier friends departing to the Gulf War. These soldiers bragged to their comrades about how well designed the knives were. Eventually, Emerson received so many orders that he shifted from making knives by hand to manufacturing them in a factory, with the goal of proving that, with proper diligence, a factory-made knife could have the quality of a forged one. He followed the example of Al Mar, a former Green Beret who in the late 1970s pioneered the modern tactical folder and became known as the father of specialty knives. An original Al Mar or Ernest Emerson knife had an auction price of several thousand dollars.

Still other knives were prized because of their place in popular culture. The prop knives for the film *The Iron Mistress* were diligently acquired by Hollywood production artist Joseph Musso: a wooden version, a rubber version, an unfinished steel version used in a forging scene, and the magnificent fully realized knife. Musso's unique collection traveled to various museums, including one in San Antonio, Texas, the site of the Alamo, where Jim Bowie had died. Musso's love for the Iron Mistress prompted him to allow skilled bladesmiths to study the knife and its studio blueprints. Copies by George Cooper, Joe Keeslar, and Gil Hibben were better made than the original and highly prized. This was the world that Cavanaugh needed to tap into as he listened to the other phone ring.

"Steve Shackleford." The pleasant voice had a Tennessee accent.

Thank God, Cavanaugh thought.

"Steve, it's Aaron Stoddard."

Both Jamie and John straightened, frowning at one another, so unusual was it for Cavanaugh to use his real name.

"Aaron, what a surprise. I haven't talked to you in…it has to be three years."

"The last time I was at the Blade Show in Atlanta," Cavanaugh said. Of the numerous knife-enthusiast conventions, the Blade Show was the hugest, with more than ten thousand attendees.

"I was afraid you'd dropped off the face of the Earth," Steve's voice said.

"Not quite. I had a lot of obligations at the ranch." As far as Steve knew, Cavanaugh was a cattleman, thus explaining the Wyoming address. "But when I told you I was a rancher, I was really referring to a sideline. My main work is in the security field."

"Oh?" A moment's thought was broken with, "I guess you get a lot of use for knives in that kind of work."

"More than you can imagine. I need a favor."

Steve sounded wary. "What kind?"

"Your magazine's subscription list."

"You've got to be kidding."

"Names, addresses, phone numbers if you've got them. The works."

"That's confidential information, my friend. I can't just…what sort of security work did you say you did?"

"Why don't I let the FBI's director of counterterrorism explain it to you? I think you're going to hear the words 'federal government' and 'national security'."

Cavanaugh gave the phone to John.

6

Five minutes later, John gave the phone back to Cavanaugh.

"*Now* can you supply the subscription list?" Cavanaugh asked.

"As important as this sounds? Give me your email address," Steve said. "I'll send the list in five minutes. Are you looking for anybody in particular? Maybe I can ask around?"

"Carl Duran."

"Your friend?"

"He dropped out of sight. I'm trying hard to find him."

"It's no wonder you can't," Steve said.

"I don't understand."

"Carl died three years ago."

"*Died?*"

"I'm surprised you didn't know."

"We had an argument. We stayed out of touch."

"Shame about arguments, especially when it's too late to repair them. He stopped going to the Blade Show about the same time *you* did."

After he was fired from Global Protective Services, Cavanaugh thought. Cavanaugh had stopped going to the Blade Show in order to avoid crossing paths with Carl.

"I asked around, wondering what happened to him," Steve's voice continued. "The word I got was that he'd been killed."

"*How?*" Cavanaugh pressed the phone harder to his ear.

"A car accident in Thailand. Or maybe the Philippines. I heard two different versions. Carl was a construction worker, right?"

That had been Carl's cover story, the theory being that it paid to pretend to have a white-bread business that no one felt a compulsion to ask many questions about.

"I heard he saved enough money to take a vacation, and that's where he got killed," Steve said. "I checked our subscription list, and sure enough, he didn't renew. Sorry to break the news to you. Even if you had an argument, I'm sure you still thought of him as a friend."

Cavanaugh didn't reply.

"I guess you won't need the list now," Steve said.

"Better send it anyhow. I've got other names to check."

7

They spread the printouts across the floor and studied them.

"Here," Jamie said. "Duran's name."

"Three years ago," Rutherford said. "But not later."

"When you're trying to disappear," Cavanaugh said, "the rule is, abandon everything about your former life. Some people can't make a complete break, though. They have ties they can't give up."

"Such as a passion for knives," Jamie noted.

Cavanaugh nodded. "Carl got fired because of discipline problems. Maybe those problems carried over into his attempt to disappear. He'd have tried to be careful. He might have used intermediaries. But I'm betting that, under another name, he continued to subscribe to knife magazines. He's been getting *Blade* since he was a kid."

"After he dropped the subscription, maybe he just bought the magazine in a store," Rutherford suggested.

"When he was working for a drug lord in South America?" Jamie looked skeptical. "A specialty English-language publication would be almost impossible to find down there."

"Then maybe he had somebody buy it in the States and mail it to him," Cavanaugh wondered.

"A big nuisance needing to depend on somebody," Jamie said. "Plus, that probably wouldn't be the only knife publication he'd want. The easy way is to subscribe, have the publishers mail them to a drop site in the U.S., and then have them forwarded."

"John, can the Bureau investigate the background of anyone who subscribed after Carl's name disappeared from the list?" Cavanaugh asked.

"No," Jamie said. "Not *after* his name disappeared from the list. *Before*."

Cavanaugh and Rutherford looked puzzled.

"Suppose Duran anticipated that someone might try to find him this way," Jamie explained. "What if he took out a new subscription using a different name *before* he pretended to be dead? It's a better way to hide his trail."

"Smart," Rutherford concluded.

"That's why I married her," Cavanaugh said.

"It's all a long shot, of course," Jamie admitted.

"But it's the only lead we've got." Rutherford picked up the phone.

8

Atlanta, Georgia.

His hands in his windbreaker, caressing a special folding knife he'd crafted, Carl sat on a bench and watched pedestrians crossing the expanse of Centennial Olympic Park. In summer, children were able to skip back and forth through what was called a dancing water fountain, a wide area of water jets that gushed twenty feet into the air. Now, ignoring a cool October breeze, Carl imagined youngsters scampering through the spray. He could almost hear their laughter.

Wouldn't it have been great to have something like that when you and I were kids, Aaron? He remembered the two of them bicycling to the swimming pool at Iowa City's park. Below, the tree-lined river meandered toward the low, summer-hazed buildings of downtown. He remembered an afternoon when they chained their bicycles to a post, and when they returned from the pool, they found four kids trying to break the chain and steal the bikes. When Aaron shouted at them to stop, the kids attacked, but Carl showed Aaron that nobody could push them around. He pulled out his jackknife, causing the kids to gape when he opened it and chased them through the trees. He remembered how surprised Aaron was. He remembered—

A man sat down next to him. Nondescript clothes. Thin. Mid-forties. Mustache. Swarthy skin. From the Middle East. "This location is too exposed."

"It shows we've got nothing to hide."

"A directional microphone can easily overhear everything we say."

"Not with my associate playing with that miniature battery-powered car." Carl indicated Raoul a hundred feet away, the young Hispanic working a remote control that made a tiny Jeep go this way and that.

"The control interferes with directional-microphone reception?" the man asked.

"Enough to cause hearing loss to anyone using earphones. It's good for us to be outside. Fresh air. Sunshine. People going about their business. Keeps us in touch with the basics of life. The 1996 Olympics explosion was over there, incidentally."

The man looked toward where Carl pointed. "Three pipe bombs wired together," he said with contempt.

"Even so, the device managed to kill one woman and wound one hundred and eleven bystanders," Carl reminded him.

"The Army of God. That's the group the bomber's note gave credit to. The Army of Amateurs is closer to the truth." The swarthy man studied the unobstructed space around them. "How are you going to deal with Cavanaugh?"

"Aaron," Carl corrected him. "I don't intend to. Not any longer. I wanted him eliminated because he could make the connection between me and the knife attacks. Some of those agents needed to be killed with blades. The plan depended on it. Now that Aaron knows I'm involved, I'm at risk. But he hasn't discovered anything that threatens the mission itself."

"He'll keep hunting you."

"That's a personal matter, but it only jeopardizes *me*. I set traps. Be sure of that. But from now on, my concentration is focused entirely on the mission. I won't waste any more resources going after him." Carl withdrew his right hand from his windbreaker and showed the knife it held. "Since we probably won't be meeting again, I have a gift for you."

The man hesitated, then took the knife, examining it with curiosity. "The handle is unusual."

"It's carved from fossilized ivory. Mastodon tusks uncovered in Alaska. Some knife-making supply stores sell the material."

"Why go to all the trouble of using ivory that old?"

"A gesture to the environment. This way, you know the ivory didn't come from slaughtered elephants or walruses."

The man studied Carl, trying to determine if he was being ironic. Seeing no reaction, he returned his attention to the knife. The pale yellow handle had two circles carved into it, one above the other. The bottom circle represented a clock with Roman numerals. An arrow depicted the clock's hand. The top circle was formed by stars. A profiled face was in the middle.

"That's the man in the moon," Carl explained.

"The details in the carving are impressive."

"I worked on that knife for a long time. Years. Waiting for missions to start."

"I'm honored." The man tried to open the blade but failed. He tried again. "Something's wrong. The blade's caught on something."

"No and yes."

"I don't understand."

"Something is *not* wrong. But yes, the blade *is* caught on something."

"I still don't—"

"That's a model of one of the rarest knives in the world. It's called a secret knife."

"Secret?" the man asked with interest.

"It was designed in the late sixteen hundreds. In France. In a royal court known for its secrecy. Hidden compartments were the rage. The original version of that knife might have been used by a spy hiding a secret message."

The man again tried to open the blade. "But how do you—"

"By figuring out the combination," Carl said. "The arrow in the clock. The profiled face in the middle of the stars. Each needs to be twisted to a precise location in order to free a catch that holds the blade in place."

"Like a combination to a safe," the man noted.

"Exactly. But in this case, there are two dials. When you get both in the correct position, the blade will open. You'll be amused to find astrological symbols etched into the blade. No one is sure of their significance. But I suspect they have something to do with alchemy. Or perhaps the Freemasons."

The man turned the dials and tried to open the knife, without success.

"It'll take you a long time to discover the combination and learn the knife's secret," Carl told him.

"I'll use it for distraction while I wait for the start of the week," the man said. He looked across Centennial Olympic Park toward a tall, impressive, gray-fronted, many-windowed building. Mounted to the top floor, bold red letters announced that this was the main headquarters for CNN. "Two days from now, broadcasters in there will exhaust themselves reporting around the clock on what we've done."

9

With an agent in front, an agent behind, and an agent on either side, Cavanaugh and Jamie crossed the cold parking garage. Rutherford was next to them, a classic protective formation. They identified themselves to guards, entered the elevator, and rode upward in silence.

Now I know what it feels like to be a client, Cavanaugh thought.

When the stern-faced group reached the fortieth floor, they flashed their credentials to other guards. Their concealed weapons set off metal detectors as they stepped through the entrance to Global Protective Services. The receptionist's jaw dropped. Several protective agents stopped in their tracks. Crossing the brightly lit lobby, Cavanaugh barely had time to note that the damage from the explosion had been erased, the place looking splendid, as if nothing had happened. Without bothering to knock, he opened a door marked ALI KARIM and heard his personnel director tell two FBI agents who flanked him, "If you're arresting me, tell me the charges, but you can't keep me here without a reason."

Standing angrily behind his desk, Ali spun toward the suddenly opened door. "Ah," he said to Cavanaugh and Jamie as they entered, "now this all makes sense."

"Does it?" Cavanaugh asked. "*All* of it?"

"As I explained, Mr. Karim," one of the agents flanking him said, "we just wanted to be sure you stayed here so you could cooperate and answer questions when everyone arrived."

"Hey, nobody's better at cooperating than me." Ali glared. "Cavanaugh, you promised to keep in touch. When you didn't, I got worried that something had happened to you."

"A couple of times, something almost did."

"You didn't need to make a production about this. If you'd let me know you were coming, I'd have canceled my appointments and waited for you. Unless you don't trust me." Ali pointed toward the stocky black man next to Cavanaugh. "Who's *this*?"

Rutherford showed his FBI credentials.

"Does this have anything to do with Kim going into drug rehab?" Ali asked.

"You know about that?"

"She phoned from the clinic. If I'd realized she was on drugs, I'd have fired her long ago. In fact, this morning I *did* fire her. It's too risky having her around. God knows how much tactical information she blabbed when she was drugged up. At least, we know who the security leak is."

"Actually," Cavanaugh said, "I promised Kim she could have her job back when she finished her rehab."

"What?"

"We're certain she's not the security leak."

"And just to guarantee we don't get fooled again," Jamie added, "we're instituting a new security measure: a drug-testing program."

"'*We*'?" Ali asked.

"Jamie's our new deputy CEO," Cavanaugh explained.

"It helps to let the personnel director know so I can get an office ready for you and spread the word and basically do my job. As far as the drug test goes, first-rate idea. I wish I'd thought of it. I'll be the first man to piss in a vial to show my loyalty. But I have to tell you, right now my loyalty's being sorely tested. Obviously, I'm not on your popularity list. What's the problem?"

"Four years ago," Cavanaugh said.

"Give me some help here. I have no idea what that means."

"You were in Rome. In charge of a team protecting a Russian oil executive."

Ali's face tightened. "That." He looked at the four agents next to Rutherford. Beyond them, GPS personnel listened at the open door. "How public do you want this to be? Do you still care about security, or are you too busy suspecting me?"

Rutherford gestured for the agents to leave.

As Cavanaugh started to close the door, Gerald Brockman came in.

"Private party?" the Afrikaner asked.

"I forgot to send you an invitation, but you might as well join the fun."

Brockman leaned against the wall and crossed his arms over his dark suit.

Cavanaugh finished closing the door and turned toward Ali. "The Russian oil executive was shot to death."

"That's right."

"While you were in his hotel suite."

"Right again. A sniper bullet through a window. One of the Russian's competitors probably ordered the hit."

"Carl Duran was part of your team."

"Duran? That son of a bitch hasn't worked for us in years. Why do you care about *him*?"

"The Russian," Cavanaugh said. "Tell me what happened. Why did the security fail?"

"He was one of those arrogant clients who thinks his protectors are butlers and bell hops. 'Carry my bags. Phone for dinner reservations. Get my shoes polished.' I told him we did only one thing, and that was to protect, but we couldn't do that if our hands were compromised and we were distracted by silly errands. I told him if he didn't like that idea, if he was unhappy with our security, then he should hire somebody else. I checked with Gerald—" Ali indicated Brockman leaning against the wall. "—who was my superior at the time, and he said I did exactly right."

Brockman nodded.

"The client loved his vodka," Ali said. "He also loved standing in front of his hotel suite's windows at night, grinning at the lights of Rome. I kept closing the draperies. He kept opening them. I kept telling him he had to stay away from the damned windows. One evening, when he was especially drunk, he yanked the draperies open, spread his arms toward the city lights, and told me, 'You see, nobody's out there, waiting to kill me.' 'Then why in God's name did you hire us?' I asked. 'For show,' he said. He chuckled, gulped more vodka, and told me, 'I must be important, mustn't I, if I need so much protection.' He laughed again, and that's when the bullet smashed through the window."

"The glass wasn't bullet-resistant?"

"It wasn't an option. *He* chose the hotel. Anyway, how many hotels have that kind of glass? We wouldn't have *needed* bullet-resistant windows if the stupid bastard had followed instructions and kept the draperies closed. The bullet caught him here." Ali touched the middle of his forehead. "Mushroomed. Blew most of his brains out the back of his head. Working with the police, we discovered that the shot came from the roof of a building two hundred yards away. It had been raining for the previous two days and nights. The shooter must have had a poncho rigged to form a low tent. We found his dry outline where he'd been lying on the otherwise wet gravel on the roof."

"Patient man."

"Or woman," Jamie said.

Cavanaugh nodded. "Nobody's more patient than *you* are." He stepped toward Ali. "How did Carl Duran fit into this?"

"He was part of the security outside the Russian's suite. The sound of the bullet shattering the glass was loud enough that he heard it and charged inside."

"Wasn't the door locked?"

"Of course it was," Ali said.

"You let him in?"

"I was too busy trying to help the Russian. When I realized I couldn't, I hurried to phone for an ambulance."

"Then Carl couldn't have gotten in unless he had a key."

"It's been a long time. But, yes, obviously he must have had a key."

Brockman straightened, pushing himself off the wall. "I was in charge of the team that investigated the shooting. There were some questions: whether Ali should have been more insistent to the Russian about staying away from the draperies, for example."

"*Insistent*? I did everything but put him in handcuffs!"

"But on balance, we saw it as a basic case of a client jeopardizing his own security," Brockman continued. "As for Duran, he was with a member of his team *outside* the suite when the bullet came through the glass. Chunks of the glass were all over the room. Clearly, the bullet came from another building. Where is all this going? Why are you so interested in Duran?"

Cavanaugh explained what they'd learned.

"He knows so much about our agents, somebody in GPS needs to be passing information to him."

"Somebody in authority," Jamie told Brockman. "We think Duran's using blackmail to get that information. The only time, you, Ali, and Duran intersected was in connection with the Russian's death, so there's a strong chance that's when the trouble started."

"You think *I'm* involved?" Brockman said angrily.

"No. You were second-in-command when Carl was fired. If Carl had a way to blackmail you, he'd have forced you not to fire him."

"So you're blaming *me*?" Ali demanded.

"You had a connection with Duran, dating back to the Russian's murder," Cavanaugh pointed out.

"Meanwhile, Kim—our company drug addict—gets a free pass?"

"She helped us," Jamie said. "In fact, she risked her life for us."

"Then what do I need to do to prove *I'm* not the leak? Jump off a building?"

"I don't see *anything* you can do," Cavanaugh told him. "Until we get this crisis settled, I'm putting you on administrative leave. We're going through all your phone records to see if you've been in contact with anyone suspicious. Jamie will analyze your computer's hard drive to retrieve emails you've erased."

"Of course, in most cases, they're never fully erased," Jamie explained.

"Why the hell don't you check my bank records, too?"

"It's being done as we speak."

Ali ran a hand through his thick, dark hair. "You know what? Shove your administrative leave. Shove your damned job." He glared at Rutherford. "Am I under arrest?"

"I don't have enough proof. "

"Then why don't all of you go fuck yourselves?"

10

No one spoke for several seconds after Ali stormed from the office.

"If he's acting," Rutherford said, "he deserves an Academy Award."

"Yeah, but if he's innocent, I'll never be able to regain his trust," Cavanaugh added.

"Welcome to the world of running a corporation," Brockman said.

"Let's think about you and Duran," Rutherford told Cavanaugh. "You haven't been in contact for the past three years, and then suddenly he tries to kill you in Wyoming? *Why?*"

"I could make the link between the way our agents were killed and his obsession with knives. He tried to keep me from drawing suspicion to him."

"But why wait so long?" Jamie wondered. "If he was worried about you, he'd have needed to eliminate you at the start—*before* the agents were killed with sharp weapons."

Cavanaugh thought about it. "As long as I was out of the business, maybe Carl didn't consider me a threat. But then his contact alerted him that someone named Aaron Stoddard might inherit Global Protective Services. Carl knew who Aaron Stoddard was. At all costs, he had to stop me from getting involved."

"Because of the knives," Brockman said. "But the pattern still isn't clear. Not all our agents were killed with knives. And only a few of the government's agents. Why only *those* agents?"

Jamie suddenly headed toward the computer on Ali's desk. "Gerald's right. We've been studying all kinds of lists. But what we *haven't* looked at is what the agents killed with sharp weapons might have in common."

Jamie typed the codes Kim had given to her, accessing GPS's security files. She typed more keys, studied something, and pressed other keys. Immediately, the printer began processing pages.

Cavanaugh grabbed them and spread them over the desk. The group joined him.

"Nothing similar in their backgrounds," Rutherford concluded. "They were born and raised in various areas. They belonged to various elite military units: Eighty-Second Airborne, Marine Recon, Army Rangers, Special Forces, SEALs, Britain's SAS, South Africa's Reconnaissance Commando unit."

"But hardly any of them served at the same time and the same place," Jamie pointed out.

"And they hardly ever worked on the same protective assignments together," Brockman said. "Maybe we're going at this from the wrong direction."

"What do you mean?"

"If there's a common denominator, maybe it isn't where they'd been or the assignments they'd been on. Maybe it's where they were going."

"Going?" Jamie asked.

"Their next assignments." Brockman drew his finger along the pages. He stopped at one item, his features tensing. "Dear God."

Staring at where Brockman pointed, Cavanaugh felt sick. He grabbed the phone. "We'd better check with the Secret Service, the U.S. Marshals, and the Diplomatic Security Service. *Their* agents who were killed with sharp weapons. We need to find out where *they* were being assigned."

"The same place?" Jamie asked.

She and the others stared at the pages.

"New Orleans."

"The World Trade Organization."

"Two days from now."

11

The GPS conference room was crammed with agents using computers and phones. Messengers hurried in. Printers whirred as Rutherford's team worked with Cavanaugh's, trying to take advantage of every second. Similar battle-plan rooms were at the FBI, Secret Service, U.S. Marshals, and Diplomatic Security Service, the groups constantly communicating with each other, updating schedules, coordinating, trying to prevent a disaster.

The room's noise forced Rutherford to raise his voice. "When the World Trade Organization had its conference in Seattle, riots nearly shut down the city."

Cavanaugh knew about the thousands of protestors and millions of dollars in damage. WTO protests had also disrupted Geneva. Indeed, wherever the WTO held its meetings, huge, violent demonstrations followed in reaction to what protestors claimed were anti-environment and labor-abuse policies that the WTO encouraged.

"You wouldn't believe the political pressure to make sure this conference happens," Rutherford said.

"And the economic pressure from mega-corporations," Brockman added. "They rely on the WTO to provide clear sailing for them in Third World countries. Billions of dollars are at stake."

Cavanaugh stood behind Jamie as she studied a computer screen that showed images of blockades and barbed wire in downtown New Orleans. "There'll be hundreds of diplomats, politicians, corporate CEOs, and heads of state. They're all targets. With the security crisis we're having, they can't get the first-class protection they're used to. Why won't the Secret Service listen to us?"

"It's the people they take orders from," Rutherford explained. "They don't call it the Secret *Service* and the Diplomatic Security *Service* for nothing. Protection's a *service* industry. They need to oblige the people paying the bills. What do politicians and diplomats know about what's involved in setting up security? They're too busy wheeling and dealing and asking their protectors to carry their luggage."

"Every available GPS agent is being routed toward New Orleans," Brockman said. "We'll make damned sure nobody gets killed on our watch."

"But some of those agents are replacing dead agents on well-rehearsed teams they've never worked with. It'll take them precious time to get up to speed," Cavanaugh said.

"Plus, now that protectors know how it feels to be the primary targets, will they worry more for their clients or for themselves?" Rutherford wondered. "Oh, sure, they're professionals. Day in, day out, hardly anybody's braver. But how can they focus on defending strangers when they're worried that *they're* the ones who'll be killed or that somebody'll blow up their families? The system's dangerously overloaded."

Jamie typed more computer keys, accessing images of the crowded docks in the New Orleans area. "While we're worrying, I hope somebody's checking those ships. New Orleans has the second busiest port in the United States. A dirty bomb would be easy to smuggle in."

"We'd better get down there," Cavanaugh said.

"Maybe not." Rutherford frowned at a message he was handed. "Maybe you can help somewhere else."

"Somewhere…?"

Rutherford showed Cavanaugh the piece of paper. "As you suggested, we checked the backgrounds of new subscribers to knife magazines, especially *Blade*. We began a year *before* Duran's name disappeared from *Blade's* list. All the names were tracked to people with legitimate identities. *Except for these three.* We're still checking. We investigated so quickly that we might have made mistakes. But do any of those names and addresses mean anything to you?"

Cavanaugh stared at the names. "The last one. Robert Loveless."

"So?" Brockman asked.

"Bob Loveless was a famous knife maker. I emphasize *was*. He's dead."

"Could be a coincidence," Rutherford said.

"But not at that address. It's a rural-route number near West Liberty, Iowa. That's where Lance Sawyer lived. The old man who taught Carl and me to forge blades."

12

As the Gulfstream took off from Teterboro airport and sped toward Iowa, Cavanaugh and Jamie unpacked two more bug-out bags.

Seated in a leather chair that swiveled, Rutherford interrupted his appreciation of the jet's luxurious interior to study the contents of the bags. "Pistols, knives, ammunition, miniature flashlights, duct tape, money. Some soldiers in Third World countries aren't as well equipped. I don't suppose you're licensed to carry those firearms in Iowa."

"Afraid not," Cavanaugh said.

Rutherford sighed. "Does this phone work?"

"Yeah, but you need to leave fifty cents on the table."

After giving Cavanaugh a dry look, Rutherford took a notebook from his suit-coat pocket, found a number, picked up the phone, made his call, and identified himself. "I need to speak to the agent in charge. …We expect to arrive around your time eleven p.m. I want to confirm that lodging has been arranged and that your team will be assembled for a six a.m. briefing. …Good. Also, I need temporary law-enforcement credentials for two civilians so they can carry concealed handguns. I'll give you the serial numbers when we land. …Thank you." Rutherford set down the phone.

"You're a handy guy to know," Jamie said.

"As long as you don't expect me to make a habit of pulling strings for you."

"Hey, we helped *you* a couple of times," Cavanaugh said.

Rutherford sighed again.

13

In lengthening shadows, Brockman stared at the glut of traffic and told his driver to leave the car in Global Protective Services' garage. "I can walk home faster. Call me in an hour. I'll tell you when to pick me up."

After the stress of the day's events, he welcomed the chance to move. Six feet one inch tall, with two hundred and ten pounds of solid muscle, he exercised ninety minutes a day, using weights, a treadmill, and a multipurpose flex machine in his apartment. Although the temperature was forty degrees and he wore only his suit, he welcomed the chill as he loosened his tie and took long strides past Madison Avenue onto 53rd Street.

Stretching his legs, dodging pedestrians, he almost broke into a run as he reached Fifth Avenue and headed north. The exertion warmed him. The blaring horns, rumbling engines, and choking exhaust of traffic blurred until he was hardly aware of them. He concentrated on the satisfaction of using his muscles, of feeling blood surge through his veins.

Fifty-Eighth Street. Ahead, beyond jewelry and designer clothing stores, he saw Central Park stretching away on his left, its leaves red, yellow, and gold in the last of the sun. Sixty-Third Street. Now only the park was on his left, its bushes, boulders, trees, and grass looking surreal in the concrete of the city. He took out his encrypted cell phone and pressed numbers.

"Case," he said, using the name of a knife manufacturer as a code word. He waited for a reply. "New Orleans," he explained to the person listening. "I'm supposed to fly there tonight. Cavanaugh has the company jet, so I need to go out to LaGuardia and take a commercial flight." He waited for a response, then added, "He went to Iowa."

Brockman put the phone away and walked even faster. He purged his mind of traffic, of pedestrians, of bicycle messengers and kids on skateboards. He imagined that he hiked through a wilderness, far from people and the messes they made. In his reverie, the only sound was the crackle of his footsteps on fallen leaves as his skin tingled and he inhaled mountain air.

At 71st, he turned right, went a block and a half, and entered his apartment building. There, he took the elevator to the tenth floor. His forehead was beaded with sweat as he walked along a corridor, reached his apartment, and unlocked it. When he opened the door, the intrusion detector began its shrill beep, giving him twenty seconds to press buttons on a number pad to the right of the door.

Despite his years in the security profession, Brockman made the error that virtually every intrusion-detector owner makes. The anxiety that the beep-beep-beep created caused him to leave the door open while he pressed the buttons on the pad. Only when the beeping stopped did he turn toward the door to shut it. But the beep-beep-beep had obscured the sound of approaching footsteps. Suddenly, Brockman felt a sharp sensation in his right thigh. Reaching to draw his pistol from under his suit coat, he saw Ali Karim's dark face glaring from the hallway. Brockman's leg felt warm. As the dart in him spread its toxin, Ali's angry features seemed to waver.

Brockman floated backward, downward, Ali's blurred hands striking him, yanking his pistol away.

14

A phone rang. Muffled. As if blankets were wrapped around it.

"Hello?" The voice seemed a far-away whisper. It sounded eerily like Brockman. "Pick me up to go to the airport? No, I changed my plans. There's something urgent I need to attend to. I won't be leaving until tomorrow. I'll call you."

Silence gathered. Slowly, Brockman understood that he was sitting upright, his back against something metallic. *Tied* against something metallic. A sudden light blazed toward his face. *Many* bright lights. He wanted to paw them away, but his arms wouldn't move.

Footsteps. The air seemed denser as someone hovered in front of him.

"Hey!" *Slap.* "Wake up!" *Slap.* "I know you're faking!" *Slap.* "Open your damned eyes, or I'll tape them open so you can't blink!"

Brockman warily opened his eyes and squinted from the pain of numerous lamps. Their shades had been tilted backward, their exposed bulbs aimed in his direction, nearly blinding him. Unable to move his head, he shifted his eyes this way and that to try to protect them, but the heat from the lights was inescapable. His right leg, where the dart from the tranquilizer gun had struck him, felt swollen and throbbed.

Ali stood close before him. Along with his dark hair, his dark features, and dark suit, he wore dark leather gloves.

Brockman strained to move. Shifting his eyes blurrily from side to side, he saw barbells, a treadmill…his exercise room. His pistol and his cell phone were on a table, along with his claw-shaped knife, its plastic sheath and the breakaway chain that Ali had found on him. He angled his eyes down, realizing that he was secured to the flex machine, his legs strapped to the leg-curl extensions, his arms raised and attached to the butterfly extensions.

"I know *I'm* not the security leak," Ali said. "And Cavanaugh was awfully sure Kim wasn't. After all, who would be stupid enough to blackmail her and trust a druggie to deliver information on time and accurately? That means *you*, my friend, and would you like to know why I'm sure you're the son of a bitch who told Carl Duran where our agents would be, on what assignments, and when?"

Brockman relied on his rugged military training, on the weeks he'd spent in the South African outback with hardly any food and water, amid brush fires, lions, and elephants. He gathered all his discipline, everything he'd ever learned about withstanding interrogation. "You're making a mistake."

Slap. "I asked, would you like to know why I'm sure you're the son of a bitch who's the security leak?"

"Have you gone out of your—"

Slap. Ali's glove burned Brockman's cheek. "Because protectors are getting killed right and left. Because all of us are constantly checking over our shoulders, wondering if we'll be next. Except *you*, my friend. I've been watching you the last few days. When you're on the street, you don't seem the slightest bit threatened or nervous the way the rest of us are. You're not acting as if you're worried that somebody's going to stick a knife in you the way *I'm* worried. Now why would *that* be? Do you suppose it's because you're *part* of this, because you know you're safe?"

Brockman didn't answer.

"Well, we've got time," Ali said. "Hours and hours. Tonight. Tomorrow morning. I heard your accent so often over the years, I can do a damned good imitation in case anybody telephones. I told your driver he won't be needed. Are you expecting any visitors?"

"A friend."

"Male or female?"

"Female. She'll get suspicious if I don't answer the intercom."

"I'll disguise my voice again," Ali said.

"She knows me too well. She'll realize it isn't me, especially if pain distorts my voice. She'll get suspicious and call the police."

"So I'd better take it easy on you, is that it?" Ali smiled. "Well, at least I got you to answer several questions in a row, even if the answers are lies. How could you be expecting a girlfriend when your driver was expecting to drive you to LaGuardia?" *Slap.* "Mustn't lie, Gerald. But we've got plenty of leisure to discuss this. First, though, I think a little exercise will relieve the tension? These flex machines are wonderful. I hope you don't mind that I took the liberty of rerouting some wires and readjusting some parts."

Nearly blinded by the lights, Brockman watched as Ali pulled a handle. Its wire was attached to a series of pressure-increasing wheels that Ali had attached to the machine. The device allowed Ali to exert minimal energy in order to move a lot of weight. In horror, Brockman watched as the leg-curl extension began to rise. Unwilled, his legs rose with it. They felt as if they were going to snap from the enormous weight of barbells tied to his ankles, weighing them down. Sweat burst from his face. His mouth opened. He thought he was going to scream.

Ali jammed a rag into his mouth.

Immediately, he pulled another handle, its cable attached to another series of pressure-increasing wheels. The machine's butterfly extensions moved forward and inward, causing Brockman's bent arms to follow.

But the weight against Brockman's arms was enormous, and his arms had been strapped to the extensions in the reverse of the usual way so that his palms faced outward rather than inward. Muscles were pulled in unnatural directions. Backbones crackled. He had a terrifying image of a roasted chicken, of its overcooked wings being torn off. Sweat dribbled down his face. The scream inside him built until it threatened to propel the rag from his mouth.

Abruptly, Ali released each handle. The machine's leg-curl and butterfly extensions shot back into place, forcing Brockman's legs and arms to shoot back with them. The excruciating impact sent a shockwave through him. Pain made his stomach heave. Ali pulled out the rag just before hot bile filled Brockman's mouth.

"Now didn't that get the kinks out?" Ali asked. "There's nothing like working the muscles a little to relax them and unwind at the end of the day and encourage conversation, right? But before we start our chat, let's review the basics of interrogation. The absolute certainties that you and I both know. No one, regardless of how strong and determined, can resist a steady assault. As sure as the sun rises, you know that the combined effect of weakness, pain, shock, trauma, fear, and disorientation will reduce you to a whimpering near animal who'll do anything to stop the agony. Knowing that, you'll make bargains with yourself. Right now, you're thinking, 'I'll hold back information as long as I can. Maybe someone will burst in to rescue me. Or maybe the person I'm trying not to betray will suspect I'm being interrogated and take steps to protect himself and the mission. That way, if I eventually confess, it won't matter. Don't think about a day from now or an hour from now or even a minute from now. Just concentrate on this moment. I can deal with this moment. That's a doable task.' Isn't that the attitude you were taught to have when you're being interrogated, Gerald? Sure.

"But this is what *I'm* going to teach you. Before tomorrow morning, you'll tell me everything I want to know, or else I'll cripple you. I'll leave your body so broken, your senses so impaired, you'll be a prisoner within yourself for the rest of your long days and nights. As I cripple you, you'll experience pain of a sort you never thought possible. Pain that won't ever end. At last, you'll talk. You know that. The question you need to ask is, since you realize you'll eventually surrender the information, why suffer the pain in the meantime? Of course, you need to prove that you're strong and brave. I understand, and I'll give you the chance to show your stuff. But the emotions that usually stop someone from talking are loyalty or fear. I can't imagine you feel loyal to whoever's killing your fellow protectors. So I'm forced to conclude that you fear this person more than you fear me. I'll make you a promise, Gerald. Tell me what I need to know, betray him, and I'll personally guarantee your protection. I'll make you another promise, Gerald. If you don't do what I ask, I'll make you fear *me* far more than you ever feared the person you report to."

Ali shoved the bile-soaked rag back into Brockman's mouth and pulled the levers on the machine faster than before, causing Brockman's legs and arms to jerk upward and forward with greater force, the weight against them threatening to tear sinews and ligaments and pop sockets.

Brockman's vision turned gray. Again, Ali removed the rag from Brockman's mouth, letting bile spew out.

"Talk to me, Gerald. Tell me about Carl Duran."

15

Even when viewed from a wooded hilltop a half mile away, the farmhouse, barn, and outbuildings were obviously in disrepair. As the sun rose, Cavanaugh, Jamie, and Rutherford lay on cold ground behind red-leaved bushes, using binoculars to peer down past the stubble of a cornfield. In the mid-distance, a dirt road went from right to left. Beyond was a field of wild grasses that belonged to one of the few cherished places in Cavanaugh's memory of his youth, the farm where he had spent so many wonderful Sundays. At least, the Sundays had *once* seemed wonderful. Not because of what he had learned about making knives. The knives hadn't been as important to him as the time he'd spent with the person he once considered—and had believed would *always* be—his closest friend.

With the sun behind them, they didn't need to worry about light reflecting off their binoculars, signaling their location. Even so, Cavanaugh took care that his were shielded.

"The place looks deserted," Jamie said. "Porch needs paint. Roof needs new shingles. The barn's listing."

"When Carl and I visited there, the old man kept it in perfect shape. He never let age slow him down."

"Sounds like someone I'd like to have known," Jamie said.

"I doubt John here would have. Not the way Lance was always cussing."

Rutherford looked amused. "Well, there's cussing, and then there's *cussing*."

"This was the latter."

"According to the local FBI office, after the old man died, an English professor from the university in Iowa City bought the place," Rutherford said. "Gentleman farmer sort of thing. Sold some of the land to the neighbors. Leased out the rest."

"Yeah. I remember. When I was a teenager." Cavanaugh felt hollow. So much had happened in the meanwhile. Except for Jamie, so much of it had been painful.

"Four years ago, the professor retired and moved to Arizona." Lying on his stomach, Rutherford scooped up black dirt and studied it. "That's when Bob Loveless bought the place."

"Seems like Duran had a yen for the good old days," Jamie said.

Rutherford kept examining the dirt in his hand. "Awfully rich soil. Excellent loam. Breaks apart easily."

"Since when do you know about soil?" Cavanaugh asked.

"My dad was a farmer in Arkansas. I grew up helping him plow and plant. What he wouldn't have given for soil like this."

"You've got all kinds of secrets, John."

"None like yours, Aaron."

"How strange it feels to be called that."

"Did the local FBI office talk to the neighbors?" Jamie asked. "Is there any indication that Duran actually lived there?"

"Someone matching Duran's description lived there off and on four years ago. A few of the neighbors dropped by to welcome him. They remember he was polite but that he didn't encourage socializing. When he smiled, it was sort of distant."

"Yeah, that's Carl," Cavanaugh said.

"As near as they could tell—tire tracks in snow, that sort of thing— he seemed to be there only a week or two at a time."

"So this is where he went between assignments," Jamie said to Cavanaugh, "the same as *you* went to Jackson Hole. This was his home."

"Close to Iowa City and Hafor Drive, where his real home was when he was a kid." *Three houses up the street from mine*, Cavanaugh thought. He remembered the two-story homes along the street. Most were painted an idealized white. Big front windows. Thick bushes. Luxuriant flower beds. Lush lawns. Again, he felt hollow.

"Then three years ago, according to the neighbors, he pretty much stopped coming," Rutherford told them. "That's when the place started looking worn down."

"Three years ago." Cavanaugh nodded. "After Carl got fired and wound up working for that drug lord in Colombia."

"The postman who drives this route says Bob Loveless gets magazines and bills. Renewal forms. Advertisements. Things like that."

"And tax forms," Cavanaugh said. "He needs to keep paying his property taxes, or else the county will take the farm. We need to assume someone comes here to check if there's mail and to forward it. Maybe the same person who pays his taxes."

"Someone we'd like to talk to," Rutherford concluded. "The mail gets delivered late in the afternoon. Yesterday, when you told us this was the address we wanted, the local FBI office had just enough time to intercept the postman and arrange for him to leave some advertisements in the box. Agents have been watching the place since then. So far, there's been no sign of activity in the house and nobody's picked up the mail. We don't dare go in there until someone stops at the mailbox. Otherwise, we might scare the courier away. We'll just need to lie here and wait."

"Maybe not as long as you think." Jamie pointed.

To the right, a dust cloud appeared, moving steadily to the left along the dirt road. Through his binoculars, Cavanaugh saw a gray SUV approaching the mailbox.

Rutherford spoke into a walkie-talkie. "Everybody stay in place until we see what we've got."

The SUV drove closer, continuing from right to left. Cavanaugh's pulse increased, although he was oddly conscious of the emptiness between heartbeats.

"Steady," Rutherford said into the walkie-talkie.

The SUV appeared to go slower as it neared the mailbox. Despite the dust the car raised, the sun reflected off the driver's window. Braced on his elbows, Cavanaugh concentrated so much that he leaned forward, trying to get closer to the car.

It passed the mailbox and continued down the road.

No one spoke for a moment.

"If that was the courier, maybe he or she sensed something was wrong and kept going," Jamie wondered.

"Maybe," Rutherford said. "Or maybe it's just someone driving into town."

Another cloud appeared on the road, this one caused by a red pickup truck that drove from left to right. It sped past the mailbox, almost obscuring it with dust. The faint drone of the engine drifted away.

A minute later, it was a blue sedan that came from right to left.

Cavanaugh felt an increased sense of being stuck in time while the world sped toward disaster. He thought of Brockman, who should have been in New Orleans by now, organizing Global Protective Services agents. Several times the previous night, Cavanaugh had tried to contact him on his cell phone. No response. He'd tried Brockman's home phone. Again, no response. Rutherford had called the FBI office in New Orleans to see if Brockman had checked in. No sign of him.

Once more, Cavanaugh pulled out his cell phone, but this time, instead of trying to call Brockman, he pressed the numbers for Global Protective Services, intending to send an agent to Brockman's apartment, only to cancel the call when he stared toward the road beyond the field and saw the blue car stop at the mailbox.

16

The dust cloud hovered. All Cavanaugh could see was a vague figure leaning out the far window of the car, opening the mailbox.

"Steady," Rutherford said into the walkie-talkie. "This could be somebody putting an advertisement or something *into* the box."

A young woman—jeans, leather jacket, blond ponytail—stepped from the car. She walked to the gate, unhooked its chain, and swung the gate inward. Then she got back into the car and drove up the lane toward the house, the sound of her engine receding.

"Not yet," Rutherford said to the walkie-talkie. "Wait until we see what happens."

The car reached the house. Through his binoculars, Cavanaugh watched the woman get out. She stepped onto the porch and tried the front door but found it locked. She looked through the windows. She proceeded around to the back, out of view.

Listening to an earbud linked to the walkie-talkie, Rutherford reported what the other watchers were seeing. "She's trying the back door. It's locked also."

Now the slender woman came back into view. She tried to get into the barn, tried to get into a shed, then gave up, returned to her car, and drove back toward the road.

"Go! Go! Go!" Rutherford shouted into his walkie-talkie.

Abruptly, the countryside was in motion. Camouflaged men with rifles rose from tall weeds near the house. Vehicles that had been hidden on a nearby farm sped from that property and raced along the road, hurrying to block the lane. A faint drone became the growing rumble of two enlarging specks on the horizon: helicopters speeding toward the farm.

The woman's startled face was visible through the windshield. Shocked by the sudden appearance of the camouflaged men, she urged the car forward.

Armed men blocked the lane. The woman swerved into a field, desperate to veer around them. But now a dark van arrived, blocking the open gate. As the men with rifles converged on her, the car's wheels got stuck in the field. Tires spun. Dirt flew. Through his binoculars,

Cavanaugh saw that the woman had her hands to the sides of her head. She was screaming.

"Hell of a start to the day," Jamie said.

Standing, they brushed dirt from their outdoor clothes. From lying on the cold ground, Cavanaugh's knees felt stiff. *A long time since I was with Delta Force*, he thought.

"You take the car, John." He pointed toward the back of the hill, where their vehicle was parked. "I need some exercise."

"So do I," Jamie said.

Rutherford considered them for a moment, then nodded.

Descending through stiff, brown grass, Jamie told Cavanaugh, "And maybe you need a little more time to get used to coming back to this farm."

"That too."

The crunch of his footsteps seemed to come from a distance as Cavanaugh gazed ahead: past the cars at the entrance to the property, past the blue car and the men searching the distraught driver, toward the house, the barn, and especially the building next to the barn. He remembered being in the passenger seat as his mother drove him and Carl up that lane for their weekly lessons. Then Cavanaugh's memory was shattered by the roar of the helicopters landing where his mother had always stopped near the barn. Instead of two boys getting out of a car, men with rifles leapt from the choppers and scurried among the buildings.

Wordless, he and Jamie reached the lane at the same time Rutherford arrived with the car. They stepped aside for a van that sped past them toward the house. Squinting in the cold stark morning sunlight, Cavanaugh watched the van stop next to a leafless oak tree, men hurrying out with dogs.

Cavanaugh pointed toward the woman. She was outside the car now, slumped against a fender. "Jamie…"

There were no other females on the team.

"Yes, I'll talk to her," Jamie said.

Taking the opportunity to postpone going up the lane, Cavanaugh watched Jamie speak to the armed men. When they stepped back, she went over and leaned against the car, mirroring the woman's slumped posture. The woman wiped away tears. Jamie approximated that gesture by pushing a few strands of hair behind her ears, using imitative body language to establish rapport.

Amid the chaos around them, they spoke for several minutes. At first, the woman talked haltingly, but soon the full torrent of her distress poured out, Jamie listening sympathetically, guiding her with questions, nodding, at last pressing a hand on her shoulder.

She returned to Cavanaugh and Rutherford. "Her name's Debbie Collins. She's a nurse in a doctor's office in Iowa City. Lives here in West Liberty. The rent's cheaper. Every morning, she checks if Bob Loveless—actually she calls him Robert—has any mail."

"What was she doing with the doors and looking in the windows?" Rutherford asked.

"That's part of her routine. She makes sure nobody's broken in, that everything's secure. In winter, she uses a key and goes inside to check that the furnace keeps the interior at fifty-five degrees and that the pipes haven't frozen."

"She does this every day?"

"For the past three years," Jamie answered. "Except when she visits her parents in Des Moines or if she takes a vacation. But she's never away for long, and she always arranges for someone to substitute for her."

"They must be lovers," Cavanaugh said.

"No."

"Then he pays her, right?"

"Sort of. A hundred dollars a month."

"What? For doing this month in and month out for the past three years? That's hardly enough. You're sure they're not lovers?"

"The opposite. He never tried to touch her. She wonders if he might be gay."

"Then I don't understand."

"A little over three years ago, Debbie was in a bar in Iowa City. Saturday night. A few beers after seeing a movie with some girlfriends. Early December. The group stayed until midnight, then split up to go home. It started to snow. Debbie was parked on a side street. She hurried to get to her car so she could drive home before the weather turned worse. One moment, she was fumbling in her purse to find her car key. The next moment, two guys grabbed her while a third pulled up in a van. She struggled. They punched her. They dragged her into the van, and before the first guy could close the side hatch, his buddy was already using a knife to cut off her clothes. The driver started to speed away when all of a sudden another guy lunged through the half-closed hatch. The stranger knocked the first attacker senseless. When the one with the knife attacked, the stranger pulled out a knife of his own. Debbie says she can still hear the scream when the stranger slammed into the guy, did something with the knife, and threw the guy out into the snow. Meanwhile, the driver stopped the van, jumped out, and ran away before the stranger could get to him."

"Duran," Rutherford said.

"Who, as far as she knows, is named Robert Loveless," Jamie continued. "The men reeked of whiskey. The knife they used makes her think they might have killed her after they raped her."

"*Then* what happened?" Rutherford asked.

"The stranger managed to get her to calm down enough to tell him where her car was. Her overcoat was in shreds. Her clothes were half cut off, so he wrapped her in his own coat and carried her to her car. Her purse was in the snow by the driver's door. The key was where she'd dropped it. He unlocked the car, put her in the passenger seat, got the car started so she'd be warm, and then told her he was taking her to the hospital. 'Not hurt,' she told him. She was thinking about being brought into the emergency ward half-naked. 'Then I'll drive you to the police,' he told her. She didn't want that, either. She'd still be half-naked, people staring at her as she clutched his coat. She'd been drinking. The police would probably think she'd asked for it. Suddenly, an engine roared. While they were distracted, one of the attackers had come back and escaped with the van. The two other men had run off. So now there wasn't any way for the police to investigate the assault. 'I want to go home,' she managed to say between sobs. 'All I want is to go home.' The stranger told her he'd drive her, but she was suddenly afraid to be alone with him. She told him that where she lived was too far, that she didn't want him to go out of his way. She kept insisting she could drive, so finally he got out of the car, and despite the storm, she did manage to drive home to West Liberty. The next morning, she discovered how bruised she was and fully realized how close she'd come to possibly being killed. She also discovered that she still had the stranger's overcoat."

"*Then* what?" Cavanaugh asked.

"Around noon, a car pulled into her driveway. A lean, lanky man got out and knocked on her door. The temperature was almost zero, but instead of a coat, he wore a sweater. Debbie was afraid to answer the door, but finally she couldn't bear watching him stand out there freezing, so she opened a window to talk to him, and that's when she discovered he was the man who'd helped her the previous night. It turns out he was so worried about her that he got in his car and followed her home, making sure she didn't have an accident or slide into a ditch. If she didn't mind, he'd like his coat back. Well, of course, she had to invite him in and offer him some coffee. He kept a respectful distance, taking care not to make her feel nervous about having a stranger in the house. She thanked him for going out of his way. That made him smile, and when she asked him why, he said he was surprised to find that they were practically neighbors. He lived two miles down the road."

"Imagine that," Cavanaugh said.

"When he reached to take the coffee cup from her, Debbie noticed the fresh bandage on his wrist. The man with the knife had cut him."

"Imagine *that*," Rutherford said.

"So they became friends," Jamie continued. "He kept treating her with respect, never making a romantic move, although she wished he would. Eventually, he told her he needed to leave the farm for a while. He was a construction worker, but because of the cold weather, he'd been unemployed for a while, and now he'd learned that his father, who lived in Miami, was sick with emphysema, so he was going to Florida to find work and take care of his dad."

"But would she please watch the farm for him, forward his mail, little things like that? He'd be glad to pay her," Cavanaugh said.

"After all, it was the least she could do," Rutherford added.

"So you get the picture?" Jamie asked.

"Classic recruitment," Rutherford concluded.

"Almost makes me proud of him," Cavanaugh said bitterly. "The guy's a natural."

"Does she realize it was all a setup?" Rutherford asked Jamie. "Duran scouted the West Liberty area, spotted her, found out she was single, followed her, learned her habits, and then paid those three guys to pretend to attack her."

"She hasn't the faintest idea."

"Nice to be innocent," Cavanaugh said.

"I wrote down the Miami address where she forwards the mail." Jamie handed Rutherford a piece of paper.

"And from where a drug courier probably forwarded the mail to Colombia," Rutherford said. "The question is, where is Duran's mail being forwarded *now*." He pulled out his cell phone, pressed numbers, and began reading the address to someone.

"The woman says Duran came back here yesterday," Jamie said. "He told her he needed to leave something for a friend."

Cavanaugh stared up the lane toward the building next to the barn. For several moments, he didn't seem to breathe.

17

Brockman's legs and arms were racked with pain, his left calf muscle feeling torn, his right rotator cuff about to snap. The pain combined with his nausea and the heat from the unshielded lamps made him sweat so much that his shirt and suit coat were drenched. The strap that attached his neck to the spine of the flex machine made him feel increasingly strangled. The glaring lights hurt his eyes, but no matter how often he blinked, he couldn't get rid of the spots that the lights seared into his vision.

Abruptly, the spots turned gray.

They swirled and wavered.

Ali slapped both cheeks with his leather gloves. "Wake up, Gerald! It's not polite to pass out when you've got company. Conversation, Gerald. That's what a guest wants. Stimulation. What I wouldn't give for an intelligent discussion about...oh...say...Rome four years ago. That Russian oil tycoon who was assassinated. Now *that* would be interesting."

Despite how sick Brockman felt, he desperately needed water to soothe his parched lips, to clear the taste of bile from his mouth.

"I bet I can read your mind. I bet you're thirsty. Right, Gerald?"

Brockman closed his eyes.

Ali peeled Brockman's lids upward. "Thirsty?"

Hang tough, Brockman thought. *Take it a moment at a time. Hope for somebody to break in and rescue me. Make Ali believe I'd rather die than tell him anything.*

But what if it comes to that? I might in fact die.

Stop thinking like that.

Ali held up a pitcher filled with water and ice cubes. He swirled the cubes, making them clink against the pitcher. On the outside, moisture beaded, trickling down like rain on a window.

"Gerald, I'm getting tired of asking if you're thirsty."

Brockman tried to nod, but the straps kept his head in place. "Yes." His voice reminded him of the sound of a boot breaking crusted mud.

"That's all you needed to say." Ali poured ice cubes and water into a glass, inserted a straw, and raised it to Brockman's lips. "Easy. Only a little at a time. You don't want to get sick."

Brockman sucked on the straw, feeling the delicious, cold water fill his mouth. Ali took the glass away as Brockman swallowed and ran his wet tongue over his crusted lips. He had thought that the crust was from dried bile. But now he tasted the copper of blood.

Ali dipped a cloth into a basin of water. He twisted the excess from it and pressed the cloth against Brockman's forehead. He stroked Brockman's cheeks with it. The cloth felt wonderfully cool.

"The Russian, Gerald. Tell me about the Russian. This doesn't need to be difficult. The Russian was long ago. Four years ago. I don't want you to talk about what's happening *now*. Four years ago. It's safe to talk about *that*. It's safe to talk about the Russian."

Through his groggy, nausea-and-pain-filled thoughts, Brockman tried to decide what to do. Stay silent; suffer more pain. Or try to string Ali along. Seem to give him information but not really tell him anything. Stop him from…

"Have more water, Gerald." Ali lifted the glass, extending the straw.

Brockman opened his mouth. At once, Ali shoved the rag into it, then yanked the handles on the flex machine, thrusting Brockman's legs up, propelling his arms inward.

Brockman's rotator cuff ripped. He could hear it give, like a zipper being yanked open. In the blazing lights, his mind went black. Fire filled his throat. He fought to breathe.

Coughing. Mouth open. Rag gone.

Water streaming over his head. Dripping. Cooling.

Shadows.

"Have more water, Gerald."

Brockman blearily opened his eyes and saw that Ali had turned off most of the lamps. The one that stayed lit had its shade adjusted properly, shielding the bulb's glare. His parched, burned skin felt refreshingly cool.

Ali took away the basin, part of the contents of which he had poured over Brockman's head. Again, Ali extended the glass and the straw. Desperately thirsty, Brockman studied it, afraid that, when he opened his mouth, Ali would again yank away the straw and shove the rag between his lips. He was conscious of his wet hair clinging to his scalp.

"Drink, Gerald."

Brockman opened his mouth and sucked on the straw. He rinsed bile from his tongue. He spit it out, unable to project it far, some of it landing on his pants. He sucked more water, swirling it, swallowing, purifying his throat.

"I promise to protect you from Carl Duran," Ali said.

"He kind of seems in control, don't you think?" Brockman murmured. "All the protectors who've already died. Nobody could protect *them*."

The shadows in the room were luxurious. He wanted to close his eyes and—

"I can fix it so you seem to disappear, Gerald. He'd never be able to find you."

Disoriented, Brockman realized that Ali had managed to engage him in a conversation, a sin of being interrogated that had to be avoided at all cost.

At all cost? Brockman thought groggily. *Look at what it's already cost me. After the last three years, do I care anymore? Do I want to keep living like this?*

He licked his coppery-tasting lips. "What if…"

Ali waited.

"What if *he's* not the one I'm afraid of?" Brockman asked.

"Then who *are* you afraid of?"

"All of you. Need more water."

Ali extended the straw.

Brockman sipped.

Ali prompted him. "Afraid of all of us?"

"Protectors. Afraid of what you'll do if you find out."

Ali set down the glass and raised an electrical box with a switch on it and numerous plugs attached to it. When he flicked the switch, the room blazed again. All the lamps were attached to the box, all the bulbs suddenly glaring.

"No." Brockman groaned. The heat swept over him.

From the shadows behind the glare, Ali asked, "What are you afraid we'll find out?"

"Suppose I did something."

"Something?"

"Sleepy. Feel sleepy."

"Don't worry, Gerald. The glare and the heat of the lights will keep you awake. What did you do?"

"How can you protect me from…"

"Stay awake, Gerald, or I might need to tear your other rotator cuff. Protect you from what?"

"Keep me from being punished."

"A deal, Gerald? Is that what you're asking me to make with you? A promise to protect you from Carl Duran *and* from your fellow protectors?"

"Can you do it?"

"I promise you this. You tell me what I want to hear, and I'll look after you as if you're my closest friend. I'll do everything in my power to get you out of whatever trouble you're in."

"It'd be a…"

"Be a *what*, Gerald?"

"Relief. The bastard held it over me for so long."

"Tell me," Ali said.

18

The building was made of weathered boards. It was twenty feet square, single-level, with dusty windows on two sides and a black stovepipe protruding from its sloped roof. The door was blank wood. On leashes, two dogs sniffed at it.

"They don't seem interested," one of their handlers said.

"The same as the other buildings. So far, no indication of explosives," the second handler told Cavanaugh.

Cavanaugh looked around—at men coming in and out of the farmhouse, whose door they'd rammed in; at other men searching the barn, whose padlock they'd cut.

"No indication of radiation, either," a man said, walking over with a Geiger counter. "A dirty bomb or anything like that."

"Or smallpox or anthrax," another man said. He held a compact device programmed to identify the DNA of selected bacteria and viruses. His hands were covered with latex gloves.

"And the place tests negative for stashes of drugs," Rutherford said, joining them.

A man with bolt cutters indicated the building's locked door. "Shall I do the honors?"

Cavanaugh walked to where a window provided an inside view of the door. Through the dusty glass, he didn't see any sign of a booby trap, but even though trained dogs had failed to indicate that they smelled explosives, he needed to be sure.

Reaching into a windbreaker, he pulled out a twist tie. "Free the lock," he told the man with the bolt cutters.

When the lock fell to the ground, Cavanaugh eased the door open a quarter inch, knelt, inserted the twist tie through the narrow gap, and slowly raised the pliant strip from the ground, alert for any sign of resistance from a wire attached to a detonator. While Jamie aimed her flashlight, searching for a reflection off a wire, Cavanaugh drew the twist tie along the entire door.

"Anybody care to step back?" he asked the group.

They thought about it.

"Wouldn't hurt to crouch behind that car," one of the dog handlers said.

"John, why don't you and Jamie go with them?" Cavanaugh asked.

What Jamie did instead was cautiously open the door.

Sunlight pierced shadows. Dust on the floor showed the footprints of someone who'd recently gone in and out. The marks were large, presumably a man's. They led past a metal stove that the old man had used for burning wood in the winter. They passed a dusty anvil and a table of equally dusty forging tools. Cavanaugh had worked with them so often that, even after many years, he recognized them as the old man's, especially the battered anvil. The footprints veered around a waist-high metal container that had a propane tank attached to it: the old man's forge. They led to another dusty table, upon which an envelope was set against a small wooden box.

The box was made of oak so polished that it reflected Cavanaugh's flashlight.

The box was open. It was lined with green felt, into which was nestled the most beautiful knife Cavanaugh had ever seen.

Hey, he warned himself, *pay attention.* He and Jamie looked for wires stretched across the shadowy floor. As Cavanaugh approached the far table, he stayed clear of the footprints, preserving them as evidence. But the closer he came, the more difficult he found it to take his eyes from the envelope and the contents of the box. At last, he stopped before them.

The envelope had handwriting on it. Neat, solid strokes. In black ink.

To Aaron

"Looks like you've got a pen pal," Rutherford said.

"It's Carl's handwriting." Trying to ignore the beckoning knife, Cavanaugh reached for the envelope but then hesitated. Turning toward the door, he saw one of the technicians peering in. "You'd better check this."

The technician followed the trail Cavanaugh and Jamie had made in the dust. He moved his detector over the envelope and the knife. "No pathogens. At least, none that this device is programmed for."

"Got any more gloves?"

The technician reached into a jacket pocket and gave him a pair.

After putting them on, Cavanaugh picked up the envelope and saw that it was sealed. He tore it open, removed a sheet of paper, and cautiously unfolded it. The handwritten message had the same neat, solid strokes. It was dated one day earlier.

Aaron,

Do you ever miss Lance? I used to lie awake nights wishing that old bastard was my father and you were my brother. All the adventures you and I had. Old buddy, you need to be reminded of the military virtues. Loyalty, courage, honor, and sacrifice. Thanks to them, we were able to fight our way out of a lot of trouble because we knew we could depend on one another.

Loyalty. That's the greatest virtue. And Aaron, as I told you on the radio, you weren't a good enough friend. You should have backed me up when I got fired. I felt like you'd cut my parachute lines. I know you thought I killed that stalker to impress that twat singer. The truth is, I did it to impress YOU. I expected you to say, "Damned good job, man. You sure showed that piece of shit." Instead, you let me get fired. Okay, I made a mistake. But a true friend doesn't turn against another friend just because of a mistake. A friendship's supposed to be stronger than that. You can't choose your parents, but you CAN choose a friend.

Trust. That's what a friendship's about. Being able to count on somebody no matter what. Well, buddy, I sure found out I couldn't count on YOU. None of this would have happened otherwise. I hope you're satisfied. Of course, you were supposed to be in a grave in Wyoming and not know any of this. You always could rise to a challenge. Not that it matters—two days from now, not even you will be able to find me. Just to show I'm big enough to stop hating you, here's a present. I think it's the best knife I ever made.

Carl

Cavanaugh showed the letter to the group.

"So now he's justifying what he's done?" Rutherford asked. "This doesn't feel right."

"And what's the significance of the knife?" Jamie wondered. "It's beautiful, I admit. The handle. Is it covered with…"

"Gold quartz," Cavanaugh said.

"And those red dots. They look like…"

"Rubies embedded in gold rivets," Cavanaugh said.

The slender knife was eleven inches long, five inches of which were the amazing handle.

Cavanaugh couldn't take his gaze off it.

"Michael Price," he finally said.

"I don't understand."

"Old San Francisco." Cavanaugh kept staring at the knife. Then he felt that *he* was being stared at. Breaking his concentration, he looked up at Jamie and Rutherford, who watched him, puzzled.

"Who's Michael Price?" Jamie asked.

19

In 1848, San Francisco had a population of about four hundred people when gold was discovered at Sutter's Mill a hundred miles away. Within a year, two hundred thousand miners passed through San Francisco on their way to the gold fields. The town was so undeveloped that necessities had to be brought in by ship.

Knives were some of those necessities. In the east, most communities had blacksmiths who could forge crude blades, but quality knives needed to be imported from manufacturers in England. Suddenly, in San Francisco, a market developed for thousands of knives, dependable ones, blades that could be trusted to hold an edge while they pried nuggets from a stream and protected those nuggets from thieves.

A shipment of knives took a year to travel from England to San Francisco. Seizing the opportunity, knife makers began setting up forges and charging top dollar. Soon a distinctive style and a high level of expertise became common. One of those knife makers was Michael Price, who came to San Francisco in the mid-1850s and whose clients were some of the richest, most powerful men in the community.

Judges, bankers, merchants, and real-estate moguls were wealthy beyond their fantasies. To show it, they dressed extravagantly, including the knives they carried for self-defense. Michael Price's elegant designs were characterized by a handle made of gold, diamonds, mother-of-pearl, and other precious materials. The blade was enclosed in an elaborately engraved silver sheath attached prominently to a dress belt. Customers vied with each other to have the most beautiful, subtle, and yet ostentatious knife.

"They're proof that knives can be works of art," Cavanaugh said. "Knife collectors search for them. Recently, a Michael Price dagger sold at auction for almost a hundred thousand dollars. One way master blade smiths prove their skill is by replicating a Michael Price knife."

Cavanaugh pointed toward the knife in the box. "Carl did it flawlessly. At the back of the handle, you see that screw? If you detach it, you can take the handle apart and spread it out in small pieces: the grip, the bands that hold it onto the tang, the various fittings that form the guard. Each of those tiny parts is perfectly crafted."

As if hypnotized, Jamie reached for it.

Cavanaugh stopped her. "I don't think that's a good idea."

"Why?"

"The blade should be gleaming. It should have a satin polish. But it doesn't. Its finish is dull."

Still wanting to touch the enticing knife, Jamie said, "Sure. It has dust on it."

"After a day?" Cavanaugh said. "There wouldn't be *that* much dust. No, Carl put something on it. Probably the handle, also. I'm betting it's some kind of topical poison, something that the pathogen detectors haven't been programmed for. You wouldn't need to cut yourself. Skin contact would be enough. You'd probably die instantly."

Jamie jerked her hand away. "Playing with us. Showing how smart he is. He's pissed at being rejected, and he's getting back at everybody."

Cavanaugh re-read the letter. "He says that in two days he's going to disappear. The message is dated a day ago. So tomorrow, something's going to happen."

"New Orleans. The World Trade Organization," Jamie said.

Cavanaugh's cell phone rang. Reluctant to be distracted, he looked at its screen. The name made him frown. "Ali Karim."

He pressed a button and said to the phone, "There's no point in trying to persuade me to change my mind. I can't even *think* about reinstating you until we finish the investigation."

"Yeah, well, I believe you'll reinstate me a lot sooner than that," Ali's voice said. "I just had a heart-to-heart talk with Gerald. He says you figured out Carl Duran is arranging an attack in New Orleans. The World Trade Organization."

Cavanaugh cut him off. "If you're the security leak, you knew that already."

"Every available agent's been sent there, right?" Ali's voice asked. "Ditto the Secret Service, the Diplomatic Security Service, and the U.S. Marshals."

"I can't discuss any of it," Cavanaugh told him.

"Then let's discuss *this*," Ali's voice ordered. "The agents are the real targets."

A chill made Cavanaugh's chest contract.

"Stay away from New Orleans." Ali's voice rose. "That's where Carl Duran wants everybody to go. *It's a trap.*"

PART SEVEN:
THE MOST EXPENSIVE KNIFE IN THE WORLD

1

"What you did to me…" Brockman's features were contorted with pain. "None of it matters. I can bear anything."

"Certainly," Ali said.

It had been a long, painful night.

"I'm as tough as *you* are. If I talk, it's not because you got the better of me."

"Of course not."

"*Carl Duran* matters."

"Then we'll need to make sure he keeps away from you."

"The only way to guarantee that is to kill him," Brockman said.

"Tell me what you know. I'll see what I can arrange."

"Don't you think *I* had plans to kill him? But first, you need to find the bastard." Strapped to the flex machine, Brockman's body was rigid with anguish. "And if anything happens to him, he left instructions for someone he trusts to release documents. About me."

"Unless you tell me, I can't help you."

Brockman took a long breath. "Duran had nothing to do with the hit on the Russian."

Ali leaned forward, concentrating to hear Brockman's faint words.

"*I* did," Brockman said. "*I* arranged the hit on the Russian."

The revelation was far from what Ali expected. Concealing his surprise, he asked, "You? Why?"

"Money."

"We get paid a lot."

"Not enough to risk our lives for strangers. Not *those* kinds of strangers. Do you ever hate them?"

"Hate?"

"I grew up in Pretoria." Anger cut through Brockman's pain. "In the alleys. I fought for a cardboard box to sleep in, for the rags on my back, for every scrap of food I managed to get my hands on." As sweat ran down his face, Brockman stared fiercely ahead. "When I got big enough, I thought, 'Hell, I've been fighting all my life. Might as well join the military.'" He took another anguished breath. "Turned out I was right—it wasn't any worse than what I'd already been through. In many ways, it was better. All the shit I had to do to qualify for special ops. Nights in the bush country with wild fires. Water holes dry. The petrol my instructors put in the only food I'd been given to eat. Even then, it was *still* better." Brockman's eyes were fierce. "Because I proved I was special. Because I had something to be proud of. My discipline. My skills."

Brockman's voice cracked. Ali put the straw in his mouth, letting him drink.

"Then I got too old," Brockman said. "Thirty. Too old. Shit. So I went to work for GPS," he said with contempt, "and was assigned to protect some of the most wealthy, attractive, and powerful people in the world. I'd read about people like that. But nothing prepared me for meeting them. They owned penthouses, villas, jets, yachts, islands, anything they wanted. In a world of poverty, starvation, and pain, they were blessed." Brockman inhaled. "They took it for granted. Vain, arrogant, domineering, greedy, and disgusting. I hated them."

Ali used a cool washcloth to rub sweat from Brockman's face.

"When I left the commandos, all I had were scars and empty pockets. These people had *everything*, but they didn't have the character to deserve it. The worst of them, the biggest pig of tall, was that Russian."

Ali listened harder.

"I'd been assigned to him two years earlier, before I was promoted. His language was filthy. His manners were..." Brockman faltered.

"Shouting, bragging, insulting. I once saw him vomit in the middle of a business dinner. On the floor next to him. 'Must have been the red wine with the fish,' he said, and told the waiter to bring him more vodka. He was a subhuman who'd bullied his way into an oil fortune."

Bound rigidly to the machine, Brockman tried to lower his eyes toward his swollen knees. "Do you think they can be repaired, or will I be crippled?"

Ali didn't answer.

"Well, my days of jumping from aircraft were probably over anyhow." Brockman stared into an imaginary distance. "I wanted what those clients had. The penthouses, the yachts, the villas, the islands. I overheard stock tips every day. These people made fortunes on insider knowledge. So when I learned about a drug company that would soon be bought by a rival for double its value, I invested everything I had in it. I borrowed heavily." Brockman lapsed into a self-hating chuckle. "The stock tip was only a rumor. The drug company went bankrupt. I lost it all."

"Rough break," Ali said.

"Wasn't it, though. The next time the Russian hired GPS to protect him…"

"The Rome assignment? The one I worked on?"

"Yes." As Ali wiped more sweat from his face, Brockman said, "The Russian's enemies were expert. They needed someone familiar with how he was protected." Another self-hating chuckle. "Somehow they got word of how much I hated the Russian. Somehow they learned about how desperate I was for money. I often wonder if they didn't arrange for me to hear the stock tip about the drug company."

"They set you up?"

Brockman tried to shrug, but he was bound too tightly to the machine. "They promised to pay off my debt. They promised to set my finances back the way they'd been. All I needed to do was arrange for a man I despised to be killed."

"You were in New York while I was in charge of his protective team in Rome," Ali said. "Every time I reported to you, you told the hit team what I said."

"You kept telling me that he wouldn't stay away from the windows in his hotel suite."

"So you passed that information on, telling the sniper where to take his position?"

"It was so easy," Brockman said. "The son of a bitch was no longer on the planet, and my debts vanished."

"Carl Duran had nothing to do with the hit?"

"Nothing. He had no influence on me. When he sliced up that stalker in front of the Plaza Hotel, I didn't have the slightest reason to keep him from being fired."

"Then how does this relate to…"

"The damned sniper. After Duran was fired, after he went to work for a drug lord in Colombia, he and the sniper crossed paths." Brockman's voice became thicker, sounding as if he'd swallowed sand.

"Try," Ali said, giving him more water. "We're almost there. This'll soon be over. Tell me about the sniper."

"Duran and the sniper compared notes, talking about former assignments."

"The sniper told Duran about your involvement in the Russian's death?"

"Everything." Brockman grimaced with self-loathing. "Duran threatened to expose me. At the least, it would have put me in prison. More than likely, it would have gotten me killed. The Russian had two brothers almost as vicious as *he* was. They'd have…" Brockman's voice trailed off.

"You didn't see an alternative. You had to let Duran blackmail you into providing information about our agents and their assignments."

"So there you have it," Brockman said with greater self-disgust.

"No, I *don't* have it. *Why is Duran doing this?*"

Brockman didn't answer, so Ali shoved the rag back into his mouth and pulled handles on the flex machine. Five minutes later, after tearing Brockman's left rotator cuff, after Brockman completed his silent scream, Ali removed the gag.

"*Why is he doing this?*"

"I don't know."

Ali reached for the handles on the machine.

"But I've got a strong suspicion."

When Brockman told him, Ali felt his stomach turn cold.

2

In the shed, Cavanaugh clutched his cell phone, listening to what Ali told him. "How do I know this is true?"

"If you don't believe me," Ali's voice said, "maybe you'll believe Gerald."

Cavanaugh heard a bump as the phone was repositioned.

Ali's voice was now muffled by distance. "Tell him, damn it. Tell him what you just told *me*."

Another bump. Then Brockman's pain-ridden voice said, "I…it was me. …I'm the security leak."

"Tell him about New Orleans!" Ali insisted in the background.

Brockman obeyed. Hoarsely. Between difficult breaths. His thick words sounded as if they were forced through swollen lips.

Cavanaugh felt that the shadows around him got darker. Staring at the Michael Price knife that Carl had expertly reproduced, smelling the dust and the old metal around him, he was hardly aware of Jamie and Rutherford reacting to his strained features.

Ali's voice returned. "*Now* do you believe me?"

"Stay with him. Don't leave the apartment. I'll send a team to protect you."

"Get a doctor for Gerald," Ali said.

Cavanaugh broke the connection, then quickly arranged the help he'd promised. As he hurried toward the door, he told Jamie and Rutherford what Ali had discovered.

After the murky interior, the glare of the cold sun was blinding. Passing members of the search team, taking long strides down the lane toward Rutherford's car, Cavanaugh said, "At yesterday's meeting, we tried to find a link among the agents who were killed with sharp weapons. Brockman steered the conversation. We were looking for a common denominator based on their previous assignments or the military units they'd been in. But it was Brockman who suggested their past assignments didn't matter. The *next* assignments. Brockman made us look at *those*. I can still hear him saying 'The World Trade Organization.' That was his final job. In case we missed the significance of the blade killings, Carl ordered him to make sure we noticed the connection. He wanted to focus us on New Orleans. The note Carl left here reinforced that idea."

"But why would he go out of his way to warn us when and where the attack will be?" Rutherford asked.

"Every available agent's been sent there. Duran wants to destroy as many targets as possible, but he doesn't care about the trade ministers and corporate executives at the conference. They're a bonus. The *agents* are his targets. He's already strained the system. Now he wants to bring it to its knees. If he cripples the entire U.S. security network, it'll take months to train new operators. Meanwhile, whoever hired him will be able to attack domestic targets at will."

3

The warehouse was next to the Mississippi. Despite dampness that rose from the floor, the building was used as a dormitory. Cots with sleeping bags formed three rows, twenty in each. Men sat on the cots, cleaning weapons. Others sat at tables, playing manhunter video games or watching action movies that emphasized accurate tradecraft. Ample food was available. After the punishing youth most of these men had known, after their prison experience, after the pride and discipline they'd acquired at the training camp, they were content.

When a side door opened, they looked toward a man silhouetted by sunlight. His tall, lanky figure and powerful-looking forearms were immediately recognizable. Dressed in hiking boots, multi-pocketed pants, and a slightly large shirt hanging over his hidden gun, he closed the door, obscuring two men outside who looked like dock workers but were actually sentries.

As he walked to a podium, the men gathered before him. Without needing to be told, each assumed a military posture with his feet apart and his hands behind his back.

"Good afternoon, gentlemen." Carl's voice echoed off the metal walls.

Eyes alert, they nodded in response to the respectful way he addressed them.

"Let's deal with the most important thing first. Are you getting enough to eat?"

They chuckled.

"Well, *are* you?"

"Yes, sir."

"Taste good?"

"Yes, sir!"

"Nothing beats New Orleans cooking. Oysters. Crawfish. Shrimp in Creole sauce. Pecan-crusted catfish. Red beans and Cajun rice. Praline bread pudding. Lord, I'm making myself hungry."

They laughed.

"When we get this job done, I'll arrange a feast worthy of Antoine's or some other of those fancy restaurants around here. In the meantime, just remember when there's ample tasty chow, make sure you take advantage. You never know when famine follows feast. That's a soldier's law. Got all the equipment you need?"

They nodded.

"If you have any doubts about the weapon you were given, get another one. Load up on ammunition. After all, you're not paying for it."

They laughed again.

"Speaking of pay, this fine-looking gentleman over here—" Carl indicated Raoul. "—has your next month's cash. You can pick it up after the briefing."

Guns, money, and respect. This was heaven.

"I mentioned work. Are you ready to get down to it?"

"Yes, sir!"

"Positive?"

"*Yes, sir!*"

"Then here's the drill. Tomorrow, a conference starts. They call it the World Trade Organization, and it brings a ton of important people to town. Politicians. Billionaires. The fat cats who run international corporations. It also brings a ton of people who think the World Trade Organization wants to chop down the world's forests and strip-mine what's left. They believe it wants to keep poor folks in the mud so rich guys can get richer by paying twenty cents an hour in an overseas factory and then slapping a big price tag on shoes and shirts or whatever they make. These protestors start a riot. It always happens. It's as sure as sunrise and sunset. They riot. Which is where *we* come in. The people we work for want us to help the rioters. They want us to make this a really impressive riot. A riot the World Trade Organization will never forget. To make them think twice about chopping down forests and strip-mining and paying poverty wages. So how are we going to make this the end-all and be-all of riots? We're going to give each of you one of these."

Carl held up a battered knapsack that looked as if it had been tied to a truck and dragged along a dirt road for ten miles. The group studied it, the only time anyone would ever pay attention to the nondescript object.

"Each of these knapsacks has a smoke canister in it. You're going to mix with the crowd. There'll be so many protestors, thousands of them, that no one'll pay attention to you. Each knapsack has a number. Go over to the map on the wall, and find your number on it. Convention Center Boulevard. Fulton Street. Commerce Street. Poydras Street. Along Riverwalk. Outside Harrah's Casino. Up past Lafayette Square. Duncan Plaza. The City Hall. Each street has one of your numbers. That's where you'll place yourself. And when the riot gets going, when they start torching cars and smashing windows and throwing Molotov cocktails, when the police march in to stop the festivities, you're going to find a place to hide your knapsack. At eleven hundred hours on those expensive, synchronized Navy SEAL watches you were given, you'll tug this cord here and trigger your smoke canister.

"Wait until the smoke's thick enough. With all these knapsacks evenly spaced, there'll be plenty. As soon as the cops can't see you, draw your gun and rapid fire above everybody's head. We don't want to kill anybody. Just scare them. Sixty guns going off. It'll sound like a war. But nobody'll be able to see you to know you're doing the shooting. The rioters'll think the cops are doing it. The cops'll think it's the rioters. There'll be screaming and yelling and stampeding.

"Use all your ammo. Drop your piece. Make sure you've got these stick-on latex pads on your fingertips so you don't leave prints, and make sure you wore gloves when you loaded the magazines so there won't be any prints on the ejected cartridges. Then get out of there. Rendezvous two days from now at the campground I told you about near Galveston, Texas. We'll celebrate and plan the next mission.

"Your part in all this shouldn't take more than a minute, but it requires steady nerves. That's why you've been training. A can-do attitude. Dependability. Resolve. Control. A cool head. That's the secret to getting along in life, gentlemen. You're not punks anymore. Prove it. Show me how professionals behave. But being a professional also means knowing your limitations. If there's anybody here who doesn't think he's ready, who needs more training, tell me now, and you can walk away with no hard feelings."

About a dozen—the least sociopathic—looked hesitant, but no one raised a hand.

"Good," Bowie said. "Then get your cash and your knapsack. Find your place on the map. Make sure your weapon's ready. Get plenty to eat and a good night's sleep. I'll talk to you tomorrow morning."

As Carl stepped from the podium, the men formed a line in front of Raoul, who distributed the money.

"Mr. Culloden," Carl said to one of the men, "when you first came to us, you looked soft and pale from solitary confinement. You were puffy from lack of exercise and the starchy crap the prison called food. Now you're solid. You've got a healthy glow. You ought to be paying *me* for treating you to a spa."

Culloden chuckled. "Right, Mr. Bowie, but if it's all the same to you, I'll keep the cash."

Carl continued his banter, making the men grin and feel part of a cherished team. Sometimes he shook hands or gave a man a good-natured slap on the back. But as he scanned the line, concealing his calculated assessment, he noticed that a half-dozen men hung back.

They waited while the majority pocketed their money and drifted back to cleaning guns, playing video games, watching action movies, and eating the best buffet in New Orleans.

"Mr. Bowie," one of them said.

Knowing where this was headed, Carl replied, "Yes?"

"We, uh…we've been wondering…"

Another man said, "Did you mean it that, if we didn't think we were up to this, we didn't have to do it?"

"This isn't a dictatorship, Mr. Todd. I believe that the best team is one that's totally voluntary."

"Then…" another man said.

"Yes, Mr. Weaver?"

"I think I've got myself in enough trouble for one lifetime. I don't need any more."

"It's not as if you're going to kill anybody," Carl said. "All you need to do is activate the smoke canister and shoot into the air."

"I guess I was more comfortable holding up gas stations, but I don't even want to do *that* now."

"Totally voluntary," Carl said. "I won't pretend I'm not disappointed. A lot of effort went into training you. But if you can't commit to the mission, you're doing everybody a favor by admitting it. You're sure you won't change your mind?"

They didn't respond.

"Okay then." Carl sighed. "Naturally, you won't get next month's wages. And naturally, you can't stay with the team any longer. But I can't let you stay in New Orleans, either. If you get drunk, you might stagger into some bar in the French Quarter and say more than you should."

"We wouldn't do that, Mr. Bowie. You know you can count on us."

"All the same, Mr. Weaver, you have an alcohol problem that made you do things that put you in prison. You also, Mr. Todd. I'll arrange for the six of you to stay in a motel for a couple of days. Outside town. Stock it with booze. Get take-in food. I don't want you out in public."

"No, sir."

"Two days from now, you can leave the motel, and it won't matter *what* you tell anybody after that."

Todd looked relieved. "Thanks, Mr. Bowie."

Bowie told Raoul, "Bring the van."

Ten minutes later, Raoul was driving them through dense traffic west on Interstate 10. The setting sun hurt his eyes. As they left the city, he said, "Mr. Bowie says the motel can't be fancy. Nothing where you need to show a credit card and leave a trail. You've got plenty of cash you haven't been able to spend. Use it. That place'll do." He pointed toward something called the Escort Inn.

"As long as it's near a liquor store," Todd said. "I haven't had a drink since an hour after I got out of prison. Then Bowie convinced me to go to his damned camp, and that was the end of that."

"Hey," Weaver said. "There's a liquor store across the street."

They stocked up with beer, bourbon, Scotch, vodka, gin, soft drinks, potato chips, onion dip, beef jerky, and a deck of cards, then drove to a parking lot at the side of the motel.

"I'll wait here while you register," Raoul said. "In case the mission turns to *mierda*, you don't want to be seen with me."

"Right. Good idea. We don't want to be linked to what goes on in town."

"Ask for rooms in back. Less chance of anybody noticing me parking back there while you unload this stuff."

"Yeah, we'll tell the clerk we want to be away from the noise of traffic."

Five minutes later, the six men returned from the motel's lobby. Raoul drove them to their rooms in back.

"Ground floor," Todd said proudly. "We won't be seen carrying all this stuff up the stairs."

Raoul watched them take the booze and food into one of the rooms. "Everybody set?" he asked from the doorway. "Need anything more?"

"A couple of hookers," Todd said, smirking.

"Mr. Bowie doesn't want you talking to anybody," Raoul warned.

"Yeah, okay, don't get bent out of shape. I was just making a joke."

One of the men twisted the cap off a Jim Beam bottle. Another popped the tab on a Budweiser can while a third turned on the television.

"See if they get the History Channel," Weaver said. "Maybe they'll have a program about machine guns or something else that's neat."

"Gotta use the bathroom," Raoul said.

He went in, closed the door, urinated, and flushed the toilet. He pulled two Beretta fifteen-round handguns from under his baggy shirt. He attached sound suppressors that he took from pouches on his belt. When he opened the door, he heard a TV announcer describing the invention of the AK-47 assault rifle. Stepping from the bathroom, he emptied both pistols into the six men. The suppressors made sounds as if a pillow fight were taking place. The nine-millimeter ammunition had fragmentation tips that disintegrated in their targets instead of passing through and piercing walls, alerting someone outside or in a neighboring room.

Raoul searched for and picked up every expelled cartridge, a few of them taking longer to find than he intended. Even if somehow he didn't locate every one, it wouldn't have been calamitous—he'd worn gloves when he loaded the weapons, taking care that he didn't leave fingerprints on the shells. But without empty cartridges, the investigators wouldn't have firing-pin marks and extraction scratches that could provide ballistics evidence linking Raoul's pistols to the crime scene. For certain, the bullets were so mangled and fragmented that *they* wouldn't provide ballistics evidence. In addition, Raoul planned to wipe his fingerprints from the pistols and abandon the weapons the moment it was safe to do so. As Mr. Bowie had taught him, survival depended on details.

He removed cash from the bodies. Then he cleaned his prints off the toilet lever and the few other things he'd touched. Leaving the unit, about to lock the door behind him, he heard the History Channel announcer explain that the Communist-era inventor of the AK-47 never received royalties from it.

4

Hearing a barge chug past on the Mississippi, Carl pressed buttons on his cell phone and yet again got a recording that told him to leave a message. He pressed a different set of buttons and got a similar message. He interrupted the transmission and brooded. It had been twenty-four hours since he and Brockman had been in touch. Brockman was supposed to have flown to New Orleans the previous evening. This morning, he was supposed to have reported to the Global Protective Services base here and evaluated the security preparations for the World Trade Organization conference. He would then have spoken with his counterparts in the various government protective services. When he knew the schedules and the routes that various agents would use to escort their clients to the convention center, he was under orders to get in touch with Carl and inform him of the details.

Had Brockman decided that he could no longer tolerate being part of this? Had he fled? Was he being detained for questioning? Because the latter had the more serious implications, Carl was forced to give weight to it. In the worst-case scenario, how long would Brockman resist interrogation? Would he be weak enough to confess his involvement in the deaths of so many operators? Would he tell the authorities that Carl manipulated them into sending as many agents as possible to New Orleans?

Disloyalty was the worst sin.

For a final time, Carl angrily pressed Brockman's numbers on his cell phone.

5

"You're lucky I'm on retainer to Global Protective Services." The doctor was a spectacled fifty-year-old, who'd once been a nurse in a mobile military hospital. She nodded toward Brockman, who lay in his bed, groggy from pain relievers.

"He'll need physical therapy on his knees and his torn rotator cuffs," she told Ali. "Considering all the damage you inflicted, another doctor would have phoned the police."

"Talk to Cavanaugh," Ali said. "He'll explain why it needed to be done this way."

Down the hall, in the exercise room, Brockman's cell phone rang. It wasn't the first time. Several times throughout the interrogation, calls had been attempted, none of which Ali had answered. Most callers had left messages, all of them related to GPS business, wondering why Brockman hadn't reported for work in New Orleans.

Only one caller had not left a message. The phone's display had shown the name William Scagel and a telephone number.

Now, as the phone rang again, Ali left the bedroom and walked to the exercise room.

After six rings, the phone stopped. Ali went to a table, where the cell phone sat next to Brockman's pistol and claw knife. Its display again showed the name William Scagel.

Troubled, he unclipped his own phone from his belt and pressed numbers.

Two rings later, Cavanaugh answered. "I hope this is good news."

"Just a question. Does the name William Scagel mean anything to you?"

"Hell, yes. Scagel was a famous knife maker. Where did *his* name come up?"

"He's been calling Brockman's cell phone and his home phone. But he doesn't leave a message."

The transmission was silent for a moment. "It's Carl."

"Hang on. Let's find out if he left a message *this* time." Ali pressed buttons on Brockman's cell phone.

"What's the telephone number on the display?" Cavanaugh's voice asked.

Ali dictated the numbers to him, then listened for a message on Brockman's phone. An electronic hiss indicated that something had in fact been recorded. Leaning against the table, shifting Brockman's weapons aside, Ali waited, hopeful. The hiss was interrupted by an electronic shriek.

The exercise room blew apart.

6

Carl clipped his cell phone onto his belt and put his small radio transmitter into a camera bag he carried. He strolled along the riverfront, nodding to tourists, pretending to admire boats on the Mississippi, although what attracted his attention were more police officers than usual and numerous barricades stacked to the side in preparation for tomorrow's demonstrations. He imagined Brockman—more likely an interrogator—listening to Brockman's phone, hoping to hear a message. But the only message was the trigger signal from Carl's radio transmitter. He reasoned that the claw knife he'd given Brockman wouldn't be far. He imagined the radio signal reaching the miniature detonator in the knife's sheath. The blast from the powerful explosive molded into the sheath would have destroyed everything around it.

7

One instant, the transmission Cavanaugh listened to was alive. The next, it was dead. That word came involuntarily to Cavanaugh's mind.

Dead. En route to New Orleans aboard GPS's jet, he felt something inside him drop. Reminding himself that phone communication on an aircraft wasn't reliable, that an electronic glitch might have interrupted the transmission, he stifled his premonition and called Ali's cell phone again, but the only response he got was a computerized voice that told him the number he had called was unavailable.

"Is something wrong?" Jamie asked.

"I'm afraid there is." Cavanaugh hurriedly called GPS headquarters in Manhattan.

The duty officer had already heard from two GPS agents outside Brockman's apartment.

"An explosion?" Tightness took Cavanaugh's breath away. He lowered the phone. "God damn you, Carl."

8

When the Gulfstream landed in New Orleans, a row of emergency vehicles waited, the lights on their roof racks flashing in the darkness. Somber officials with handguns under their jackets formed a protective square as Cavanaugh, Jamie, and Rutherford stepped from the jet into Louisiana's humid air.

"The phone number your man read to you before he was killed has a local area code," a Secret Service agent told Cavanaugh. "William Scagel bought the phone yesterday in St. Charles twenty miles from here."

"Carl probably didn't do it in person. Someone working for him did the honors so the clerk couldn't provide an accurate description."

"The address the buyer gave was bogus."

"What a surprise."

"I'll bet several other phones got purchased in various other stores—by the same person using more fake names and IDs," Rutherford said.

Police officers flanked a van. Accompanied by FBI agents, Cavanaugh, Jamie, and Rutherford scrambled inside. The moment the side door was secured, the driver headed toward an exit gate, cruisers to the front and back.

"We can't assume Carl will keep that phone much longer," Cavanaugh said as they sped onto a freeway. "Is the satellite in position?"

"Ready and willing," an agent answered. "The eyes and ears of the sky are aimed at New Orleans."

"Then do it. "

The agent spoke into a walkie-talkie. "Baker to Butcher, do you copy?"

"Affirmative," a voice replied.

"Commence tracking."

"Tracking engaged."

The agent nodded to Cavanaugh, who pulled out his cell phone and pressed the numbers Ali had dictated to him seconds before he was killed.

The group watched intently, but Cavanaugh was conscious only of the phone pressed against his ear and the sound of ringing at the other end.

One.

Two.

Three.

"He got rid of the phone," Rutherford said. "If anybody does answer, it'll probably be a junkie."

Cavanaugh's heart sped as Carl's voice said, "Hello, Aaron."

The van swayed, veering around car lights on the freeway.

"Good guess, Carl."

"No guessing involved. I know you, old buddy. I can predict what you'll do."

"Same here." Cavanaugh noted that there was something odd about the sound. He heard music and laughter in the background. Carl's voice was muffled and distant. "You were sure I'd call?"

"Unless you were interrogating Gerald Brockman, in which case you'd be a smear across a wall right now."

Acid burned Cavanaugh's throat. He wished he could reach through the phone and—

With effort, he kept his voice steady. "You also blew apart Ali Karim, plus two protectors and a doctor."

"Karim. Good man to work with. Knew his stuff. Sorry to hear he's gone."

"Try to sound more sincere."

"Who were the other…" Carl's voice faded, although the music and voices strangely persisted.

"I can barely hear you," Cavanaugh said.

The voice strengthened. "Who were the other protectors?"

Cavanaugh gave their names.

"Didn't know them. They must have been brought aboard after I was fired," Carl's voice said pointedly.

"I told you, I had nothing to do with getting you fired."

Headlights blazing, the van veered down an exit ramp, forcing Cavanaugh to grip the wall for balance.

"But you didn't do anything to prevent it, buddy," Carl said, "and deep in your heart, you know you could have."

"You kept exceeding orders. You were out of control. When Duncan fired you, it was the right thing to do."

"Ah, so finally I'm getting some truth. You *admit* you could have stuck up for me, but instead you went along with firing me."

"The incident outside the Plaza Hotel wasn't the only time you lost control. Blame *me*? How about blaming *yourself*?"

"Take some personal responsibility, is that what you're suggesting?"

"Stop what you're doing, *that's* what I'm suggesting."

"How long did you figure you could keep me talking?" Carl's voice asked.

"As long as it takes to persuade you to stop this."

"Are you triangulating the signal from my cell phone, old pal? Figuring out which microwave stations are relaying my voice?"

"Needs to be done. You know the procedures in a situation like this. Nothing personal."

"That's a laugh. You certainly proved, as far as you're concerned, nothing is ever personal. Cold, Aaron. I never realized how cold you are."

"And *you're* not? Listen to me, Carl. Stop whatever you're doing."

The van veered around a corner and stopped abruptly, forcing Cavanaugh to grip the wall again. Even before the vehicle was motionless, the agent in charge yanked the side door open, revealing men with rifles silhouetted by lights flashing on emergency vehicles.

"Now why would I want to stop something that took so long to set up?" Carl's voice asked.

Pressing the phone to his ear, Cavanaugh jumped to the pavement and followed agents toward a one-story brick building. The pungent smell of the nearby Mississippi filled his nostrils. "Carl, if it's me you're getting even with, name the place and the time. I'll give you all the security you want. No tricks. One on one. You can show me how much you hate me."

An agent opened a metal door. Bright light spilled out. A huge room was filled with radio equipment, computers, video and audio recorders, and closed-circuit monitors. The screens depicted hundreds of views of the streets around the New Orleans conference center, busloads of police arriving, barricades being set up.

At least two dozen technicians worked the equipment, but as one, they became silent, turning toward Cavanaugh as he entered.

"Hate you, Aaron?" Carl's voice came from speakers next to a monitor.

A technician turned down the volume.

"The reason I'm so pissed at you is I *love* you, man. Not like I want to bang you. Not *that* kind of love. But you were the only person I felt close to, and you walked away like I had the plague. Getting even with you? No way. What I'm doing is making a point. I'm proving I'm not out of control anymore. And now that your satellite technicians had their chance to try to find where I am, *adios*."

"Carl, wait."

The only sound was the music and the voices.

"Carl, how do we stop this? *Tell me what you want.*"

No answer.

"Carl!" As the music and voices persisted, Cavanaugh lowered his phone. He had to leave the transmission open in case Carl said anything else. But by leaving it open, he allowed Carl the opportunity to overhear what was being said in the room.

"Clever…" Stifling the impulse to curse, he gave the phone to a technician and told him to take it outside.

"Do you have his location?" Rutherford asked a technician.

"The French Quarter. He must have set the phone down and walked away."

"But why did his voice sound distant?"

"Maybe he wasn't speaking directly into the phone."

"The signal's coming from the corner of Bourbon and St. Peter," another technician said.

"Is there a team close to there?" Rutherford asked. "The police must have plenty of officers in the bar district."

A third technician finished speaking into a microphone. "A half-dozen teams converged on that area during the conversation. More teams are on the way. The streets are being blocked."

"One thing bothers me." The first technician pointed toward a monitor that showed a map of the French Quarter and a stationary, pulsing dot.

"Only *one* thing?" Rutherford asked.

"He never moved while he was talking," the technician said.

Jamie got it first. "Never moved? Why would he stay in one place when he knew we were using satellites to get a fix on his position?"

9

The van stopped on Chartres Street between Jackson Square and St. Louis Cathedral. Protectors converged on

the vehicle as Rutherford opened the side door.

Cavanaugh stared out at the glow of streetlights, at numerous tourists passing in the shadowy background, plastic cups of beer in their hands.

"Are you sure you want to do this?" Rutherford asked. "He could be baiting you."

"I'm positive he *is* trying to bait me."

"Then why are you playing his game?"

"Because it's the only game we have. How many agents are mingling with the crowd?"

"Almost enough that they *are* the crowd."

Cavanaugh looked at Jamie. "Want to stay here?"

"And miss the excitement?" she answered.

"Let's hope there *isn't* any excitement."

Flanked by agents, they got out and headed up narrow St. Peter Street. Passing the majestic cathedral and its gardens, approaching the glitter and activity of Bourbon Street, Cavanaugh slowed his pace. The sound of music and partying filled the night. Door-to-door bars and restaurants, most of them open to the street, were crammed with customers.

"If we stick together like this," Cavanaugh told the agents, "we won't be able to surprise him."

"But if we *don't* stick together," one of them said, "we can't shield you."

At night, Bourbon Street was closed to traffic. The agents scanned the raucous bars and the rowdy crowd in the middle of the street. They switched their attention to the ornate wrought iron of the numerous balconies, many of which were occupied by revelers.

Sweating, Cavanaugh crossed to where a man with a German shepherd stood next to a garbage bin. The dog's owner seemed to be enjoying the music and the enthusiasm of the crowd, as were a man and woman on the other side of the bin, and another couple amused by a man dancing in the street. All of them, including the dancer, were part of the team.

The man with the dog told Cavanaugh, "Arnold here is the best in our canine unit. He never fails to locate explosives. So far, the area seems clean." The man indicated the two couples and the dancer. "*They* have radiation and pathogen detectors. Negative readings."

"Show us what you found," Rutherford said.

The man and woman on the other side of the bin shifted garbage bags away, revealing two cell phones duct-taped together. There was also an apparently mystifying object next to them.

For now, Cavanaugh concentrated on the duct-taped cell phones. "Son of a…"

"This is one instance where I think your language is needlessly restrained," Rutherford said.

Cavanaugh took latex gloves from a pocket and put them on, hating the chalky feel of the powder inside them. He crouched, removed his compact flashlight from his belt, and studied the phones taped together. Their ear and mouth areas were positioned against one another.

An agent lowered his phone and said, "One of the phones is still on. Back at headquarters, they hear our voices coming through it."

Cavanaugh looked at the man with the German shepherd. "Have Arnold sniff this again for explosives."

"Happy to."

Then Cavanaugh asked the couples near him, "How about another scan with those detectors?"

They obliged, but the readings on the handheld monitors continued to be negative for radiation and pathogens. They did it so discreetly that the hundreds of tourists who passed them didn't notice.

Cavanaugh picked up the phones, holding them at the bottom where he was less likely to smudge fingerprints. He unclipped his knife from his pants. After studying the way the phones were secured face-to-face, he sliced the duct tape, separating the two.

"The second phone is on also. It's receiving a signal," Cavanaugh said, pointing toward the lit display screen.

"It would require *three* phones," Jamie said.

Cavanaugh nodded.

"The one you called," Jamie said. "The one taped to it. And a third phone that Carl used to phone the second one."

Again, Cavanaugh nodded.

"I'm missing something," an agent said. "What are you talking about?"

"Carl assumed I'd eventually call the number for the phone he used to contact Brockman. He knew Brockman's caller ID would keep a record of the number, but even if both Brockman's phones were destroyed in the explosion, the phone company would still have a record."

"Okay, I'm with you so far," the agent said.

"Carl and a companion waited for the call." Jamie pointed toward one of the phones. "Before Carl answered it, he turned on the second phone. Then he used a third phone to call this second one. He put the first and second phones together and used the third phone to relay his voice through the second into the first. While he spoke, a companion taped the phones together so they'd be secure. Then Carl and his companion hid the phones behind these garbage bags and walked away."

The agent nodded. "Because we didn't have information about the third phone, he could talk to you as long as he wanted, without worrying that we'd use a satellite to track him wherever he was talking—probably outside the French Quarter."

"And he's listening to us right now," Cavanaugh said.

Rutherford straightened. Cavanaugh noted with approval that the agents kept their attention where it belonged: on the crowd and the raucous buildings along the street.

"Isn't that right, Carl?" Cavanaugh said into the second phone. "You're listening to us right now."

He didn't get an answer, but a slight electronic hiss told him that the connection was still active. He showed the phone's display to the agent in contact with the communications center.

Noting the incoming number, the agent stepped away from the group so that he wouldn't be heard when he told the communications center the new phone number. They would track its signal.

"Are you there, Carl?" Cavanaugh asked.

Again, he didn't receive a reply.

"I hope you're having fun listening to us."

"What about the other thing he left?" Rutherford asked.

"The knife?" Cavanaugh referred to the apparently mystifying object.

"Yeah. It's one of the meanest-looking blades I've ever seen."

Cavanaugh picked it up. His latex gloves protected him from any dermal poison that Carl might have put on it. "It's called a 'khukri'."

The knife had an impressive ivory handle and a thirteen-inch blade. What made the blade intimidating was that it curved like a sickle. It was designed for chopping, its sweet spot almost anywhere along its curve.

"The Gurkhas use these," Cavanaugh said.

Rutherford nodded. The Gurkhas were a military tribe in Nepal. Their main source of income came from being mercenaries in various armies. They never drew their knives unless they intended to draw blood, and if they didn't wound or kill an enemy, they allegedly felt obligated to draw blood from themselves.

"When an enemy hears the Gurkhas are coming, the sweat starts to flow." Cavanaugh raised the second phone and said, "Carl, you did a fabulous job on this. The engraving on the ivory handle is magnificent.

I thought the Michael Price dagger at the farm was fabulous, but the craft on this one is better. Excellent work."

"*Fossilized* ivory," Carl's voice said from the phone.

Cavanaugh smiled slightly in victory.

"Lance taught us nothing should die in order to be used to make a knife," Carl's voice said.

The agent in contact with the communications center gestured to indicate they were tracking the signal from the third phone.

"Mastodon ivory," Cavanaugh said. "From Alaska, right? I like the way you put black epoxy over the main part of the blade and then let the edge of the blade retain its natural shiny metallic look. Contrasts beautifully with the ivory."

"Coming from you, that's high praise, Aaron."

"Nothing should die in order to be used to make a knife?"

"You heard Lance say that often enough."

"So the killing's justified only after the knife is made?"

"Hey, don't get moralistic, Aaron. In Delta Force, you did your share of work with a blade. Did you figure out why I left you the khukri?"

"A threat?"

"Well, let's just say a warning." Carl's voice was faint. "For all you know, I'm watching you right now. Maybe I've got a rifle trained on you. Maybe I could blow you to hell at this very moment."

"I doubt it, Carl. You're blocks away. You made sure this phone registered the number you're using. You want us to track the signal you're using, but all we'll find is another set of phones taped together. Are you enjoying yourself?"

"Just like when we were kids and pretended to be soldiers hunting one another in those woods at the bottom of our street."

"But we're not kids any longer."

"Exactly. Do you remember the last time we were in New Orleans? The blast we had, drinking, listening to jazz all night? Except for the club behind you, there's hardly any place that has jazz anymore. The bar down the street features karaoke, for God's sake. When I was there earlier, some kid with rings in her nose was screeching the lyrics to 'Love Shack.' The jazz clubs were turned into strip joints and sex-toy shops. Pitiful. This town'll destroy your memories if you don't get out as fast as you can. Ease off. Go back to Wyoming."

"Not much there for me now. You burned my house, remember?"

"Rebuild it. Occupy your time with something constructive. Stay out of my business. Aaron, do you want to make a bet?"

"What do I get if I win?"

"I'll stop whatever I'm doing if you can tell me what's the most expensive knife in the world."

"Then I win, Carl. The most expensive knife is the solid gold replica of King Tut's dagger that Buster Warenski made."

"Wrong," Carl's voice said.

"Come on," Cavanaugh said. "When Buster made that knife in the 1980s, it was valued at fifty thousand dollars. Two years ago, the estimate was raised to a half million. But then the collector said it wasn't for sale at any price."

"Yeah, Buster did a great job on that dagger. But it's still not the most expensive knife in the world. You want to know what *is*?"

"Sure, Carl. Go ahead and tell me."

"The knife that costs you your life."

Carl made the statement sound so final that Cavanaugh had the sense that the conversation was over.

"Whatever you're doing," Cavanaugh said, "stop it. You've got so many people looking for you, you can't expect to get away. Negotiate with me. What can we give you to make this stop?"

The phone's subtle electronic hiss stretched on and on.

"Carl?"

Suddenly, Cavanaugh heard voices coming through the phone: angry men cursing.

The agent in contact with the communications center lowered his phone and said, "They tracked the signal to the Garden District. A team found two phones taped together in a flower bed outside one of those old mansions."

"*Both* phones are active?"

"Yes."

"Sure. Carl did it again. He relayed his voice from a further location. If I go there, he'll start talking to me through another relay phone. He'll lead me all over the city. A cemetery or the river will probably be next."

"Anything to distract you from trying to stop whatever's going to happen tomorrow," Jamie said.

"Oh, we're going to stop it."

10

As a police car hurried Cavanaugh and Jamie through the busy night, he noted increasing signs of the trouble that was coming. More law-enforcement officers on the streets. More barricades. In several parks, large groups of demonstrators were gathered, some of them sprawled on sleeping bags, others gesturing in animated discussions. Distant sirens wailed.

Jamie looked at her watch. "Almost one o'clock. Not much time."

They reached the Delta Queen Hotel, one of several on Canal Street. The district's proximity to the convention center made it a logical place for many of the delegates to stay, although Cavanaugh hated the idea of so many influential people being grouped so close to each other.

He and Jamie showed their ID to guards and ran past barricades into the ornate hotel's lobby. Next to the check-in desk, the concierge directed them to a banquet room on the hotel's second floor. They ran up a staircase and along a thickly carpeted corridor to where they showed their ID to more guards and entered the brightly lit command post for Global Protective Services.

Tables filled the huge room. Computers and monitors seemed everywhere, phones ringing, printers whirring, dozens of agents working to keep up with the massive influx of information. Outside the hotel, more sirens wailed.

For several weeks prior to the conference, GPS advance teams had traveled to New Orleans and studied the security layout of this and other hotels where clients were staying. They assessed possible routes to the conference as well as to various tourist spots that the delegates would insist on visiting. The agents took photographs. They made diagrams of streets and the room patterns of floors and suites. They created time charts of how long it took to get from one building to another. They did background checks on limousine services and arranged for armored cars to be available. They hired guards to make certain the limos weren't tampered with and that the guards inspected each vehicle on a regular schedule. They arranged for medical personnel to be on call and made detailed notes about how to reach the nearest hospitals. These and numerous other preparations were the hidden part of the protective world, each security measure made to look effortless when in fact everything was the result of intense planning.

Amid the organized commotion, a tall woman looked up from a printout she studied. A former Marine who was also a former member of the Defense Intelligence Agency, she wore dark slacks and a dark blouse that could be made to look formal or casual, depending on the type of client she needed to blend with. Her red hair was cut short. Her strong features had only faint makeup and were tight with fatigue. Looking as if she welcomed the distraction, she approached Cavanaugh and Jamie.

"I hear you're the new boss."

"Just my bad luck," Cavanaugh said. "Jamie, this is Dawn Finch, the best advance agent we have."

"Flattery, flattery."

"Dawn, this is my wife, Jamie."

"Word came my way about that, also. You're full of surprises."

"Let's hope *tomorrow* doesn't bring surprises."

"Here's how it lays out." Dawn led them to various charts mounted on a wall.

Cavanaugh studied them. "I don't like the pattern of the choke points." He referred to the potential attack sites common to every route that the attendees would need to use.

"Yeah, the convention center's in a centralized area. The Warehouse/Arts district, Canal Street, the French Quarter. Everything's within a few blocks. No matter how we try to vary the routes, everybody has to pass through the bottlenecks here and here. Bombs and snipers are the big worry, of course. We tag-teamed with the police and the government agencies to reinforce security at those points, keep the protestors back, occupy roofs, watch for movement at windows, that sort of thing."

"How many agents?"

"Eight thousand and more on the way."

For a moment, Cavanaugh thought he hadn't heard correctly. "*Eight thousand?*"

"To hit that many people, you need a dispersive weapon, a dirty bomb, something like that," Dawn continued. "Homeland Security has radiation and pathogen detectors all over the waterfront. Any vehicle that enters the downtown area is being scanned."

"Give me a list of the most influential delegates."

"What do you have in mind?"

"To make sure tomorrow doesn't happen."

11

"Remember almost the first thing I told you when I brought you to our training camp?" Carl asked Raoul.

They paused outside the warehouse. Insects swarmed around the overhead light. A tugboat sounded from the Mississippi's gloom.

"I told you rest was the operator's friend, that you should take advantage of it whenever possible. You put in a good day, Mr. Ramirez."

Raoul stood straighter in response to the term of respect.

"You did what you were instructed. You executed your orders perfectly. Now it's time to reward yourself with sleep. It'll be difficult. Plenty of exciting things going on. But tomorrow's where we're headed, and the most important thing you can do now is stretch out. Even if all you manage to do is keep your eyes shut, you'll still get the benefit. Clear?"

"Yes, Mr. Bowie."

"Okay then." Carl slapped him on the back and gave an approving nod to guards near the door. Then he opened it and ushered Raoul inside.

The warehouse was in shadow, only a few dim lights near the lavatories. A male smell filled the area, the musky odor of men primed for action. Bodies shifted on cots, occasionally snoring and coughing.

Carl gave Raoul another reassuring slap on the back and watched him go to his cot, where the young man obediently closed his eyes. Carl surveyed the other men, then switched his attention to the knapsacks against the wall to his right. Sixty of them.

"Nerve gas," Carl had told the swarthy man weeks earlier. Blazing noon. They were at the training camp, far from the shots and explosions of the conditioning exercises at the main part of the facility.

Sweating from the heat and humidity, his suit sticking to him, the man peered into a corrugated metal structure large enough to hold one hundred chickens. The birds clucked, pecked at each other, and scratched the dirt floor, looking for food.

"I got these from a farm-supply outlet a hundred miles from here," Carl explained. "Just another customer. Nobody paid attention."

Stepping among the chickens, sending them scurrying noisily, Carl set a knapsack in their midst. "As you know from your experiences in Iraq, detonation devices of this sort require a two-step process, one to arm them, the other to set them off. The two stages guarantee that the devices won't go off prematurely—in our hands, for instance."

The man eyed the knapsack and took several steps back from it.

"After all, we want to make sure the detonations occur at the scheduled time and place. So this is step one." Carl pulled a cord on the side of the knapsack. Then he made his way through the clucking chickens, emerged from the structure, and shut the door. He walked around the building and lowered metal panels over the screened windows.

The van was a hundred yards away through ferns and weeds. Some of the ground was spongy and caused the man to look annoyed at the seeds on his pants and the mud on his dress shoes.

Carl opened the van's side hatch and indicated a television that received signals from a camera in the concrete-block structure. The image came from high in a corner, angling down toward the chickens.

"The pull-cord on the knapsack activates a radio receiver attached to the detonator," Carl said. "On the day of the event, all the receivers—sixty of them—will be calibrated to a common frequency used by law enforcement. God knows, there'll be plenty of law enforcement in the area, all of them eager to stay in radio contact with each other. One of them will inadvertently set off the detonators. But just in case, I'll send a radio signal of my own. For the safety of this demonstration, I chose an uncommon frequency so a radio broadcast from a police car that happens to be in the area won't get us killed. Ready?"

The man nodded.

Carl pressed a button on a transmitter and drew the man's attention toward the television.

A black cloud billowed from the knapsack. Ominously silent, it filled the structure so thickly that the chickens could no longer be seen.

"Of course, the nerve gas is colorless," Carl said. "The smoke is for dramatic effect. For the TV cameras. Otherwise, all the viewers at home would see is people falling down. Terrifying enough. But this way, the cameras will see mysterious black clouds spreading and joining. The viewers will watch with rapt attention as the clouds clear, and then the thousands of corpses will slowly come into view. Bear in mind, there won't be any on-site announcer to describe what's happening. Everybody in the area will be dead."

On the screen, the black cloud continued to be all that was visible.

Carl pressed another button. At the distant structure, metal clanked. The window coverings opened. The black cloud emerged from the gaps. On the TV screen, daylight struggled through the black haze.

"The gas kills only when breathed," Carl said. "This particular batch isn't full strength. It'll lose its potency by the time it disperses this far. Even so, you might want to put on *this*."

He gave the man a gas mask. Then he too put on a mask.

A bird flew over the structure. Skirting the edge of the dispersing black cloud, it folded and fell, crashing onto the building's roof.

Another bird fell.

Then another.

"As you see," Carl said, pointing toward the screen, where the black cloud dispersed enough to reveal that all the chickens were dead, "it's extremely effective."

Another bird plummeted.

In the warehouse, Carl glanced from the knapsacks and made a final assessment of the men on the cots. They slept restlessly, primed for the morning. Satisfied, he took his own advice and left the building. He closed the door and went down an alley to a parking space where he entered the van Raoul had used to transport the six men who'd chosen not to participate. Crawling into a sleeping bag, he reviewed what needed to be done the next day. His knife in one hand, his pistol in the other, he practiced hard-learned bio-feedback techniques and drifted off to sleep. The last thing his mind considered was the end of the conversation at the training camp.

"For the actual event," the man asked, "the gas will be full strength?"

"Absolutely."

"How much area will it cover?"

"Spreading the men out, arranging them in a strategic pattern? All of downtown New Orleans."

12

"I once had the privilege of meeting Frank Sinatra when he performed in my country," the Japanese trade minister said. He wore a white bathrobe over gray pajamas. His thinning hair was rumpled. With sleep-puffed eyes, he peered over slim spectacles.

Seated across from him, Cavanaugh waited.

"Indeed, some months later, in Los Angeles, I was invited to an event at Mr. Sinatra's home, something one of his Republican politician friends asked him to host," the official continued. "There was a sign next to the intercom at the gate. It said, 'You'd better have a damned good reason for ringing this bell.' I assume *you* had a good reason for waking me at this hour."

"I apologize." Cavanaugh bowed slightly.

The official gave no indication of caring about apologies.

"I want you to think twice about continuing with the conference, Mr. Yamato." Out of habit, Cavanaugh scanned the suite, pleased that the draperies were closed and that security personnel were on duty. "You're one of the most influential members of the World Trade Organization. I strongly recommend that you persuade your associates to move the conference to another location."

"Because of your friend."

"*Former* friend," Cavanaugh said. "He's capable of anything."

"And *you* aren't capable of anything? Such as *stopping* him?"

"It doesn't make sense to risk—"

"You think this is about money, don't you?" Yamato asked.

Cavanaugh didn't reply.

"About multinational industries and power," the official continued. "Or pride? Do you think this is about pride? Six months ago, the demonstrators forced us into a premature conclusion of a conference. Now we refuse to be humiliated again. Is that what you believe?"

"That's one of the theories I've heard," Cavanaugh said.

"This isn't about wealth or power or pride. This is about survival."

Cavanaugh leaned forward, listening closely as more sirens wailed outside in the darkness.

"And this isn't about demonstrations as a voice in a debate," Yamato said. "If you're right, your former friend wants to extend the rioting into something far more extreme."

"The only motive that makes sense to me is that he's being paid by terrorists."

"Whose purpose, by definition, is to destroy the underpinnings of our system."

"That's right."

"If we allow them to intimidate us, if we run and hide, we surrender to that intimidation. Eventually, it becomes easier to continue running and hiding. If we don't resist at every opportunity, we can never win. Am I afraid? Yes. Do I believe people will die tomorrow? Yes. Perhaps I myself will die. But if there's an atrocity, perhaps public outrage against the terrorists will make it less likely that future atrocities will occur. You fight in one way. *We* fight in another. I cannot recommend canceling or moving the conference."

"I admire your bravery," Cavanaugh said, "but—"

"It's not bravery," Yamato told him. "It's the refusal to act like a coward."

An alarm suddenly blared.

Shrill. Ear-torturing. Outside the suite.

Cavanaugh and Yamato swung toward the door.

Someone pounded on the door. "Mr. Yamato!"

Cavanaugh drew his pistol.

"Mr. Yamato!" a voice yelled. "Cavanaugh!"

Through doors on each side of the suite, Japanese protectors rushed in from adjacent rooms. They held pistols. Cavanaugh took for granted that they'd been electronically monitoring the conversation and knew that he wasn't a threat. Stepping in front of the trade minister, shielding him, they directed their fierce attention toward the main door as the alarm kept blaring and the pounding persisted. Next to it, a television camera revealed the corridor outside and a security agent yelling Mr. Yamato's name.

Cavanaugh hurried to the door, glanced back at Yamato's protectors, got a nod of agreement from them, and freed the lock.

Inching the door open, ready with his weapon, Cavanaugh saw other agents pounding on other doors, shouting the names of occupants.

The agent told him, "Smoke in the elevator shaft!"

Before Cavanaugh could respond, another shouted, "And the front stairwells!"

"Fire?"

"Or toxic gas! We don't know yet!"

As the alarm blared, sirens wailed outside the hotel, presumably from fire trucks and other emergency vehicles.

"What about the *back* stairwells?" Cavanaugh asked.

Protectors and trade ministers peered starkly from doors along the corridor, security agents talking urgently to them.

"So far, they're clear."

"This could be a way to funnel us into a trap," Cavanaugh said.

Behind him, the suite's phone rang. Past the open doors in the corridor, Cavanaugh heard other phones ringing.

At the end of the corridor, abrupt movement made Cavanaugh stare toward an agent who jerked his gaze from the elevators and frowned at the ceiling. Gray vapor swirled above him. "The air conditioning vent! Something's coming from the—"

"Gas! I smell it!" another agent yelled. Coughing, he shifted back from a vent in the ceiling.

Cavanaugh pivoted toward a security agent, who set down the phone in Yamato's suite and raised his voice to be heard above the fire alarm. "I've just been told that the hotel lobby is filled with smoke."

"Can we use the service elevator?" Yamato asked.

"No. Even if it's clear of smoke, you can't use it. What if it stops between floors? Plus, we don't know what we'll face when the door opens."

Yamato headed toward the corridor. "Can we use the back stairs?"

"Seven floors. Do you have a heart condition, any problem that makes the distance too far for you?"

"No." Yamato hurried along the corridor. "But what if, as you noted, this is a way to funnel us into a trap?"

Cavanaugh smelled the acrid vapor wafting from the air-conditioning vents. Along the corridor, agents and clients were coughing as they rushed. Peering back, Cavanaugh saw black smoke at the bottom of the elevator doors. "At the moment, all we know is we can't stay here."

An EXIT sign marked the door to the rear stairwell. Eyes burning, Cavanaugh turned toward Yamato and the other officials. He gestured to the GPS agents who'd been watching the elevator and the stairwells. "Tony, use your phone. Tell the FBI what's happening. Arrange for plenty of vehicles to meet us downstairs. The rest of you, let's clear the way."

One man banged the door open, trying to startle an enemy as Cavanaugh aimed into the stairwell. All he saw were harsh lights, concrete steps, and metal railings. Using the metal door for cover, he pivoted around it, showing only enough of his body to allow him to aim toward the higher levels. No one confronted him.

"Clear!" he shouted.

An agent hurried past him, jumping three steps at a time to the lower landing, crouching and aiming downward. "Clear!"

Footsteps scraped on concrete as an agent scurried upward to make sure that the higher levels didn't conceal a threat. Hard to do when the eighth-, ninth-, and tenth-level doors crashed open, other hotel occupants rushing to escape. Amid the blare of the fire alarm, Cavanaugh heard their echoing clatter as he and the other agents added to it, charging methodically downward, checking the next level.

"Clear!"

"Clear!"

Someone groaned. Cavanaugh turned toward a commotion behind him, an elderly man in pajamas tripping, falling down the stairs, two young men catching him.

"Is he all right?"

The man's face was twisted in pain.

"He broke his leg!" someone shouted.

Urgently, Cavanaugh motioned for Yamato's protectors to accompany him down the stairs. Flanking their client, they led the way, the rest of the officials and their protectors following. Adding to the din, cell phones rang. Officials shouted into them, trying to be heard, having even more trouble hearing.

The door to the fifth level banged open. A GPS agent aimed into the stairwell, saw Cavanaugh, reacted to the swarm of people descending from the upper floors, and urged his own group of officials and protectors downward. The fourth and third doors remained closed, the hotel offices behind them unoccupied at night.

At the second floor, Dawn Finch and the communication team escaped into the stairwell. Smoke followed them.

Dawn slammed the door, telling Cavanaugh, "We waited as long as we could. I grabbed these." She showed him a handful of computer discs, the security data she'd accumulated about the conference. "Is anybody hurt?"

"A trade minister broke his leg." Staring down, watching for threats, Cavanaugh hurried with her toward the ground floor.

"Wait," Dawn said. "I don't see Jamie."

"She isn't here. There were so many officials to try to convince, we split up. She's talking to trade ministers at the Southern Belle."

"*That* hotel's being evacuated, too."

"*What?*"

"*Four* hotels were hit."

"I need to find her."

Reaching the ground floor, Cavanaugh spun toward the officials and security teams who pressed toward him. His agents knew immediately what to do, no need to discuss forming a barricade in front of the door and holding out their arms.

"Everybody, relax!" Cavanaugh shouted. Amid the fire alarm and the reverberation in the stairwell, he could barely be heard.

"Stop!" he yelled.

The other security teams shifted into the proper mode, calming the officials.

"You're safe!" Cavanaugh told them.

The footsteps stopped clattering. The reverberation diminished. In a few seconds, the only sound was the fire alarm.

"The door behind me is metal. The walls are concrete. There's a firewall. Nothing's going to happen to you here. I'll check outside. Vehicles are supposed to be on their way. We'll evacuate you as soon as possible."

"What if there's a sniper?" an Italian trade minister demanded.

"Too much commotion. Too much to aim at," Cavanaugh said. Noticing that many of the officials wore pajamas, he said, "Find a security agent who's your size. Put on his jacket. That'll make it hard to distinguish you from the team. A sniper wouldn't be able to decide who's a target and who's a protector. By the time, he managed to sort everybody out, you'd be gone from here."

As protectors took off jackets and gave them to their clients, Cavanaugh noticed the elderly man who'd fallen. Two young men cradled him.

"We'll get an ambulance as soon as possible," Cavanaugh assured him. He nodded to Tony, the agent he'd spoken to earlier. Again, without the need to discuss it, Tony understood what needed to be done.

"The password's Treadmill," Cavanaugh said.

Tony freed the deadbolt lock and opened the door. Aiming, Cavanaugh scanned the chaos in the street behind the hotel, then rushed outside.

13

The rumble of parked emergency vehicles was so loud that Cavanaugh barely heard Tony locking the door behind him. Sirens approached. Exhaust fumes choked the street as men in uniforms rushed through a panicked crowd. Lowering his weapon, Cavanaugh saw a van creeping through the commotion, other vehicles behind it. Emergency workers set up more barricades, preventing pedestrians from getting in the way.

Before the van came to a full stop, Rutherford was already jumping out, hurrying toward Cavanaugh. "*Are you all right?*"

"Confused as hell, but not hurt. I've got at least thirty trade officials behind this door. We need evac vehicles and an ambulance. A trade minister broke his leg."

"On the way." Rutherford indicated more headlights coming toward them.

"Someone told me this happened at *three* other hotels," Cavanaugh said.

"Smoke, but no explosives. Gas, but it wasn't lethal," Rutherford said. Like the security agents in the background, he scanned the rooftops.

"It smelled like *tear* gas," Cavanaugh said, his throat raw, his eyes still burning.

"We think the demonstrators couldn't wait until tomorrow and started early. To give us a taste of what to expect from them."

"Yeah, I can taste it all right."

"Someone had a heart attack in another hotel. The paramedics think he'll survive. But if this had been Duran's work…"

"We'd all be on the way to the morgue," Cavanaugh said.

Across the street, an insistent woman—tall, with a runner's build and long, brunette hair—emerged from the darkness. Lights flashing across her, she forced her way through the crowd. She wore rubber-soled, low-heeled street shoes and dark slacks, her long legs increasing her stride. Veering around an approaching van, she rushed toward Cavanaugh, who broke into a smile and hugged her.

"*Are you okay?*"

Jamie gripped him tightly. "Yes. What about *you?*"

Cavanaugh smelled smoke in her hair. He was so relieved to have her safely with him that the smoke might as well have been perfume. "I couldn't be better now that I know you're safe."

Rutherford, a widower, looked as if he wished somebody would be overjoyed to greet *him*. He knocked on the door and shouted, "This is John Rutherford! FBI! We have the area secured! Evacuation vehicles are waiting for you!"

Cavanaugh shouted, providing the code word, "It's okay, Tony! You can get off the Treadmill!"

Slowly, the door opened. Wary security personnel stepped out, their principals in the protective box they formed.

14

Carl squirmed in his sleeping bag, sirens disturbing his rest. More sirens than usual at night, even in a city renowned for being festive. More than expected as police tried to contain protestors gathering for the demonstrations in the morning. His pistol and knife close to him, he instantly cleared sleep from his mind and sat up.

The van didn't have windows at the sides or the back. That made him feel sheltered and yet vulnerable to a sneak attack. He knelt and stared past the front seats through the windshield toward the end of the dark alley. The flashing lights of a police car sped past, its wail peaking.

A major accident, Carl thought. *Or a fire. Or perhaps a collision on the river. Nothing to concern me.*

Wrong. Everything *concerns me.*

He squirmed from his sleeping bag and climbed into the front seat, getting behind the steering wheel. Driving from the alley, he followed the direction of the lights and the sirens. When he realized they were leading him toward the heart of the downtown area, he found a safe side street on which to park. Then he got out, locked the vehicle, secured his weapons under his loose-hanging shirt, and went the rest of the way on foot. Passing barricades and growing groups of demonstrators, he avoided the conference center and angled toward the nearby business district, where he encountered so many uniforms and barricades that he was reminded of occupation zones he'd seen years ago in Bosnia.

At last, he reached his destination: fire trucks and other emergency vehicles surrounding a hotel on Canal Street, smoke spreading from the ground floor.

No, not *one* hotel, Carl realized. A further commotion led him to another hotel on Canal Street, more fire trucks and smoke. And another.

And another.

It's amateur night, he thought.

A guy with a sweat shirt labeled OUTSOURCE THE WHITE HOUSE TO INDIA on one side and KEEP AMERICAN JOBS AT HOME on the other told a buddy, "Man, if it's starting this early, tomorrow's gonna be wild."

A group chanted, "Stop burning the rain forests!"

Keeping a distance, avoiding the appearance of any association with the protestors, Carl drifted into the shadowy background. About to return to the van, he paused for a final look at the smoke coming from the hotel.

Tomorrow's going to be wild? he thought. *You have no idea.*

15

"Good morning, gentlemen."

The men looked up from cleaning their weapons as Carl entered the warehouse. Walking toward the podium, he rubbed his hands together enthusiastically.

"I trust you had a restful sleep."

They gathered before him.

"We've got another fine breakfast for you. Sugared beignets and chicory-flavored coffee. Eggs with Creole sauce and Cajun sausage. Hash browns. Steak. Biscuits. Gravy. Your basic Heart Association, cholesterol-friendly meal."

They chuckled.

"Eat up because you might not have a chance for another meal until tonight. No complaints? Everybody happy?"

They nodded.

"Outstanding. So are you ready to earn your pay, to do what you've been training for, to prove how skilled you've become, and show me an honest morning's work?"

"Yes," they answered.

"I can't hear you."

"Yes!"

"Damned straight. An honest morning's work. Once we get to Texas, you can let off steam. But right now and until noon, we're all business. Finish your breakfast. Roll up your sleeping bag. Fold your cot. Set it over by the door. Put the TVs, DVD players, computers, and video games over there as well. Pretty soon a truck'll arrive, and we'll load everything. Those of you on KP duty will take the leftover food and deliver it to a homeless shelter, a different one from the one yesterday's KP team delivered to. No point in wasting food. Share and share alike. Camp without a trace. Words to live by, gentlemen. As soon as this warehouse looks the same as when we arrived, you'll put on your knapsack and double-check its number with the corresponding number on the map. You'll make sure you know how to get to the street you've been assigned. I don't want anybody wandering around asking directions from a cop."

They chuckled again.

"Control. Discipline. That's what you've been training for. Otherwise, you're just the street thug you were when I took pity on you and brought you to the training camp. Make sure you're wearing your Navy SEAL watch. They're each set to exactly the same time. After you put on your knapsack and go to your assigned street, you'll mingle with the demonstrators. The conference starts at nine. There'll be delays because the protestors will try to block the streets. Some of the trade ministers will want to make an impressive late entrance. But let's assume that by ten o'clock, all the participants will be there and the opening ceremony will be in full swing. Exactly at ten on your watch, take off the knapsack and pull the cord on it. Everybody clear on that?"

They nodded.

"When the black smoke comes out and mingles with all the other black smoke and covers your area, pull out your pistol and empty it into the air. Enjoy yourself. Stampede the protestors. But for God's sake, don't shoot any of them. We've been hired to disrupt the conference, not kill people. Clear on *that?*"

Again, they nodded.

"Okay, clean up this warehouse. Put on the knapsacks. Make sure you know where you're going. Don't bunch up after the event. Go your separate ways, and regroup two days from now at the campground near Galveston. Gentlemen, you want to make a bet?"

They studied him, eager to hear his next words.

"I bet you make me proud. I bet you prove that I was right to choose you, that you're worth all the training you received. You're not thugs anymore. You're operators. I can't think of a higher compliment to give anyone. Operators."

16

Cavanaugh felt a hand on his shoulder and jerked awake. It took him a moment to realize that he was in a hotel room, that sunlight struggled past the draperies, and that Jamie, who looked as tired as he felt, was leaning over him, nudging him.

"William's here," she said.

Cavanaugh squinted up toward William, who stood at the foot of the bed, holding a briefcase. Despite the long plane trip, William's expensively tailored, pinstriped suit was impeccably pressed. His pristine white shirt was perfectly starched, his striped tie dramatically authoritative. With his coiffed gray hair and projecting chest, he had never looked more like a high-powered attorney.

"He brought us beignets." Jamie bit into one.

"...coffee," Cavanaugh murmured.

"That, too." Jamie handed him a Styrofoam cup.

Groggy, Cavanaugh sipped the hot bitter liquid. "You're the best attorney anybody ever had, William."

"Maybe I should open a catering service."

"What time is it?"

"Six-thirty."

Cavanaugh turned toward Jamie. "You let me sleep this long?"

"You were dead on your feet."

"Unfortunate choice of word. *You* were exhausted too, but you still got up earlier than I did."

"Things on my mind. Not to mention nightmares."

"I know all about nightmares." Cavanaugh sat slowly, his head feeling as if ball bearings rolled inside it.

"On the phone last night, you told me to get here as quickly as possible," William said.

"And by God, you did. Thank you, William."

"Is there a legal emergency?"

"There's going to be," Cavanaugh told him. "And that's probably not the only emergency."

"When the Gulfstream picked me up at Teterboro airport, my escorts said that I wouldn't be needing their protection any longer."

"That's right," Jamie said. "You're not in danger now. Or perhaps I should say, you're not a specific target."

"As opposed to being part of a general target?" William frowned.

"I'm going to need your help," Cavanaugh said. "But I can't lie to you. You'll probably be risking your life to help me. Are you willing to do that?"

286

"As I recall, you saved *my* life back at your ranch—not to mention, several times you kept some of my litigation opponents from trying to strangle me."

"Then you'll do it?"

"When do we start?"

"Good man," Cavanaugh said. He stood from the bed and looked down at his rumpled slacks and shirt. "Don't have a change of clothes."

"There's no time to change them anyhow," Jamie said, peering down at her own wrinkled slacks and blouse.

"Or shave." Cavanaugh scraped a hand over his beard stubble.

"We're going to hell," Jamie said.

"*Carl* is." Cavanaugh went into the bathroom, shut the door, and urinated. He put his head under the cold-water faucet and soaked his hair. He toweled it, ran a comb through it, then came out and took a bite from what was left of the beignet in Jamie's hand. After snapping his pistol holster to his belt, he put on his sport coat, which reeked of tear gas and smoke. "Knives. Two spare magazines. Looks like I've got everything but a winning lottery ticket."

Jamie attached her gun and knife to her belt, then hid them with her blazer. "Ready?"

17

Seven a.m.

The communications center was even more crowded and noisy than the evening before, radios crackling, keyboards clattering. But in contrast with the chaos of yesterday, everyone in the room seemed paralyzed. Motionless agents stood before a vast array of closed-circuit television monitors that showed intense crowds assembling on various streets around the conference center. Helmeted police officers and military reservists formed a line behind barricades, holding shields and batons, ready to respond if the crowd pushed beyond the checkpoints.

Somber, Rutherford sensed movement behind him and glanced back, frowning toward Cavanaugh and Jamie. His gaze lingered on William.

"Any developments?" Cavanaugh asked, reaching him.

A stranger shifted next to Rutherford. A mustached man of fifty, he had gray hair, the severely short cut of which exposed a crescent of skin above each ear. His tie was rigidly knotted, his suit meticulously pressed, his shoes obsessively shined. Of medium height and weight, with pallid skin suggestive of a career spent at a desk, he wore a white shirt whose style communicated the impression he gave: buttoned-down.

"The demonstrators are getting ready to try to block the streets so the trade ministers can't reach the conference," Rutherford said.

"It starts at nine?" Jamie asked.

"It was supposed to," the severe-faced stranger said.

Cavanaugh studied him, puzzled. "I don't believe we've met."

"This is Deputy Director Mosely." Rutherford subtly emphasized the stranger's title, as if giving Cavanaugh a warning.

"Pleased to meet you." Cavanaugh extended his hand. "This is my wife Jamie, and *my* name's—"

"You've got *plenty* of names, I hear." Mosely ignored the offered hand. "I'm surprised you can keep them all straight."

Cavanaugh looked at Rutherford and then back at Mosely. "Is something wrong?"

"You got what you wanted," Mosely said.

Two FBI agents edged toward them.

"I'm not sure what you mean."

"Four hotels needed to be evacuated," Mosely continued. "The ones with the most trade delegates. There wasn't any way to put them in rooms in other hotels in the area. Every place was full. In fact, there weren't enough available hotel rooms within twenty miles. We had to take them to the nearest city: St. Charles. All the confusion forced the WTO to cancel today's meetings."

"They *did?*" Jamie asked.

"Don't act so surprised," Mosely answered.

Other agents stepped closer.

"Hey," Cavanaugh said, "if the conference got postponed, it's a good thing, right? It gives everybody more time to try to find Carl and stop whatever he's doing."

"Oh, it's a good thing. Definitely," Mosely replied with sarcasm.

Frowning with greater puzzlement, Cavanaugh turned toward Rutherford. "John, on the flight here, you and I talked about how important it was to get this thing canceled, how crazy it was that the WTO wouldn't allow itself to appear to give in to the demonstrators. Now the trade ministers did what we hoped they would. A lot of lives have probably been saved."

"Oh, I'm all for saving lives." Mosely stood more rigidly. "But when you couldn't convince the WTO to change its mind, do you think it was right to change their minds for them?"

"You're not making sense," Jamie said.

"Who's *this* man?" Mosely pointed toward William.

"My attorney," Cavanaugh answered.

"You suspected you'd need one?"

"William has one of the most attentive, logical minds I've ever come across. I thought it would be a good idea to include him. Maybe he'll notice something we haven't thought of."

"Well, he's definitely going to come in handy," Mosely emphasized.

On the various TV monitors, the crowd kept getting larger.

"Wait'll they find out the conference isn't happening today," someone said.

Mosely pointed toward a door. "We need to talk," he told Cavanaugh. "You too," he told Jamie. He looked at William. "And by all means, *you're* invited, counselor."

18

The door led to an office that was bare except for a metal table and chair. Two FBI agents joined the group. In the cramped quarters, everyone remained standing.

Although Rutherford shut the door, Mosely still had to raise his voice to be heard above the noise outside. "You were seen entering all four hotels."

"Of course," Jamie said. "We visited trade ministers in those hotels, trying to persuade them to cancel the conference. We identified ourselves to security personnel."

"Someone went to the bottom of the elevator shafts and put smoke bombs in them," Mosely told her. "Someone went to the roofs, opened the air-condition vents, and put tear-gas grenades inside. Spray paint disabled the lenses on the security cameras in those areas."

"That makes sense," Jamie concluded. "That's the way *I'd* have done it."

"Which begs the question," Mosely said.

"Wait a minute. Are you suggesting *I* did it?" Jamie sounded indignant.

Cavanaugh looked at Rutherford. "What's going on here, John?"

"Sorry. I'm afraid it's out of my hands."

William stepped forward. "Before this conversation goes any further, are you arresting my clients for what happened at those hotels?"

"Counselor—" Mosely put rancor into the title. "—I invited you to listen, but I don't believe you're licensed to practice law in the state of Louisiana."

"That doesn't mean I can't act as a concerned knowledgeable friend." William pulled out his cell phone. "But if you want to put this on an absolutely legal basis, I'll make a call to my good friend Lester Beauchamp. He and I went to Harvard together. He's also my brother-in-law and the former assistant attorney general for the state of Louisiana, not to mention the most respected defense attorney in New Orleans. I'm sure he'll be more than happy to represent my clients."

"Let's be clear, counselor. Are you advising your 'friends' not to answer my questions?"

"If you're arresting them, I'm advising *you* to read them their rights."

"We don't have anything to hide," Jamie insisted.

"A man and a woman matching your description were seen in the area of the elevator shafts and the roofs just before the incidents happened," Mosely said. "Your height, your build, your clothes."

"Where are your witnesses?" William challenged.

"They worked the night shift at the various hotels."

"That doesn't answer the question. The witnesses are where? My friends are more than willing to stand in a lineup and be identified—or *not* be identified, which is what's going to happen."

Mosely's gaze almost faltered. "We haven't been able to contact them this morning."

"Perhaps because they're drug addicts semiconscious from illegal substances," William continued. "Until you find these so-called witnesses and prove their reliability, these accusations are hearsay and possibly slander."

"I was speaking with the Japanese trade minister when the smoke and the tear gas went off in his hotel," Cavanaugh said. "How could I have been in two places at one time?"

"Did I neglect to mention that the detonation devices were on timers?" Mosely asked.

"And where are we supposed to have gotten all that stuff?"

"Your file emphasizes how resourceful you are. You have an obsession with being close to what you call 'bug-out bags' that have all sorts of equipment in them. Your wife carries a specialty knife that has numerous tools in the handle. She wouldn't have had any trouble opening the air-conditioning ducts. For all I know, your corporate jet is loaded with other equipment you needed."

"Then search the jet," Cavanaugh told him.

"But not before you get a warrant," William pointed out.

Mosely's eyes flared. "You present yourselves as such ethical people, so concerned about protecting your clients. You claim you're the edge between right and wrong. Then you show how irresponsible you are by putting all those trade ministers at risk. Thanks to your stunt, one of them broke his leg. Another had a heart attack. Two cars rammed into emergency vehicles speeding toward the hotels."

"Was anybody killed?"

"No, but that doesn't mean what you did is right!"

Cavanaugh looked at Rutherford. "Make him understand, John. Whoever's responsible saved a lot of lives. Now that the conference has been postponed, Carl will need to change his plans. Meanwhile, we've got time to catch him."

Mosely's pallor mutated to a fiery red. "You think you deserve a medal? Well, *I* think you took a privilege the Bureau gave you and abused it. You're a guest here! A civilian. You don't have any authority, but you decided you were running this operation, breaking God knows how many laws. If it's up to me, you'll go to prison."

"Thank heaven, it *isn't* up to you," William said. "After I talk to Lester Beauchamp, I'll phone the district attorney and—"

The door opened. Everyone turned toward an agent.

"There's been a new development," the uneasy man told them.

"Don't tell me the riots have already started," Mosely said.

"Fifteen minutes ago, a man and a woman were caught trying to put tear gas into the conference center's air-conditioning ducts."

"*What?*"

"And smoke bombs in the elevator shafts."

Mosely groaned.

"Do the suspects look like these two?" William asked the agent in the doorway.

"Yeah, in a way. Sort of. They're white and more or less the same age."

"You're not deceiving me," Mosely told Cavanaugh and Jamie. "Those are copycats."

"Without talking to the suspects, how can you be sure?" William asked.

"Because, unlike your friends, they don't have the skills to manage that kind of sabotage. Because the man and woman today got caught."

"An interesting distinction but without legal merit. If you're not going to arrest my friends, I trust you have no objection to allowing them to go about their business."

"Not here. They don't have *any* business in this area."

"Uh, sir," Rutherford said.

Mosely stared. "Yes, Executive Assistant Rutherford?" He emphasized "Assistant," reminding Rutherford of who had the greater authority.

"If I could make a suggestion."

"By all means." Mosely clearly wished that Rutherford had kept quiet. "Everyone knows I'm always open to constructive ideas."

"I think it might not be a bad idea to let them stay. Cavanaugh understands Duran's personality better than anyone. As events develop, he might be able to predict what Duran will do. Plus, Cavanaugh's the only person here who can identify him."

Mosely continued staring.

"We need to seem to use every available resource," Rutherford said. "Otherwise, in an inquiry, there might be questions."

Mosely's narrow gaze pivoted toward Cavanaugh and Jamie. To Rutherford, he said, "This time, keep them under control." He yanked open the door and entered the communications room, followed by the agents.

Except Rutherford.

As the noise from out there filled the small area, Cavanaugh said, "Thanks, John."

"I feel my job dangling in the wind."

"I owe you. I'm sure it wasn't easy disagreeing with him."

Rutherford looked pained. "Please, remember what he warned you about. You're civilians. Don't make me sorry I trust you."

Cavanaugh solemnly followed him into the communications room.

19

On the TV monitors, the crowd got bigger.

On one of the screens, a woman carried a large, heavy purse. She hid an object in her hand and periodically looked at it.

"Part of the radiation detection team," someone in the communications room explained.

On another screen, a man held what looked like a smartphone: a pathogen detector.

"Two hundred members of the Homeland Security team are out there, weaving through the crowd, scanning it. But how many diseases can they program their detectors to test for? They can't possibly scan for *everything*," someone said.

"How big is the crowd?"

"Fifteen thousand."

"And getting larger," an agent said. "What difference does it make if the conference was postponed? As long as they think it's happening, there'll be a riot."

"And maybe worse," Rutherford murmured.

Next to him, Cavanaugh said, "Right now, somebody needs to send agents into that crowd. Make them act like the protestors. Tell them to spread the word, sounding pissed off that the conference was canceled."

Mosely's gaze was icy as he turned toward Cavanaugh. "And I bet you're dying to get out there and show us how it's done."

20

Seven-thirty.

On the podium, Carl faced his men and said, "To tell the truth, I'm jealous. You're going to have so much fun, I decided to join you. There are six knapsacks that aren't being used because of the men who opted out. I might as well take one and enjoy myself. Mr. Ramirez is going to put on a knapsack and join the fun also."

Raoul looked up, not having expected to hear that. But to Carl's approval, Raoul concealed his surprise and nodded firmly.

"Has everyone got a watch?" Carl asked.

They did.

"Is your knapsack on? You know where you're going?"

They did, obviously pleased that Carl would be joining them.

"Leave here in groups of six. Split up as soon as possible. New Orleans has an excellent bus system, so you won't have trouble getting to the target area. But those buses are equipped with video surveillance cameras, so sit separately and look out the window, not at the camera. Remember, when it's ten o'clock, take off your knapsack and pull the cord at the side. Make sure you're wearing these fingertip pads so you don't leave prints when you drop your gun. Everybody clear? Good. Gentlemen, show me how disciplined you are."

21

Eight.

Mingling with demonstrators across from the conference center, Jamie felt pushed and shoved. The heat of so many bodies increased the humidity, making her sweat. Someone stepped on her shoes. They had steel caps under the leather: standard equipment for protectors. Even so, she felt the jolt. But she was less concerned about damage to her body than she was about someone bumping against the weapons under her blazer, realizing what they were and trying to take them. She kept her elbows tight against her sides, bracing them against her handgun and her knife.

Although the conference wasn't scheduled to start for another hour, the demonstrators were already shouting their complaints about Third World sweatshops, increased pollution, climate change, the vanishing rain forests, the over-fished oceans, and chemicals in the food supply.

"Wait'll the motorcades arrive," someone said. "We'll stop those greedy bastards from getting into the building."

"If we need to, we'll push their cars over," someone else vowed.

Jamie pretended to be listening to her cell phone. She hurriedly lowered it and blurted to the people around her, "My friend says she saw on television that the cars won't be coming."

Someone overheard and asked, "What?"

"They just announced the conference was postponed."

"Bullshit."

"No, it's true," Jamie said, the crowd banging against her. "The chief of police just made an announcement. Something happened at four hotels last night. Smoke and tear gas. The trade ministers were moved out of town."

"…ministers were moved out of town," Cavanaugh said.

"Harry, listen to this guy. They canceled the conference."

"Like hell."

Cavanaugh pointed toward his cell phone. "That's what my friend just told me. He saw it on television."

"A trick. They want us to give up and leave. Close to nine o'clock, those pigs'll arrive in their limos. Bet on it."

22

Eight-thirty.

The spreading chaos forced Carl to park a half mile away. Even from that distance, he heard the shouting.

"Sounds like the party started." He grinned at Raoul. "This is what it's all about. Everything else is just waiting."

He and Raoul stepped from the van and made certain their loose shirts covered their weapons.

"Here's your party favor," Carl said, handing Raoul his knapsack. He put on his own.

They followed Magazine Street six blocks north of the convention center. As they neared the shouting, they saw a bus come to a stop. Amid numerous departing passengers, six members of their group emerged, keeping separate as instructed. Like good operators, they never glanced at each other as they took separate directions through the crowd.

"Don't you love it when a plan comes together?" Carl asked Raoul.

Progress became difficult. Carl passed one of his men halfway down the block, exactly where he should be. Although they didn't acknowledge one another, their brief eye contact told Carl how much the man was reassured.

And so it went. Shifting through the crowd, passing various members of his team, Carl verified that everyone was obeying instructions. That gave him reason to believe they would *continue* to obey.

By nine, he and Raoul reached the conference center, where the crowd was so immense, the protestors so animated that the four-lane boulevard in front was almost totally blocked. Behind barricades, police officers readied themselves to push back.

"*Where are the cars?*" a demonstrator demanded to his friends. "They should have been here by now!"

Energized by anticipation, Carl continued through the turmoil, buoying his widely separated men with his presence while he made sure they were in place.

23

Nine-thirty.

Cavanaugh and Jamie pushed through the crowd, reached the back of a large delivery truck, and showed their IDs to a camera above the rear doors. A moment later, one of the doors opened, hands helping them up.

Against the inside wall, armed men were ready in case Cavanaugh and Jamie were not who they claimed or someone charged in after them.

The truck's interior was a compact version of the communications center. Computers, two-way radios, and closed-circuit monitors seemed everywhere. An electronic glow filled the compartment. On the screens, the police and the protestors shoved at each other outside the convention center, but because the police had body armor, helmets, shields, clubs, and Tasers, they had more success. The silence of the images contrasted with the tumult outside.

"I told as many as I could about the radio announcement that the conference was postponed," Jamie said.

"We've got plenty of other operators blending with the crowd, spreading the word," an FBI agent said.

"Doesn't seem to be doing any good." Cavanaugh frowned toward the violence on the monitors.

"Wait." An agent pointed.

On one of the screens, Cavanaugh saw the protestors shifting back from the police. On another screen, the shrubs that separated the four lanes of Convention Center Boulevard were becoming visible. Protestors stared both ways along the thoroughfare, baffled that the motorcade hadn't arrived.

At a two-way radio, an agent said, "I'm getting reports that portions of the crowd are beginning to realize the conference isn't going to happen."

"Look," Jamie said. "At the end of the boulevard. Near the casino. On Poydras Street. Some of them are drifting away."

24

Nine forty-five.

A cloud crossed the sun, casting a cool shadow. Then the sun returned, the heat again as palpable as the humidity. The press of bodies smelled of sweat as Carl and Raoul made their way through them. After crisscrossing the target area, they entered Girod Street, moving away from the conference center. Carl verified that the final man he needed to check was in place.

As Carl reached the intersection of Tchoupitoulas Street, where Raoul was scheduled to wait until ten o'clock, he noticed that the going seemed easier, that he no longer needed to struggle against the crowd. Then he realized that the tide had turned, that the demonstrators were moving *away* from the conference center instead of toward it, that he was being carried by the flow.

He stopped an angry-looking man and woman. "What's going on? Why are you leaving?"

"Damned thing's been canceled."

"No," Carl said, jostled by the passing crowd.

The woman held up an iPhone. "It's all over the Internet. Four hotels got smoked-bombed and tear-gassed last night. The trade ministers were evacuated."

"But that can't be!" Carl insisted.

"I'm telling you, the bastards left town."

"*No motorcade? No opening ceremonies?*"

"Nothing. Down at the convention center, they're getting their heads cracked for no reason."

As the disgusted man and woman moved onward away from the pointless battle, Carl stared down Girod Street. Except for a truck parked two blocks away, all he saw were demonstrators moving in his direction, a steady mass of them filling the pavement and the sidewalk.

Four hotels? Furious, Carl remembered following last night's sirens and arriving at hotels that were surrounded by the flashing lights of emergency vehicles while smoke streamed from the buildings.

Aaron? he thought. *Was that* your *doing?*

"Is it over?" Raoul asked.

For a moment, Carl didn't hear him. "Over?"

"If the conference isn't going to happen, what's the point of the smoke?"

"Quiet." Carl pulled him toward a wall. "Somebody might hear you."

"But we don't have much time. We need to split up and hurry so we can tell the men to forget about ten o'clock."

"Forget about ten o'clock? No way."

Carl's employers were more frightening than anyone could imagine. Good God, the last thing he needed was them hunting him because he took their money and didn't follow through on what he promised.

"But what's the point?" Raoul demanded. "You told us we were hired to make sure the conference didn't happen. *Mierda*, look around you. It *isn't* happening."

The point, Carl couldn't tell him, was the Secret Service, the U.S. Marshals, the Diplomatic Security Service, and the Homeland Security Response Team, not to mention operators from Global Protective Services and other major non-government firms. They'd been lured into coming to New Orleans to safeguard the World Trade Organization. In eleven minutes…

"We're going to do what we promised," Carl said.

"But—"

"This isn't some stupid-ass street gang. We don't act on impulse. We don't change our mind whenever we feel like it. We follow orders."

"But what if the orders stop making sense?"

"If a man pays me to do something, I do it. Maybe he didn't tell me all his reasons. My job isn't to think. It's to follow through on an assignment. Are you a coward?"

"Of course not," Raoul said, his face reddening. "You know I've done everything you asked."

"You're supposed to be an *operator*."

His face even redder, Raoul said, "I *am* an operator."

"Then show me!" Carl tugged Raoul along the wall. "Here. The middle of the block. This is where you're supposed to wait!"

More disappointed protestors went up the street.

Carl checked his watch. "In ten minutes, follow the plan!"

"Okay!" Raoul said angrily. "All right!"

Stop, Carl warned himself. *What am I doing? Keep control.*

He touched Raoul's shoulders with apparent affection. "Don't take it personally. I'm just stressed, keeping track of all the details. You're my most dependable operator. Never doubt that."

Raoul didn't reply, but the compliment clearly made him less angry.

"When you're in *my* place, you'll understand the burden of responsibility. I'm sorry." Carl gripped Raoul's shoulders harder. "I know you won't let me down."

Raoul didn't answer.

"Is everything straight between us?" Carl asked.

"Yes."

"Then make me proud." Carl stepped away.

"Where—"

"I need to hurry and get to my spot," Carl said over his shoulder. He struggled to conceal the irritation he felt for losing control.

What the hell's wrong with me? This is almost over. Keep cool. Don't screw things up.

The crowd carried him toward the edge of the killing zone. He reached the middle of the next block, where nine minutes from now he was supposed to pull the cord on his knapsack.

He shifted toward a wall. Freeing himself from the passing crowd, he took off the knapsack and shoved it into a garbage bin. Rejoining the protestors, he was eager to let them propel him to safety. He had plenty of time to get to the van and flee the area. A few seconds after ten, he would press a button on the transmitter in his jacket pocket. If the police frequencies hadn't already set off the detonators, the signal he sent would do the job.

Something made him glance back.

Raoul was at the refuse bin, gaping at the discarded knapsack.

25

When Raoul had started to ask "where," his intention hadn't been to find out where Bowie was going. What he wanted to know was whether he should meet Bowie at the van or whether he was supposed to get to Galveston on his own. Because of their argument, they hadn't finalized their arrangements. The way Raoul felt, he wasn't sure he *wanted* to meet Bowie at the van. Talking to me like he's a *chingado* guard in the joint. But as seconds passed, the heat of Raoul's anger lessened. He didn't want trouble between them. The truth was, what Raoul felt for him was what he was supposed to feel for his father.

Nine minutes. Plenty of time to ask him and get back here.

Raoul slipped into the crowd, moving toward the next block, where Bowie would be waiting for ten o'clock to occur. There. Ahead. Raoul saw the lanky man, slightly taller than those around him, flowing with the crowd.

Bowie shifted toward a wall. *Exactly where he's supposed to be*, Raoul thought, working toward him. But then Raoul frowned, seeing Bowie take off his knapsack. Raoul frowned harder when Bowie shoved the knapsack into a garbage bin. Bowie rejoined the crowd.

Stunned, Raoul came to the garbage bin and gaped at the knapsack Bowie had abandoned. He raised his eyes, searching the crowd. Bowie was glaring back at him.

The force of it made him dizzy. The fury in Bowie's eyes was so overwhelming that Raoul felt shoved. He actually took a step backward, his dizziness intensifying. The world he thought he knew spun. The reality he depended on seemed to ripple beneath his feet, making him unsteady.

At once, another world took its place. A mask seemed to slip from Bowie's face. The man Raoul thought of as a father suddenly became a stranger. Worse than that: an enemy. The rage and hatred on Bowie's face shot across the distance and made Raoul lurch back another step.

Immediately, Bowie pushed through the crowd, hurrying toward him. A terrible heat primed Raoul's muscles. The most searing fear he'd ever known fired his protective instincts and sent him fleeing.

26

No! Carl thought. Shoving protestors out of the way, he charged toward Raoul. *The look on his face! He suspects! If he warns the others…*

The constant stream of demonstrators held him back. Turning sideways, ramming his shoulder through the crowd, he was reminded of playing in high-school football games, his father yelling drunkenly from the bleachers.

"Hey!" a man said. "Watch where you're going!"

"Out of my way!"

"Don't ram into me, jerk-off!"

The man gasped, struck in the stomach, baffled by the blood streaming from him.

His knife at his side, Carl shoved harder through the oncoming crowd. Ahead, Raoul stayed close to the wall, gaining distance, managing to reach the next block.

A young man with a knapsack saw them coming.

Raoul shouted a warning.

The team member looked confused.

Raoul shouted again.

The team member saw Carl chasing Raoul. Fear tightening his face, he turned and ran.

27

"What's *this* about?"

In the communications truck, an FBI agent pointed toward a monitor.

"Where?"

"Here. *This*."

Cavanaugh and Jamie walked toward it.

"Somebody's in an awful hurry to go the wrong way," the agent said.

"Not *one* person. Three," Jamie noted.

The camera was angled downward from a roof. The screen showed the crowd filling the street, countless protestors shifting away from the conference center. Breaking the pattern, a line of three men charged in the opposite direction, thrusting their way through the demonstrators.

"Seems like the guy in back's chasing the others," the agent said. "Look at how frightened they are. They keep glancing back to see if he's gaining on them."

"And what about *this*?" Another agent pointed toward a monitor that showed a commotion nearby. People formed a circle around a man scrunched sideways on the pavement. He held his stomach, which was dark with spreading liquid. A woman raised her face and soundlessly screamed.

"Looks like he's been shot," an agent said.

Cavanaugh concentrated on the three men forcing their way south as everyone else went north. "Can you get a closer view of the guy in back, the one who seems to be chasing the others?"

"Sure."

The agent twisted dials. Immediately the camera magnified the man at the rear of the line.

As the face got larger, Cavanaugh felt a chill speed along his nerves. "Not shot. Stabbed."

"How do you know?"

"Because the guy chasing the others is Carl."

28

Eight minutes before ten.

Fighting his way through the crowd, Carl saw another young man with a knapsack. Raoul shouted a warning. When the man, already on edge, looked behind the team members charging toward him and saw the rage on Carl's face, he too broke into a run. Carl shouldered through more protestors.

"Hey, dickhead, watch who you're slamming into," a man said, only to groan and double over as Carl lunged past.

Ahead, Raoul hurried straight ahead while the team members he'd warned dropped their knapsacks and split to the right and left, racing down side streets.

They'll alert the rest of the team, Carl thought in a fury. *I trained them to feel they belong to a tightly knit unit. That's how they'll act now, protecting each other.*

Because of Raoul. All the effort I spent on him, he's still a punk.

Ramming through the crowd, getting nearer, Carl angrily calculated that he had sufficient time to teach him the consequence of disloyalty.

Ahead, the son of a bitch hurled his knapsack away and shouted to a team member waiting farther along the block.

29

"What are they throwing away? Knapsacks?"

"They seem to be shouting at people at the side of the crowd." Cavanaugh stared at the monitors.

"Men standing against walls," Jamie said. "They all have knapsacks. Here, here, here, and…my God, once you notice them, they seem to be everywhere."

"I hate to imagine what's in them." An agent picked up a microphone. "Surveillance One to all units."

As the agent described what he saw on the screens, Cavanaugh pointed toward the one that showed Carl. "What street is he on?" he asked another agent.

"Girod near Fulton."

Cavanaugh grabbed a lapel microphone and an earbud. "Keep telling me which direction he's taking."

Before Jamie had a chance to think about going with him, Cavanaugh opened the door and jumped to the street.

"Grab the guys with the knapsacks!" the agent said into a microphone. "For God's sake, be careful. We don't know what's in them."

When Jamie jumped to the street, Cavanaugh had disappeared into the crowd.

30

Seven minutes before ten.

Without looking back, Raoul had a visceral sense that Bowie was gaining on him. His stomach felt on fire. His lungs ached. His legs felt wobbly. Although he stayed along a wall, there were still too many people in front of him. Crashing, shoving, he shouted to another team member, "Bowie lied! Something's wrong! Get rid of the knapsack!"

The already-nervous team member seemed to be grateful for the excuse to run. Raoul leapt over the dropped knapsack and veered left onto Fulton Street. The side street had fewer departing protestors, giving Raoul a chance to run faster.

But he continued to have that visceral sense that Bowie was gaining on him. He saw yet another team member and shouted his warning. For proof, all the man needed was a frightened look behind Raoul toward where Bowie was getting closer. The man dropped his knapsack and raced toward the next corner.

Perhaps Raoul only imagined the footsteps pounding behind him. But he didn't imagine the increasing tightness in his lungs, the worsening unsteadiness in his legs. Never having been tested, never having passed five missions, he was ruled by fear instead of using adrenaline to give him strength. *Gotta breathe. As long as I'm running, he has the advantage. Gotta stop.* On the opposite side of the street, an archway beckoned. *Gotta fight.*

Raoul crashed past retreating demonstrators, knocking a man to the pavement. "Damn it!" he heard behind him, but all he cared about was reaching the protection of that archway. He charged inside, but there wasn't a door that he could slam and lock. A musty brick corridor led to metal stairs angling up. Shadows beckoned as he raced to the stairs. He heard footsteps rushing behind him. Drawing his pistol, he spun and saw a blur as Bowie shouted, *"Want to make a bet?"*

The shout boomed off the bricks. Along with the fright of Bowie's swiftly enlarging figure, the noise was loud enough to startle Raoul. His knees bent. His shoulders hunched. His hands rose to shield his chest. He fumbled to squeeze the trigger, but at once, he felt Bowie walloping into him, jolting the remaining air from his lungs. He landed hard on the stairs, their sharp edges chopping his back as Bowie continued hurtling into him, punching him repeatedly, except that the punches were stabs and now it was blood instead of air that escaped from Raoul's lungs.

31

"You dummy, didn't you learn *anything?* Don't bring a gun to a *knife* fight!" Carl drove the blade deep into Raoul's chest, his stomach, his throat, again and again, each thrust sending a shudder through the body. Gas escaped. Blood flew. He kept pounding until the torn mass beneath him was barely recognizable. With each frenzied blow, he felt as if he were out of himself, smiling down at the punishment he inflicted. Courage. Honor. Sacrifice. But the greatest military virtue is *loyalty.* This is what you get for—

Carl was suddenly in his body again, conscious of the gore beneath him, the blood dripping from his hands, his shirt, his face. A tremor went through him, a spasm of release that raised his head and arched his back. His vision turned gray. Then everything was vivid before him, Raoul's death-contorted body, the black metal stairs now sprayed with red, the crimson-covered knife in his hand.

How long have I been…my God, what time is it? His watch was so covered with blood that he had to wipe it on the back of his shirt before he could see its display. Four minutes to ten. The last thing he remembered was charging into the passageway at *six* minutes to ten. Several quick slashes with his knife. That was his plan. Thirty seconds to teach Raoul his lesson. In and out. Five minutes to get away. Not all the team members would be warned that something was wrong. Some would pull the cords on their knapsacks and activate the detonators, releasing the gas. Not enough to save the mission, although the target area was still dangerous. He needed to run.

Looking like this? Straightening, he felt the wet heaviness of the blood on his shirt. *Every security agent in the crowd will converge on me. Damn you, Raoul.* He kicked the body, cursing Raoul for making him lose control.

Think! There's got to be a way to—

He tore off his shirt. In muggy New Orleans, a man without a shirt attracted little attention, but someone with a blood-soaked shirt was another matter. He hurried to a faucet next to the stairs, rinsing the blood from his hands and face. He almost ran back along the alley toward the street, but a commotion out there told him that somebody was charging in this direction.

Trying a door on his right, he found it locked. He tried a door on his left, with the same result. Terribly aware of time passing, he charged up the stairs, all the while folding his knife and shoving it with his pistol into one of the baggy pockets of his pants. His shoes clattering on the stairs, he reached the top and turned the knob, groaning when he found that *this* door, too, was locked.

Past a closed window next to it, he heard two women talking. When he pounded on the door, their voices stopped.

"Let me in! It's an emergency!"

Below him, footsteps sounded in the passageway. He stared down, feeling his heart skip.

32

"The middle of the block! The south side!"

Listening to the voice give instructions through his earbud, Cavanaugh veered through the crowd on Fulton Street. Reaching an archway, he heard the voice say, "That's where they went! Backup's on the way!"

"No time!"

Staying to the side, he drew his pistol and listened. With the noise of the departing protestors behind him, he thought he heard the echo of footsteps on a metal staircase.

Working to control his heartbeat, he took a breath, held it, counted one, two, three, exhaled through his mouth, one, two, three, and inhaled through his nose, one, two, three. Pivoting into view, he aimed along a brick passageway and saw the lower half of a man climbing the stairs. A blood-covered body lay at the bottom. A blood-soaked shirt was near a faucet.

Continuing to aim, Cavanaugh eased along the passageway, shifting his feet carefully, taking care to place them firmly and maintain his balance. Nearing the stairs, he heard pounding on a door above him. Ignoring the corpse at his feet, he aimed upward.

Carl.

Slowly, Carl's surprised look changed to a welcoming smile. "My, my." The smile widened. "How are you doing, Aaron?"

"I've been better." Cavanaugh tightened his finger on the trigger.

"Yeah, I'm not having a great day, either." Carl's lanky chest was bare, his ribs showing through his lean muscles. His narrow face dripped water. He held up his wet, powerful-looking arms in surrender. "It's been too long, Aaron. You must be taking a lot of vitamins. Either that, or marriage agrees with you. You don't look any older."

"For certain, *you* haven't changed. I see you're still having control problems."

"Well, he turned against me. I know disloyalty doesn't bother *you*, but it makes me furious."

"Apparently, a lot of things do."

"Only people who trick me into believing they're my friends when they're actually the opposite."

"Come down the stairs, Carl."

"I don't think so."

"Slowly. Carefully."

"What happens if I tell you to screw off? You'll shoot me?"

"Yes."

At the top of the stairs, voices behind a door made Cavanaugh frown.

"Not today, good buddy."

The door opened. Before Cavanaugh could fire, Carl vanished into the building.

Cavanaugh raced up the stairs, but not before the door slammed shut. He yanked at the knob. Locked. He pounded on the door. Beyond it, he heard shots. The door was metal. Carl knew that pistol bullets wouldn't go through it. That meant the bullets were intended for someone else: whoever had opened the door. Cavanaugh thought he heard footsteps running along a corridor.

"He's in a building on the second floor!" Cavanaugh said into his lapel mike.

"We'll seal off Fulton and the opposite street!" the voice promised.

Loud noises made Cavanaugh spin and look down the stairs. A half dozen agents rushed along the passageway. The person he focused on was Jamie.

"He went through here!" Cavanaugh yelled to them. Seeing flowerpots at the top of the stairs, Cavanaugh grabbed one and hurled it through the window next to the door. Convinced that Carl wouldn't have risked staying, he reached through, freed a lock, and raised the window. Air conditioning cooled his hand.

As Jamie and the agents ran up the stairs, Cavanaugh peered through the window, studied an office, decided that he had to take the chance, and crawled inside. Two women lay on the floor, streaming blood.

"We need an ambulance!" Cavanaugh shouted into his lapel mike. Rushing, he unlocked the door.

Jamie and the agents hurried in but stopped at the sight of the gunshot victims. One agent knelt, trying to help them while Cavanaugh and the others raced along a corridor.

In an office, a man peered up, hiding behind a desk. In another office, a man lay bleeding.

Reaching a lobby, Cavanaugh saw a receptionist trembling in a corner behind her desk. Glass doors led to an elevator and stairs.

"We've got operators waiting on the street outside! He can't get through!" an agent told him. Gun drawn, the agent ran past Cavanaugh and charged down the stairs, the others following.

But Cavanaugh and Jamie lingered.

"What's above us?" Cavanaugh asked the trembling receptionist.

She opened her mouth. No sound came out.

"You're safe now," Jamie said. "What's above us?"

"Other offices."

"And?"

"A roof garden."

33

Three minutes to ten.

A team member stood against a wall as the crowd passed. Impatient, he checked his watch, looked up, and paled when two men confronted him, aiming pistols.

"Hands up!"

"Turn around! Against the wall!" an agent shouted to another team member, this one a block away. "Jay, get the knapsack off him!"

"I think it's safe to take the knapsack!" an agent yelled to his partner three blocks away. "If it's a bomb, it doesn't have a manual trigger. Otherwise, he'd have blown himself up by now."

Someone in the crowd overheard. "*Bomb*?"

"Where?"

"A bomb!"

"Run!"

"Keep your hands away from the knapsack!" an agent shouted.

When the team member drew a pistol, the agent protected the knapsack and shot the man in the head.

The dying man fired into the sidewalk, fragments hitting the crowd.

Panicking, a woman tripped. Stampeding, three men fell over her. Screams filled the street.

34

Cavanaugh and Jamie hurried up the stairs. An office door was open, startled faces peering out.

"Close the door," Cavanaugh told them.

"Take cover," Jamie warned.

Continuing higher, they reached an open door, sky beyond it.

"Stay here," Cavanaugh said. "You don't need to do this."

"Babe, I'm not letting you do it alone."

Cavanaugh went first, aiming to the right while Jamie aimed to the left. Amid blazing sunlight, potted trees and shrubs surrounded them. Patio tables, chairs, and sun umbrellas provided a lunch area through which Cavanaugh and Jamie darted, searching for a target.

"Over there," Jamie said.

Fifty yards away, a shed-like structure had an open door. With the Mississippi spread along their right, they raced toward the exit.

"He used the roof to head east! Farther along the block!" Cavanaugh shouted into his lapel mike. "The corner!"

They entered a stairwell in time to hear footsteps rumbling below them.

"He's almost onto the street!" Cavanaugh shouted.

"We're waiting!" a voice shouted through his earpiece.

Shots made Cavanaugh pause. Even in the stairwell, he heard screaming along the street.

35

Two minutes to ten.

Nearing the ground floor, Carl heard shots outside. Beyond a window, a frenzy swept through the crowd, people swarming to get away. He veered into an office, where workers stared in alarm at the chaos outside. Turning toward him, they reacted with greater alarm to his bare chest, the water dripping from his face, and the gun in his hand.

"Out!" Carl yelled. When they didn't respond, he chose a man with red hair and shot him. "*Out! Out! Out!*"

The survivors collided with each other, all of them trying to get through the door at once. Firing above their heads, Carl watched them surge out, joining the turmoil on the street. Agents out there would be totally overwhelmed.

He grabbed a suit coat off a chair and put it on. He picked up a chair and hurled it through French doors. He surged through and joined the screaming, stampeding crowd.

36

Reaching the ground floor, Cavanaugh saw that the door was open, people rushing past. Taken aback by the chaos, he heard a window shatter in an office to his left.

"Go *that* way," he told Jamie, indicating the open door. "I'll take the side!"

He rushed into the office in time to see Carl leap through the window and charge into the crowd. Immediately, Cavanaugh followed, shouldering past men and women, straining to keep Carl in sight. Another distant shot increased the crowd's panic. "Bomb!" he heard somebody say. The hysterical need to get away was so powerful that, for a moment, Cavanaugh was actually lifted off his feet by the crush of people around him. It was like being swept along in a flood while he tried to break free of the current and maintain a direction.

Ahead, he saw Carl struggling to go sideways through the crowd. But that didn't make sense. Where Carl seemed determined to go— to the right—was a dead end. He couldn't escape there. Abruptly, Cavanaugh realized he was mistaken. What he thought of as a dead end was actually the Mississippi River. *The river.* That was how Carl planned to get away.

37

One minute to ten.

No matter how hard Carl strained to break free from the crowd, it caught and squeezed him, carrying him with it. The force was so great that he had trouble breathing. Jabbing with his elbows, ramming with his shoulders, he managed to clear a space and thrust closer to the river.

He was too confined to be able to look at his watch. But he sensed that ten o'clock was almost upon him. Any second, the few remaining members of the team would pull the cords on their knapsacks, the police radio frequencies would trigger the detonator, and black clouds filled with nerve gas would drift across the remaining demonstrators.

Vaguely aware of a building on his right, he jabbed harder with his elbows and cleared enough space to draw his pistol, firing into the air. The deafening shots made people scream and run faster. Several fell, others piling onto them. Carl scrambled over them.

Ahead, part of the crowd raced across train tracks, up steps, and into a tunnel. He fired several more shots to keep the crowd hurrying and charged into the shadow of the tunnel. When he broke into sunlight, a wide expanse of concrete ended at the water. Barges and tugboats chugged along the Mississippi. He vaulted a waist-high fence and dove past a paddle wheeler moored at the shore, plunging beneath the surface.

38

Racing after him, Cavanaugh saw Carl sprinting toward the river. He stretched his legs to their limit and sped closer, but not enough. There wasn't sufficient time to close the gap. As Carl vaulted the fence, Cavanaugh didn't have time to stop and try to control his exertion-trembling body enough to aim. In a blur, Carl dove past a paddle wheeler into the river. Three seconds later, Cavanaugh vaulted the fence. Afraid of being weighed down, he dropped his gun and the knife on his belt. He threw off his jacket, tugged his claw knife from its neck sheath, gripped it securely, and dove.

The river was cold. Gritty. Greasy. Submerged in the weight of the muddy water, he heard the muffled vibrations of engines. The water was so murky that when he opened his eyes, he couldn't see. All he could do was keep kicking with his heavy shoes, blindly sweeping his arms, following the course that Carl had taken into the water. As he thrust with his hands, he gripped his claw knife, slicing, hoping to wound Carl's legs. Already short of breath from running, he felt pressure in his chest, his lungs demanding air. He kept thrusting, his clothes weighing him down.

Caught in the current, no longer hopeful that he was on Carl's trajectory, he thrust again with the knife. The engine vibrations were louder. Then he realized that what he heard was the pounding of his heart. Lungs feeling as if they'd explode, he kicked upward, pawed through the water, broke the surface, and gaped at a tugboat looming toward him. It was so close that he had to shove his feet against its hull, thrusting his body away before he was struck. Nonetheless, the suction of the current pushed him back against the hull. *The propeller,* he thought.

A row of tires hung from the tug's side, buffers that kept it from banging against a dock. Stretching up, Cavanaugh snagged a hand into one of the tires and felt an agonizing strain in his shoulder as the tug carried him along. Staring back, he saw Jamie standing at the side of the river, helplessly watching his struggle.

In the distance, a black cloud rose.

Farther over, so did another.

Suddenly understanding Carl's plan, he prayed that Jamie would realize what she needed to do. As a third black cloud rose, he raised his free hand, the one with the knife, waving insistently that he was all right, urging her to go. She returned his wave, and with a frightened look behind her toward the isolated black clouds, she broke into a run.

PART EIGHT:
THE FELLOWSHIP OF THE KNIFE

1

"So far, we know almost one thousand people died," Dawn Finch told him, "including forty federal agents and fifteen GPS operators."

Cavanaugh was too overwhelmed to reply. He sat in a Coast Guard office, where a patrol boat had brought him after he was transferred from the tug. Although he clutched a blanket wrapped around him, he shivered—only partially because of his wet clothes.

Jamie brought him a steaming cup of coffee. "At least, another two thousand needed medical care, enough to fill the emergency wards in every hospital in the area."

"But it could have been significantly worse," an FBI agent said. "The canisters were so carefully sealed, none of the toxin detectors in the crowd registered what was in them. If the conference had occurred, if all the protestors had remained in the area, if all the knapsacks had been detonated and all the gas released…"

"The preliminary estimate is that at least fifteen thousand protestors would have died, plus the thousands of tourists and business people in the downtown area," another agent explained. "Lord knows how many others would have needed medical attention. This came close to being the worst—"

Outside the office, boat engines rumbled. A door opened. Everyone turned toward a Coast Guard officer who entered. Rutherford and Mosely followed, neither of them looking happy.

The Coast Guard officer reported, "No luck finding him. We're beginning to think he might have been hit by boat traffic on the river. Perhaps he was knocked unconscious and drowned."

"He didn't drown," Cavanaugh said.

"One of our men saw you chase him," an FBI agent reported. "Our man was too far away to help, but he managed to see both of you go into the water. Only you came up."

"Maybe he struck his head on something under the water. Maybe his body's caught on something down there," the Coast Guard officer hoped. "We're dragging the area. We sent for divers."

"And you're searching the banks all the way up and down the river?" Cavanaugh asked. "Using helicopters as well as boats?"

"Of course."

"Still think you're running things?" Mosely demanded.

The hostile interruption made everyone turn.

"Just contributing to the conversation," Cavanaugh said.

"Sure."

Except for the rumbling of the boat engines, the room became silent.

"Don't mind me," Mosely said.

Cavanaugh told the Coast Guard officer, "Carl's an expert swimmer. In high school, he was state champion. On our Delta Force team, it was one of his specialties. I once saw him swim under water for a minute and forty-five seconds. Given the current, he could easily have gone quite a distance downstream before surfacing, probably using a boat for cover. He's miles away by now."

"We'll explore every possibility."

"Yeah, definitely running the show," Mosely said.

Again the room became silent. Next to Mosely, Rutherford's dark face brooded.

"Have you got a problem?" Cavanaugh asked.

"Yeah. But you've got a bigger one." Mosely turned to the Coast Guard officer. "Does this office have a DVD player?"

"On this computer."

"Then let's take a look at *this*." Mosely handed him an unlabeled disc.

The officer inserted it and pressed buttons on the keyboard.

Everyone stepped close.

For a moment, the screen was blank. Then it showed a corridor. At the far end, elevator doors were visible.

"This is from the Delta Queen Hotel's security-monitor system," Mosely explained. "Very up-to-date technology. No blur. No haze."

The screen continued to show the corridor and the elevator doors at the end.

"Not too interesting so far," William said. "How much of this do we need to—"

"I'm just setting the scene, counselor. Building suspense. The camera's on the hotel's maintenance-room level. There's also a camera at the end of the corridor, near the elevator doors, and one on the stairwell leading down. *Those* cameras had their lenses spray-painted, but I guess you didn't know about this one," Mosely told Cavanaugh.

"There's no way you can prove my clients had anything to do with spray-painting those cameras," William protested.

"Keep watching, counselor."

A man appeared at the end of the corridor. Crouching, moving past the elevator doors, he aimed a can and sprayed paint at something above him.

"This still proves nothing," William said. "That man is so far away, he's impossible to identify. He could be *anybody*."

"I knew you'd say that, counselor, so for your edification, I had the image magnified."

The man at the end of the corridor now filled the screen.

"A good likeness, don't you think?" Mosely asked.

The man was unmistakably Cavanaugh. He finished spraying paint at something above him. Then he used lock picks to open a panel next to the elevator. He pressed a button inside the panel, causing the elevator doors to open. The floor of the shaft was empty, the elevator at a higher level. After flicking a switch on a box, he lay on his stomach and stretched down to set the box at the bottom of the shaft. Finally, he closed the doors and stepped out of sight.

"This proves nothing. The image could have been manipulated," William insisted. "With fifty dollars of software from a computer store, I could make it seem as if *you* opened those elevator doors."

"Yeah, but the person who magnified that image is an FBI computer technician who'll testify under oath that the face wasn't altered."

"I can't wait to cross-examine that agent."

"Not in *this* state, counselor. You're not licensed. Also, I did some checking about your famous brother-in-law. The great defense attorney Lester Beauchamp is on vacation in Europe."

On the monitor, a green-tinted image showed a flat roof.

"The green comes from a night-vision camera," Mosely said. "At the Southern Belle. *That* hotel has a state-of-the-art surveillance system also. The management even put a camera on the roof. Those are air-conditioning units you see in the background. And here comes our co-star, who spray-painted the surveillance cameras on the stairway to the roof but who didn't know about this other camera."

On the screen, silhouetted by the lights of the city, a faraway woman came into view. She knelt, removed a knife from her belt, and unscrewed its cap. Abruptly, the image was enlarged. The woman was clearly Jamie.

"No objections this time, counselor?" Mosely asked.

"I'll save them for court."

"You do that."

The group watched as Jamie pulled tools from the knife's handle and used them to unscrew an air-conditioning duct. Next, she flipped a switch on an object and put it inside. Finally, she used the tools from her knife to close the duct.

"The switch activated a timer on a tear-gas bomb," Mosely said. "The switch Cavanaugh tripped was on a smoke bomb. Naturally, he and his wife used latex gloves. No fingerprints. But seeing's believing, don't you think?"

"You already know my opinion about that," William responded.

"Well, here's *my* opinion. Cavanaugh or Stoddard or whoever you are, you got lucky. The trade minister who broke his leg needed a pin put in it. The one who had a heart attack is still in intensive care. The people whose cars hit the emergency vehicles are also still in the hospital.

You put four hotels out of business for the days it'll take to repair the damage. Millions of dollars have been lost."

"Now you sound like you belong to the Chamber of Commerce," William said.

"Counselor, shut your mouth. You have no legal authority here." Mosely stared at Cavanaugh. "You're under arrest."

"Don't do this," Cavanaugh said.

"You have the right to remain silent. You have the right to an attorney. If you can't afford an attorney, one will be appointed—"

Cavanaugh turned toward Rutherford. "John, isn't there any way you can stop this?"

"The time for him to have stopped this was last night," Mosely interrupted. "Trusting civilians is one of the first things an agent learns not to do."

2

"Bankrupt?"

In a stark interview room in the New Orleans detention center, Cavanaugh and Jamie listened in disbelief to what William told them.

"You knew Global Protective Services was in precarious financial condition."

"That's why I ordered the cancellation of the planned Tokyo office and cutbacks at the others," Cavanaugh said.

"Both were good ideas, but the downsizing came too late. It's not your fault. Duncan overextended the corporation, and this is the consequence. In normal circumstances, the cash outflow and inflow might have been balanced enough for Global Protective Services to rebuild its strength. But the attack on the New York office and the tremendous resources you put into security for the conference tipped the balance. It's only a matter of weeks before GPS collapses."

"Couldn't you have waited a while longer before you gave us more bad news?" Jamie asked.

"Unfortunately, that wasn't an option. The judge set bail at a half million dollars for each of you. I tried to persuade the bail bondsman to accept GPS as equivalent value for the bond. But even a hurried examination of the corporation's finances was enough to show how wobbly its balance sheet is. If you want to be released on bail, you need to use your personal resources as collateral."

"Personal resources?" Cavanaugh seemed not to understand.

"Your Jackson Hole property," William said. "Because the government owns most of the valley and only four percent is available for private ownership, the area's land values keep surging. Even without a structure on it, your ranch is worth several million dollars."

Cavanaugh exhaled in what was nearly a gasp, not because of the worth of his home but because he suddenly realized how threatened he was. "Carl tried to kill us. He burned our home. He destroyed my business. Because of him, we'll probably go to prison, which means I'll lose my security status."

"Don't assume you're going to prison," William said. "Mosely arrested you because he's in line to be the Bureau's director. By refusing to ignore the laws you broke, he shows he can't be influenced, doesn't play favorites, or make exceptions. But a lot of people are on your side. Here are copies of as many national newspapers as I could find. *USA Today*, *The Washington Post*, *The New York Times*. You're on the front pages and, more important, the op-ed pages, where you're favorably presented as preventing an even greater disaster. You're the topic of every talk show. Every network called, asking for an interview."

"Hard to do an interview when we're in custody," Cavanaugh said, "not to mention, protectors shouldn't put their faces on national television programs. Removes our effectiveness, don't you think? Assuming we're ever allowed to work again."

"The point is, a lot of people understand the difficult choice you had to make."

"What matters is what the court thinks," Jamie said.

"What a *jury* thinks. Lester Beauchamp's on his way back from Europe. He's extremely persuasive. I believe there's a good chance you'll be exonerated."

"When? The trial might not happen for a year."

William's cell phone rang.

"One moment." He pulled the phone from his pocket and raised it to his ear. "William Faraday." He listened. "Yes." He listened further. "Yes." He concentrated. "That's very generous of you. ...I agree—if things had gone the other way, you wouldn't have had the opportunity to be generous. You'll make the arrangements? …Thank you."

William lowered his phone. "In the vernacular, it looks as if you'll be sprung."

"What *happened*?"

"Do you know someone named Mr. Yamato?"

"He's one of the leaders of the World Trade Organization. I tried to persuade him to stop the conference. I was with him in his hotel suite when the tear gas and smoke bombs went off."

"He credits you with saving his life and those of the other delegates if the conference had occurred." William's smile showcased his perfectly capped teeth. "I hope it's a sign of the outcome of your legal trouble that he persuaded the World Trade Organization to post your bail."

Cavanaugh would have been speechless, except for the need to ask the most important thing on his mind.

"Has anybody figured out where the hell Carl is?"

3

The river was cold. Gritty. Greasy. Submerged in the weight of the muddy water, Carl heard the muffled vibrations of engines. He kept kicking with his heavy shoes, in too great a hurry to take the time to stop his momentum, unlace them, and push them off. He had no doubt that Aaron was close behind him, possibly already in the water, thrusting after him. *Kick!* he ordered himself. *Claw at the water! Swim harder! Faster!* After chasing Raoul, killing him, and rushing to get away from Aaron, Carl felt that his lungs were strained to their capacity. His chest ached with the desperate need to take in oxygen.

No! I won't give up! I won't let Aaron win!

He swept his arms with greater determination, surging through the mucky water, feeling the current add to his momentum. *Fifty, fifty-one, fifty-two,* he mentally counted. He had to swim as far and fast as possible. *Sixty, sixty-one, sixty-two.* His mind spun. Even with his eyes closed, he saw swirling spots. *Seventy-one. I once swam underwater for a minute and forty-five seconds,* he reminded himself. *Aaron saw me do it. He knows how strong I am, how far I can…*

Carl's body took control of his mind. No matter how fiercely he willed his lungs not to do it, they insisted on inhaling.

Frantic, the vibrations around him even louder, he propelled himself upward, taking in water, coughing as he broke the surface. A barge sped close, threatening to strike him. Instantly, he took a breath and dove, kicking, aiming toward the opposite shore. He had to surface one more time, breathe, and submerge again. Then his sweeping arms touched silt, and he raised his head slightly from the river, blinking filthy water from his eyes, wanting to cheer when he saw boats against the shore. A wharf. *See, Aaron, I can still do it!*

But there were too many people on the shore, too many chances of being noticed. Word of the attack in the downtown area would travel fast. A man seen crawling from the river would attract so much attention that the police would be alerted. They might corner him before he could find a hiding place. Better to stay where he was, under the dock, behind its pilings, close to the shore, where no one would notice him. A helicopter thundered overhead. A Coast Guard boat roared past. He held his breath and slipped underwater.

4

After dark, as voices and rumbling footsteps faded from the wharf, he eased past a piling, listened harder, studied the few details he could see above him, and climbed a dirt embankment, squirming into shadowy bushes. Seeing nothing to alarm him, he crept past a warehouse. He worried about the trail of water he left, but gradually it lessened as a night breeze dried his clothes. He hugged his chest, shivering. Then he heard voices and ducked behind a Dumpster bin. When the voices receded, he skirted the glare of lights, creeping deeper into whatever gloom he could find, craving darkness.

By one a.m., his clothes were dry enough for him to be inconspicuous enough to emerge onto a street. His cropped hair looked the same as before it had gotten wet. Granted, he was dirty and had an earthy smell from the river, but he appeared no different from many homeless people he passed. He bought peppermint-flavored brandy from an all-night liquor store. He approached an alley, where several ragged men lay against a wall. When he sank next to them, they made fists.

"This place is *ours!*"

"Here. I'm too sick to drink this."

He handed the brandy to the most aggressive man. After the leader got his share, the others shoved at each other, grabbing for the bottle.

Meanwhile, Carl found a space far into the alley, next to garbage cans. With his back and side protected, he gripped his folded knife in his pants pocket, his pistol having been lost in the river. He watched his companions warily until they finished the bottle and sank against a wall. Eventually, he allowed himself to doze, although several noises woke him in the night.

Plenty of time to think. During the progress of the mission, he'd accepted two payments of five hundred thousand dollars each, with a promise of another million when the assignment was completed. That did not include the considerable expense that his employers had paid for him to set up the camp, fly across the country to recruit trainees, and bring the team to New Orleans. The receipts he'd presented to his employers were detailed and accurate. After all, he was a principled man, although even if he'd been tempted to cheat them, these people were far too scary for him to risk it. But in round numbers, the cost to his employers for two years of planning and execution was three million dollars, and that did not include his two-million-dollar fee. Serious money, even for a group that got much of its funding from the narcotics trade. Several times, his employers warned him that their investment had better pay off. He'd given them repeated assurances, pointing to the progress he had made.

They will not, he decided, *be happy.*

I wouldn't have gotten involved if I hadn't been confident these guys would let me spend the money, he thought. *I was sure they'd want me to work for them again. I was also sure I could slip away from New Orleans and enjoy life in southern France. Hey, I was supposed to be anonymous. But thanks to you, Aaron, none of that's going to happen. Everybody'll be hunting me.*

As the sun rose, Carl remained still. Only at nine o'clock, as the craving for alcohol prompted his companions to stagger from the alley, did he leave. Every action needed to be calculated, every decision analyzed from every angle. He never went anywhere without a thousand dollars in twenties in a money belt, so for the moment, he didn't need to worry about cash. He bought unremarkable clothes in a discount store. He bought jogging shoes. He ate two sandwiches from a take-out place.

That's where he noticed the *Times-Picayune* in a vending machine. The attack was all over the front page. On a secluded bench, he studied the newspaper and found a detailed description of him. No photograph, but one would eventually be found. Because Brockman had scrubbed Carl's file from the GPS records, the only source for a picture would be the military. But information about Delta Force was secret, and the Pentagon's bureaucracy would take a while to declassify it. The photo would show him in uniform, younger and thinner—enough differences that it might not draw attention to him.

The newspaper had plenty to say about Aaron and his wife. It gave Carl bitter satisfaction that the reporter actually referred to Aaron by his given name and revealed that the mysterious single word "Cavanaugh" by which he was known in the protection business was actually an alias.

But the greater satisfaction came when Carl learned that Aaron and his wife had been arrested and why they were being charged. *So that* was *you at the hotels,* he thought with angry admiration. *Clever move, Aaron. But now you're in jail while I'm on the street. I bet you think everything's upside down. It's only starting. I'll deal with you later, pal. Right now, I've got problems to solve.*

A bug-out bag. Always make arrangements for a bug-out bag. The van Carl had abandoned contained one, but members of the team might have been captured and interrogated, in which case the authorities would know about the van. Even if that weren't the case, by now all vehicles left overnight in the conference area would have been investigated. He didn't dare return to it.

Always have a back-up plan. The jet was no longer available, having been abandoned at the camp. His alternative bug-out bag was in a spot that was now off-limits to him: a New Orleans bus station. In theory, the arrangement would have worked perfectly. Get the bag. Get a ticket. Get out of town. But now he took for granted that the authorities would be watching the bus stations, the airport, the train depot, and the car-rental places, looking for anyone who matched his description.

"Hey," he said to a street musician near the bus station, "want to earn fifty bucks?"

The guy, a skinny guitarist with his case open in front of him, a couple of dollars in it, stopped singing a nasally version of "The City of New Orleans" and asked, "What do I have to do, pull your putz? Get out of here, man."

"Nothing funny. Just a straight business proposition. I need you to run an errand for me. In the bus station. Five minutes max."

"And there's a reason you can't run the errand yourself?"

"Let's make it a *hundred* reasons," Carl said, showing the money.

"And maybe I walk into trouble in there?"

"I guess you don't need the dollars." Carl turned away.

"Wait," the scruffy guy said. "What's the errand?"

"This." Carl showed him the key to a locker. "I'll tell you where the locker is so you don't need to wander around searching for it. Five minutes. In and out. You bring me what's in the locker."

"For a hundred. Right?"

"Did I say a hundred? I made a mistake."

"A scam. Damn it, I figured this was too good to be—"

"What I meant was *two* hundred."

"You're kidding."

"One hundred now. One hundred when you bring me what's in the locker."

"And what's in—"

"A briefcase."

The guy's eyes reacted.

"Want to make a bet?" Carl asked.

"Bet?"

"That I know what you're thinking. You figure the briefcase must contain something really valuable for me to pay two hundred dollars to get it. And you're right. There are many valuable things in it. So your plan would be to take the hundred dollars and steal the briefcase. After all, if I don't feel comfortable going into the station, I must have a reason I don't want to be seen, and that means I won't report the theft to the police. Right?"

The guy's face now radiated suspicion. "Something like that."

Carl gripped the arm that wasn't holding the guitar. Immobilizing him, he removed the guy's wallet from his back pocket.

"Hey," the musician said, struggling.

"Shut up, or I'll break your guitar." Carl studied the driver's license. "Okay, Kenny Barrington." Carl read the address out loud. He found a photograph of a young woman. "Pretty. She your girlfriend?"

No answer.

"*Four* hundred dollars, Kenny. Half now, half when you come back with the briefcase. If I don't see you back here in five minutes, the next time you see *me*, it'll be the sorriest night of your life. And your girlfriend's life. Sound fair?"

"Uh…"

"Here, Kenny. Here's two hundred dollars and the key. I'll hold your guitar for you. Be cool, my friend. Easy money."

Minutes later, when the musician came back with the briefcase, Carl watched from a distance. The guy looked around in bewilderment, then focused on a black kid sitting next to his guitar.

Carl imagined what the kid told him. "Somebody paid me ten bucks to tell you to go into that Starbucks over there and buy some coffee."

If the musician had warned the police about a man who paid him four hundred dollars to get a briefcase out of a locker, Carl would see if anyone followed.

No one did. As the musician carried his guitar and the briefcase into the Starbucks front entrance, Carl came in from the side entrance, took the briefcase, gave him the other two hundred, and told him, "Nice to meet an honest man."

5

In one of the city's lovely parks, Carl sat, watched a bicyclist go past, nodded to a woman with a stroller, smiled at children on swings, and worked the combination lock on the briefcase. The case was dull brown, attracting no attention. He slid his hand inside and felt past five thousand dollars, a pistol, an extra magazine, fifty rounds of ammunition, a knife, small rolls of duct tape, fake ID, and other necessities. He gripped a cell phone. His previous phone had been destroyed by the river. He pulled the new one out, closed the briefcase, and enjoyed the pleasant morning.

Then he couldn't postpone his business any longer. He pressed numbers on the encryption-equipped phone and waited. After two rings, the connection was completed, although the person on the other end didn't speak, presumably waiting to learn which language to use.

"This is Bowie," Carl said.

"You disappoint us."

Carl felt his chest harden. "Things went wrong. They couldn't be helped."

"You accepted our money but did not produce results."

"I got *some* results. The mission isn't a total failure."

"You sound like a child making excuses."

Carl's muscles tightened, now because of anger. "It was a unique situation. The next time, the person who caused the problem won't exist."

"Your friend? If *he* had been available to us, the mission would have succeeded."

Carl bit the inside of his cheek.

"You will return the fee we already paid you," the voice said. "One million dollars. An electronic transfer. By noon tomorrow."

"Of course."

"You will also return the money we paid for expenses and preparations."

"You know it's been spent. Where am I going to find three million dollars?

"Perhaps from your friend," the voice said acidly. "We need to meet. To discuss what has happened."

I'd never survive the meeting, Carl thought. "Well, at the moment, that's a little difficult. The authorities are hunting me. I'm trying to get out of New Orleans."

"I don't mean today. That's impossible. I'm flying to the Philippines."

"And you feel comfortable talking about this on a plane?"

"A private jet. I arrive in an hour. When you reach a secure location, contact me again. I'll tell you where to meet me."

Carl felt a weightless sensation, as if a trap door opened beneath him. *As soon as I arrange an electronic transfer of the money, he'll invite me to a meeting and have me killed. Perhaps he'll do it himself.*

"On a plane? Are you passing the time, trying to figure out how to open the secret knife I gave you?"

"That's another way you disappoint me. Your ridiculous knife doesn't work. I tried every possible combination."

"Sure, it works. Have you got it with you?"

"In my pocket."

"On the top combination, turn the man in the moon to two o'clock. On the bottom combination, turn the arrow to Roman numeral X."

"I already tried that! Nothing happened!"

"Try it again."

Impatient, the voice said, "The same result! Nothing!"

"Did you release the catch?"

"*What catch?*"

"Recessed into the bottom of the handle. See the little hook?"

"You didn't say anything about that. It's barely visible!" the voice complained.

"Pull it."

"This had better—"

The transmission ended.

6

Near the Philippines, the newly married couple strolled the deck of the cruise ship. Holding hands, they admired the glorious radiance of the stars.

"You can't see this in Philadelphia," the man said. "All the light pollution in the city interferes with—"

The woman pointed. "What's *that?*"

"Oh, my God," the man said.

One of the stars exploded. It blossomed like a rocket on the Fourth of July. Flaming debris plummeted toward the water.

Seconds later, the rumble of the blast echoed over them.

7

"Don't call a knife I made 'ridiculous'," Carl said.

He shut off the phone, worked to calm his heartbeat, then directed a melancholy look at the children playing on the swings in the park.

Detonating the explosive in the knife hadn't solved anything. There would be others to take the swarthy man's place, and those others, too, would demand the return of their money. He couldn't possibly come up with millions of dollars. When the electronic transfer did not occur, they would insist on meeting with him, something to be avoided with every effort. From now on, his life would be a matter of running and hiding.

No, blowing up the plane definitely didn't solve anything, Carl thought, *but it certainly gave me a world of satisfaction. Maybe Aaron's right. Maybe I do need a few more lessons about keeping control.*

The children. He couldn't take his sad gaze from the children. *Hey, Aaron, wouldn't it be great if we could go back to being kids? If only life could be simple again.*

The game. All that mattered now was the game. He picked up the newspaper he'd set next to him. After reading about Aaron and his wife one more time, he turned to the classified ads. The area's airports, train stations, bus depots, and car-rental agencies were being watched. But there were other ways to get out of town.

8

"Sounds a little rough," Carl said.

"Hey, I'm not pretending she don't need a tune-up. I figured that into the price."

"What about oil changes, regular maintenance, stuff like that?"

"Four months ago. Then the twins got born. I'm so tired working two jobs to pay the bills, I ain't driven her since. Truth is, I didn't take her out much *before* the twins got born. Guess I'm getting too old for kid stuff."

"Naw, you're never too old to act like a kid."

"Tell that to my old lady."

"Well, if you're sure you want to sell…"

"Need to. Don't have two jobs anymore. That's how you caught me at home. The factory where I worked my day job got shut down and moved to Mexico. I really need the money. But like I told you on the phone, I won't take a check."

"Don't blame you. Can't be too careful. Here's the three thousand in cash. Now all you need to do is sign the ownership papers, and I'll make sure the title's transferred to me."

"Hate to part with her."

"Well, you can count on me taking care of her for you."

"Thanks, mister."

"I don't suppose you've got a helmet."

"In the garage some place. My wife got it for me, but I never bothered. Always made me feel trapped."

"Bad for your health. Gotta stay safe you know."

"You're a decent enough guy. Tell you what, I'll throw in the helmet and my goggles."

"Naw, that wouldn't be right. Sounds like the twins are waking up. As you say, you can use the cash. I wouldn't want to take advantage. Here's another fifty bucks."

"Much obliged, mister."

A minute later, his helmet and goggles adjusted, Carl fired up the old Yamaha and drove from the modest neighborhood.

By then, it was twelve-fifteen. The sun was pleasantly warm. The breeze created by the motorcycle soothed him. It had been years since he'd driven a bike, and now he wondered why he had ever stopped: the mobility, the freedom, the independence. Plus, unless you wore leathers and a Hell's Angels scowl, people tended not to pay attention to you, as the number of accidents in which cars ran into motorcycles confirmed.

Enjoying the vibration of the engine between his legs, Carl passed a police cruiser. Looking straight ahead, he concentrated on traffic and obeyed the speed limit, confident that the cops in the cruiser wouldn't pay attention to him. The goggles and helmet indicated how safety-conscious and law-abiding he was.

He found his way to Interstate 10 and headed west, skirting Lake Pontchartrain. Impressed by the expanse of the water, he reached Interstate 55 and proceeded north, soon passing Lake Maurepas: the fishing boats, the waves, the evocative smell of the water, the feeling of freedom. Blending with the flow of cars, he luxuriated in each moment and discovered that eighty miles went by like they were nothing. Before he realized, he was in the small Louisiana city of Hammond, which for his purposes had one major asset: an Amtrak station. He knew this because familiarity with the train routes out of New Orleans was part of his contingency plan, just as he'd known the bus routes.

But after getting directions to the train station, he decided that if the station in New Orleans would be under surveillance, didn't it make sense that the nearest Amtrak station in another city would be under surveillance also? Hell, eighty miles was nothing. He stopped for a burger, fries, and a Coke at a drive-in restaurant. They tasted as delicious as when he'd been a kid. Then he returned to Interstate 55 and headed farther north.

In an hour, he crossed into Mississippi, and now he felt less threatened, although he didn't delude himself that the hunt for him would not continue to be urgent and widespread. The next Amtrak station was twenty miles farther in another small city, McComb. But again, his instincts warned him away. Too small a station. Too easy to be spotted. By then, it was four in the afternoon. Fatigue insisted, but he couldn't rest until he was confident that he'd found sanctuary. And food. He couldn't seem to get enough to eat. But there wasn't time.

He drove another ninety minutes to the large Amtrak station in Jackson, Mississippi. Making sure that his fingerprints were wiped clean, he left the motorcycle on a side street a few blocks from the station. By midnight, the bike would be gone, no way to trace it to him.

Trying not to attract attention by hurrying, he went to a convenience store. He kept his back to the security camera while he bought shampoo, toothpaste, a toothbrush, shaving soap, a razor, and a packet of Kleenex. Subduing his urgency, he shaved in a men's room in the train station, making himself as presentable as possible. He went into a toilet stall, locked it, then stuffed Kleenex under his lips and into his cheeks, changing the profile of his face, making it look puffy rather than gaunt-cheeked, as the newspaper described him.

He leaned forward at the ticket counter, reducing his height.

"Chicago," he said. "This evening."

"You just made it. Arrives at nine tomorrow morning."

"Got anything in the sleeping car?"

"Let's see. Yep. One compartment left."

"Must be my lucky day."

9

"Your honor, my clients request that the conditions of their release be relaxed sufficiently to allow them to leave Louisiana and fly to New York City. Their corporation, Global Protective Services, requires their immediate presence to oversee urgent financial matters relative to the continuing existence of the company. If my clients are unable to perform their corporate functions, the result will be calamitous, destroying their livelihood and that of hundreds of employees. The charges notwithstanding, Mr. Stoddard has an exemplary record as a protective agent credited with saving the lives of numerous international figures who function at the highest levels of finance, government, and entertainment. Prior to that, he defended the United States as a member of the elite military unit Delta Force. You have heard the respect that Mr. Yamato and other members of the World Trade Organization have for him and his wife, so much in fact that they guarantee bail. My clients offer to surrender their passports."

10

The rhythm of the wheels on the railroad tracks gradually soothed him. Clickety. Clickety. For a half hour, Carl sat next to the small table in his compartment. His hand on his pistol, he expected that at any moment, the door would burst open and men would throw flash-bangs at him. He kept the window shade drawn, but then he worried about what he wasn't able to see. Raising the shade, he saw only passing countryside and gathering shadows. After his heartbeat calmed, he went to the compartment's sink, removed the wads of Kleenex from his mouth, and brushed his teeth (no matter how filthy he was on a mission, he always felt clean if he had a chance to brush his teeth). Then he washed his hair in the sink and used a wet towel to swab the dirt and river smell from him, all the while keeping his pistol close and his gaze on the locked door.

Hunger demanded to be satisfied. At the convenience store, he'd bought a Coke, two ham sandwiches, and a bag of potato chips. He'd wanted much more, but he'd been afraid of being remembered if he bought too much food in addition to his other purchases. Clickety. Clickety.

The sandwiches were stale and tasteless. He washed them down with the now-warm Coke, seasoning them with the equally stale potato chips. Clickety. Clickety.

Outside the window, the countryside rolled by, vague trees and hills in the darkness, glowing windows in farmhouses, then the glare of towns. He shut off the light, eased onto his bunk, set his knife and pistol next to him, and stared at the ceiling. The passing shadows rippled over it. Mercifully, he slept.

But then the clickety, clickety slowed. The change of rhythm woke him. Hearing the squeal of breaks, he grabbed his pistol and peered out the window, only to see a small train station, a passenger departing into the gloom. No one else was in view. Nothing to be alarmed about.

He started to lay back but then noticed a sign on the station's wall: NEWBERN-DYERSBURG, TENNESSEE. A hand seemed to reach inside his barely full stomach and twist at his guts. The northward Amtrak line passed through the extreme western edge of Tennessee, he knew. A hundred miles to the east was Nashville, where Carl's father had taken the family after his drunkenness caused him to lose his stockbroker's job in Iowa City.

In Nashville, the arguments and beatings had worsened. One night, Carl found his father unconscious at the kitchen table at three in the morning. The lights were on. A half-empty bottle of peppermint brandy sat next to him. The peppermint soothed the stomach inflammation that years of too much alcohol caused.

Carl had laid out bread, mustard, mayonnaise, lettuce, dill pickles, and a chunk of ham, as if his father had decided to make a sandwich. His father was so stupefied that the muted sounds didn't wake him. Carl applied mustard and mayonnaise to one slice of bread. He took a sharp knife and cut into the ham. He used a dishtowel to wipe his fingerprints from everything. He used the same towel while he held his father's hands and applied fingerprints to bottles, plates, and the bread wrapper.

"Uh," his father said.

"Ssshh," Carl said.

He raised his father from the table, then hefted him to the counter and the half-prepared sandwich. He put the sharp knife in his father's right hand and knocked his father's legs from under him, making sure that the knife plowed into his father's stomach when he hit the floor. His father tried to moan, but Carl pressed his hands over his father's mouth. As a pool of blood spread, his father trembled, then lay still. Avoiding the blood on the floor, taking care that none was on him, Carl went back to bed. He enjoyed the most satisfying sleep of his life.

Now Carl wished that the same peaceful sleep would come to him. Watching the ripple of shadows across the train compartment's ceiling, he tried to think back to when, if ever, his life had been the way he wanted. There had been a time, he decided.

11

Daylight. The Illinois train stations went by. Champaign-Urbana. Kankakee. Homewood. That name filled him with bitterness. Next stop: Chicago.

He used his cell phone.

A woman's pleasant voice said, "Grand Cayman bank."

"I need to wire-transfer nine thousand dollars to my bank account in Chicago." That account, under an assumed identity, had been carefully established two years earlier. The nine thousand dollars was less than the ten-thousand-dollar transaction amount that banks were required to report to the federal government.

"Certainly, sir. May I have your account number and your password?"

Carl recited the number from memory. "The password is 'stiletto.'"

"Thank you, sir." A moment lengthened. "Sir, would you please repeat that account number?"

"Is there a problem?"

"I may have mistyped it."

Carl repeated it.

"Sir, our records fail to show any funds in that account."

"But there should be a million dollars!"

"No, sir, I'm afraid there aren't any funds."

"Try that number again." Carl recited it slowly.

"Yes, sir, that's the number I'm accessing, but the account does not have a balance."

The undigested sandwiches from the night before soured Carl's stomach. "Was there *ever* any money in it?"

"Yes, sir. As you mentioned, a million dollars. Yesterday afternoon, it was wire transferred to another bank."

Carl swallowed something bitter. "Thank you."

"You're welcome."

12

Cavanaugh admired the Gulfstream's interior, the last time he would see it.

"The jet needs to go back to its base in New Jersey anyhow," William said. "The expense is the same whether we're aboard or not, so we might as well take advantage."

"It never occurred to me to ask how much it costs to fly this."

"Four thousand dollars an hour."

"And we crossed the country several times. No wonder the company's going bankrupt."

"When you're protecting a Saudi prince, the fee's high enough to earn out," William said.

"But when I'm fighting to stay alive, it's too expensive."

The powerful engines whispered as the jet reached its scheduled altitude, streaking through clouds.

"Less than a week ago, you didn't want anything to do with Global Protective Services," Jamie said, "and now you hate to lose it."

"Yes," Cavanaugh told her bitterly. "Because of Carl."

13

The train arrived in Chicago ten minutes late. Slouching, Carl blended with the departing passengers on the damp, shadowy concourse. He carried his briefcase in his left hand while his right hand was primed to reach for a weapon. He had strips of a towel under his lips and inside his cheeks, altering his features. His ears had Kleenex wadded neatly into them.

Keeping in the thick of the crowd, he entered the brightly lit terminal, the din of which was muffled by the padding in his ears. He tensed when he saw two policemen studying everybody. They stopped a tall, thin man, who looked somewhat like Carl, and asked him questions.

Carl showed no reaction. Face blank, eyes forward, shoulders drooped, he kept moving, not breaking rhythm, just another zombie. *Take it easy*, he thought. *You'll be fine.* The "you" was deliberately chosen, a way of disassociating from the moment and keeping his emotions in check. *If they really believed you were on a train that arrived here, there'd be a small army to welcome you, not a handful of cops*, he tried to assure himself.

Approaching an exit, he glanced at a newsstand, then looked ahead, as if the newspapers meant nothing, even though a large photograph of him stared from the *Chicago Tribune*, the *Chicago Sun-Times*, and *USA Today*.

Not a military photograph. Not him young and in uniform. This was a recent photograph of him among a crowd on a street. New Orleans. Taken by a security camera, it depicted him chasing somebody. Raoul. Digitally magnified and enhanced, alarmingly clear, the image showed Carl in profile. More than in profile. Three quarters of his features.

Silently cursing, he saw another policeman scanning the crowd and warned himself, *Be cool. No one'll recognize you from that picture. It isn't a full face, and the angle's downward. Everything's going to be fine.*

Yeah, sure, right. He could no longer objectify. Suddenly "you" became "I." *I'm being hunted by the bastards who hired me and by every law-enforcement agency in the country. Every intelligence agency, also. I've got fifty rounds of ammunition and two thousand dollars. What the hell am I supposed to do?*

Play the game.

For the rest of my life.

A policeman appeared at the exit ahead. Shielded by businessmen, Carl kept walking. The policeman straightened, paying attention to him. Immediately, Carl reached into a pants pocket and removed an object he'd taken from the briefcase. A small canister. As the policeman blurted something to a microphone attached to his shoulder, Carl pulled a pin from the canister and dropped it behind him. The canister *clanked* onto the floor and made several people turn to look.

The policeman drew his gun and stepped toward Carl, raising a hand to warn him to stop. Carl pretended not to notice.

The policeman shouted, "Stop right there!"

At once, the canister, a flash-bang, detonated. Having counting the seconds until it did, Carl knew when to close his eyes. Even then, and even though the flash was behind him, the searing brightness pushed through his eyelids. Anyone facing that direction, including the cop, would be blinded. The *bang* from the device was literally deafening, except for Carl, who'd used Kleenex to protect his eardrums.

The force of the two onslaughts stunned the policeman and shoved him backward. People screamed. They scrambled over each other.

"Terrorists!" Carl shouted. "A bomb!"

The panic worsened, everybody charging toward the exits. Carl moved with them. Instead of fighting their fierce momentum, he allowed it to take him. The next thing, he was outside, the stampede spreading into traffic while he blended with people charging along the sidewalk.

14

The Manhattan headquarters for Global Protective Services looked as busy and professional as ever, but Cavanaugh knew that the strength and solidity were only apparent. With Jamie and William, he entered his office. An outsider would not have realized that, less than a week earlier, the place had been littered with bomb wreckage. Now a close look showed Cavanaugh that the hasty cleanup was only cosmetic, that the damage had been disguised, not repaired. *Like the corporation*, he thought.

"I can't imagine how expensive our lease is."

"A half million dollars a year," William said.

"Amazing that the company stayed in business as long as it did."

"Two executive officers dead and one in a detox ward." Jamie slumped in a chair.

"It's going to be hard dismantling the various operations," Cavanaugh said. "Jamie, you're the one with a business background. How do we handle this?"

"For starters, we alert the heads of our foreign offices and tell them to cancel all upcoming assignments. Then we negotiate to terminate all our office leases and have other protection firms take over the jobs already in progress. After that, we—"

15

A cold October wind breathed a premonition of winter. Especially after the warmth of New Orleans, it made Carl shiver. But as he retreated along the walkway next to the Chicago River, maintaining a disciplined, inconspicuous pace, appearing to enjoy the view of the water, he was determined not to go into a store and risk buying a jacket. After all, the photograph in the newspapers was likely to be on television as well. Word would have spread quickly that he'd been spotted in Chicago. People would pay attention to strangers.

His discomfort gave him a glimpse of the future: decreasing possibilities and increasing deprivations.

What happens when my money's gone? Do I start holding up liquor stores? Hell, I can't show my face to spend the money anyhow. Where am I going to sleep tonight? I can't risk going to a hotel, even a seedy one. It won't be long before the government offers a reward. Do I hide in an alley the way I did two nights ago? Do I hole up in the woods?

Play the game.

Hide and seek.

He passed a newspaper that someone had stuffed into a garbage bin. Making sure than no one was near him, he pulled out the paper and studied his photograph on the front page. *Aaron, you son of a bitch, I should be getting laid on the Riviera right now.*

In a fury, he read that Aaron and his wife had managed to post bail and been released. It gave him savage pleasure to learn that Global Protective Services was about to collapse. *Only a fraction of what you deserve, you bastard.* Aaron and his wife had been allowed to leave

Louisiana and fly to New York to begin the process of dissolving the company.

"If *he* had been available to us, the mission would have been a success," the swarthy man had said before Carl blew him up.

Well, let's see about that, Carl thought.

Hide for the rest of my life?

Aaron, I'll prove to you how good I am.

On a bench ahead, a man slept next to a bicycle. The man had beard stubble and matted, dirty hair. He wore a ragged jacket and filthy jeans. Attached to the rear of the bicycle, a small cart contained plastic bags of what appeared to be even more ragged clothing. A cord led from the man's wrist to the bicycle, a burglar alarm.

Carl checked that no one was paying attention. He unclipped his knife from his pants pocket, thumbed the blade open, and sliced the cord. He wheeled the bike out of earshot (it had only one gear and didn't make the clicking sound of sports bikes). He stopped just long enough to pull a ragged blue shirt from a bag and pull it over the brown shirt he'd bought in New Orleans. Then he got on and bicycled away. Like a motorcyclist wearing goggles and a helmet, a ragged homeless man on a bicycle, towing his few meager possessions, was invisible.

He still had the newspaper from the waste bin. When he felt that it was safe to stop, he planned to study the personal ads and buy another used motorcycle. There was always the risk that he'd be recognized, but he would sense if that happened and make sure the man selling the motorcycle couldn't warn anyone. He didn't have enough cash to buy as good a bike as the Yamaha he'd abandoned in Mississippi, but then the bike didn't need to function long. His destination was only five hours away.

16

After Cavanaugh canceled yet another assignment and set down the phone, he sensed the receptionist standing in his office doorway. "Yes?"

"You had a dozen more calls."

Exhausted, Cavanaugh glanced at his watch. The time was shortly after five p.m., and he had several more clients to talk to. "Anything urgent?"

"They *all* seem urgent."

At the desk, Jamie typed computer keys as William spoke into a phone, arranging an auction for the Gulfstream.

"One caller's more insistent than the others," the receptionist said, holding up a list. "So far, he contacted us eight times."

"Must be a really angry creditor. What's his name?"

"Lance Sawyer."

Cavanaugh straightened.

Overhearing, Jamie frowned. "But isn't that the name of the old man who taught you and Carl how to make knives?"

Cavanaugh grabbed the list and pressed the phone number on it.

William looked puzzled. "What's going on?"

Cavanaugh activated the speaker function on his phone. On the other end, the phone rang only once, its tinny buzz filling the room.

Immediately, the three of them heard a man's voice. "Hey, Aaron, how's it going?"

Cavanaugh clenched his fists as he leaned over the conference table. "Fabulous."

"Not likely. I read in the newspaper that you spent time in the slammer yesterday. Sorry to learn about all the trouble you're having."

"Try to sound sincere." Cavanaugh watched Jamie and William approach the phone, listening to the smooth voice that came from its speaker.

"Is the FBI trying to locate where this call's originating from, or are you and the government not on such great terms any longer?"

"To tell the truth, Carl, I was so eager to talk to you, I didn't think to alert them."

"The truth's always nice, not to mention rare, coming from you. Half the directional work's already been done for them anyhow. They know I'm in Chicago."

"Chicago?"

"Haven't you been watching television? The Carl Duran show?"

Instantly, Jamie went to a cabinet in a corner and turned on a television.

"Afraid I missed it," Cavanaugh said.

"Oh, it's getting big ratings. Lots of action, suspense, and mystery."

The television was tuned to CNN, where a reporter stood in what looked to be a train station, nervous-looking passengers going past. The words LIVE FROM CHICAGO appeared at the bottom of the screen. The program changed to video from a security camera mounted in a corner. The image showed passengers crossing the terminal. The picture became magnified, focusing on a man who resembled Carl (the cheeks were fuller) as he approached an exit. A policeman hurried toward him. A flash filled the screen. Even with the television's sound at low volume, Cavanaugh heard a powerful detonation. The crowd screamed, charging toward the doors.

"I'm watching it now," Cavanaugh said. "Nicely done."

"That's high praise, Aaron, considering that you don't believe anybody can do anything better than you."

"I always admitted you made knives better, and you're certainly a better swimmer."

"Gosh, all these compliments are going to my head."

"Turn yourself in, Carl."

"Right."

"You can't hide forever."

"I can give it a try. That abortion-clinic bomber lasted five years in the woods."

"Freezing his ass in the winter. Living off acorns and lizards in the summer."

"Yeah, good buddy, but he wasn't trained the way you and I were."

"I'm serious. Turn yourself in, Carl. I can arrange for you to do it safely."

"Golly. I appreciate your concern."

"You can bargain with the authorities. Give them information about the bastards who hired you. Negotiate for a bearable prison sentence."

"Don't I wish. See, the problem is, I don't have anything to reveal. I dealt with one guy. He told me nothing about his organization. I don't even know what his real name was."

"Was?"

"He's dead. An unfortunate plane explosion. Aaron, don't bullshit me. We both know if I turn myself in, the government'll go for the death penalty. A thousand people are dead, for God's sake. The government'll snuff me the way it did that guy who blew up the federal building in

Oklahoma City. I don't like that option a whole lot. My only chance is to play the game."

"Game?"

17

Carl lied. He wasn't anywhere near Chicago. His newly acquired motorcycle had taken him two hundred and fifty miles west, where he now sat on a picnic bench, watching a shallow creek meander through autumn-brilliant trees while he spoke to the phone.

"The game, Aaron. That's all there is. That's all there ever was." A chill wind bit into him. "So here's the deal. I'm offering you one last chance to play. Tomorrow night. The usual place. But if you don't show up or you bring help, you'll piss me off even more than you already have. If you betray me again, I'll come to *you*, but the next time, you won't get fair warning. It'd be nice to meet your lovely wife."

Through the phone, Carl heard a noise as if a hand slammed a table. *"Now you're threatening my wife?"* Aaron shouted. "You cocksucker!"

"That's the spirit, Aaron."

Carl broke the connection.

18

Hearing the dead air, Cavanaugh slowly lowered the phone and deactivated its speaker function. His heart pounded with rage. Gradually, he became aware of Jamie and William staring at him.

"'One last chance to play. Tomorrow night. The usual place'," Jamie said. "He's challenging you to a fight."

"Sounds like it."

"One on one."

"That seems to be the idea."

"Do you know the place he means?" William asked.

Cavanaugh thought for a moment. "Yes, I believe I do."

"Where?"

Cavanaugh didn't answer.

"You're not seriously thinking about accepting the challenge," Jamie wanted to know.

"I hate him so much. Everything he's done to us. You have no idea how much I'd like to."

"But," Jamie said, "you won't."

"You heard him. He's giving me a chance at him. If I don't take it, his target will be *you*."

"Not if you phone Mosely and Rutherford and tell them about this," William said. "It'll go a long way toward getting the FBI on your side again. They'll order the place—wherever it is—surrounded. A SWAT team will take care of this."

"But what if they *can't*. The place I think Carl means, there are too many ways for him to see if I betrayed him and brought help. Too many ways to escape. I'm willing to bet *my* life, but not Jamie's."

"Don't *I* have something to say about that? What if he wins?"

"Then he'll leave you alone. But he isn't going to win."

"Did he ever win before?"

"When we were kids."

"Well, you're not kids any longer! If the FBI doesn't get him, we'll deal with the consequences together. But I won't let you use me as an excuse to satisfy your hate and possibly get yourself killed."

Cavanaugh studied her.

"William," he finally said. "I assume it's easier for you to negotiate in person than on the phone."

"That's correct."

"Then arrange a meeting with Mosely and John as soon as possible." Cavanaugh picked up the phone and made a call of his own. When a voice answered, he said, "Get the Gulfstream ready to fly in an hour. ... Selling it? Not just yet."

19

"I'm amazed," Mosely said. The lights of Washington's Capitol Building gleamed beyond his office window. "Shocked, in fact. You're actually following proper procedure instead of showing everybody what a hotshot you are."

"All I ever tried to do was the right thing," Cavanaugh told him.

"Sure. Of course, it would have been even better if you'd alerted us before you made the call so we could try to trace it. But I guess I'm asking for too much. This 'usual place' he referred to. I assume it's the farm where the old man taught you and Duran to make knives."

"No."

"Then where *is* it?"

Now Cavanaugh looked at William.

"Do we have an understanding?" the attorney asked.

"Counselor, I don't make deals."

"We're not asking for a deal. My client is willing to cooperate to the fullest extent. But he wants that taken into consideration when his case comes to trial."

"Consideration. Oh, he'll get plenty of consideration if he *doesn't* cooperate."

Rutherford sat next to Mosely at the conference table. He leaned forward, one friend to another. "Where's 'the usual place,' Aaron?"

"A park in Iowa City. It's down the street from where he and I used to live."

"A park?"

"Willow Creek. Carl and I played there often when we were kids. We used to pretend we were special-operations soldiers shot down behind enemy lines. We hid in the bushes and trees and kept the enemy… people walking through the park…from noticing us."

"Keep talking, Aaron."

"Then we changed the game and pretended we were on opposite sides. We had rubber knives, and we hunted each other. We got so good at hiding that sometimes it took all day before we finished the game."

"Who won?" Rutherford asked.

"Sometimes I did. Sometimes Carl did."

"So you assume he's inviting you to have one last go-around?" Mosely asked.

"Yes."

"Instead of trying to escape."

"Maybe Carl doesn't think he *can* escape. Maybe he figures he might as well amuse himself in the little time he has left."

"Well, it's for sure he *can't* escape," Mosely said. "You're one hundred percent confident about this hunch of yours?"

"It's not a hunch. Carl wouldn't have been vague about the location unless he knew it was the only place I'd think of. The usual place where we played the game."

"You'd better be right," Mosely emphasized. "If this is part of his strategy, if he's using you to jerk us around and you fell for it, I won't be happy, and that means *you* won't be happy. Tomorrow night, he said?"

Cavanaugh nodded.

"The fallout from what happened in New Orleans is so complicated, I can't possibly get away. In fact, I'm expected right now at another meeting." Mosely stood and looked at Rutherford. "*You're* in charge of counterterrorism. Make sure you catch this guy. Assuming this isn't just a big joke on us."

Mosely picked up a briefcase and left the room.

Cavanaugh thought, *He's setting up John to take the fall if anything goes wrong.*

"John," Cavanaugh said, "your friendship means a lot to me. I believed I was doing the right thing. I still do. I never meant to put your job at risk. I never thought it would seem I abused your trust."

"Things don't always turn out the way we want," Rutherford said.

"I'm sorry."

The office felt cold.

"Tomorrow night?" Rutherford asked.

"Yes, but he'll start earlier."

"Have you got room on your fancy plane for an FBI SWAT team? And this time, you don't carry guns. This time, you're truly a civilian."

20

Cavanaugh wasn't prepared for the changes. Driving into town from Iowa City's airport, he asked the FBI driver to head toward the park.

"Might be risky," Rutherford said. "If Duran sees you in a van full of people…"

"At eight in the morning, we're just one in a stream of vehicles going to work. He won't even try to monitor traffic at this hour. What he'll look for is stationary surveillance."

"I made sure there isn't any," Rutherford said. "I don't want to scare him away. Tonight, after he has a chance to go in and get settled, we'll surround the park and tighten the noose. Assuming you're right about this."

"I guarantee he's in there at this very moment."

As their driver turned left onto West Benton, one of the streets that flanked the park, Cavanaugh couldn't adjust to how much traffic there was. In his youth, this had been a sleepy area of town, on the verge of farmland. Now, except for the park itself, the area was thick with houses and apartment buildings.

With greater surprise, Cavanaugh peered to the right and saw that the park wasn't the same, either. Dense woods had been cut down, leaving trees only along Willow Creek. Clearing the area had made room for more soccer fields. On the opposite end, near where there had once been a cornfield, a children's climbing gym area had been added.

"In there right now?" Rutherford said. "It doesn't look to me as if he has many places to hide."

21

"I've got a bad feeling," Cavanaugh murmured to Jamie and William as they followed Rutherford and his men into Iowa City's modest-sized police station.

The noisy lobby was crowded with law-enforcement officers, the overflow from a crammed conference room. Two men in uniforms, one police, one military, pushed through and spoke to Rutherford.

"Not enough room for a briefing," Rutherford said when he returned. "We're switching locations to the National Guard armory."

Time, Cavanaugh thought. *Even though it's eight-fifteen in the morning, we'll soon run out of day.*

"For that matter, I'm told the armory might not be large enough," Rutherford said, hurrying with them from the police station. "The current estimate is, we need at least a thousand people to seal off that park. Police officers and sheriffs are coming in from all over the state. We've got FBI agents and U.S. marshals flying from as far as St. Louis, Denver, Minneapolis, and Chicago. Through Homeland Security, we also received permission to use the local detachment of the National Guard."

"Another alert," William said. "Another stress on a severely stressed system."

"Reminds me of New Orleans," Jamie said. "Let's hope for a simpler outcome."

"Damn it." A policeman pointed. "Here comes a reporter."

22

The armory filled rapidly. Its high ceiling caused a harsh echo as hundreds of military and law enforcement personnel gathered in front of a platform. Behind a podium, a large map of Willow Creek Park hung from a portable blackboard.

Standing to the side, Jamie said, "I don't see how they can get organized soon enough."

"John has a lot of amazing skills," Cavanaugh told her. He pointed toward where Rutherford spoke to a half-dozen intense civilians, all of them holding notepads and tape recorders.

"…let you observe the briefing," he heard Rutherford say. "…let you take notes and—"

"Photographs? What about photographs?" a reporter demanded.

"Only at the end. But I don't want you printing anything until I tell you."

"We can't promise that."

"It's a matter of national security."

"What are you talking about? What's the emergency?"

"In return for complete access, I want you to swear you won't leak the story. If word about what's happening reaches the general population, we'll have so many curiosity seekers at the park, our target might slip away."

"Park? Target?"

"Watch, listen, and learn," Rutherford said, mounting the podium.

He did indeed have a lot of amazing skills, not the least of which was the clear, authoritative way he conducted the briefing. As the disparate group concentrated on what he said, they stood straighter, assuming similar body language, showing signs of coalescing into a unit. The information that their objective was related to the terrorist attack in New Orleans and the subsequent nationwide manhunt certainly got their attention.

"At three hundred hours tomorrow morning, we'll secure the four approaches to the park." Using a red flashlight beam, Rutherford indicated areas on the map. "Once we know he can't escape, we'll wait until daylight. There's no use going in blind. The northern flank will progress into the search area, checking every conceivable place where someone might hide. The other flanks will remain in position to make sure the target stays trapped. Some of you might be wondering why *every* flank doesn't converge on the park, squeezing him into the center. That way, all of you would be part of the action. The answer is, we don't want you shooting each other in a crossfire if the target puts up a fight."

The group was so confident about their skills that they assumed Rutherford was joking. They chuckled, continuing to bond.

"We've got a great deal to accomplish in a very short time. Equipment. Weapons. Transportation. Timing. There'll be two staging areas: here and a high school a half mile from the park." Rutherford looked toward an official at the side. "West High. Is that right?"

The official nodded.

"After the students go home, we'll conduct practice drills in the track behind the school. Before we enter the search area, the streets near the park need to be blocked off. We also need to evacuate the homes that border the park. This is Special Agent Murphy from the FBI office in Des Moines. She'll organize you into north, south, east, and west units, as well as traffic diversion and evacuation teams. After that…"

One hour later, with the briefing almost concluded, Rutherford said, "Finally I want to introduce a man who knows the target intimately. They grew up here. They played in that park so often that it was practically their backyard. They served in the military together. They worked as protective agents together."

Cavanaugh climbed to the platform. Hundreds of faces studied him. New personnel entered through a door in back. He took the microphone from Rutherford. It made an electronic hum, then settled down.

"I won't take long. You're tired of listening. You want to get started."

They nodded, their eyes bright with the urge to hunt.

"When you see the park, you might conclude that there's little cover and it won't be hard to find him. You might feel confident because there are so many of you and you're going against only one man. Those attitudes could get you killed. Never forget that your quarry is ex–Delta Force. He has world-class training in camouflage and concealment. Fighting in unexpected ways is one of his specialties. Death is one of his specialties. When you go into that park tomorrow morning, you're entering his world. Suspect everything."

An FBI agent raised a hand. "But surely he realizes there's a good chance you won't show up alone tonight. Why would he gamble you won't turn him in?"

"Actually, I think he expects me to betray him by bringing help," Cavanaugh said.

The group looked puzzled.

"He wants to prove how superior he is," Cavanaugh continued. "For him, everything's a competition. He doesn't care if I bring even a small army to catch him. He's telling me he can outsmart *all* of you."

23

"Ten feet apart! No more than that!" Rutherford shouted. "We don't want any gaps in the line. On command, you'll step forward at the steady pace you've been practicing. Supervisors will follow, making certain each line remains straight. Most of you will keep your eyes toward the ground. Every eighth man will study the trees in case the target tries to hide in one. Each hollow. Each pile of leaves. Each fallen tree limb. Assume they conceal the target. Some of you will be in the creek bed. Look for tracks. Look for evidence that someone dug into a bank. If any of you think you've spotted something, blow the whistle you've been given. The line will stop while a team behind you checks the area in question. Your supervisors will tell you when to move forward again.

"Each of you has a firearm. Remember to keep it aimed ahead of you toward the ground or, if you're the eighth man, upward toward the trees. You know the basics. Do not point your weapon at anything you don't intend to destroy. Do not put your finger on the trigger unless you intend to pull it. Do not fire unless you're aware of what's behind your target. In other words, gentlemen and ladies, don't shoot each other. The rules of engagement are as follows. Capture, if possible. But remember, the target is ruthless and dangerous to an extreme. We want to interrogate him, but not at the expense of anyone's life."

24

"The personnel at the armory will be driven to the high school before dark," Rutherford told Cavanaugh after the briefing. "We'll use school buses. No one will pay attention to school buses going to a school. Starting at two hundred hours, each unit will walk the half mile from the school to the park. I don't want the noise from a lot of buses warning the target that we're coming. He might slip away before we're all in place. En route to the search area, the teams will be under orders not to talk. Can you think of anything else?"

"Rig a plane with an infrared camera," Cavanaugh said. "Tonight, have the pilot fly over the park while someone takes photographs. Maybe you'll get Carl's heat signature on the pictures. You might find out where he's hiding."

"Please, remember my client's cooperation when his trial starts," William said.

25

The teams consumed hundreds of pizzas and sodas in the school's cafeteria. Afterward, they sprawled in the corridors and the gymnasium. Knowing that they'd soon be on the move, they dozed as best they could. At 1:30, they were wakened. They used the toilets whether they felt the urge or not. At two, they left the building. In the dark, a cold breeze made them zip their coats shut and shift from one foot to the other. As they assembled in their assigned groups, they heard a plane fly over.

Obeying the command not to speak, they hiked to the park. By three, they reached their appointed areas, spread out in lines that flanked the park, and waited. Lights came on in houses behind them. Troubled questions prompted orders to evacuate, automobiles soon driving away. Then the night became quiet.

Just before five, it started to drizzle.

26

"Rain!" Rutherford's voice was loud inside the van. "The forecast predicted it wouldn't start until late afternoon!"

"Inexact science," Cavanaugh said.

"By then, we'd have caught Duran! We'd have been out of here!"

The downpour pelted the van's window. At 6:30, what should have been a brilliant dawn was a dismal gray.

"Where are we going to find rain gear at this hour!" Rutherford complained. "The men are soaked! They'll get hypothermia!"

A car sped toward the van and skidded to a stop on the slick pavement.

"Finally," Rutherford said.

A man hurried from the car. Flecked with moisture, he scrambled inside the van and handed a manila envelope to Rutherford. "Here are your photos."

Impatient, Rutherford sorted through them. Frowning, he handed them to Cavanaugh. "See anything?"

"A few hot spots," Cavanaugh said. "This one's so small it's probably a squirrel. This other one looks like a dog."

"But no heat signature that looks like it came from a human being?"

Cavanaugh studied the photos a final time. "No."

"Then he lied to you, or you misunderstood the place he meant. He's not in there."

"Wrong," Cavanaugh said. "This is definitely the place, and this is part of his game."

"But a human being gives off heat. The infrared image would show it if he's in the park."

"Unless he shielded himself so a camera wouldn't detect the heat."

"Buried himself?"

"It's one possibility."

"In that case, we don't have to worry because he's drowned by now!"

"He might not even be wet. After all, he was trained to plan for the worst. But even if he *is* soaked, he doesn't care. These conditions are luxurious compared to some of what we went through in Delta Force."

"You know," Rutherford said, "I'm getting tired of hearing about the good old days in Delta."

"You did say you wanted my opinion."

"And what's your opinion of what we ought to do now?"

"Get started."

27

"*...your chance to end this peacefully and give yourself up!*" Rutherford's amplified words drifted across the park. He used a public-address system, the speakers of which were mounted to the top of the van.

He waited. Two minutes became five. He turned from the rain on the windshield. "Counselor, I asked him three times. I put a lot of sincerity into it. Do you think that's enough fair warning?" Without waiting for an answer, he raised his microphone and said, "*Go!*"

On the right, the northern flank moved into the park while those on the south, west, and east formed barricades.

Cavanaugh opened the van's side door.

"What are you doing?"

"Getting some exercise."

The van was on Teg Drive, a street that bordered the eastern side of the park. Feeling the cold rain pelt his head, Cavanaugh passed through the line of men on that side and followed the northern flank as it continued into the park.

Initially, there weren't any obstacles, just the creek flowing through a grassy field. Then the searchers reached trees along the creek and slowed their advance. Dead wet leaves lay along the creek, their autumn colors now dull.

Sensing someone next to him, Cavanaugh turned and saw Jamie. He smiled.

"You'll get soaked," she said.

"So will you," he replied.

"Yeah, but walking in the rain is romantic," she told him.

While some searchers examined the area among the trees, others came to a playground: swings, slides, climbing equipment. They passed metal picnic tables. They reached a shelter and checked its washrooms as well as its rafters. They looked under a bridge that crossed the creek. They attempted to pry up a storm-drain lid, but it was too heavy. They peered into various garbage cans secured in wooden frames. More trees. Another bridge. Another. They arrived at the new playground that a sign said was called Kiwanis Park. Climbing equipment was nestled in a grotto surrounded by rock walls and fir trees. An open shelter had picnic tables under it. Its rafters were exposed, no place to hide.

That was it. They'd come to the southern flank of men, houses behind them. The end of the park.

Suddenly, Rutherford crossed the soaked grass toward Cavanaugh and Jamie.

"Nothing!" he said, flicking rain from his face. "Mosely was right! Duran's playing games with us! He isn't here!"

"That was just a first pass." Cavanaugh's wet clothes stuck to him. "They checked the obvious things. Now they should go through the park again, noticing details."

"What about the neighboring houses? He might be hiding in a garage or a shed."

"No. The houses aren't in the park. When we played the game, we never broke the rules and went out of bounds."

Rutherford shook his head unhappily and walked to the men who'd searched the area. He spoke to the officer in charge, who looked eager to get out of the rain but who nodded and shouted orders, motioning for the line to reverse direction.

Rutherford came back to Cavanaugh and Jamie. "Show me the details that bothered you."

"The ground under every picnic table needs to be checked," Cavanaugh said, walking.

Rutherford thought about it. "Sure. The grass under some of them is worn away until there's only dirt. If he dug a hole there, it would be easier to disguise than if he dug up the grass. The problem is, he'd need a cover, something solid that he could put dirt on and slide over the hole after he got in."

"When we drove into town, I noticed a half-dozen construction sites," Cavanaugh said. "The night before last, he could have grabbed a square of plywood and something to dig with."

"Where would he have put the dirt from the hole?"

"Spread along the creek bed. Covered with leaves."

"How would he have carried it?"

"In a bag he found at a construction site. An empty cement bag is strong enough to hold forty pounds."

"But the dirt on the plywood lid would look freshly dug."

"Not if Carl packed it down until he was satisfied that it looked like the dirt under all the other benches. Leaves on the lid would hide the cracks at the edges."

"Ventilation?"

"A tube coming up next to a table leg."

"Well, if that's where he's hiding," Rutherford concluded, "he's in rising water. He'll need to climb out soon."

"You'd be surprised how snug and dry you can make a hole in the ground with a little help from a plastic sheet."

"More of the good old days in Delta?"

"Actually, the good old days when Carl and I were kids. This is one of the tricks he used against me."

28

In the rain, the line searched the park in greater detail, moving picnic tables, looking under play equipment, examining the edges of shelters for signs that someone had dug under the concrete pads. They found nothing.

"They need to do it again," Cavanaugh said. "Those garbage cans in wooden frames. Let's push them aside and see if Carl's in a hole under one of them."

Carl wasn't.

"That storm-drain lid needs to be pried up. The tunnel needs to be checked."

But the tunnel was filled with water.

"Look for evidence that Carl dug under the concrete paths."

Four hours and five crossings later, Rutherford said firmly, "We're wasting our time. He isn't here."

"But—"

"Either he tricked you, or else you made a mistake about the place he meant."

"This is it. There's no other place."

Rutherford studied the shivering, wet, exhausted men. Many of them coughed. Wind gusted. Dark clouds thickened. "I'm calling off the search."

"No. Please."

"They've been out here since three in the morning," Rutherford said. "Somebody'll end up in the hospital."

"Just one more time."

"To prove that you're wrong? As far as Mosely's concerned, that would be the only good thing to come out of this. Okay, Aaron. Just for you. One more time."

They probed the sand under the playground equipment. Farther along, they did the same to the wood chips around the climbing gym.

Yet again, they found nothing.

Water trickling down his face, Rutherford pointed toward TV news cameras near the park. "They should air this after a Three Stooges marathon. I can only hope the rain blurs any shots they took of me." He turned toward the searchers. "We're finished, everybody! The buses will arrive soon! We'll take you somewhere warm and dry!"

"Coffee," someone said.

"Steaming pots of it," Rutherford promised. He stared at a puddle in the grass. "A thousand men. Some flew in from across the country. Food. Lodging. Buses. Vans. Weapons. Equipment." He gazed up at Cavanaugh. "Nothing to show for it. Mosely's waiting for me to report to him. I can imagine his reaction when I tell him how much everything cost. This time tomorrow, I might be looking for a new job."

Shoulders bent, Rutherford walked toward Teg Drive and the van. The lines disintegrated, soaked men wandering toward the nearby streets.

Burdened with discouragement, Cavanaugh remained in the middle of the field. Jamie stood next to him, the rain gusting at them. Emptiness made him feel colder.

"Want to take a stroll?" he asked.

"It's been a fabulous experience so far. Let's prolong it as much as possible."

He couldn't help smiling. "I love you."

"Of course, you do. I don't want diamonds or fancy clothes. All I want is to share the glamour of your life."

29

They walked east of the park and reached an upward-sloping street called Hafor Drive. As the rain strengthened, Cavanaugh held Jamie's hand and went a half block before stopping in front of a gray, two-story colonial house. It had carefully pruned evergreen shrubs, an ambitious flower garden (now wilted in autumn), and a well-maintained lawn.

"This is where I lived. In my memory, every house on the street is a brilliant white. But as you see, they're all different in reality. Gray. Brown. Blue. Maybe they always were. I guess I only imagined they gleamed." Cavanaugh pointed toward the second level. "There, on the left, that was my bedroom. The house on that side had the dog I played with."

"The one that disappeared?"

"Yes. The house farther along on the left is where Carl lived. Now that I think about it, in my memory *that* one definitely doesn't gleam. I knew too much about Carl's father and what went on inside that house. So long ago." Cavanaugh turned to look down the street toward the rain-veiled park. "I can see Carl and me on the sidewalk, heading for the creek and those trees."

Cavanaugh became silent.

The rain gusted.

"I know he's down there."

30

They lay under blankets on a motel-room bed, but despite a long, hot shower, they still had trouble getting warm. Beyond closed draperies, the sound of the rain lessened. Afternoon became evening. Shadows deepened. They held one another.

Someone knocked on the door.

A blanket around him, Cavanaugh crossed the room. Standing next to the door, avoiding the peephole, which could be a target for a bullet, he asked, "Who is it?" The response made him open the door, allowing William to enter.

"Hi, Jamie," William said cheerily, as if accustomed to seeing her in bed.

"Hi, William," she said from her pillow, as if receiving a visitor in this manner was the most natural thing in the world.

Cavanaugh locked the door.

William had two garment bags draped over an arm. "Here are the clothes you asked me to bring from the Gulfstream. Jeans. Pullovers. Jackets. Socks. Shoes. Underwear. I'm quickly becoming the most expensive errand boy in the legal community."

"Except that we can't afford to pay you any longer," Cavanaugh said.

"The distraction factor is payment enough. Rutherford says that he still has some loose ends to take care of, that we won't be flying out of here until the morning."

"Does that ruin your schedule?"

"Not at all. I went to Harvard with the dean of the University of Iowa's law school. I'm having dinner with him tonight."

"Every city you come to, you have a connection."

"I win friends and influence people."

"Intimidate them into submission is more like it."

"Oh, I almost forgot. I needed to set something down when I knocked." William opened the door and retrieved a large paper bag marked with the logo for Kentucky Fried Chicken.

"How could you forget you brought food?" Jamie asked with delight.

31

In the night, she wakened, reached for Cavanaugh, but didn't feel him. Outside, the night was quiet, the rain having stopped. She glanced toward the bathroom. Its door was open. Its light was off. She switched on the bedside lamp, went to the closet, and found that his clothes were gone.

32

Cavanaugh told the taxi driver to let him off at a convenience store on the end of West Benton Street. He paid and waited until the taxi pulled away. Then he left the harsh lights of the store and walked down the street toward the park. It was on his right, and he was pleased that fog obscured the fields and the creek, making it unnecessary for him to take elaborate precautions to hide his approach.

Where the creek entered the park, he left the sidewalk. Immediately, he unclipped his knife from his pants pocket, allowing the hook on the back of its blade to snag on the pocket, the resistance causing the blade to open. The creek was on his left. He used it as a guide but stayed far enough away that he could respond to the sound of an attacker lunging up from the bed. Soon the hazy glow of the streetlights behind him dimmed, then vanished. As he proceeded over the wet grass, the fog's moist tendrils drifted around him, their chill dampness seeping through his jacket.

He unfocused his eyes, emphasizing the periphery of his vision. The effort produced a strain comparable to forcing himself to be cross-eyed. But in this uncomfortable way, trying to look sideways while peering ahead, he activated the rod-shaped cells in his eyes, the cells that were sensitive in darkness. The technique made it possible for him to see distinctions among shadows, gradations within shades of gray and black.

Having crisscrossed the park numerous times during the day, he had a sense of how far objects were from each other. Strong boyhood memories reinforced his estimate. The spongy grass absorbed his footfalls. Only when he judged that he was within thirty paces of the first stand of trees did he crouch and assess what was ahead. He listened for a long while. Lingering moisture dripped from the trees and bushes. Water trickled along the creek bed. A breeze scraped branches.

He crept ten paces forward and listened again. Hearing nothing to alarm him, he went another ten paces, then turned to the right toward a fog-shrouded field while the periphery of his left eye concentrated on the vague shadows of the trees. With his rod-strengthened vision, he looked for movement that couldn't be attributed to a branch swaying, for a shape that didn't fit the pattern of tree trunks. The rain had caused many bushes to lose their leaves, creating gaps that enabled him to notice if there was a solid shape behind them.

He crept farther ahead. In his experience, nothing was more tense or exhausting than stalking someone in darkness. Patience was everything. Discipline. Control. The irony wasn't lost on him that, because Carl's lack of discipline had been the cause of so much misfortune, Carl would take extra care to prove that he now had more control than Cavanaugh did.

Knife ready, he entered the trees. From the rain, the dead leaves were so soggy that they made no sound under his shoes. In his youth, this section of trees had been almost fifty yards wide and long, but now it was barely ten yards wide and thirty yards long. As wisps of fog drifted past, he crouched with his back against a trunk and turned his head slowly one way and then the other, using his peripheral vision to scan the indistinct branches and bushes.

One minute.

Two minutes.

Three minutes.

This is what you planned, Carl. You knew I'd be forced to act responsibly and betray you. You knew even a small army wouldn't find you. You knew, when the search failed, I'd finally come.

So here I am. Ready when you are. Wherever you're hiding, come out. This is what you wanted, so let's do it. But take your time. I don't want to rush you. I've got all night.

Eight minutes.

Nine minutes.

Ten minutes.

Cavanaugh couldn't risk staying in one position much longer. The chill creeping into his muscles might cramp them if he remained immobile. The same liability applied to Carl. He, too, would need to shift his body. Inching forward, Cavanaugh expected that at any moment a figure would rocket from under leaves, a knife plunging toward him. Despite the cold, he felt nervous sweat trickling down his face.

At once, a noise made him flinch. On his right. Something crashing through the bushes. Low. Breathing hard, a huge dog bounded toward him. Black, it suddenly noticed him and veered through the trees. With equal suddenness, it howled in agony. The howl became yelps as it thrashed grotesquely, snapping branches off bushes, twisting, thudding against a tree. Its frenzy dwindled, its yelps getting weaker. Finally, it lay still.

At distant houses, dogs howled in response. Gradually, the night returned to the quiet of moisture dripping off leaves, the wind scraping branches, and water trickling along the creek. Cavanaugh eased toward the dog—a Labrador retriever, he estimated—and found the stake that had catapulted into its chest when paws tripped a wire.

A booby trap, Carl? After dark, you crawled from your hiding place and arranged a surprise for me? I'm disappointed. Since when are traps in the game?

Rage heating him, Cavanaugh yanked the stake from the dog. He felt along the wire. It was the sort of item routinely discarded on a construction site. He coiled it, put it in a pocket, and inched forward, holding the stake.

33

At the open door to his room, wearing hastily put-on clothes, Rutherford squinted at his watch, his eyes puffy from having been wakened. "Maybe he just went for a walk."

"At one in the morning?" Jamie asked skeptically.

"It was a tough night and day. He must have a lot on his mind, a lot to rethink."

"He's gone to the park."

"You don't know that for a fact."

"I know *him*. There isn't anywhere else he'd go."

"What do you expect me to do, tell those thousand men to go back to the park? Even if I wanted to, I couldn't get them organized before dawn. Did you watch the evening news? Did you see how foolish we looked? For sure, Mosely would demand my resignation if I repeated today's farce."

"No," Jamie said, "I don't expect you to tell those thousand men to go back to the park."

"Thank heaven."

"I expect that *you and I* will go to the park."

"Shit," the Southern Baptist said.

34

Sweat blended with moisture from the fog and trickled down Cavanaugh's face. He lay on his chest on wet grass, assessing the gloom of the next stand of trees. He was sure that a booby trap waited for him in there, also. He tried to imagine Carl's reaction to hearing the dog's agonized howl.

Carl needs to assume I realize what killed the animal. He also needs to assume that I'll now avoid the trees and any other areas where traps can be easily set. He'll decide that I'll shift to the open spaces. He'll focus his hunt in those areas.

That meant Cavanaugh needed to do the opposite of what Carl expected and go farther into the trees. But first he rolled toward a nearby picnic bench. He crawled under. It was a space that would appeal to someone who wanted to hide his silhouette while looking for his prey. Cavanaugh used the wire to bind the stake to a metal leg, the point projecting outward at head level.

Then, ready with his knife, he squirmed from beneath the table and studied the closer gloom of the trees. Probing with the knife, moving it up and down, then right and left, he crawled past a bush. He waited. He listened. With his peripheral vision, he stared at the fog and the shadows. In the distance, the muffled drone of a car proceeded along West Benton Street. His nerves tightened until the sound was gone and he could again concentrate on the faint noises around him.

He shifted deeper into the trees. Immediately, he froze when his knife met resistance. Something thin and taut. A wire. Moving to the side, he discovered a low branch bent sideways and down. Feeling in the darkness, he found that the wire was attached to a rock that weighed down the branch. A stake was tied to the branch. If Cavanaugh had disturbed the wire, the rock would have shifted, the branch would have sprung, and…

He held his breath—one, two, three. Silently exhaled through his lips—one, two, three. Quietly inhaled through his nose—one, two, three. The technique calmed his heartbeat and steadied his lungs. Then he pushed the rock off the branch. With a *whoosh*, the branch vaulted noisily past him. Simultaneously, he grunted as if he'd been hit, then crashed against a bush. His groan became faint as he remembered the groans of wounded comrades becoming faint when death claimed them.

Holding his breath again (one-two-three), exhaling (one-two-three), he crawled silently to the edge of the trees, doing his best to make his crouched silhouette indistinguishable from a stump.

One minute.

Two minutes.

Three minutes.

Ten minutes.

A whisper on his right made his heart lurch. "Getting tired of waiting, Aaron?"

The words came from a cautious distance, perhaps as much as thirty feet away, muffled by the fog.

"I'd have joined you sooner," Carl's voice continued, "but I had to check the rest of the park and make sure you didn't bring company like you did this morning."

Cavanaugh's pulse was so rapid that his veins felt swollen.

Something crashed among the trees. Instantly, Cavanaugh squirmed in that direction. He knew that was the one place Carl *wouldn't* be. The noise was intended as a distraction. Right now, Carl would be hurrying around the stand of trees, intending to enter them from behind while Cavanaugh theoretically remained in place, his attention directed toward the noise.

All the while Cavanaugh squirmed forward, he used his knife to probe the air. Abruptly, he felt the resistance of another wire. At the same time, he thought he heard a slight noise behind him, Carl entering the trees.

He rolled to the side, threw a branch on the wire, heard a *whoosh*, and relied on *that* to distract Carl while he snaked to the side of the grove, emerging onto the grass. He sprinted soundlessly onto a soccer field and spun with his knife, waiting for Carl to charge through the fog.

"How do you like the traps?" Carl asked from the murk of the trees. "Makes the game more interesting, don't you think?"

Cavanaugh didn't answer, refusing to be baited into revealing his location.

"I figured, if *you* can break the rules, so can I. Honestly, don't you feel embarrassed that you brought all those guys to look for me? Can't you fight your own battles?"

Cavanaugh remained silent.

"All that manpower, and they couldn't find me. Aren't you dying to know where I hid?"

A crash among the trees. Cavanaugh flinched. Instantly, he recovered and tightened his grip on his knife, knowing that Carl had used the noise to hide the lesser sounds he made as he hurried from the grove.

Now they were both in the open. In the fog.

"The truth is, I counted on you to betray me again." Carl's voice came from straight ahead. "After all, betrayal's in your nature."

Cavanaugh crouched, making himself a small target while priming his arm muscles to strike with his knife.

"I wanted you to bring help, lots and lots of help." This time, Carl's voice came from the darkness on the right.

Cavanaugh moved in the opposite direction.

"So much help that, when they didn't find me, they'd figure this was the last place in the world to look for me." The voice was farther to the right.

He's tempting me to charge, Cavanaugh thought.

"The only flaw in the plan was the chance you'd feel so ashamed that you wouldn't show up tonight." Now Carl's voice came from the *left*.

Cavanaugh reversed direction and headed to the *right*.

"Even though they'll never find your body, they'll be forced to assume I was here." The voice was closer, to the right now.

Cavanaugh stopped moving.

"After you disappear, they'll focus on this area."

Cavanaugh glimpsed a shadow in the fog.

"But of course, that'll be too late. I'll be far away by then."

Taking advantage of Carl's distraction, Cavanaugh charged.

From experience, he knew that the surprising rush would provoke Carl's startle reflex, gaining the second he needed to strike a lethal blow, but as he raced toward the shadow, plunging his knife into flesh, feeling blood on his hand, he realized with sickening dismay that what he stabbed was the dog.

Carl held the corpse in front of him. Before Cavanaugh could pull the blade free, Carl twisted the carcass sideways, wrenching the knife from Cavanaugh's hand. Carl shoved the dead animal at him, knocking him backward, the dog's weight thrusting him to the ground.

The impact jolted Cavanaugh's breath from his lungs. Wheezing, he rolled. Simultaneously, he felt a sharp impact in his right side as a crack and a flash came from Carl's direction. *Jesus, he has a gun! He shot me!*

Continuing to roll, his lungs wheezing, Cavanaugh realized that the bullet had passed through the dog before it struck him. The bullet had penetrated him but not deeply enough to hit a vital organ. Lunging to his feet, he ran. But now his urgent footfalls were forceful enough to make sounds on the wet grass. He heard Carl chasing him. The collision had been so disorienting that he lost his bearings in the fog. Possibly, he raced toward West Benton Street, possibly toward the creek, possibly toward—

A branch struck his face. The trees! He'd run back to them! As Carl's footsteps pounded closer, Cavanaugh scurried into the bushes. A sudden glow struggled to pierce the fog—from a flashlight Carl held. Frantic, Cavanaugh shifted deeper into the trees.

"I did play fair, sort of," Carl said. "The gun's part of a knife. You remember those combination models Lance showed us?" He referred to an antique style in which a barrel formed part of the back of a blade. The hammer was the top of the guard, the trigger the bottom of the guard. "Of course, you can't get much accuracy and power. You got hit with a thirty-two. I expect *that* won't kill you."

Feeling blood swell from his side, Cavanaugh backed from the searching flashlight and bumped against something that stung his leg. Peering down, he saw a stake on the end of a branch, one of the booby traps he'd sprung.

The weak light pivoted through the darkness and the fog, moving in his direction. He moved farther backward, forcing the branch to bend behind him.

The flashlight beam settled on him.

"You don't look like you're hit bad at all." Carl shifted toward him through the bushes. "Not to worry about taking another bullet. It's a single shot. I don't have another round for it. Always had a fondness for this thing. Two weapons in one. Saves room in my bug-out bag."

Cavanaugh kept backing away. He bumped against a tree trunk.

Holding the oddly shaped knife, a barrel along the back of the blade, Carl stalked toward him. "Hate to do this. A knife against bare hands. But as you're dying, I want you to bear in mind, I'll be going for your wife next."

Carl lunged.

Cavanaugh jumped free of the branch.

It whipped forward.

Carl screamed as the stake plunged into his thigh.

35

Jamie and Rutherford drove past the park. Two exits along West Benton Street, they turned right and then right again, finding themselves on the street where Cavanaugh had lived. The fog kept the van's headlights from reaching the park. As they got out, a dim streetlight allowed Jamie to realize that Rutherford had parked in front of what had once been Cavanaugh's house.

They secured their jackets and started down toward the invisible park, only to pause when they heard a distant *crack*.

They waited. The sound wasn't repeated.

"What was that?" Jamie whispered.

"It sounded like a—"

"Shot?" Jamie's face tingled, only partly from the chill of the fog.

"Low caliber, I think."

They waited a moment longer. Then Rutherford crouched, as if tying a shoe. He straightened and handed her something.

"A gun?"

"My emergency pistol. I keep it in an ankle holster."

"You're trusting me with this?"

Rather than discuss it, Rutherford continued through the fog. As Jamie caught up to him, she heard what might have been muted voices in the park, too low and indistinct to be identified. They walked faster, then started to run when they heard a scream.

36

"You cocksucker!" Wailing, dropping his flashlight, Carl stumbled backward, the stake in his thigh tearing flesh as it pulled free.

Cavanaugh rushed him, then dodged away as the flashlight on the ground glinted off the knife Carl swung at him.

Cavanaugh grabbed a thick limb from the ground, the size of a baseball bat. He braced himself to strike as Carl hobbled toward him, slashing his knife up and down and from side to side in a buzz-saw blur.

Cavanaugh swung the club. Carl dodged. Cavanaugh swung again, wincing from the wound in his side. Carl leapt back. Breathing heavily, facing one another, they turned in a circle, looking for an opening, ready to strike, the flashlight casting shadows across them.

At once, Cavanaugh realized that Carl had maneuvered so that his left hand now pulled back the branch with the stake. Lurching away as Carl released it, Cavanaugh struck a fallen bough and dropped backward, the stake zipping past him. Shouting, Carl charged, and all Cavanaugh could do was roll away from the light. Keeping his hand on the club but in no position to use it, he surged to his feet and raced from the trees.

The picnic table, he thought. Its dark shape was suddenly before him. He almost banged into it but managed to slow in time to drop to his knees and scurry under it, carefully avoiding where he'd secured the stake. He groaned as Carl's blade sliced across his back. But he forced himself to keep crawling, sensing Carl leaning fiercely under the table to stab him.

Something made a grotesque, liquid, popping sound. Carl's scream communicated sanity-threatening pain. Cavanaugh tightened his grip on the club. Rising beyond the table, he swung over it, aiming toward Carl, who twisted in a frenzy, his left hand clutching his left eye.

The club whistled past Carl, who now did an amazing thing, the one mistake an experienced knife fighter never makes. Don't throw your knife at your enemy. You might miss, and then you're without your weapon. But in this case, it wasn't a mistake. At so close a range that the sounds Cavanaugh made guided Carl's aim, relying on surprise, Carl threw the knife. Hurled it with all his might. Cavanaugh wailed from the pain of the knife striking his ribs, chipping bone. The only thing that saved him was that the blade was upright and didn't slip between ribs to puncture his ribs or his heart.

Nonetheless, he felt dizzy, in shock from blood loss. Gasping, he wavered. He fumbled, trying to find where the knife dropped, but Carl was suddenly on him, knocking him to the sand, his fingers around his throat, squeezing.

Blood dripped from Carl's missing eye onto Cavanaugh's face.

"Want to make a bet, Aaron?"

Wheezing, Cavanaugh grabbed a handful of dirt from under the table and threw it at Carl's bleeding eye socket.

Carl hissed as if the dirt were hot coals. But his hands remained firm on Cavanaugh's throat.

Flesh separating on his sliced back, Cavanaugh reached painfully up to shove a thumb into Carl's empty eye socket. He actually got it in, feeling blood stream down his thumb. But before he could probe, his hand sank, his mind swirling, Carl squeezing harder.

Carl's head jerked up, his remaining eye scanning the fog. Distant footsteps ran across the invisible soccer field.

"You still can't do this without help, huh?" He leaned down, so close that he breathed against Cavanaugh's left ear. "I bet your friends never find *either* of us."

As Cavanaugh's mind swirled faster, Carl's last words echoed and faded.

37

Running toward the park, Jamie and Rutherford heard a shout. Reaching the grass, they heard a scream. Charging across a fog-shrouded field, they heard another. Instinctively, they knew when they were close enough that they needed to slow their frantic pace or risk giving away their position in the dark and being shot.

Pistols aimed, they shifted carefully toward the last sound they'd heard.

38

Cavanaugh woke in darkness. Not the darkness of the night and the fog in which there'd been gradations of blackness and shadow. This was absolute darkness, made worse by foul air and the press of Carl's body against him. His neck felt swollen, the inside of his throat burning from having been choked. His sliced back felt on fire, blood streaming from it, making his mind swirl again. His wounded side throbbed. He almost vomited. It took him several moments before he overcame panic sufficiently to realize that he and Carl lay on their left sides, Carl's chest against his back. He felt Carl's labored breathing against his neck.

"Awake, Aaron?" Carl whispered.

Cavanaugh felt breath against his ear. He didn't respond.

"Sure, you are," Carl said. "I feel your heart beating faster."

Cavanaugh didn't see a point in pretending any longer. "Where are we?" The words stung his irritated throat.

"Home, sweet home. Check out the expert workmanship. Feel the fine wood."

Cavanaugh's arms were pinned along his side. The narrow space, which increasingly reminded him of a coffin, made it impossible for him to touch what he now identified as wood against his cheek (a floor) and against his forehead (a wall).

Carl's right arm was free. In the absolute darkness, he reached over Cavanaugh and tapped the wood, causing a muffled echo. "The best plywood available on the junk heap of a construction site. A sheet of plastic's above the roof so water can't seep in. Comfy, huh? Just the thing for spending a couple of days and nights. Of course, I didn't plan for company. When I was the only occupant, I had room to drink from a water bottle and eat beef jerky. Not too much, of course, because I didn't want to foul my dream house with more piss and crap than was necessary."

Cavanaugh almost threw up.

"So relax. We'll find out if I win my bet. But I'm sorry to say, this is going to be a one-sided conversation from now on. You might try to shout and attract your friends. There's an air hole above my head. I can't take the chance they'd hear you. Open your mouth."

Cavanaugh didn't. In the darkness, he felt something sting his neck. The point of a blade.

"I picked up my knife before I carried you here. Open your mouth, or else I'll slice the artery in your neck."

Cavanaugh obeyed. He felt a gritty, musty rag being shoved into his mouth.

"I hope you don't have asthma," Carl whispered. "I wouldn't want you to suffocate. So here we are, snug as two bugs in a rug. How do you suppose we should pass the time?"

Behind him, Carl's voice was so soft that Cavanaugh could barely hear it. His hushed breath drifted past Cavanaugh's ear.

"Why don't I give you a little lesson? You know the old saying, 'You can't pick your family, but you *can* pick your friends.' Isn't that the truth? If only Lance had been my father. Wouldn't *that* have been great? Me and the old man making knives. As for friends, well, most people throw that word around. What they really mean is 'acquaintances.' They mean people they spend time with because they happen to live next to each other or work together or play sports with each other or belong to the same club or whatever. People who don't make trouble. People who don't ask for much, who don't inconvenience them.

"But a true friend, Aaron. That's rare and special. A friend is somebody who accepts your faults, who's there for you always, even when you're not your best, somebody who'll do anything for you, somebody you can count on totally, just as a friend can count on *you*. It's the most powerful relationship there is. Most marriages don't come close, because in a lot of marriages the partners aren't really friends.

"I chose *you* as my friend, Aaron. My *only* friend. I never felt closer to anyone. There isn't anything I wouldn't have done for you. Imagine how I felt when I realized that you weren't *my* friend, that you were just another self-centered asshole who said *adios* when the going got rough."

In the pitch-blackness, the gag absorbed moisture in Cavanaugh's mouth. It made his throat dry. It made the fetid air he breathed tickle his bronchial passages. He feared he would cough. He feared he would choke.

"When you think about it, we've never been closer than we are right now," Carl said. "It's not a bad way to die. Pressed against the person we love."

Fighting not to panic, Cavanaugh held his breath in the hopes of stifling his impulse to gag. He failed. His stomach heaved. Bile soared up his throat.

39

Where? Jamie mentally yelled, not daring to speak and make herself a target. Where *are* they?

Rutherford moved next to her, aiming to the right while she aimed to the left. They continued slowly, warily, into the fog. As much as she could estimate in the darkness, the screams had come from straight ahead. With her attention focused there, the ground beneath her suddenly collapsed. She fell, sliding downward, tumbling into water. Rutherford splashed next to her, sprawling, the creek flowing over them.

They scrambled upright, but any element of surprise was now lost, and Jamie's stomach seemed filled with sharp heavy stones as she peered over the top of the opposite bank. More darkness and fog awaited them. She aimed to the left, listening intensely for any indication of where Cavanaugh might be. But what caught her attention wasn't a sound.

It was a glow so faint that it might have been marsh light. Climbing from the creek, aiming, she crept toward the pale illumination, Rutherford moving next to her.

They reached trees. The glow was stronger. On the ground. Among bushes. A flashlight. When Jamie picked it up, she did what Cavanaugh had taught her to do, keeping it away from her center of mass so that a bullet aimed toward the light wouldn't hit her chest.

She scanned the trees and bushes. Rutherford pointed, crimson attracting her attention: blood on a stake tied to a branch. Her mouth sour, she aimed the flashlight toward the ground, seeing more blood. Following it, they left the trees. The blood went in two directions. Some of it formed a trail on the left, where the flashlight revealed a dead Labrador retriever, a knife sticking into it.

"What the hell happened here?" Jamie murmured.

"Hell," Rutherford said. "Exactly."

The blood trail on the right led to a picnic table, and here Jamie found an astonishing amount of blood, a spray of it everywhere. The sharp stones in her stomach now felt like cold barbed wire twisting inside her. Rutherford pointed again. The blood led toward the creek. They peered down at the water, where the blood was no longer in sight.

40

"Take it easy," Carl whispered, pulling the rag from Cavanaugh's mouth as bile rushed into his mouth. "We don't want you to choke to death. Especially when you've got the alternative of the dreaminess of bleeding to death."

Cavanaugh spit acid and gasped for air. He understood. Carl had spoken about the plastic sheet above the roof, the barrier that kept water out. But the floor was now wet, the fluid rising, and the only explanation for that was blood—from Cavanaugh's wounded side, punctured chest, and sliced back as well as from Carl's stabbed thigh and bleeding eye socket.

"Aren't we a pair?" Carl said. "Just like being in a womb. From the cradle to the grave. Drifting away. On the path to dreamland. What's the best time we ever had together. No. Don't answer that. Instead of whispering, you might scream. I'm afraid I need to gag you again."

Carl crammed the rag into Cavanaugh's mouth, then nestled against him. "Blood sure smells like copper."

But Cavanaugh couldn't smell anything. Indeed, he had trouble feeling the wet, slippery wood beneath him. His mind again swirled.

"The best time we ever had was when we went camping in Colorado and..."

41

Screaming inwardly, Jamie shifted along the creek, scanning each side of it while Rutherford aimed toward the top of the bank in case a dark figure attacked them. *Where?* she kept demanding. *Where's the blood?* She almost did scream when it occurred to her that they might be heading in the wrong direction. Rather than searching deeper into the park, perhaps they should have gone in the opposite direction. Her trembling hand made the flashlight waver, its beam flicking this way and that. Time seemed suspended, yet she felt that ten minutes went by in an instant. *The blood! Where's the damned...*

There! She saw it, the crimson rising from the creek, blending with deep footprints that struggled up the bank on the right. She and Rutherford hurried to the top, and now Jamie felt the barbed wire in her stomach become molten. It expanded, threatening to burn through her belly. The blood formed a pool in the grass in front of her.

But it didn't go farther.

42

"Looks like I'll win my bet," Carl whispered. "If they were going to find us, they'd have done it by now. I cut a piece from my jacket and tied it around my leg so I wouldn't drip blood on the ground. I came back here and got one of the plastic sheets I stole from a construction site. I wrapped it around you so you wouldn't drip blood when I carried you here. As far as whoever's out there is concerned, we vanished. Ain't that great? Our last game of hide and seek."

Cavanaugh managed to nod. His consciousness wavering, he thought about all the things he regretted—not kissing Jamie more often, not telling her often enough how much he loved her. He regretted the beatings Carl had received from his father. He regretted not having spent more time with Carl in the weeks before his father's disgrace forced Carl's family to move to Nashville. He regretted having treated Carl's letters and phone calls as a nuisance. He regretted not having kept in touch with Carl after Global Protective Services fired him.

What do you say we go out for a drink, Carl? How about a movie and a burger afterward? How about visiting my ranch in Wyoming? You'll love my home. Sunset over the Tetons. A friendship. All this happened, so many people died, because of a friendship that went bad.

His suffocated mind couldn't find the words. *Who's the self-centered asshole, Carl? You think I let you down? Pal, you* let *me* down.

He knew he ought to feel angry. Furious. And he *was*. If he had the strength, he'd find a way to grab Carl's head and pound it until…

But he felt something else as well, and as tears streamed down his face, his blood and his life seeping from him, he tried to say it, tried to spit out the gag and tell Carl….

"Choking again, good buddy?"

Carl's hand pulled out the vile rag. Cavanaugh's mouth was almost too dry to force out the words.

"Got something to say?" Carl asked.

Cavanaugh nodded weakly.

"Let's hear it."

"I'm…"

"Yes? Keep trying. Get it out. Last words and all that."

"Sorry."

"Ah."

Cavanaugh's mind seemed to plummet.

"Sorry? You know what, my friend?" Carl said. "I am too. Three years ago, maybe I should just have kicked the shit out of you. Maybe I was afraid I couldn't do it. But hey, I sure kicked the shit out of you now."

Cavanaugh felt more tears streaming down his face. What he had tried to say was that, Jamie aside, he was sorry that he and Carl had ever grown up. I wish we were still kids, he thought. His head thudded onto the blood-soaked wood.

43

"John, help me think," Jamie said. "Where did they go?" Jamie aimed the flashlight through the fog. Frantic, she stumbled forward into the darkness.

"What's that over there?" Rutherford said.

"Where?"

"*There.*" Rutherford guided her hand, the flashlight dimly revealing a children's climbing gym: rods and railings and tubes in a rock-walled grotto whose sides were topped with bushes and evergreen shrubs.

Jamie entered the grotto and shivered as if in another dimension. She scanned the dim light over everything, the wood chips on the ground, the little bridge over a culvert through which children could crawl, the beams that formed a sandbox, the picnic tables.

"There's no blood." A sob escaped her. "I don't know what to do."

She stepped farther inside the grotto. She aimed the light at everything, lingering, staring. Finally, desperate to search somewhere else, she turned away. Her flashlight swung past something.

"Wait."

She redirected the light.

"Tell me if I'm seeing things."

"*Where?*"

"There!"

She and Rutherford walked toward the children's bridge. It spanned a cement culvert that children would find exciting to crawl through. On the right, there was a second culvert, smaller, more exciting. Between the two was the rock wall, huge boulders embedded in a dirt slope.

"That boulder," Jamie said. "The one in the middle. Why are–"

"Wood chips on it?" Rutherford asked.

"There aren't any on the others. Help me," Jamie pleaded.

They rushed to the boulder. Rutherford grabbed its top.

"Stand back," he told Jamie. "Aim the light."

Jamie did. She also aimed the gun. Rutherford pulled with all his broad-shouldered strength, unprepared for how easily the boulder toppled away, revealing a nightmare, two men smeared in blood, the smell of excrement streaming out. Next to them lay the strap that Carl had wrapped around the boulder, hoisting the rock back into place, then pulling the strap through slits on either slide.

At first, it was impossible to tell the difference between them, both were so mired in gore. One wasn't moving. But the other raised his head and peered out. His left eye was missing. His lips were crusted with blood.

"Looks like I lost the bet." Carl's voice sounded like his throat was filled with sand. "No matter. I was never going to let you win it, Aaron."

Carl lowered a knife to slit Cavanaugh's throat.

Jamie shot out Carl's other eye.

44

Cavanaugh saw lights in his coffin. Blinding. Panicked, he jerked up a hand to shield his eyes.

Fingers startled him, grasping his arm, lowering it.

"You'll pull out your IV line," Jamie said.

His eyelids felt as if they were sewed shut. Slowly, he managed to break the imaginary threads and open his eyes.

Jamie sat next to him. She was haggard with exhaustion, her green eyes dull, her brunette hair lusterless from tension, and yet she looked as beautiful as he'd ever seen her.

He was in a hospital bed. His side and back throbbed. Stitches and bandages squeezed him. His lips felt thick, his tongue swollen and dry.

Jamie put a straw in his mouth.

Grateful, he sipped. The water was tasteless for a moment. Then it became exquisite. But weakness made it difficult for him to swallow. He drooled. Jamie used a cloth to wipe it away.

"Afraid I'm not at my best," he said.

"Nonsense. You're perfect."

Weariness drifted over him.

When he wakened again, Jamie continued to sit next to him.

She squeezed his hand. "Asleep, you look like a little boy."

Mustering his strength, Cavanaugh managed to ask, "Carl?"

"Dead."

"How?"

She told him. He had to concentrate to take in all the details.

"The boulders and wood chips were wet from the rain," she said. "When Carl lowered the boulder that hid him, wood chips stuck to it. They were *under* the boulder. He couldn't have seen them when he pulled the boulder back into place. He must have been so delirious with pain that he didn't realize."

"The second person you've killed."

"Don't talk about it."

"I understand. I've been there."

"No," Jamie said. "You *don't* understand."

Cavanaugh's lips felt numb. "Even justified, it's a terrible—"

"I'd do *anything* for you. That's not what I meant. I mean you can't talk about it. You can't let anybody know I'm the one who shot him."

Jamie looked around. Her voice was so low that he could barely hear it.

"John lent me his gun," Jamie whispered intensely. "He'd lose his job if anyone found out. After I shot Carl, he took the gun from me and fired it a second time, hitting a boulder next to the hole as if a first shot missed. That way, he had gunpowder residue on him. The investigators took his word. Nobody thought to test *me*."

"*John* did that?" Trying to analyze the implications, Cavanaugh drifted again.

The next time he rose out of blackness, he heard hushed voices. Looking for Jamie, he saw Rutherford and her talking quietly in a corner.

Rutherford glanced over. "Sleeping beauty's awake. How are you feeling?"

"Ready to take up ballroom dancing."

They smiled at the feeble joke.

"Want the first waltz?" he asked Rutherford.

"Thanks for the offer, but I'll sit this one out."

"Reject me. See if I care."

They smiled again.

"Carl wanted it," Cavanaugh said.

"Wanted?" Rutherford asked, puzzled.

"To be shot."

"He didn't act like it! He was trying to slit your throat!" Jamie insisted.

"To force John to shoot," Cavanaugh said as a nurse went past the doorway.

Jamie looked at him with new appreciation. He was more alert than she thought.

Even so, Cavanaugh had to concentrate to form the words. "Carl knew he had nothing ahead of him except probably a death sentence. Sitting in a narrow cell waiting for the seconds to tick by and somebody to stick a needle in him. He hurried things along. John, you did him a favor," Cavanaugh said, looking at Jamie.

"The bastard didn't deserve a favor," she told him.

"When he and I were kids, we had wonderful times," Cavanaugh said. Melancholy made him feel as if Carl's hands were again around his throat. He had difficulty getting his voice to work as he changed the subject. "So what happens now?"

"You lost a lot of blood. Your doctor says you'll need to stay here a few more days while you get more strength back."

"And then we go back to New Orleans to prepare for the trial," Cavanaugh said.

Rutherford and Jamie looked at one another.

"What aren't you telling me?" Cavanaugh asked.

"Mosely dropped the charges," Rutherford answered.

Cavanaugh needed a moment to adjust to that

"What happened in the park attracted a lot of media attention," Rutherford continued. "A lot of sympathy for you. God knows why, but many people think you're some kind of hero." He half-smiled. "The hotels don't want to look like corporate bullies. They put pressure on Mosely. So did the officials for the World Trade Organization. It seems my boss isn't as unbendable as he maintains."

"How's he treating *you*?" Cavanaugh asked.

"Apparently, *I'm* some kind of hero, also," Rutherford said. "For now, we're best buddies."

"Knock, knock," a voice said.

Glancing over, Cavanaugh saw William in the doorway. With his coiffed hair, his gleaming teeth, his brilliant white shirt, his authoritative pinstripe suit, and his powerful-looking chest, he looked more the celebrity attorney than ever. "Do you feel strong enough for more company?"

"You're always welcome," Cavanaugh said.

"I considered bringing flowers, but I decided on *this* instead." He gave Cavanaugh an envelope.

"What's *this* about?"

"A letter of credit from a dozen of your wealthiest clients. It seems they quaked in their billionaire boots when they realized that Global Protective Services and in particular *you* weren't going to be available to keep them alive."

"From the Cheshire-cat look on your face," Jamie said, "I have a feeling you took pains to remind them."

"Quite a few phone calls, yes. You'll receive an itemized bill now that you can afford my services again. Of course, you'll need to downsize Global Protective Services considerably, but I suspect you prefer it that way."

"As long as it allows me to protect people who deserve it but can't afford me." Cavanaugh felt Jamie squeeze his hand.

"Whatever you want. It's your company," William said.

"And Jamie's."

"Yes," Rutherford said. "I've seen firsthand that she's an excellent protector."

Cavanaugh studied him. "So are *you*, John. You helped save my life. Thank you."

Rutherford thought about it and shrugged. "That's what friends do."

ACKNOWLEDGMENTS

I'm indebted to many operators who have firsthand experience in the high-risk activities depicted here and who were kind enough to teach me. To the best of my knowledge, much of their tradecraft (the bug-out bag and the use of twist ties for searching vehicles, for example) has not appeared in fiction before. My thanks to the following:

Linton Jordahl, former U.S. marshal. The U.S. Marshals Service ranks with the Secret Service and the Diplomatic Security Service as one of the premier protective units of the United States government.

Don Rosche and Bruce Reichel of the Bill Scott Raceway's Executive Training course. Various U.S. government agencies, including the Diplomatic Security Service, send their personnel to BSR to learn defensive and offensive driving techniques.

Lt. Dave Spaulding of Ohio's Montgomery County Sheriff's Department. His unit contributed to the high-level of security for the 1995 Dayton (Bosnian) Peace Accords. He is one of America's foremost firearms instructors. In addition to giving me invaluable lessons, he arranged for me to attend sessions of the International Association of Law Enforcement Firearms Instructors. See his *Handgun Combatives* and *Defensive Living*, the latter co-written with retired CIA operations officer Ed Lovette.

Marcus Wynne, former paratrooper with the 82nd Airborne, former federal air marshal, and one of the few thriller novelists who knows what he's writing about. See his *No Other Option*, *Warrior in the Shadows*, and *Brothers in Arms*. Marcus was one of my literature students when I was a professor at the University of Iowa. Years later, he returned the favor and taught me many aspects of the world of high-risk operators.

Dan "Rock" Myers, former member of U.S. Special Operations/military intelligence and former contract officer for the Diplomatic Security Service.

Dennis Martin of CQB Services. He teaches VIP protection in some of the most dangerous places in the world and introduced me to the close-quarter combat theories of W. E. Fairbairn.

Scott Reitz, primary firearms instructor for the Los Angeles police department's elite Metropolitan Division. Visit www.internationaltactical.com.

Tom Evans of Sotheby's International Realty in Jackson, Wyoming. Only four percent of the Teton valley is available for private ownership. I needed an expert to help me find Cavanaugh a home, finally locating it in the northeast corner of Jackson Hole, near Turpin Meadow.

Barbara and Richard Montross for refreshing my fond memories of Iowa City and Willow Creek Park.

Jake Eagle, practitioner trainer in neuro-linguistic programming. The "visualization" theory dramatized in *The Naked Edge* and practiced by some elite military units is a good example of NLP, as is my main character's habit of manipulating verb tenses in order to reduce stress. Years ago, when I learned that the CIA and other intelligence services require NLP as part of their training, I took certification classes in it.

Steve Shackleford, editor of *Blade* magazine.

Knife makers Gil Hibben, Joe Keeslar, Jimmy Lile, Al Mar, Chris Reeve, and Michael Vagnino.

Ernest Emerson. In addition to being one of the best manufacturers of tactical knives (several of his blades are featured in this novel), Ernest is also a top-level knife instructor who works with various elite military and law-enforcement units. My ineptitude was entirely to blame when I took one of his courses (trying to play with the big boys) and broke my collarbone.

Larry Haight and Paul Dwyer of Sierra Aviation flight school in Santa Fe. My research into flying finally motivated me to get a pilot's license.

If I presented the details correctly, my teachers deserve the credit, but if there are mistakes, I'm solely to blame.

David Morrell
Santa Fe, New Mexico

DAVID MORRELL

David Morrell can be contacted at his website, www.davidmorrell. net. He is the award-winning author of *First Blood*, the novel in which Rambo was created. He was born in Kitchener, Ontario, Canada. When he was seventeen, he became a fan of the classic television series, *Route 66*, about two young men in a Corvette convertible traveling the United States in search of America and themselves. The scripts by Stirling Silliphant so impressed Morrell that he decided to become a writer.

In 1966, the work of another writer (Hemingway scholar Philip Young) prompted Morrell to move to the United States, where he studied with Young at the Pennsylvania State University and received his M.A. and Ph. D. in American literature. There, he also met the esteemed science-fiction author William Tenn (real name Philip Klass), who taught Morrell the basics of fiction writing. The result was *First Blood*, a ground-breaking novel about a returned Vietnam veteran suffering from post-trauma stress disorder who comes into conflict with a small-town police chief and fights his own version of the Vietnam War.

That "father" of modern action novels was published in 1972 while Morrell was a professor in the English department at the University of

Iowa. He taught there from 1970 to 1986, simultaneously writing other novels, many of them international bestsellers, including the classic spy trilogy, *The Brotherhood of the Rose* (the basis for the only miniseries to be broadcast after a Super Bowl), *The Fraternity of the Stone*, and *The League of Night and Fog*.

Eventually wearying of two professions, Morrell gave up his academic tenure in order to write full time. Shortly afterward, his fifteen-year-old son Matthew was diagnosed with a rare bone cancer and died in 1987, a loss that haunts not only Morrell's life but his work, as in his memoir about Matthew, *Fireflies*, and his novel *Desperate Measures*, whose main character lost a son.

"The mild-mannered professor with the bloody-minded visions," as one reviewer called him, Morrell is the author of thirty-three books, including such high-action thrillers as *The Protector*, *Testament*, and *The Spy Who Came for Christmas* (set in Santa Fe, New Mexico, where he lives). Always interested in different ways to tell a story, he wrote the six-part comic-book series, *Captain America: The Chosen*. His writing book, *The Successful Novelist*, analyzes what he has learned during his four decades as an author.

Morrell is a co-founder of the International Thriller Writers organization. Noted for his research, he is a graduate of the National Outdoor Leadership School for wilderness survival as well as the G. Gordon Liddy Academy of Corporate Security. He is also an honorary lifetime member of the Special Operations Association and the Association of Intelligence Officers. He has been trained in firearms, hostage negotiation, assuming identities, executive protection, and car fighting, among numerous other action skills that he describes in his novels. To research the aerial sequences in *The Shimmer*, he became a private pilot.

Morrell is an Edgar, Anthony, and Macavity nominee as well as a three-time recipient of the distinguished Stoker Award, the latest for his novel, *Creepers*. The International Thriller Writers organization gave him its prestigious career-achievement Thriller Master Award. With eighteen million copies in print, his work has been translated into twenty-six languages.